Dear Reader,

This year has been a very successful one for *Scarlet*! Our particular brand of romance fiction has captivated readers in North America and the UK, and we are also reaching audiences as far afield as Russia and New Zealand.

So, what delights are there in store for you this month? Characters from Angela Drake's book *The Mistress* are featured in *The Love Child*. Naughty-but-nice Ace Delaney from *Game, Set and Match*, returns in Kathryn Bellamy's new novel, *Mixed Doubles*. (But don't worry if you didn't read the authors' earlier titles – both of these books stand alone.) We are also absolutely delighted to announce the return to writing of much-loved romance author Margaret Pargeter, with a brand new book, *Misconception*, written especially for *Scarlet* readers. And finally, we are proud to bring you another author new to *Scarlet*: Tammy McCallum has produced an intriguingly different novel in *Dared to Dream*.

I believe this time there is something to appeal to all reading tastes. But if there is a type of romance (say, time travel, ranch stories, women-in-jeopardy novels) we are not featuring regularly enough to please *you*, do let me know, won't you?

Till next month,

Sally Cooper

SALLY COOPER,
Editor-in-Chief – *Scarlet*

MARGARET PARGETER

MISCONCEPTION

Enquiries to:
Robinson Publishing Ltd
7 Kensington Church Court
London W8 4SP

First published in the UK by Scarlet, 1997

Copyright © Margaret Pargeter 1997
Cover photography by J. Cat

A copy of the British Library Cataloguing in
Publication data is available from the British Library

ISBN 1-85487-997-9

Printed and bound in the EC

10 9 8 7 6 5 4 3 2 1

CHAPTER 1

Sixty miles from London Brett Deakin gave up. It was snowing heavily. The roads were growing increasingly treacherous and he knew he would have been wiser to postpone his journey until the morning. It was snowing when he set out, but he had dismissed the possibility of a heavy fall so early in November.

Irritable at having been proved wrong, he left the motorway at the first exit he came to. Being in countryside he was familiar with, he soon found his way, despite the weather, to a small hamlet he knew and parked his car outside a quiet hotel on the main street.

Once inside he asked for accommodation and a room was quickly found for him. It was clean and adequate, if not up to the high standard he was used to. He didn't quibble, he was glad to get anything. After a late dinner, rather than linger in a half-empty bar, he went straight to bed.

On a chest in his room lay a few magazines. Picking one up, he leafed idly through it. Seeing it was dated from earlier in the year, he was about to put it impatiently down again when his glance fell on a picture at the bottom of the page he was looking at. Cleo, the caption read, daughter of Sir Ronald and Lady Delroy of Constead, happily able to walk again after being badly injured in a car accident twelve months ago.

Instead of closing the magazine, Brett Deakin continued to hold it. His mouth tightening, he stared at the photograph closely, his narrowed eyes devoid of expression. Then, as if suddenly realizing what he was doing and quickly releasing himself from the thoughts that held him captive, he placed the magazine back on the chest and moved away from it. He had never seen or even heard of Cleo Delroy before, but it served to remind him of the injuries sustained by another girl in an accident he was partly responsible for. It also reminded him of the plane crash that had killed his mother, for which he might also have been partly responsible. His mother had been beyond help, but he still did a lot for Eve Martin, who had been crippled since the accident. Yet nothing he had done so far had managed to alleviate the guilt he still felt because of these two women and, as he stood there, he wondered broodingly if he would ever find anything that would?

'Are you sure there is nothing we can do?' Miranda Ferris asked her father in a hollow voice.

'Very sure.' Harry Ferris's tone and the paleness of his face left no room for doubt. 'Do you think I haven't tried to find a way out? If there had been any way at all of keeping the firm, do you think I would have sold it?'

'I suppose not.' Miranda frowned, trying to control both shock and bewilderment. She had come home full of joy after her successful operation, to find her father practically bankrupt. Five years ago, because of an accident, the very foundations of her life had been shaken. Now it seemed that the same thing, if in a different way, was happening again. Despair clouded her grey eyes as she gazed at her father in consternation. 'Did you say the house will have to go too?'

'I'm afraid so.' Harry sighed heavily. 'I won't have a penny left after everything is settled, and the house is part of the deal.'

'Wouldn't this Mr Deakin let you keep it? Couldn't we rent it from him?'

Harry shook his head. 'Men like Brett Deakin aren't interested in the personal affairs of their victims. They would rather help their own kind. They have no room for failures. Of course,' he admitted grimly, 'one has to be fair. If Deakin hadn't taken the works over, it would have been someone else. And he didn't drive so hard a bargain that I'll be left with a lot of debt.'

With more anger than she'd previously betrayed, Miranda exclaimed, 'That, for him, would probably be a minor consideration. I suspect he is more interested in his public image than in your welfare or feelings. Any concession he made in your direction could be well calculated to boost that. Brett Deakin may be successful, but when it comes to a business deal I don't think much sentiment would be allowed to come into it.'

'You've heard of him?' Harry looked puzzled.

'And others like him,' she said curtly. 'You forget, Dad, that apart from studying for my degree, reading and looking at TV is about all I've had to do for years. The business news can be very enlightening, and because I expect it's in my blood I've always found it interesting.'

'Sorry, love,' Harry said anxiously, 'I didn't mean to be tactless.'

'I know you didn't,' Miranda hastened to assure him. 'And I'm not criticizing your choice of a buyer. The Brett Deakins of this world are probably necessary for a healthy economy. It's just that sometimes I think they go a bit too far. What difference, I mean, could one house make to him?'

'But haven't I told you?' This time Harry spoke sharply. 'It was part of the final settlement.'

'You don't have to snap,' Miranda said.

'Sorry, love,' Harry repeated bleakly. 'That was uncalled for, I agree, but I've been so worried lately . . .'

'It doesn't matter, darling. I'm the one who should have more patience.' Miranda was unable to bear the haggard look on her father's face. It was four months since she'd last seen him and she could scarcely believe the change she saw in him. Four months ago when she left for Switzerland he had been – or he had appeared to be – happy and full of confidence. Now he was a broken old man.

'I wish there was something I could do,' she murmured impotently. 'If you hadn't spent a small fortune on me since my accident, you might have had enough to see you through a bad patch.'

'I didn't spend as much as would have made any

4

difference,' Harry denied quickly. 'I was hit by the recession more than anything. Nothing to do with you.'

Miranda didn't contradict him, though she doubted this was completely true. After her accident, when it was thought she would never walk again, Harry, in his determination to do everything possible to help her, spent incredible amounts of money having the house altered and specially geared to her needs. Rooms were fitted with everything imaginable to make it easier for her to get around. He'd had lifts installed to take her expensive wheelchairs so she could still go upstairs to bed, and her bedroom and bathroom had been completely remodelled, again with no expense spared. Many of the ground-floor rooms in the lovely old house had been on different levels and the architect Harry engaged had redesigned them so she could go anywhere.

On top of this, she'd had a nurse, a car with a chauffeur always at her disposal, and her father had taken her to Europe on wonderful holidays which, because of the extra arrangements often to be made, had not been cheap. And, at regular intervals, there had been specialist fees for various treatments and operations, none of which were successful. Not until the last one in a Swiss clinic which miraculously, for there was no guarantee, had enabled her to walk again.

After leaving the clinic, she had remained nearby under constant supervision, until her doctors were sure she was almost completely recovered. Alice, Harry's sister – who had kept house for them ever since Miranda's mother died when Miranda was a baby – had stayed with her. Otherwise, no one but

Harry had known where she was. Having endured so many exploratory and seemingly hopeless operations, Miranda had agreed to this one only if her father promised to pretend she was on holiday, so she might avoid the disturbing, if well-meant sympathy of friends and neighbours if she returned yet again in her wheelchair.

With a sense of wonder and even excitement, Miranda had come to realize that, this time, she could dispense with her wheelchairs for good. During the weeks of her convalescence she had felt increasingly grateful and delighted to be restored to near-perfect health. Full of high spirits she had arrived home, only to find her mood of eager anticipation cruelly shattered by the news her father had reluctantly broken to her.

Tears misting her eyes, she glanced from Harry's bent figure to Alice, who sat listening to them silently. 'If there was only something I could do,' she reiterated huskily. 'If we had been able to continue living here, I shouldn't have minded about the works so much.'

Raising his head, Harry turned his drawn face towards her. 'I did ask Deakin if he would rent the house back to me, but he refused.'

Alice spoke for the first time. She was a woman of sixty, some years younger than her brother with a much stronger will and personality, something she disguised so cleverly that, though she had lived with them now for twenty-three years, neither Harry or Miranda ever considered her anything but self-effacing. All this time she had been virtually mistress of Well House, a role she was determined not to

6

relinquish easily. She loved her brother, but was quite aware of his weaknesses. It was not the money he spent on Miranda that was responsible for his downfall. It was his gambling debts, of which Miranda knew nothing, and the added folly of trying to recoup his losses on the stock market and in ways he knew little about. The damage was done, of course, but she hoped the fright he had got over losing almost everything might have cured him. Whatever happened, she was resolved not to be parted without a struggle from the home she had devoted a large part of her life to.

She said crisply but quietly, addressing her brother, 'This has been a great shock to me as well as Miranda, but if Mr Deakin believed she was still a cripple, I wonder if he might reconsider? You did mention,' she added, as both he and Miranda stared at her in bewilderment, 'that he is coming here later today.'

Harry frowned at his sister uncertainly. 'I'm not sure that I follow you, Alice. Miranda isn't – er – disabled any longer.'

'She could pretend to be.' Alice returned Harry's confused glance impatiently. 'Don't you see?'

As Harry suddenly did, his mouth opened and closed again like a fish. With the appearance of a man grasping at straws, he exclaimed, 'By heavens, Alice, that sounds crazy but it might just work! And what have we to lose? After this one visit Deakin isn't likely to be here again. Once, I believe, when he took over a business, he stayed with it personally until it was on its feet again. Now he just puts a good manager in as he spends most of his time abroad. Anyway, to get back to the house, men like Deakin, though they can be hard, often have a weak spot somewhere. As you say, Alice, if he saw Miranda in a wheelchair, he could change his mind about the house.'

Miranda, who had sat in stunned silence throughout this exchange, suddenly found her tongue. She jumped furiously to her feet, still marvelling, despite her agitation, that she could. 'Are you both out of your minds?' she cried. 'Oh, Dad,' she appealed to him, 'I realize that losing the firm must have been a terrible blow and you aren't yourself. If you had been, I know you wouldn't be giving Alice's suggestion a second thought.'

'I lost the firm,' Harry returned piously, 'because none of those I turned to for help would help me. All my fairweather friends deserted me. I learned the hard way that most people are only interested in looking after themselves, so why should I try to be different?'

'Rubbish!' Miranda snapped, then paused remorsefully. 'I don't mean to sound unsympathetic, Dad, but when people refuse to help there's usually a good reason. In your case, they probably didn't have sufficient spare cash, or at least not enough to have made any difference. Besides,' she pointed out, as her father continued frowning, 'if Mr Deakin did allow us to stay on, he might demand an enormous rent and houses like this are not cheap to run.'

'I'll still have enough to cover things like that. If we were careful and perhaps you found a job,' Harry muttered tersely. 'If Deakin felt sorry enough for us, he might even let us have it rent free.'

8

Before Miranda could ask incredulously where his pride was, the telephone rang. As he hastened to the study to answer it, she turned to Alice accusingly. 'Whatever possessed you, Alice, to think of such a thing, filling his head with foolish ideas you must realize would never work? He's a broken defeated man, desperate enough to try anything, but you should know better.'

'How can you be sure it wouldn't work?' Alice's voice was sharper than Miranda had ever heard it, her brown eyes harder than Miranda had ever seen them. 'You could at least try. Though your father may deny it,' she went on harshly, believing, in the circumstances, a little deviation from the truth to be justified, 'he would not be in the straits he is in today but for you. Darling . . .' she softened her voice as Miranda paled visibly '. . . I don't enjoy saying this, but don't you think you owe it to him to help him – if this might be possible – to keep the house? Would you ever be able to forgive yourself if you didn't?'

'It's not a case of being able to forgive myself,' Miranda replied shortly. 'I don't need to be reminded of all Dad has done for me, but was it my fault that he spent more than he could afford? If he didn't tell me, how was I to know? And of course, now that he needs it, I'd like to help. Your scheme sounds so absurd, that's all. And it's not as if we had nowhere to go. We still have the flat in London, don't we?'

'What would we do in a poky little flat in town?' Alice asked angrily.

'Other people manage,' Miranda said, more optimistically than she felt.

'We aren't used to living in a city, though,' Alice argued. 'We shouldn't last a week,' she exaggerated. 'Or if we did, your father wouldn't. It would kill him.'

Helplessly, Miranda clenched her hands, feeling despair eating into her. She hated seeing her father so beaten and down and Alice looking at her with censure in her eyes. She wasn't used to being found fault with. Since her accident, everyone had made much of her, pandering to her every whim. It was a new and unpleasant sensation to be disapproved of by those who loved her. It made her feel curiously lost and disorientated, as if she was treading on ground that was less than firm under her feet. Suddenly nothing seemed more important than that her father and Alice should be smiling at her again.

As Harry returned to the lounge she drew a sustaining breath and asked him nervously, 'When, exactly, is Mr Deakin coming to see you?'

'This afternoon.' Harry sat down and gazed at her unhappily. 'That is why I had to break my bad news straight away. I had hoped to give you a few more days but he said to expect him about three. I told him I wouldn't be in this morning, when he rang last night, though I didn't mention I was picking you up at the airport.'

'So we have no time to think about what Alice is proposing – really think about it, I mean?'

Harry ran two shaking fingers under a shirt collar which appeared to be choking him. 'Listen, love . . .'

Alice, suspecting from the strangled note in his voice that he was about to tell his daughter to forget the whole thing, cut in sharply. 'What is there to think about, Miranda? Mr Deakin hasn't made any definite decision regarding the house yet, has he, Harry?' As Harry shook his head, she went on, 'He might easily let us stay until he does and it couldn't possibly be cheating if we were paying him a fair rent.'

Miranda frowned, still feeling reluctant. 'It would be cheating, though, if we got it under false pretences; if he only let us stay because he thought I was crippled.'

'Nonsense!' Alice countered immediately, throwing back her grey head in an almost belligerent fashion. 'But, if it is, how many people like Brett Deakin have got where they are today without doing a little cheating themselves?' As Harry attempted to intervene she ignored him. 'You may not need to even speak to him.'

'That's true,' Harry murmmered weakly, subsiding beneath her warning glance.

Miranda wasn't sure why her conscience was struggling so desperately to make itself heard. Was it her conscience or just a strong sense of self-preservation? What did she know of Brett Deakin, what kind of man he was? How he would react if he discovered they had deceived him? No one appreciated being made a fool of, and it was in this light that he might view their transgression, should he ever find out about it. And what then?

Though she tried to shrug off such fears, she found herself saying flatly, 'If he did agree to letting us stay, then discovers I can walk, he might be angry enough to throw us straight out. Which could be worse, don't you think, than making a dignified exit in the first place?'

11

'All your father requires is some breathing space,' Alice said quickly.

With a nod Harry confirmed this. 'Given time, we might find a nice country cottage somewhere. But it's unlikely that Deakin would discover anything, as he wouldn't be here.'

'If he did,' Alice put in, 'we could always pretend you had your operation after he met you. I'm more inclined to agree with your father, though, that if he consented to let us have the house he would probably just go away and forget all about us.'

Miranda sighed, knowing she couldn't continue objecting to something that could result in making her father and Alice happy again. She owed them that much, surely? And she had to admit she hated the idea of leaving the house herself and having to hand it over to a stranger. While recovering in Switzerland, she had decided, when she came home, she would find a job and a place of her own, but she had never thought that Well House wouldn't always be there to come back to.

Resolutely, she turned to her father. 'You did say that I might not need to see this man for more than a few minutes?'

'He probably won't even wish to speak to you,' Harry said drily. 'I hardly think he will wish to spend much time with a disabled young woman confined to a wheelchair. If you do intend going through with this, it might be wise to let him see you in one, but that's all.'

'How old is he?' Miranda asked, suddenly curious. 'You haven't given us even a hint of what he is like.'

'Late thirties, I should say. Could be younger, but I shouldn't think so, as you rarely achieve his kind of success much under that age. As to what he is like, I don't really know. Charming enough on the surface, but a lot, I would guess, which isn't so charming underneath. The only thing about him that seems to be common knowledge is that he is fond of getting his own way. And usually gets it.'

'He sounds interesting.' Miranda shrugged, trying to hide her persistent uneasiness with a dry observation. 'I can hardly wait to meet him.'

'You'll do it, then?' Alice asked eagerly, her strained face registering relief.

Miranda hesitated, then nodded. 'You make me feel I have to try, but I'll never forgive you if I'm forced to tell a lot of lies.'

Alice ignored this, though she did colour slightly. Recovering swiftly, she rose from the chair in which she was sitting and touched Miranda's arm with grateful fingers. 'While I go to see to a few things in the kitchen, as we no longer appear to have a cook, you'd better go upstairs and freshen up. That suit you are wearing looks rather crumpled and, if Mr Deakin is arriving shortly, we have no time to spare.'

Upstairs, Miranda sank wearily on to her bed. Though she had recovered well from her operation, she hadn't had time to build up any great reserves of energy, and the conversation she'd had with Harry and Alice, then with Harry after Alice left the lounge, seemed to have depleted what little she had. Despite her aunt's warning of Brett Deakin's imminent arrival, she had been determined to extract from her father more of what had happened while she was away. Possibly, because he had got into the habit of protecting her during the years she was disabled, the habit lingered. She suspected he had told Alice far more than he told her – or was it just that Alice had guessed more? Whatever it was, Miranda was resolved not to be kept in the dark any longer.

Her interview with Harry, however, had gained her little. It appeared that the firm had been losing money faster than he made it and he'd had no other option but to sell. This was why he never visited Miranda in Switzerland. Until the last moment he had hoped to find something to save him. Poor Harry, Miranda thought, wishing she had been there to help him. The worry of having to bear it all by himself must have been nearly too much for him.

She had tried to tell him how sorry she was, how much she regretted that the money he had spent on her must have contributed towards his downfall. But Harry would have none of it, which somehow only made her feel worse

Suddenly she felt very frightened. Believing she was coming home to a wealthy father, while she had planned a new future for herself, she hadn't worried about it. She had decided to enter the family firm – as she liked to think of it – so she could carry it on when Harry retired. But most of all she had looked forward to leading a normal life, to having fun and doing all the things she'd missed out on after being confined for years to a wheelchair. Now, without any money to support her until she at least found her feet, the future stretched before her, presenting a challenge she felt in no way equipped to meet.

Gazing despairingly around her familiar bedroom, she realized how much she loved it and had missed it while she was away. It was wonderful to be back but dreadful to know she might shortly be leaving it for good. Desolately she buried her face in her hands, trying not to look at it any more, for fear she break down completely and had to present herself to their visitor with swollen eyes and red cheeks.

She still felt tired. Since her accident, travelling had always tired her – which was why they had seldom gone further than Europe when on holiday – but she hadn't thought that the journey from Switzerland, now she was better, would have the same effect. Fighting a desire to sleep, she dragged herself reluctantly from the bed and began pulling off her clothes. Absently she let them fall to the floor, forgetting there was no longer a maid around to pick them up. Briefly she even forgot she was capable of picking them up herself. It wasn't until she realized what she was doing that she remembered and, with a half-stifled exclamation, retrieved her discarded suit and threw it over a chair.

Why, she wondered impatiently, was she still so shaky? Catching sight of her white face in a mirror, she decided ironically it might not be so difficult to fool Brett Deakin, or indeed anyone, over the state of her health. For the first time she was willing to concede that Alice's plan might make sense. If one short plane journey could exhaust her, where was she to find the immediate strength to set about finding a job and earning a living? Her doctors in Switzerland had warned her to be patient, to give herself time; neither they nor she had realized this was the one thing she was going to be short of.

The dress she found to replace the suit she had just taken off was a model in the finest blue wool. Moodily she regarded the rows of expensive dresses in her huge, walk-in wardrobe. They were something she must definitely learn to do without. The next dress she bought would have to be off the peg, always supposing she could afford to buy another one, off the peg or otherwise, she thought gloomily.

When she was ready she went along to the room at the far end of the upstairs corridor where Harry said he had stored her wheelchairs until they decided what to do with them. Miranda had thought she wouldn't need them again but, for the next hour or so, seemingly she was going to. Viewing the one she chose, she was surprised to find none of the aversion she had expected to find. Strangely, though she was sure she must be mistaken, she was conscious of regarding it more as an old and trusted friend. The chair seemed to represent a way of life which, though far from satisfactory, had been entirely safe. As she sat tentatively down in it, she was immediately back in the world she had known since she was nineteen and somehow felt more secure in it than she did out of it. Unhappily, as she tried to block out the chaos she had come home to, she actually wished she could go back. If she had been content to remain in a wheelchair for the rest of her life and refused all the costly things that had been contrived to help her, she was sure, for all he denied it, her father wouldn't be in the dreadful position he was in today.

Trying to shake off what threatened to become a terrible burden of self-recrimination, Miranda swiftly manoeuvred herself back along the corridor, into the

16

lift and down to the lounge. Setting her chair deter-
minedly in front of the TV set, she switched it on. She
wasn't interested in any particular programme, but
hoped to find something distracting. Her father was
on the phone again. It seemed to ring continually. She
had heard him shouting into it at someone as she
passed the study.

She tried to concentrate on a cookery lesson which
was being shown, but as tears began again to run
down her cheeks, she gave up. All at once she felt so
angry and miserable about everything that she didn't
care any more. She was quite prepared to dislike
Brett Deakin before she even met him. Alice must
have spoken the truth when she hinted that men like
him were rarely honourable. Harry, when it came to
terms, couldn't have been in any position to argue
with him. A situation which must have been mostly
favourable to Mr Deakin. If they did succeed in
fooling such a man, might it be no more than he
deserved?

CHAPTER 2

'May I come in?' As a strange voice broke through the sudden acrimony of Miranda's thoughts, she jerked her chair around so quickly to see who it was that she forgot, in her haste, the telltale dampness on her face.

The man approaching her saw it and frowned and, though he didn't say anything, his surprise was evident. 'Who are you?' he asked, his dark brows drawing together as he stared at the girl now confronting him and watching him warily.

Abruptly he halted beside her. Despite the careful blankness of his gaze, Miranda had the odd feeling that, for all he tried to conceal it, he had received a distinct and unwelcome shock. It was as if she reminded him of something, or someone, he would rather forget.

Taking advantage of whatever it was that had diverted him for even a few seconds, Miranda surreptitiously wiped a tear from her cheek and studied the stranger closely. If this was Brett Deakin – and who else could it be – he had a tall well-built body giving the overall impression of fitness and strength. And if his face had not been so hard she might have thought it handsome. He would have a very forceful personality, she sensed this instinctively, and there was something else about him that sent a funny shiver down her spine which she couldn't put a name to immediately.

His deep blue eyes continued to regard her intently as he carefully repeated his question. Almost as if the answer was of some importance to him.

'I'm Miranda Ferris,' Miranda said hastily.

'Harry's daughter?'

Miranda frowned. 'Didn't you know he had one?'

'No,' he replied, still scowling. 'He never mentioned one, if that's what you mean?'

'He probably didn't think it necessary. Are you,' she asked, though she knew she didn't need to, 'Mr Deakin?'

'Brett Deakin. Yes.'

No apology for letting her guess. Miranda's grey eyes were fleetingly hostile. 'My father is expecting you,' she said. 'Didn't he let you in?'

'No one answered the door when I knocked so I just walked in,' he replied absently, before reverting to what still obviously puzzled him. 'I find it strange, when we've been seeing quite a bit of each other over the past few months, that your father never told me about you. Especially as you are apparently crippled.'

Miranda coloured at such unvarnished frankness, though she sensed he would not be a man to prevaricate simply to spare one's feelings. Harry wouldn't have told him she was a cripple as she had not been one for weeks. But how could she tell him this when it was what both her father and Alice had asked her to keep quiet about?

'He probably believed that, if he did, you would think he was appealing for pity, or a better deal.'

'A better deal?' Brett Deakin's eyes hardened and he opened his mouth as if to say something, but, appearing to have second thoughts, closed it again abruptly. After a slight pause he said. 'I still find it rather strange that he didn't say something.'

Why couldn't he just leave it alone? And why didn't he stop staring at her? She was beginning to feel like a specimen on the end of a pin. Surely one girl in a wheelchair couldn't be of that much interest to him? She recalled her father saying she wouldn't be, but now she didn't feel quite so sure. Of course, there were people who were morbidly intrigued by anything injured or maimed. Not many, but they did exist. 'Would it have made any difference if he had?' she asked coldly.

'Perhaps not,' Deakin conceded. Then, leaning closer, inquired bluntly. 'How long have you been like this?'

Miranda was always reluctant to discuss her disability with anyone and people had learned to be tactful and avoid the subject. Even though she was now completely recovered, with her long slender limbs bearing no evidence of what she had been through, she found herself still unwilling to talk about it. But when she didn't reply immediately Deakin startled her by catching her firmly by the shoulders, making her look at him as he repeated his question insistently. 'How long, Miranda?'

Miranda's breath caught sharply at the way he said her name, and though he wasn't hurting her she felt the impact of his strong fingers burning through her dress to her bare skin. 'Five years,' she said, trying to control her suddenly erratic breathing. 'A car I was driving skidded on black ice and went over an embankment.'

Straightening abruptly, Brett Deakin let go of her and, almost as if he wasn't aware of what he was doing, strode to the window. The room was large, he was some distance away, but Miranda noticed the tension in his powerful body and broad shoulders as he stared out over the gardens. What was it that appeared to be bothering him? Why did he seem so disturbed by the sight of someone in a wheelchair when thousands spent their entire lives in one? She thought suddenly and apprehensively that Alice's crazy plan could have a better chance of working than any of them had ever imagined.

'I could have been killed,' she pointed out prosaically, as something about Brett Deakin's tall still figure began making her feel uneasy.

He turned again swiftly and came back to her. 'Could that have been any worse?' he asked curtly. 'Doesn't what you are left with seem like a life sentence? Stuck in a wheelchair all day, unable to walk? How old were you?'

'When it happened?' Miranda still found it hard to meet the brilliant blue eyes. For some reason they seemed to arouse something inside her she didn't recognise. 'Nineteen but, in a way, I got used to it,' she said, and was surprised to find she was speaking the truth. She had become used to being disabled. In

21

fact, looking back, she wondered if it had not been preferable to how she was now? Without her chair and the protection and attention it had guaranteed her from those who loved her, she felt strangely vulnerable. It was the same kind of apprehension that she'd experienced a few minutes ago upstairs. It was as if fate was pushing her from one stage of her life to another too quickly, before she was ready for it.

Brett Deakin was clearly doubtful over what she said. 'You may be used to it, but you can't like it. Not when it means you can't lead a normal life. No boyfriends or parties, for instance.'

'Sometimes I go to parties,' she said.

'As an onlooker.' Grabbing a small chair, he swung it around and sat down facing her, so that their eyes were almost on the same level. 'That might be worse than not going at all.'

'In a way.' Her heart began beating faster from both his nearness and perception. 'I used to think it was better for me, though, than staying at home and feeling sorry for myself.'

'But it must take a lot of courage.'

Miranda breathed a silent sigh of relief that he seemed to be so busy examining her face that he obviously hadn't noticed the mistake she had made. With a panicky gulp she looked away from him and murmured quickly, 'I can't think where my father has got to. Perhaps I should let him know you are here? He may not have heard you come in.'

'Don't worry,' Brett said, 'I'm in no hurry.'

Well, she was – to get rid of him! Stirring uncomfortably under his prolonged scrutiny, she reminded him stiffly, 'This is your house now,

Mr Deakin, you don't really have to wait for him. You could start looking around on your own. You don't need his permission.'

Ignoring the unconscious resentment in her voice, Brett stayed right where he was. He continued as if she had never spoken. 'Where will you go when you leave here?'

'We have a small flat in London.'

'Flat?' His dark glance fell grimly on her wheel-chair. 'A ground-floor one?'

'Third,' she answered briefly, wishing he would stop asking questions. His apparent concern, even though she couldn't be sure it was genuine, made her feel very uncomfortable. Handicapped or not, she couldn't believe a man like Brett Deakin could possibly be interested in what happened to her, once he took over her father's business and the house. Yet, despite this, deceiving him, even for a short time, was leaving a horrible taste in her mouth.

'Is there a lift?' He sounded as if he was in the boardroom, interrogating someone over something he didn't like the sound of. As Miranda reluctantly shook her head, he asked curtly, 'Then how do you manage to get up to it when you are there?'

'I haven't been there since my accident,' she told him. 'Daddy only uses it when he has some business to see to in town. It's in a nice area, though, and I'm sure a few stairs will be no problem, once I get used to them.'

Right then, Harry appeared. Miranda couldn't remember being more pleased to see anyone in her life. She had been praying he would come, but had almost given him up. When he caught sight of Brett

Deakin sitting talking to her, he obviously received a shock. Flashing Miranda an anxious glance, he apologized hastily to the man beside her.

'I'm sorry, Deakin. Didn't hear you arrive. That's the worst of these confounded telephones.'

'I've been getting to know Miranda.' Brett rose unhurriedly to his feet and shook hands. 'I just walked in but I'm sure she didn't mind.'

'I'm sure she wouldn't.' To Miranda's dismay, Harry placed a protective arm along the back of her chair, every inch the caring father. 'Good of you to be so kind, Deakin. She's often lonely, I'm afraid, even though she bravely denies it. Has she told you about her accident?'

'Briefly, but it was more than you did.'

'Sorry,' Harry said again. 'I was going to once or twice, but Miranda's my favourite topic, you see, and I was afraid, once I got started, that I wouldn't know where to stop. And then again, I didn't think the two of you would ever meet.'

Brett Deakin frowned. 'I'd've appreciated knowing, all the same.'

Harry nodded, as if he didn't want to disagree with him. 'Remiss of me, I suppose, but she will be all right here while I show you over the premises.'

'Couldn't she come with us?'

Though it was phrased like a question, Miranda recognized it as a request. Harry must have received the same impression as he raised no objections. It soon became obvious, however, that Brett Deakin's interest in the house was, in some inexplicable way, almost entirely bound up with Miranda. For the next hour, to her growing dismay and embarrassment, he

24

made Harry demonstrate every device there was installed to enable her to cope with her wheelchair and disability. Once started, Harry was like a child showing off a new toy, in no way reluctant to explain everything he had done to make life easier for his beloved daughter.

As time passed, Miranda became increasingly disconcerted. And, as the strain of this and the earlier stress of the day began hitting her, she began feeling curiously light-headed. While Harry talked with renewed animation, she wilted and grew paler. And when Miranda lost her colour, with her lint-fair hair, grey eyes and slight figure, anyone might be deceived into thinking her eighteen again and on the verge of collapse. She wasn't aware of Brett Deakin's eyes frequently on her, or of the mixture of both concern and speculation in their depth. After they had been outside and toured the gardens, along the specially levelled paths, he called a halt.

'I think your daughter has had enough for one day,' he said to Harry and, without waiting for him to reply, promptly took hold of Miranda's chair and wheeled her back inside.

'Will you have a drink before you go?' Harry asked awkwardly as they returned to the lounge. He looked somewhat downcast, as if he had just realized how far his enthusiasm had mistakenly taken him.

'I've just made a cup of tea.' Alice entered behind them. She had met Brett Deakin when they were in the kitchen and Miranda could see she had taken to him immediately. Which was more, Miranda thought wryly, than she had done.

25

She hoped he would refuse her aunt's invitation, but he didn't. Smiling at Alice warmly, he assured her there was nothing he'd like better.

'Tea is something I rarely make time for,' he confessed.

Miranda tried to excuse herself and escape to her room, but he thwarted her. 'You look worn out,' he said, removing the light shawl she had flung carelessly around her shoulders as they went outside and putting it over her knees.

As his hands caught the nape of her neck she shivered, as she had done before when his hands had touched her. She wondered why he should have such an effect on her? While she hadn't taken to him, she didn't actually dislike him, she told herself.

'You'd better have some tea as well,' he advised, quietly, his eyes darkly compassionate on her pinched face. 'Better than locking yourself away. You are cold, we shouldn't have taken you outside. It's not very warm in here, either.' He glanced at Harry grimly. 'Can't you turn the heating up?'

'Our oil is low.' Looking abashed, Harry cleared his throat gruffly. 'The gardener always kept his eye on it, but after he went I forgot all about it, I'm afraid.'

Alice, beginning to pour out their tea, paused and sighed, all too explicitly. 'As we are leaving it won't be worth ordering another load, even if we could afford it.'

Attempting to conceal her distaste of a situation which, even if it was as bad as it seemed, shouldn't, in her opinion, be given a public airing, Miranda said quickly, 'I'm sure Mr Deakin isn't interested in our problems, Alice. He must have enough of his own, and if we are cold we can always light a fire.'

To her surprise, his mouth still grim, Brett Deakin, clearly used to taking the law into his own hands, immediately produced a lighter. Bending swiftly, he flicked it forcibly under the dry tinder in the wide fireplace. Miranda watched, startled, while neither her father nor Alice seemed able to find a word of protest as the bright yellow flames leapt up among the piled-up logs in the grate, as if they dared do nothing else. Even the fire seems to obey him, Miranda thought cynically.

Soon they were all drinking tea and basking in the warmth from the crackling logs. Miranda, conscious of Brett Deakin's eyes frequently studying her, felt increasingly tense. She drank her tea and ate a rather stale biscuit without being really aware of what she was doing.

To her relief Harry enquired at last, 'Are you returning to London this evening, Deakin?'

'That was my intention, but now I don't think I will,' Brett replied smoothly. 'We still, as you know, have a lot to agree on and, if we do, I'd like to get a new manager settled in before I leave. I also have some private business in Birmingham which, while I am here, I may as well see to as well. And I'd like to spend more time considering this property before you move out, if you don't mind?'

There followed a brief but uncomfortable silence during which he was the focus of three pairs of apprehensive eyes. Miranda's hands clenched over clammy palms as she experienced again the feeling of being trapped. If he intended popping

27

in unexpectedly over the next few days, what was she to do? she asked herself.

Harry, observing the obvious plea for help on Miranda's face, made a visible effort. 'My dear chap,' he exclaimed, 'as the house belongs to you now – well, more or less, you can, of course, do what you like. I'm not sure, though, what kind of hospitality we can offer you. Not with the servants gone unfortunately, and,' he added, as if inspired, to Miranda's growing alarm, 'Alice having to do their duties as well as looking after her niece.'

'Doesn't Miranda have a nurse?' Brett Deakin asked curtly.

'She had. An excellent one.' Harry sighed.

'Where is she now?'

'Looking after someone else. She left a month ago.'

'Really, Mr Deakin,' Miranda intervened quickly, not liking the condemning expression on his face as he looked at her father, 'the staff would have had to go in any case. We couldn't possibly have taken them to London with us, as the flat I told you about has only three small bedrooms.'

'It was your nurse I was asking about, not the rest of the staff,' Brett Deakin said before turning to Alice. 'There's no need to put yourself out, Miss Ferris. I'm quite happy for the moment in my hotel.' He named a five-star one, twelve miles away. 'If I did decide to come and stay, or to drop in for a meal, I would see to it that you wouldn't be out of pocket. Now how would you all like to dine with me at the Ruteridge, this evening? I presume that Miranda does dine out occasionally?'

28

Before Alice could reply, Miranda exclaimed. 'I don't want to go out this evening, Mr Deakin.'

'Don't be silly.' He dismissed Miranda's protests as if she wasn't old enough to know her own mind. 'You told me yourself that you do go out sometimes, and it's better for you to mix with people than to hide yourself away.'

Was he an authority on the handicapped? If he wasn't, he sounded like one, Miranda thought, though she knew this would be unlikely. The whole thing was getting out of hand. She stared at him frustratedly. Surely her father and Alice must be aware of this? If they didn't do something, the whole situation might develope into a disaster of some kind which would be no longer possible to control.

'And you can call me Brett,' she heard him continuing.

Miranda shook her head, but more because of the folly of what she had got herself into than at what he was saying.

'Don't you like my name?' Deakin asked, half-humorously, misjudging the frown on her face.

Somewhat desperately, Miranda glanced at her father, willing him to think of some excuse – if he couldn't bring himself to confess the truth – as to why Brett Deakin must leave immediately and not try to see them again. Didn't he understand that if Deakin even just stayed around, he might easily, inadvertently, discover she was able to walk. Even if he didn't, how long might she have to go on pretending she couldn't? It could be weeks! 'It's not that,' she muttered, as Deakin repeated his question.

'What is it then?'

'Ask my father.'

Harry, however, was apparently unable to come to her rescue. It was Alice who did this, though it soon became clear that she was only adding to the web of deception they were caught in, rather than freeing them from it.

'Miranda,' she began, to Miranda's astonishment, 'is inclined to be too sensitive, Mr Deakin. I'm sure she doesn't mean to sound ungrateful, but when she does go out, though I know she would never admit it, I suspect she often feels self-conscious. Thinks everyone is looking at her, you know, that kind of thing. I suppose, though,' she added, as if there was no one in the room but Deakin and herself, 'this is only to be expected, as she can't get about like most people.'

Deakin gave Alice his full attention. 'I realize this, but is it mostly transport that's the problem?'

'No, Miranda has a specially adapted car. It will have to be sold along with everything else, but until it is, it is still in the garage.'

'The trouble is,' Harry broke in, feeling on safer ground, 'neither Alice nor I can handle it. It wasn't necessary, of course, when she had a chauffeur.'

Brett Deakin hesitated a moment, his eyes resting briefly on Miranda's strained face. 'It doesn't matter about this evening,' he said to Harry, 'we can always go out some other time. I can call tomorrow, instead, and perhaps take her out for a run, when she isn't feeling so tired. We can take my car.'

'I can't do it, I tell you!' Miranda exclaimed in a strangled voice, an hour later, as he drove away and the receding sound of his car emphasized the silence that fell heavily on the three in the lounge, even after it faded completely. 'It's crazy!' Her voice rose hysterically. 'And I don't believe for a moment he has any intention of letting us keep the house.'

'Miranda, love . . .' Harry began.

'Don't Miranda love me!' Miranda cried. 'No lies, you said. He will only be here a few minutes, you said. You may not even need to speak to him, you said. You will *have* to tell him the truth, Dad. I'm too old to be taking part in a charade like this.' Her grey eyes glittered angrily. 'I think I will leave straight away for London. There's a train at eight. When he comes back in the morning, or whenever, you can tell him this wheelchair thing was my idea. I don't mind taking the blame.'

'How can I tell him that?' Harry mumbled unhappily. 'My affairs aren't completely settled yet and he isn't a man to appreciate that kind of a joke. He won't believe you thought it all up yourself.'

'Then say I was called away suddenly,' Miranda suggested distractedly. 'You don't have to confess anything. Just say someone came to collect me and I've gone to stay with friends.'

'You don't understand.' Harry looked apprehensive, if not frightened. 'He implies it is the house he is interested in, but I rather think it is you. Call it intuition, if you like,' he said, as Miranda's eyes widened incredulously, 'but somehow I feel convinced that there are certain concessions he might be willing to make if he thought that, by doing so, it could help you. If he came back tomorrow, though, and you weren't here, well . . .' he spread out his hands '. . . I just don't know what he would do.'

Miranda knew her father too well not to be able to read between the lines. He'd said everything was settled, but was it? Heaven knew what sort of a muddle he had got himself into, if the truth were known. Briefly she closed her eyes. Perhaps it was better she didn't know, but he was obviously relying on her to help him out. Somewhere to live might be the least of their problems. Harry, now she came to think of it properly, had latched on to Alice's plan to keep the house too quickly, maybe hoping that, somehow, it might help him to solve his other problems. She could be wrong – she hoped she was – but it wasn't easy to get rid of her suspicions.

Taking pity on him against instincts warning her not to, Miranda sighed and said, 'Being used as a scapegoat, Dad, doesn't appeal to me, but you've done so much for me that I won't let you down. I'll stay, but have you considered,' she asked him tersely, 'what people are going to say if I'm confined to a wheelchair while Deakin is here, then I suddenly begin walking again when he leaves?'

'You will have to go to the flat for a few weeks,' Alice said, having already thought of this. 'We will pretend you have returned to Switzerland for another operation. You might even enjoy a few weeks in London. And if Mr Deakin won't let us keep the house, we will merely join you there.'

Miranda ignored this. 'What about Doctor Richardson?' She referred to their family practitioner. 'When he calls and finds me still in a wheelchair, what's he going to think? It may be nothing to what he's going to *say*!' she added sharply.

32

'He's on holiday,' Harry answered hastily. 'If his partners enquire, I'll tell them you are fine and don't need to see anyone until he comes back. The practice is miles away, anyway, and Deakin will only be here a few days. With any luck he'll have let us keep the house and be gone, even before that long.'

'What if he hasn't?' Miranda challenged them, throwing off the rug Brett Deakin had placed solicitously over her knees. 'I'm sorry,' she cried, as panic overtook her again. 'I can't do it! I must need my brains examined for even thinking of it. I'm going away . . .'

Rising too quickly after sitting so long, she was confused to find she was dizzy to such an extent that the room began spinning around her. Though she tried to keep her balance, she felt herself falling. It was the stress of the day catching up with her, but she didn't realize this. For a frantic moment she believed her legs were failing her again, that her cure had been a myth. As sheer terror flooded her, a peculiar darkness seemed to press down on her and – before the man who appeared suddenly in the doorway could reach her – she fell in a crumpled heap at his feet.

When Miranda came to, she was lying on her bed with Alice sitting beside her. She stared at her aunt dazedly, unable to remember how she got there. 'What happened?' she whispered as Alice, seeing she was conscious again, gave a sigh of relief.

'You fainted,' Alice told her, in the matter-of-fact way she had.

'Fainted?'

'It's been a long day.' Alice seemed to think this should explain everything. 'We forgot how much you've been through and when you tried to get up, it obviously was too much for you. You passed out.'

Miranda frowned, trying to take this in. She recalled how frightened she had felt when her legs wouldn't seem to support her and she began to think her operation had only been a short-term success. Moving her legs slowly, relief washed over her as she realized she was mistaken.

'How did I get here?' she asked, for some reason feeling suddenly uneasy again. 'Neither you nor Dad could have carried me.'

'Fortunately – ' Alice smiled, ' – Mr Deakin had forgotten his briefcase. Said he wouldn't have brought it in, but that it contained important documents which he never likes leaving in a car. He arrived just in time to carry you upstairs. He wanted to call a doctor, but we persuaded him not to.'

Miranda felt herself tense. 'Where is he now?'

'Waiting downstairs in the lounge with your father. He refuses to leave until he hears you are all right.'

CHAPTER 3

Miranda thought about this slowly. Brett Deakin had come back. He had seen her fall and carried her upstairs. Suddenly the unease she felt was replaced by a feeling of release.

'So he knows I can walk,' she cried, as she recalled getting out of her wheelchair. 'Well, at least that is one problem solved. What did he say?' she asked more uncertainly, as a worried expression crossed her aunt's face.

Alice stirred uncomfortably. 'I think he thought you were only trying to walk.'

Miranda stared at her uncomprehendingly. 'Trying to walk . . .?'

'Yes. You see, when you fell, just as Mr Deakin walked in, I saw at once that Harry didn't know what to say, so I said quickly that you sometimes tried to. Which you did.'

'Not for a long time.'

'I knew that, but Deakin didn't. I could hardly tell him the truth now, could I?'

'It would have been better.' Miranda looked at her sharply. 'What did you tell him, exactly?'

'Only that you'd been worried about the house. Nothing else, but I could see he blamed himself. He went quite pale and wouldn't allow us to touch you. I was surprised that he seemed to know just how to pick you up – the way your nurse used to do.'

Miranda went cold. She shivered at the thought of being held even briefly in Brett Deakin's arms. They would be strong enough, she didn't doubt, but instead of gratitude she was consumed by a feeling of revulsion.

'Did he really believe I would faint just because of the house?'

'Well,' Alice confessed defensively, 'I had to elaborate a bit. I told him, when he got you upstairs, that is, that your father had sent you abroad while he was trying to save the firm and we had just returned today and learned about it. I said that the journey and the bad news waiting for us must have been too much for you, but that it wasn't necessary to send for your doctor.'

'Did that satisfy him?' Miranda asked, trying to ignore the lump in her throat as this also reminded her of all her father had endured alone.

'It seemed to.'

'But for how long? When he's had time to think about it, isn't he going to start suspecting I'm not quite what I appear to be?'

'You could be wrong about that,' Alice said emphatically. 'I feel certain there is something about you that has made a deep impression on him.'

'You aren't suggesting he is attracted to me?' Miranda asked scornfully.

'Why not?' Alice frowned. 'You're not exactly short of good looks, and you do have a good figure.'

'So must dozens of women he meets every day.'

'He isn't married.'

What did Alice mean by that? Miranda looked at her in grim exasperation. Surely she wasn't getting any ideas in her head in that direction? If Brett Deakin wasn't married, she was sure he would not allow a girl whom he believed to be crippled to alter his bachelor status. Not that she would wish to, even had it been possible. Since her accident, though she knew disabled people did marry, she had never considered marriage seriously for herself. While confined to her wheelchair, she had ignored her natural instincts to such an extent that now she couldn't be sure she had any. If she had, shouldn't the thought of being in Brett Deakin's arms, even while unconscious, have aroused a feeling of something? Something other than antipathy?

'Whether Brett Deakin is married or not is none of our business, is it?' Miranda swung her legs over the side of the bed as if she suddenly realized she must be lying exactly where Deakin left her. 'Shouldn't you –' she turned to Alice again ' – be going downstairs to tell him I'm quite recovered, or at least that I'm feeling better? Then perhaps he will go away and leave us in peace?'

'If it were not for your father . . .' Alice said, inserting a clever little catch in her voice and leaving her sentence unfinished.

When Alice looked so distressed, Miranda swallowed the tart retort she was about to make. Remorsefully she hesitated. What was the use of being angry? Hadn't Alice and Harry devoted themselves to her for years? Since her accident, hadn't they looked after her assiduously, with scarcely a thought for themselves? Hadn't they given her more affection and attention than she would ever have got from anyone else? It made her feel ashamed that she'd had to keep reminding herself of this all evening.

'All right, Alice,' she said heavily. 'You win, though I refuse to see Brett Deakin again tonight. I just don't feel up to it, I'm afraid.'

The following morning, Alice and Miranda ate breakfast alone. Harry didn't join them. Alice told Miranda that he'd arranged to meet Brett Deakin in Birmingham, shortly after nine, so had set off in good time.

'Some things still to be settled,' Alice said lightly, then went on quickly, just as her niece was about to ask what they were. 'I didn't say anything last night, Miranda, for fear of upsetting you, but until he left Brett never stopped talking about you.'

So it was Brett now, was it? Resignedly Miranda put down the piece of toast she was trying to eat and glanced at her aunt enquiringly.

Alice wasn't reluctant to go on. 'He asked so many questions about your accident, how you'd coped, and the treatment you'd had since then, that your father and I had difficulty in keeping up with him. He appears to know far more about your kind of injuries than one might have thought he would. Which means – ' she frowned worriedly ' – we may have to be extra careful.'

'You might have known what to expect from a man like him,' Miranda said stiffly. 'He's the kind who makes it his business to know a bit about most things,' she added disparagingly,

'But I didn't expect him to want to know so much about you personally.'

Miranda shrugged. 'I told you before, he probably has a morbid mind. If he does turn up to take me out, I'm afraid he will get some very short answers if he starts asking me a lot of questions.'

Alice said, 'I'm sure he won't.'

Miranda looked out of the window. 'It seems to be a better morning. I was going to get up early and go for a run. Do you realize how long it is since I've been able to? Not counting Switzerland, of course. Now I'm reduced to pretending I can't,'

'Only for a day or two.'

'It will seem like a year or two. When will Dad be back, by the way?'

'He didn't say.'

'I wish . . .' Miranda sighed '. . . I'd been able to help him.'

'I wish I'd been able to, as well.'

'Didn't you ever want to go into the firm?' Miranda asked, suddenly curious.

'No, not really,' Alice confessed, omitting to mention how relentlessly she had worked behind the scenes to prevent Harry from selling up years ago. It was better that Miranda didn't know, she decided. Especially when it might reveal too much to her about her father.

Miranda had hoped that Brett – as she was unconsciously beginning to think of him – would not return until the evening, as she didn't fancy spending the day in a wheelchair. Yesterday the idea might have appealed to her, but today it did not. Consequently she could have wept when he arrived early to take her out. She was upstairs at the time, but she heard him speaking to Alice in the hall.

Fuming inwardly, she grabbed a coat, then propelled herself into the lift and went down. He was standing with his back to her so didn't see her immediately. He was wearing a pair of jeans and a casual jacket, and even before he swung around to look at her she could see he looked very attractive. This didn't occupy her nearly so much, though, as the excuse she was trying to find to avoid going out with him. With last-minute panic inspiring her she pretended, after greeting him, that this morning for some reason she couldn't face the special car her father provided for her to ride in.

Brett Deakin merely smiled and, after another brief word with Alice, simply picked her up and carried her outside where he deposited her gently but firmly in the passenger seat of a large and extremely comfortable Mercedes.

Miranda strove to recover her departing breath. 'Do you always act like this?' she exclaimed when she found it.

'Only when I know I am right,' he replied, draping a seat belt around her before getting in beside her.

'You could have hurt me,' she cried, still feeling oddly shaken from being held so close to him. A pulse beat in her throat and the emotions she had experienced startled her, though she judged most of them to be fright.

The chiselled mouth quirked at the corners. 'I lifted you so I shouldn't. Stop acting like a spoiled brat.'

Miranda gasped as, though he spoke carelessly, his remark stung. She said coldly, 'I've never been that.'

'Then I owe you an apology.' He laughed.

Miranda subsided. She was aware he was only teasing her but she wondered if there were those who considered the handicapped spoiled because they had to have a lot done for them? Some, she supposed, were spoiled, some even enjoyed having other people running after them and never tried to help themselves. But most of the disabled people she had known had struggled to be as independent as possible and achieved this, often to a remarkable degree. It was sad that many of those injured, as she had been, might never find anything that might cure them, or be able to afford it if they did. Again Miranda was reminded, as she was almost every day, that she must owe her father far more than she could ever repay. Even if she could help him to keep the house, it would never be enough.

As this knowledge briefly silenced her, Brett Deakin, as he left the drive and turned on to the main road, glanced at her sharply. 'You aren't cold, are you?' He frowned as he thought he saw her shiver. 'I've turned the heating up.'

'No, of course not,' she said, meeting his penetrating gaze briefly. 'Maybe,' she added as, despite reasoning with herself, his cavalier treatment of her still rankled, 'I'm not used to being so roughly handled.'

He glanced at her again, this time in exasperation. 'I thought we'd settled all that. I was as gentle as a lamb.'

'I know,' Miranda admitted reluctantly. 'I'm sorry.'

As he shrugged and turned his eyes to the road again, she pondered on this. He hadn't hurt her and she knew he wouldn't have done, even had she still been unable to walk. She wondered if he'd had some experience of people in her condition, or what used to be her condition? Or was it just another piece of knowledge he had picked up in order to enhance his public image? The trouble was she knew nothing about him and could only guess.

Out of the corner of her eye she watched him driving. He was good at it, she noticed. He drove well and swiftly, without taking unnecessary risks. She was surprised to find she felt entirely safe with him.

As they left the suburbs of Birmingham behind them, she decided to ask him a few questions about her father's business, questions which Harry seemed reluctant to answer in any detail himself. It was difficult to know where to begin, though.

As she hesitated, Brett asked, almost as if he sensed her confusion, 'What is it this time, Miranda?'

His astuteness startled her, but she managed to reply coolly, 'I've been wondering why someone like you should wish to take over my father's firm. It can't be up to much the way it is.'

'It isn't, but it has potential. And it's the fashion today, is it not, to take over as much as possible?'

'It sounds a bit ruthless, going after something that another man has probably devoted years of his life to.'

His mouth quirked. 'What a dramatic little thing you are, to be sure. A lot of firms I've taken over were never the object of any man's devotion. Which is why they failed.'

Miranda bit her lip. If she was trying to discover why her father's business had failed, perhaps she was going about it the wrong way. But before she could begin again, Brett went on.

'I didn't take advantage of your father, Miranda, if that is what you are thinking. However, though I hope to buy him out, nothing has actually been settled yet. There are still a few things we can't agree on.'

'Is that why you are taking me out – being nice to me and everything, so that, even if you take your time, he won't be inclined to change his mind?'

Brett laughed. 'You're quite wrong about that. Your father's firm has been on the market for months. Unfortunately, I'm the only buyer who seems to be considering giving him anywhere near what he is asking for it.'

'But, fundamentally, it is a good business?'

'Basically,' Brett agreed. 'But he told me himself that it has been going downhill for years. I knew this, of course, even before my accountants saw his books, and he didn't try to cover up. He just wants to be rid of it. So he can retire and spend more time with you, I suppose?'

While Miranda digested this in silence, he pulled up near the doorway of a large hotel.

'Where are we?' Miranda asked, trying to shake off her worries and doubts over her father as she looked about her. She hadn't realized they were going to stop anywhere. She thought she recognized the hotel, but couldn't believe they had come as far as this.

'Little Benton,' she was informed. 'Have you been here before?'

'Once, a long time ago. Why have you stopped?'

He paused, his hand on the door at his side of the car. 'We're going to have lunch. It is all arranged. You just have to wait here for a minute while I collect one of the wheelchairs they provide for guests like yourself.' Getting out, he turned to lean back in again. 'There is also help should you wish to go to the cloakroom or something. I would assist you myself,' he grinned, 'if I thought they wouldn't throw me out!'

He was outrageous, Miranda thought, yet, as he disappeared into the hotel, she couldn't help smiling at his sense of humour. During his visit last night, she had sometimes thought he didn't have one. She would make sure, though, that she needed no assistance, other than a wheelchair. She would feel a big enough fraud in that without perjuring her soul any further.

In other circumstances Miranda might have enjoyed her lunch as Brett seemed to manage everything so cleverly that she was spared even one embarrassing moment. He was also excellent company and Miranda had a lively and intelligent mind which she had never allowed to grow lazy. It was only when she found herself wondering, as she had done all morning, why a man like Deakin should choose to spend so much time with a young woman whom he believed to be crippled, that her pleasure in the conversation and the meal they were sharing dimmed a little.

On the way home, she kept praying that as soon as they reached the house he would tell her father he could keep it. And, after buying the business, would go back to New York, or wherever it was he usually lived and spent most of his time. She had a curious feeling at the thought of not seeing him again, though she knew that, if she did, the strain of having to keep pretending she couldn't walk might become intolerable.

When they arrived home and he deposited her in the hall, then informed a beaming Harry and Alice that he would be back the following evening perhaps, if Miranda wished, to take her out again, she could have screamed with fright and frustration.

On the other side of Birmingham, near Sutton Coldfield, in a smart modern bungalow in a pleasant suberb, Eve Martin was pacing up and down. She had discarded the stick which she used when her father was around. He had gone out for the day, leaving her alone with her thoughts.

They were not happy ones. Brett had come to see her the previous evening. Although he never failed to keep in touch she hadn't seen him for several months. But in all the years since her accident, he had never grown any closer to her. She sometimes wondered if he ever would, and if all her secret planning and manipulation would come to nothing.

Her thoughts went back to the evening of the work Christmas party, years ago. Brett Deakin, whose business reputation arrived before him, had just taken over her previous boss's huge electronic company and agreed to keep her on as his secretary. Eve was thrilled to see such a devastatingly impressive young bachelor sitting in the chair that had formerly held Hugh Cramp's corpulent, elderly figure. She was attracted to him immediately, and though she tried to hide it, it didn't prevent her from dreaming and planning. Two of her friends, both secretaries, had married their bosses. Why not her? she asked herself. It was only slowly that she realized that Brett Deakin was as immune to her not inconsiderable charms as old Hugh Cramp had been.

She didn't give up. Brett received plenty of phone calls from other women, but there didn't appear to be anyone special. Like a lot of men immersed in their work, he probably just needed a little jolt of some sort to make him realize he could do with a wife and that she wasn't just a part of his office furniture. With this in mind, she began scheming in earnest.

On the night of the party, to which she knew he would feel committed to at least show his face, she pretended that, in all the contagious excitement, she had overlooked some important papers which needed his immediate attention. Fortunately he didn't explode, as she had thought he might, which strengthened her suspicions that business parties weren't exactly his favourite thing.

Having to deal with the extra correspondence made them late, but with his usual good manners Brett offered to escort her to where the party was being held – which was exactly what Eve had hoped for. He said, when she made a great thing of protesting, that it was the least he could do, as he was responsible for delaying her. The entrance they made, along with the secretly seductive little smile she pinned on her face gave, if slightly raised brows and speculative looks were anything to go by, exactly the impression she had anticipated.

Brett Deakin never so much as hinted she was becoming a nuisance, not even when she clung to his side and, after a few drinks, slipped a triumphant hand through his arm. She might have noticed, had she looked for it as she did this, a slight narrowing of his eyes as he glanced at her, but she was happily oblivious, especially when he made no immediate effort to free himself. This happened a few minutes later when Dan Greenly, the head of one of the data processing sections, bumped clumsily into them, spilling Eve's wine.

'Never mind,' Brett said, cutting through the other man's profuse apologies smoothly. 'Miss Martin's dress seems none the worse, but perhaps you ought to take her to the bar and replenish her glass. I think I must circulate for a while.'

Before Eve quite realized it, Greenly was whisking her away and Deakin, she noticed a few minutes later, appeared to be concentrating on the blowsy blonde supervisor from accounts. So much for circulating, she thought acidly.

Nevertheless, she regarded this as only a minor setback. Dan Greenly, she knew, had fancied her for a long time and, while she didn't return his feelings, she felt quite entitled to use him to try and make her boss jealous. Brett might not come near her again that evening – instinct told her he wouldn't – but if he saw that other men were interested in her, it might make him think.

The party, which amounted to little more than a few drinks and light talk, wouldn't go on for long.

Before it finished she asked Dan if he would take her home. He was drinking a lot, but he always did and it never affected his driving. She never told Brett that she had asked Dan to take her home, or that, as they left, when Dan said he'd had too much to drink and suggested they should leave his car and take a taxi, she had merely laughed at him.

After the crash, when Dan swerved over the road right into the path of a huge transporter, so was not alive to contradict her, she told Brett that, though she had suspected Dan was drunk and pleaded with him not to drive, he had taken no notice of her. And she'd been too miserable over the embarrassment she'd belatedly realized she had caused Brett earlier in the evening to argue.

Once she saw that Brett blamed himself for the accident, she played on this theme continually. She let him know, seemingly innocently, that if he had not more or less thrust them together, she would never have gone anywhere near Dan Greenly. Her own injuries were not extensive but, as they guaranteed her a lot of Brett Deakin's attention, she pretended they were. She claimed, though her doctors could find no physical reasons for it, that she couldn't walk properly and spent most of her days, when other people were around, anyway, in the wheelchair Brett provided for her. When Brett insisted on calling in specialists, Eve was clever enough to convince even the best of them that she was suffering from a form of involuntary paralysis. He also paid for some plastic surgery she needed for scars that burns from the accident had left on her arms and shoulders.

As well as all this, when she swore the accident had shattered her so completely, both mentally and physically, that she was too distressed to work again, he arranged to pay her a monthly allowance which amounted to more than her previous salary and topped this up annually, along with generous payments to her father for looking after her. When John Martin occasionally accused her of taking advantage of her former boss, she would turn on him viciously and tell him to mind his own bloody business, that she wouldn't put up with any interference from him! She was certain if she kept fanning Brett's peculiar guilt over the accident which, surprisingly, still seemed to linger, that he would eventually ask her to marry him.

This belief was reinforced when he brought his sister to meet her, and when his sister still rang her occasionally. But when he left Birmingham, then London, to spend most of his time abroad and she saw him less frequently, her hopes of an early proposal gradually faded.

She didn't let his long absences discourage her altogether and while he was away she enjoyed the freedom that being financially independent and unencumbered by a necessity to work gave her. But it was now eight years since he had, by chance, followed her from the works' party and personally helped to rescue her from the almost-unrecognizable wreckage of Dan's car. And she wasn't getting any younger. Yesterday, when he came to see her and took her out to dinner and waited patiently while she pretended to hobble painfully, with her stick, she decided she must do something to get him to make the kind of committment she had worked so long and hard for.

To this end, she had teased him about remaining single for so long, then later had wondered fretfully what was to happen to her once her father was gone. But in neither instances had he replied with more than an inscrutable smile and an oddly disturbing silence.

CHAPTER 4

When Brett Deakin arrived at Well House the following evening, he found the Ferris family waiting for him in the lounge and he wondered a little at the tenseness of the atmosphere. He didn't dwell on it, however. He believed that the situation over the house and business was the cause of it. And for that, Harry Ferris had only himself to blame.

It was Miranda he felt sorry for, not her father. Without preamble, after bidding them all good evening, he told Miranda he had booked a table at the same hotel where they had lunched the previous day. Then, without satisfying Harry's obvious curiosity as to why he should be taking such an interest in his disabled daughter, he quickly got Alice to find a wrap for her and a few minutes later they were gone.

Miranda knew better now than to protest at Brett Deakin's high-handed manner. The less she said, she decided grimly, the sooner this ridiculous charade might be over. Sooner, rather than later, he was going to tire of wasting both his time and pity on an ungrateful and crippled girl, and she would be the first to sigh with relief. If he didn't, she would have even more to say to her father and Alice than she had said today. And that had been plenty!

She wondered if the strain of it wasn't, in some way, beginning to affect Brett Deakin as well, as he spoke very little during the meal they shared and his appetite seemed little better than her own. She was relieved, on looking around the hotel dining-room, to see no one she knew, though this didn't seem to matter anymore. All that did matter was how to get rid of Brett Deakin without hurting her father and Alice, but she acknowledged that if she knew how it might be easier.

Brett Deakin was thinking of the remarks Eve Martin had made the previous evening about him still being single. He had ignored the heavy hints she was throwing out, being well aware that she imagined she was in love with him and would marry him tomorrow, should he be willing, which he definitely was not.

Miranda Ferris, however, was something else again. He studied her broodingly over dinner, as a connoisseur might study a picture he was considering. The delicate, almost classical lines of her face, framed by pale blonde hair that moved like thick gleaming silk whenever she did. She was beautiful and, even casually dressed, would stand out in a crowd. If she could walk.

As soon as he saw her he knew she was going to mean something in his life. That in some way she was going to be instrumental in laying the ghosts which had bothered him for so long. *How* had not been immediately clear to him, but it was now. He would marry her, make the kind of personal commitment to her that would not be possible otherwise. Marriage would enable him to spend time as well as money on her, to do everything possible to help her to walk again. And, at the same time, to alleviate the mysterious jinx in his conscience which continued to plague him.

Aware of his appraisal without knowing the reason for it, Miranda suggested, after they had their coffee, that they went home. She felt she could stand only so much of this man's company, and, for one evening, that she'd had enough.

The moonlight was bright. It was a beautiful night for November, with no hint of the inclement weather there had been at the beginning of the week. The snow Brett had encountered on his way here from London might never have been. There was a slight frost, which made the trees and the grass around them sparkle in the moonlight, but that was all.

To Miranda's dismay, Brett pulled into a deserted lay-by a few miles from Well House and parked his car.

'I want to talk to you,' he said.

She turned to him with a frown. 'You've been talking to me all evening . . .'

'This is something else.'

Miranda stared at him as his magnetic glance held hers. She swallowed. 'Is it about my father? His business?'

'It could involve him.'

She felt suddenly sick. 'You don't want it?'

'I haven't said that. But whether I take it off his hands or not might be entirely up to you.'

'Me?' Her eyes widened. 'How could that be?'

'I'm trying to tell you. I want to help . . .'

Miranda interrupted quickly, before he could continue, hoping to secure a quick decision and somehow end this travesty she was so tired of taking part in. 'You could help if you bought the works and perhaps let him keep the house. I'm young and adaptable,' she added, though she realized she was probably just repeating what she had said yesterday, 'but Dad isn't.'

'Miranda –' leaning over her, he flipped a strand of hair gently off her smooth forehead '– will you please shut up and just listen to me for a change? I'm trying to ask you to marry me.'

'M-marry you?' Her eyes widened.

He nodded. 'Why not?'

They stared at each other in the moonlight, the suddenly apprehensive girl and the tall powerful man. Miranda couldn't believe what she was hearing. She couldn't believe Brett Deakin could possibly wish to marry someone confined to a wheelchair – which was what he believed her to be. 'I don't appreciate a joke like this,' she said.

'I shouldn't expect you to – if it was a joke,' he assured her soberly.

'So you've decided to marry a cripple!' she choked scornfully. 'Would you mind explaining, Brett, where such a crazy notion suddenly came from?'

He smiled slightly at her incredulous tones, but it didn't alter the look of determination on his face. 'Let's just say that I'd like to have the right to look after you.'

'But we've only just met,' Miranda exclaimed. 'And you can't possibly want to saddle yourself with someone like me.'

Brett laughed. 'You don't flatter yourself, Miranda, but I know what I'm doing. Do you really think I would marry you if I didn't wish to? If you will stop querying my motives, for a minute, I might tell you what I have in mind.'

'I don't care what you have in mind,' Miranda said tightly. 'When two people marry it's usually because they care for each other in some way; as we haven't had time to do that, I don't think I am wrong in querying your motives. In any case, before you go on, I think I should tell you that I wouldn't marry you if you were the last man on earth.'

His mouth quirked. 'You'd probably be killed in the rush if I were, but you obviously don't believe in boosting a man's ego.'

She didn't deign to answer him.

He studied her for a long moment while she appeared to be having trouble with her thoughts. 'Joking apart, Miranda,' he said at last, 'it might pay you to remember that your father has a business he needs to sell for more than it is worth in order to pay off his debts. And, if you won't marry me, I don't buy it. It's as simple as that.'

'And – if I do?'

'Then I'll give him everything he is asking for it.'

'And the house?'

'That as well. And an income for life.' How many more people would he be keeping in Birmingham before he was finished? Brett wondered cynically.

But what was money if it could help him get rid of the overdose of conscience that plagued him?

'And what would you be getting out of it?' Miranda raised her eyes to his dark blue ones. 'Married to someone who couldn't be a proper wife. No chance of having children.'

This didn't deter him, as she had hoped it might. 'I will worry about that kind of thing when I have to.'

Miranda shivered. He didn't realize she couldn't marry him, even if she wanted to, but he still hadn't answered her question. He said he wished to marry her so he would have the right to look after her, but she doubted that this was the real reason. And, if for her father's sake she was tempted to say yes to him, and he really did want to marry her because he believed she was disabled, what would he say when he discovered she wasn't? The whole thing was impossible. Despair rioted through her. She had to go home and tell Harry and Alice she was going to tell Brett the truth, regardless of the consequences. She would have told him now if she hadn't felt she owed her father and aunt at least some kind of warning first. Whatever fate had in store for them after that, it couldn't be worse than this, she thought, looking at Brett dully.

Brett, thinking she looked tired, took pity on her. 'Look, Miranda,' he said, 'as I don't suppose, in your position, you've ever given marriage much thought, I'll give you a few days to think about it. But I promise – ' he smiled, being supremely confident of getting his own way in the end ' – that if you do decide to accept my proposal, it won't be something you will ever regret.'

* * *

After taking Miranda home and exchanging a brief word with Harry and Alice, Brett left. He felt more than satisfied with his evening's work as he drove back along the drive. It wasn't until he was almost at the end of it that he noticed the metallic gleam of Miranda's small evening bag, lying half-concealed under the passenger seat where she had been sitting. Damn, he thought, pulling up impatiently. With so much on her mind she must have forgotten about it, but perhaps he should take it back for fear she discovered it was missing and began worrying over it. Girls were funny about that kind of thing. She might even think she had left it at the hotel they'd been in. Picking it up, he sat staring at it abstractedly. It was small and beautifully made, like its owner. Expensive without being ostentatious and looking as if it belonged to a fastidious woman. Turning it over, without quite realizing what he was doing, he found himself wondering idly if Miranda really was a woman yet, or had time suspended her, since her accident, in the same state as she was in at nineteen? Would he ever know? Brett wondered. So far he had got no further than trying to ensure he had the legitimate right to try and make her well again.

He walked back to the house. It wasn't worth risking getting stuck by trying to turn his car on the soggy sides of the drive and the house was not far away. With his long swift strides it took him no more that a few minutes to reach the front door.

The door had no bell, only an old-fashioned knocker that was almost useless. No one came, not even when he knocked again. He recalled how, on his first visit here; no one had heard him either. That time he had, eventually, just walked in. This time, however, when he tried the door he found it was locked.

Brett frowned as he stepped impatiently away from it. As he approached the house he had noticed that the upstairs lights were on, but that there was also a light in the lounge. As it wasn't yet eleven o'clock he hoped Miranda might still be up. He decided, before doing anything else, to see if she was. If he stood well back from the lounge windows, he should be able to see in without being seen, and so avoid running the risk of scaring anyone. It looked, though, as if her handbag was going to have to wait until the morning.

Very quietly he walked around the corner of the building, taking care to keep several yards away from it. The lounge curtains were conveniently undrawn and he could see inside the room quite clearly. As he did so, he felt himself go rigid. Miranda was there, all right; so was her father. As Brett halted abruptly, he saw Harry suddenly laugh and kiss her lightly on her cheek, as if he was congratulating her about something. But it wasn't this that made cold anger shoot through him. It was the sight of Miranda – poor, *crippled* Miranda – actually standing on her own two feet, without aid or assistance. And when her father let go of her, she smiled at him then walked quickly to one of the French windows and let herself out. While Harry, after calling something after her, sat down to watch the television, Miranda obviously intended going out for a breath of fresh air before turning in. Brett, smothering a rasp of rage, withdrew further into the shadow of the trees he was concealed under and watched icily as she walked straight past him.

Miranda had just had another row with her father and Alice. It went on for over fifteen minutes, until at last they had agreed that, since Brett had proposed to her and marriage was out of the question, they would have to tell him the truth. Even Alice had conceded it would not be feasible now to do anything else. Miranda was too agitated to pretend to be anything but relieved that they were at last being sensible. But it had taken her all her time to say goodnight to Alice, when her aunt, still clearly disgruntled as she retired to bed, said she couldn't pretend to be pleased about it.

Harry, after she was out of sight, had suddenly surprised Miranda by laughing and kissing her and declaring lightly that something would turn up. That, though Brett Deakin might be wealthy, he wasn't the only buyer in the haystack. Miranda almost asked if he hadn't got his metaphors mixed up. Instead she had nodded, smiled stiffly and told him she was going for a short walk before turning in, or otherwise she would never sleep. She left her father settling down in front of the TV, where he said he had better wait until she came in.

With his warning to be careful ringing in her ears, Miranda slipped out through the French windows at the side of the lounge and quickly closed them behind her. The argument they'd all had had been so angry and recriminatory that it had left her feeling drained. When she had laid all the facts before them, both Harry and Alice had looked as if she had deprived them of a fortune. Alice, to begin with anyway, even had the nerve to suggest that there must be something Miranda could do about it, and she'd had a hard time convincing her that there wasn't – even had she been willing to – which clearly had not suited her.

Nevertheless, Miranda had won eventually. In the morning she would get in touch with Brett and ask him to call. Then, when he did, she would tell him she could walk. She would confess how they had tried to deceive him and how everything had got hopelessly out of hand. And he need no longer try to make a martyr of himself by marrying her and buying Harry's business. She didn't doubt he would be furious, but if a good tongue-lashing was the worst she could expect, she should perhaps consider herself lucky. As for the family firm . . . well, as Harry said, someone might eventually be interested enough to buy it. Meanwhile something was bound to turn up to enable them to manage until this happened. Even if nothing did, whatever the future held, she decided, it could never be as harrowing as the last few days had been.

Miranda walked on, unaware of the man silently stalking her. She'd come out, not so much for a breath of fresh air as to try and forget Brett Deakin for an hour or two. But just as she thought she was managing to do this by concentrating on other things, she was startled to hear herself not only saying his name aloud, but tacking a Mrs on in front of it, as if she was unconsciously practising the sound of it. Appalled at what she found she was doing, she almost stumbled on the path she was following. For heaven's sake, Miranda, she told herself sharply, pull yourself together! You won't be seeing Brett again after tomorrow, and you'll certainly never be his wife now.

Miranda's new-found optimism, if that was what it was, might have faded a little had she known that Brett Deakin was standing only a few yards away from her and, on hearing what she said, felt his jaw go tight with increasing rage. Her reluctance earlier in the evening to commit herself had clearly only been a ruse to whet his appetite, as here she was, obviously trying out her future title. Mrs Brett Deakin, indeed! Both she and her disreputable family must have spent the last hour spending his millions. Before he finished with Miss Ferris, he vowed, she might well be incapable of spending anything!

With the quick changes so common to the capricious British weather, the frost disappeared as a rising wind blew heavy dark clouds over what had been, until a few minutes ago, a clear star-lit sky. This enabled Brett to continue following Miranda without being seen. Another time she might have sensed his presence, but for the moment she was so busy fighting the incomprehensible trend of her thoughts that she didn't realize that the person they were so stubbornly centred on was almost immediately behind her. In an effort to stop herself from wondering what it was going to be like not to see Brett again, she began to jog. This was a form of exercise she had enjoyed and excelled in before her accident and had taken up again in Switzerland, though she'd had to be careful to begin with.

Now, though not yet up to her old standard, she soon covered the few hundred yards to the edge of the grounds.

Brett followed, noting with tight lips her agile performance, the way her slight body moved as if one with the wind. She appeared to have changed into a pair of tight jeans since he dropped her off, and with them wore a white hooded top over which her hair streamed in pale golden strands in the moonlight. Slowly he came out from the protective shadows of the trees, no longer bothering to hide himself. He was so filled with icy anger that he had no intention now of doing anything other than confronting her. His eyes narrowed, he considered her. He couldn't remember anyone ever making a fool of him to this extent and he meant to make her pay for it, if it was the last thing he did!

Miranda felt her heart jerk with fright as she heard a footstep crunch on the grass behind her and swung around apprehensively to see who it was?

'Brett!' With all kinds of terrifying possibilities flashing through her mind, she had never thought it would be him. She knew her voice must sound hoarse, but she was surprised she could speak at all, with his tall figure looming threateningly over her. 'What,' she gasped, 'are you doing here?'

'Hello, Miranda,' he drawled, in tones which reminded her of silk laced with steel. 'Don't you think I should be asking you that question?'

'I . . .' Hastily she licked dry lips, her eyes still wide and startled as she groped fruitlessly for words.

'Go on,' he snarled.

She didn't pretend to misunderstand him. 'I know you must be feeling angry,' she said. 'But we were going to tell you.'

'When?' He stared at her contemptuously. 'After the wedding?'

'No – in the morning.' With his icy gaze flicking her like raw lightning, she was only able to answer him dazedly. Seeing he still looked dubious, she made a greater effort. 'We really were!'

'You expect me to believe it?'

Did she? Could she? In order to give herself time to recover a little and think, she asked quickly, 'Why did you come back tonight and follow me like this?'

'You left your purse in my car and I thought you might be worried about it when you missed it.' Taking it from behind his back, he almost thrust it at her.

'You shouldn't have bothered,' Miranda said numbly and she suspected, in the circumstances, inanely.

'Don't you think it's as well I did?' he asked. 'Didn't it ever occur to you, in the midst of all your scheming to procure a rich husband, that if I had not discovered you could walk until after the wedding, I might easily have killed you?'

He looked furious enough to kill her now. Miranda went paler than she already was and felt herself tremble. Brett's face, even in the poor light, might have been made of stone and his eyes glittered coldly. She couldn't help feeling very frightened. People were murdered for lesser crimes than the one she'd committed. She wouldn't have thought Brett was a man to lose his head – whatever the circumstances –

but he was, after all, still almost a stranger. What did she really know about him? Before he was tempted to do anything as rash as he was clearly contemplating, perhaps she ought to try and talk to him?

'I can explain,' she said, forcing herself to speak meekly. 'If you would just calm down for a minute and listen . . .'

CHAPTER 5

Unfortunately, Miranda's suggestion appeared to merely add fuel to Brett's fury. 'I doubt you could explain anything,' he rapped. 'At least, not to my satisfaction.'

His anger, being of a coldly calculating nature which Miranda had not encountered before, made her feel even more frightened and brought an unwelcome sense of inertia.

'May I sit down first?' she begged, groping behind her for the garden seat they were standing beside, as her legs felt suddenly too weak to support her.

'Tired?' As she collapsed on to it, without waiting for his permission, his dark brows rose hatefully. 'I can't say I'm surprised, considering the considerable energy you must have put into hoodwinking me. Are you sure you have enough left to concoct a plausible excuse for what you've done? If so, I'd be surprised to hear it.'

Did he think she intended concocting excuses – as he put it? Miranda's heart sank as his contempt somehow hurt her. She felt even more dejected as he sank down beside her. The seat was not very long and suddenly she was so conscious of his aggressive male body that she wished she had made more effort to stay on her feet.

'Well?' Brett taunted her, as she stared at him silently. 'Don't you know where to begin? Why not why you decided, under false pretences, to marry me?'

Miranda flinched, still having difficulty in marshalling her thoughts. His fury scared her more than it might normally have done if she hadn't sensed something behind it she didn't understand. She might almost have suspected she had shattered some kind of a dream for him but, as he was not in love with her, this couldn't be possible. But there was something, she felt suddenly sure, that had nothing to do with her or, if it had, it was only indirectly.

Aware that the line of thought she was pursuing might be irrelevant to what mattered now, she said slowly, 'You seem to forget I never promised to marry you. You asked me to, for some reason . . .'

'You must have known because I believed you to be crippled.'

'But you didn't say why –'

'Then you must have a bad memory,' he cut in. 'Didn't I tell you it was because I wished to look after you?'

'Yes, but, surely that could mean anything –?'

'Look,' he interrupted again, 'let's forget my motives – which I think I've already explained – and concentrate on yours for a change.'

Miranda clenched her hands. While Brett was obviously twisting the truth a little, he would expect total honesty from her. Yet anything she said might be suspect unless he could be persuaded she had been going to confess everything in the morning. As it was, it might be far from easy to convince him she had intended confessing anything.

'Do you want me to begin at the beginning?' she asked, when a restless movement beside her warned her he was getting impatient.

'I know you had an accident,' he said, without mentioning he had checked it out in an old newspaper. 'What interests me more is how long you've been able to walk. Years?'

'No.' She shook her head, believing it pointless now to try and keep anything from him. His curt voice and breath on her cheek was still having a disturbing effect on her, but she forced herself to go on. Briefly she spoke of her accident, then began telling him about Switzerland. 'I had so many operations which proved disappointing, but the last one was a success. I was there almost four months and Alice came with me. We only came home the day before yesterday.'

'So why pretend you weren't cured?'

Miranda's cheeks burned as she turned to look at him, then dropped her eyes from his harsh face. She hadn't thought it would be so difficult. 'I got it into my head,' she said, 'that if you believed I was disabled you might let us keep the house. Or at least to go on living in it.'

Brett's teeth snapped together. 'Whose brainwave was this? Hardly yours, I think.'

Even as his voice warned her it could be dangerous to continue being evasive, Miranda still found it difficult to involve her aunt. Alice had, after all, only been trying to help.

'It was Alice, wasn't it?'

Catching another glimpse of his smouldering eyes, as her own widened and flickered towards him, Miranda, feeling like a traitor, found herself nodding unhappily. 'She didn't mean any harm, though. She is concerned for my father, and is convinced that having to leave Well House might eventually kill him.'

'An ingenious plan with only about a thousand drawbacks,' Brett sneered contemptuously. 'Only a fool wouldn't have considered the pitfalls. I'm surprised you went along with it, Miranda. You may be misguided, but I shouldn't have thought you lacking in intelligence.'

She flushed and hoped the darkness would conceal the heat in her cheeks. 'My father believed you would only stay a few minutes – when you first came to see the house, that is.'

'Ha!' Brett's derisive laughter grated like sandpaper on Miranda's nerves. 'So, I put a spoke in your wheel straight away, did I, by outstaying my welcome?'

Miranda shrugged but didn't speak. What was the use of denying the undeniable?

As if her indifference, or what he took for indifference, infuriated him afresh, Brett grasped hold of her and swung her swiftly around towards him. 'Please look at me, Miranda, while I'm speaking to you, will you? Surely that much is not beyond you.'

Miranda shivered as something she had felt before when he touched her raced through her. It made her feel hot which, in turn, made her feel flustered and out of her depth and quite unable to snap back at him.

Apparently satisfied he had subdued her, at least for the time being, Brett went on. 'What about yesterday when I took you out, couldn't you have told me about your aunt's ridiculous plan then?'

'She still thought it had a good chance of working,' Miranda said.

'Well, what about this evening, when I proposed to you? What excuse do you have for concealing the truth from me then?'

Miranda closed her eyes defeatedly. The grip of his hands on her shoulders seemed to be threatening to break her very bones. The hot feeling he was generating was increasing but, though she wished he would let her go, she dared not struggle for fear of rekindling the anger she still felt in him.

'I don't have an excuse,' she told him stiffly. 'That is, not what you might consider a good one, Mr Deakin. I realize I should have told you everything as soon as you asked me to marry you – and I would have done had I not felt I owed it to my father and Alice to give them some sort of warning first.'

'What for?'

His abruptness made her flinch; she had to steel herself to go on. 'I wasn't sure how you would react. My father, you see, has a slight heart condition, and I thought that if you lost your temper and suddenly confronted him, accusing him of trying to gain your sympathy by false pretences and other things, it could prove fatal.'

'You obviously didn't think it might be me who would have the heart attack?'

69

'You?' She almost laughed. Anyone less like having a heart attack she had yet to see. Brett Deakin was one of those extremely tough individuals who had probably never known even a day's illness in his life. He might even have to consult a dictionary to discover what a headache was! 'Despite what you think, Brett, both my father and Alice have done a lot for me. I've had a small fortune spent on me since my accident and they've always been very kind and patient. I don't imagine you know much about the disabled. If you did, you might realize how much time and attention they often need.'

He considered her narrowly. 'Did you not say yesterday that you didn't?'

'Well, some of us can manage without it, but most of us can't. Not to begin with, anyway.'

'Would you ever have been able to cope on your own?'

'If my last operation had not been a success, I was going to try to.'

'So,' Brett did a mocking reappraisal, 'you weren't going to marry me, but you wanted to warn Harry and Alice before telling me? And what did they say when you did?'

'They agreed there was nothing for it but to tell you the truth.'

'But I only have your word for that.' Scepticism made his eyes glitter in the moonlight. 'Wouldn't it be nearer the truth to say you intended going through with it?'

'Going through with it?' Parrot-like, she repeated his question and suddenly her outraged feelings gave her the strength to wrench herself away from him.

Her legs still felt too weak to enable her to rise from the seat, but at least she could put a little distance between them. 'You're insane!' she gasped. 'And you have no proof . . .'

'I have more than you think,' he snapped. 'After bringing you home, when I reached the end of your drive I came back.'

'We didn't hear a car.'

'Because I decided to walk, rather than bother to turn the car around. It only took a few minutes.'

'But – why?'

'Haven't I already told you – to deliver your purse. And when I couldn't get an answer at your door, I went around the corner of the house to the lounge.' Here Brett paused, as if to allow the full implications of his words to sink in. 'I had noticed that the lights there were still on when I passed, and I thought I would see if you were still up before I knocked again. I kept my distance from the window so as not to risk giving anyone a fright, which I might have done had you looked out and seen me. But what I saw there made me think you would have deserved a fright, had I given you one.'

Miranda went cold, though she wasn't sure why. She felt bewildered and it showed in her beautiful uncertain eyes. 'There was only me and my father.'

'Laughing together.'

Had it looked like that? Miranda shook her head as she tried to remember. 'He was . . .'

'Obviously congratulating you on the deal you were about to make, concerning our future nuptials. Whatever you set out initially to achieve, it was apparent that his clever daughter had succeeded beyond his wildest dreams. A wealthy son-in-law, an income for life. No more work, no more strife. I'm getting quite poetic, aren't I?' he jeered.

Miranda stared at him for a moment, too aghast to speak. She had to admit that what Brett had seen could easily have been mistakenly misconstrued as some kind of celebration. He had seen she could walk, and how cheerful Harry was, or had pretended to be, and there was no way she was going to convince him that his interpretation of the scene he had witnessed was not the right one. She could only apologize again and hope he would agree to forget everything.

'I'm sorry,' she said. 'I realize how it must have seemed and I can't blame you for thinking the worst of us. I can only repeat what I told you earlier, that I was going to tell you the truth in the morning and have no intention of marrying you – ever! And you are mistaken about my father. He was not congratulating me on anything. He was merely trying to reassure me that someone was bound to come along eventually and buy his business.'

'I don't believe you,' Brett said curtly. 'I think you would have married me – taken me for every penny you could get. You made quite a fool of me, didn't you?'

Suddenly stung by his obvious opinion of her, Miranda retorted sharply, 'You can always congratulate yourself on your narrow escape. Even if you had to snoop to achieve it.'

Brett's eyes narrowed cynically. Did she really believe he was going to let her off that easily? He had planned to marry her and by doing so had

72

intended to help them both. He had felt sorry for her, taken pity on her and, in turn, she had cheated and lied and expected, after being exposed, to be let off scot-free. Well, she was about to discover that very few things were ever that easy. He would marry her – it was not as if he was thinking of marrying anyone else. After that he would treat her indifferently for a year or two, then divorce her. It might cost him – alimony was seldom cheap, but if she was deprived of the status that being his wife would give her, along with the life of luxury she would soon grow used to, she might be truly repentant instead of only making a great show of pretending to be.

Taking his time, he smiled thinly into her flushed, indignant face. 'I'm still going to marry you, Miranda, but I'll be doing it now with my eyes open.'

Miranda froze. 'You can't be serious?'

'You'd better believe it.'

She drew a shaken breath, trying to tell herself he couldn't force her to do anything, while, for reasons she didn't understand, something seemed to be telling her exactly the opposite. Feeling, because of this, as if there was something very threatening hanging over her, she almost whispered, 'You said you wanted the right to look after me, but you surely can't wish to do that now?'

'Why not?' he shrugged. 'I need a wife. They can be very useful, I believe. And I find I still want to marry you, despite everything.'

'But why me?'

'How desperate you sound.'

She didn't tell him that this was the way she was beginning to feel, especially when it was obvious he wasn't going to answer her question. 'I didn't mean to sound desperate – ' she looked at him, to try and give emphasis to what she was saying ' – but I can't marry you.'

His eyes glinted as they met her entreating grey ones. 'Do you find me physically unattractive?'

'I don't love you,' she replied evasively, 'if that is what you mean?'

'Love needn't come into it. It seldom does, in this day and age.'

She didn't like the sound of that. 'Then it should.'

'Don't be so naïve, Miranda. There are other things far more comfortable and transferable than being fond of someone.'

'Transferable?'

'Something one can take from one relationship to another. Sex, for instance. If people contented themselves with that, it might prevent them getting hurt.'

Miranda frowned. Was Brett deliberately trying to shock her, or was it really the way he looked at life? The crease in her forehead deepening, Miranda stared at him, while he stared back, his eyes glinting with mocking amusement.

'This has to be the craziest idea I've ever heard!' she exclaimed. 'I think, before you go any further, you'd better leave.'

'No way.' He shook his dark head. 'Not until everything is settled.'

'I'll never agree to marrying you, if that's what you mean. How many times do I have to tell you?'

He took no notice, except to suggest smoothly, 'Shouldn't you be thinking seriously, Miranda, of what you are refusing? My terms are the same as what they were after dinner. They still include your father and aunt and the roof over their heads. Against which, what do you have? A business I could be tempted to make sure your father is never able to sell – and probably arrange a prison sentence for him as well, if he isn't able settle his not-inconsiderable debts. Need I go on?'

Miranda countered, more defiantly than she felt, 'I'll get a job.'

'Which, as far as his debt is concerned, wouldn't pay off a fraction of it.'

She hated him. 'I'll find something!'

'I don't think you will.'

Miranda suppressed a defeated sob. What he said was unfortunately true. She was both untrained and untried. It could be months, in the present state of the job market, before she found someone willing to employ her, and even longer before she was earning more than a basic salary. And if Harry couldn't sell the heavily mortgaged factory, and the London flat had to go towards settling what he owed, they might have nothing left. Miranda dared not even try to envisage what her father and Alice would do if that happened. A life of penury, without a penny to their names. If she condemned them to a future such as that, would she ever be able to live with herself again?

Aware of the answer, almost before the question crossed her mind, she turned bitterly to Brett. 'I seem to be left with no alternative but to do as you ask. Though I don't know what you are going to get out of it? A marriage of convenience . . .'

'We'll see.'

'What else could it be?'

'Perhaps what we make of it,' he replied enigmatically.

'And what would that be?'

'I think, in this case, I might be better at demonstrating than explaining,' he said and, before she could move, his arms went out to pull her to him and he kissed her expertly on her startled lips. At first his lips only touched hers lightly and she was more conscious of the way her heart began racing. But as if it surprisingly ignited some kind of unexpected feeling between them, the pressure of Brett's mouth swiftly deepened until, far from wishing to escape him, she became, as his arms tightened, boneless and frighteningly acquiescent.

Miranda had never been kissed like this before, not even in the years she could vaguely remember before her accident. She wasn't sure what it was doing to her. It seemed to be rendering her mindless and every pulse in her body was beginning to throb. But just as her blood seemed in danger of taking on fire, Brett raised his head abruptly and, as suddenly as he had taken hold of her, he was thrusting her none too gently away from him.

Taking no notice of the dazed way she reacted to this, he said crisply, 'Perhaps that will prove that anything but a normal marriage between us may not be necessary. I won't rush you, though, Miranda. You have a lot of catching up to do and taking an inexperienced and reluctant woman to bed never appealed to me.'

Miranda was trying hard to regain her composure and, at the same time, to keep her temper, as what he said sounded more insulting than reassuring. 'I don't want to marry you,' she reiterated, between her teeth.

'You won't be getting such a bad deal.'

'You could be the one getting that.'

'I don't think so.'

Why was he so determined to go through with this? Miranda had hoped he might change his mind, but he obviously wasn't going to. Her gaze wandered blindly over the gardens, not seeing where the fountain played, where she had sat in her chair through many a summer's day, after manoeuvring herself along one of the special paths her father had made. Her whole world was changing so rapidly she wasn't sure she could endure it. For years she had relied almost entirely on other people. Now it seemed she had no one to rely on but herself. She felt like she'd been thrown ruthlessly from a safe harbour into stormy seas with no idea as to whether she would survive or not.

Brett watched her changing expressions shrewdly. 'You may think you aren't ready for marriage, Miranda but, as you can't just put your life on hold any more, you might find you can cope with it better than you could a job. The outside world can be very unsympathetic and you are used to being waited on hand and foot, are you not? Married to me, you'll have servants and every assistance to make your path smooth. You will be able to adapt at your own pace, without any pressure being put on you.'

Miranda turned to look at him again, her eyes questioning in her small face. 'Adapt to what?'

His blue eyes met hers with a hint of impatience.

'Leading a normal life, I suppose. Learning how to be fully mobile again after spending years in a wheelchair. Learning how to be a meaningful part of an adult world again. Need I go on?'

Miranda shook her head, not wishing to hear any more. He was merely quoting the obvious and ignoring what she suspected she would really have to worry about. Brett Deakin had the kind of looks and charisma that women found exciting. She had noticed them looking at him when she was out with him, and she felt terribly apprehensive over having such a man for a husband. The thoughts of the demands he might make on her, even if not immediately, were disturbing. Yet how long might she be able to fight him if he claimed what he might consider his rights? She could still feel the touch of his mouth and could not deny the way her blood had surged in response. But somehow the thought of belonging to him without love was suddenly abhorrent to her.

She thought wistfully of the light-hearted young girl she had been until the time of her accident. She had laughed about sex then, and even if she had not yet indulged in it, she had taken it for granted that one day she would, with or without a wedding ring. She'd had so many other interests that she hadn't actually given much thought to it, but she couldn't remember shrinking from it, the way she was doing now.

'I think I'd better go in before my father comes looking for me,' she said quickly, in an effort to break the train of her thoughts.

'I'll come with you.' Brett jumped up beside her. 'He may be surprised to see me, but I think I should see him this evening and tell him that you have decided to marry me after all.'

'He will never accept it, just like that!' Miranda protested feverishly. 'Not after what he and Alice just agreed to. Shouldn't you wait?'

Brett laughed drily and steadied her as she swayed. 'I think you'll find he will accept it, and without asking too many questions. Especially when I mention the concessions attached. Once he realizes how well off, and worry free, he's going to be, you can take my word for it that the fact that I've discovered you can walk will be glossed over – like the fiasco of the last few days, as if he'd known nothing about it. He will be only too willing to pretend it never happened. And when I inform him that we are going to be married almost immediately, I guarantee he will be delighted.'

Which, to Miranda's despairing amazement, Harry was.

CHAPTER 6

Eve Martin was in shock. Brett Deakin had called the previous evening and told her he was getting married. He had asked her to congratulate him and wish him well, and she still wasn't over it.

At first Eve was too stunned to speak. She'd simply stared at him, a tall, powerful man, whose air of authority never seemed to diminish. What about me? she had felt like screaming. What about all the years I've waited for you to propose to me? She might have done, had not the same self-protective instincts which had served her so well in the past, warned her just in time that to reproach Brett in this way could result in her not seeing him again. Wait, the voice of caution had advised. You may come out of this better than you think. Like lightning her thoughts had continued. How long do marriages last, today? Some were of very short duration. And if Brett tired of his and got a divorce, might he not eventually turn to her?

Meanwhile, she would do everything possible to make sure his marriage failed. To many it might seem that she wasn't in a position to do anything, but it was surprising what could be achieved if one tried hard enough. There was Brett's sister, for instance. Eve knew, from one or two things Gaby had said when she rang, that she was ready to hate any girl Brett married since she considered herself Brett's heir and would never be prepared to welcome his wife. At first Eve wasn't able to take her seriously, until it suddenly occurred to her that, far from being unbalanced, Gaby might have deliberately chosen this way of warning her off. Why Gaby should have been suspicious of Brett's intentions towards her, Eve wasn't sure, as she had never said anything to make Gaby believe there was anything romantic between them. But if that had been Gaby's intention, instead of scaring her, it had only had the opposite effect. Rather than discouraging her, it had given Eve reason to think that Brett must have said something to his sister about his relationship with her, to make Gaby suspicious of her in this way. Eve, therefore, had continued to live in hope – a hope at least temporarily shattered by Brett's unexpected announcement the previous day.

Aware that Brett was waiting for her to say something, Eve had found her voice at last and managed to wish both him and his future bride every happiness. After that, with the tension between them seeming to ease, she'd enquired if the girl he was marrying lived in Birmingham? To her surprise, for she had thought it would be someone from New York, where he usually lived, he'd said she did, and added briefly that her name was Ferris. He also told her that the wedding was to be very quiet, which Eve took to be a hint that she shouldn't expect to be invited. And when she had asked where she could send a wedding present, he said that if she really felt obliged to get them something, just to keep hold of it until he saw her again. And when she asked when that would be, he had merely laughed and said he had no idea. Probably not until well after the New Year.

He had stayed just long enough after that to assure her that his marriage would make no difference to the allowance he made her and he would still pay her father for looking after her. Eve had tried not to feel humiliated as she'd said goodbye to him, but when she thought how it might have been, had he been going to marry her instead of this other girl, she'd felt positively murderous.

She couldn't wait until her father came home, but when he did, he hadn't been much help. He was quite certain he did not know any young woman called Ferris. He knew a Harry Ferris, he said, but they were acquaintances more than friends. He seldom saw him, though he had bumped into him about a week ago. And while he did have a daughter, she was a permanent invalid, he believed, and on holiday with her aunt, in Switzerland. Harry had mentioned this when he was explaining what he meant by joking wryly about being womanless at the moment and having to look after himself.

'Ferris isn't an uncommon name in Birmingham, Eve,' John had protested as she looked at him coldly. 'There must be quite a few Ferrises with daughters, but how would I know which one Brett is marrying? Why didn't you ask him?'

Why, indeed? Eve had wondered angrily. She knew her father was surprised that she hadn't, for she wasn't usually so reticent. She didn't tell him that something about Brett had seemed to be warning her against asking too many questions and, suddenly, she had found herself almost afraid to.

But now, the next morning, having had time to think, though she still felt stunned at the thought of Brett marrying someone else, she had decided what she would do. She would ring Gaby in America and pretend she was delighted with Brett's news. She would say he had been in a hurry when he came to tell her he was getting married and she wasn't sure she had congratulated him properly. And, if she hadn't, would Gaby please do it for her and tell him how sorry she was?

This, Eve felt certain, would result in one of two things. Either Gaby would know about the wedding and exactly who her brother was marrying, or Brett wouldn't have told her anything and she'd be furious.

If it was the latter, Eve might easily gain a valuable ally when it came to causing trouble between Brett and his bride. And even if Gaby knew about the wedding and was attending it, Eve doubted she would be pleased at the thought of being disinherited when Brett made his new wife his heir, and consequently would be only too willing to supply Eve with information which it might not, even yet, be too late to use for her own ends.

With this in mind, Eve waited impatiently until her father went out. He'd been going out a lot by himself lately, but for once she didn't ask what time he would be back. Yet though she rang New York repeatedly, she got no reply from Gaby's penthouse.

83

There was only an answering machine with its usual irritating message to leave one. Damn, she thought, wondering, if Gaby wasn't on her way here already, where she could be?

She was just considering trying the penthouse one more time when she heard something draw up on the gravel outside. To her surprise, when she went to look through the window, she saw a car she didn't recognize, and her father being helped out of it by someone she hadn't seen before, either. As she stared, frowning, they started towards the front door which, suddenly feeling alarmed, Eve rushed to open. Believing something was very wrong, she forgot to limp, or even to reach for the stick she always used.

'What's happened?' she cried, as she noticed how heavily her father was leaning on the other man's arm. 'You've had an accident?'

'Not really.' John Martin smiled ruefully. 'A slight mishap, that's all.'

'I should let your father in, if I were you, Miss Martin,' the stranger advised coolly, 'He is none the worse, or not much the worse, anyway, for his mishap, but he might feel better sitting down.'

Eve flushed as she stepped aside quickly, indignant at what sounded like a critical note in his voice. What on earth had John been up to? She followed them to the living-room and watched while her father sank with relief into the chair he usually sat in.

'Well, what happened?' she asked, this time more belligerently, as she thought it a question that one of them, by this time, should be prepared to answer.

The stranger merely looked at her again and said sharply, 'Do you have any brandy?'

Feeling she was being judged and found wanting, Eve hesitated for a moment, then went to get some. As she opened the drinks cabinet at the other side of the room, her father called after her, 'They very kindly offered me something on the site, but I said I'd rather wait until I got home.'

On the site? Wherever had he been? Her eyes wide, she half-turned to glance at him, but suddenly she knew. He'd been visiting that new housing estate over at Thourly, the one he'd been trying to persuade her to come and look at for ages. He was always enthusing about it, the wonderful job the builders were making of it. She was quite aware that he had never liked the large, rambling bungalow they had lived in since her accident. Brett had bought it for them and, while he hadn't actually given it to them, it was theirs free of any charges, for as long as they wanted it. Eve knew he would rather have stayed in the two-up and two-down he had built for his late wife, and it was only for Eve's sake that he had consented to leave it. There was scarcely a day now, however, that he wasn't pointing out that, since Eve was so much better, there was nothing to stop them from finding a smaller place again, where he wouldn't always be so tired by too much housework and gardening.

'I told you to stay away from Thourly,' she said tightly, giving him his brandy – she'd offered the stranger one but he'd refused. 'So, what happened? If,' she added sarcastically, 'you're ever going to tell me?'

The stranger did it for him. 'There was an open hole on the side of the road, where some men were busy connecting a water supply. They had gone for lunch, leaving everything securely covered up, but unfortunately a gang of youths removed the covers off the top of it, along with the warning notices, and your father unwittingly drove into it.'

'Should have seen it, of course, but didn't.' John Martin, recovering a little with the brandy, took up the story. 'Broke something in the front of my car, I'm afraid. Simon, here, rang Jentor's Garage and they came and took it away. Then he kindly offered to drive me home.'

'Simon?' Eve looked at him.

'Simon Wentworth.' The man bowed slightly, a faint smile on his lips. 'I was at the site.'

'Simon's the architect in charge of it,' John said.

Which explained it, Eve thought drily. Her father had been an architect himself until her accident, when he'd decided, at almost sixty, to take early retirement, and he still liked to snoop – as Eve called it – around building sites, or any other form of construction he could find.

Reluctantly she shook the hand Simon Wentworth held out, but didn't speak. Then she said to her father. 'Haven't I told you that building sites can be dangerous? There are always hazards, as you should know.'

John sighed wistfully. 'The new houses at Thourly, though, are lovely. All detached, with their own small plots of land.'

'We have all we need here.'

'Yes,' John said meekly. 'I suppose so.'

Eve said firmly, as if to suggest that, as far as she was concerned, the subject was closed, 'You still don't look too good. Would you like some more brandy?'

John shook his head. 'I'm beginning to feel fine again, Eve, really I am, and surprisingly hungry. Perhaps Simon would care to join us for a spot of lunch?'

'Well, of course,' she said, not too politely. 'But we usually just have a sandwich at midday, and Mr Wentworth is probably used to something more substantial.'

If Simon Wentworth noticed she didn't address him directly, he didn't retaliate. 'You're mistaken, Miss Martin.' He smiled. 'I usually just have a sandwich myself.'

Feeling annoyed, Eve shot him a hostile look and flounced into the kitchen. Was this Wentworth man so thick he couldn't take a hint? She felt even more put out when he followed her into the kitchen. Why couldn't he depart gracefully, instead of obviously doing everything possible to prolong his visit? Couldn't he sense she didn't want him?

'I'm sorry, Miss Martin – ' he met her resentful gaze head on ' – your father has just told me you are disabled. Can I help?'

Yes, you can, she thought, by taking yourself off, but she merely said, 'No, thank you.'

As if not hearing, he took hold of the kettle and began filling it. 'You don't look disabled.'

'Looks can be deceiving.'

'Yes, of course.' Wentworth switched on the kettle, then watched as she got some ham from the fridge and began buttering bread for the sandwiches. Eve felt her cheeks burning and her hands growing clumsy under his close scrutiny, and hated the way he seemed so easily able to embarrass her. She felt angry as well when, apparently undeterred by the shortness of her replies, he asked bluntly, 'In what way are you disabled?'

'I'd rather not discuss it,' she said.

He merely shrugged. 'You have a wheelchair, I see.'

Did he never give up? Eve had forgotten it was standing in the corner of the kitchen. She usually kept it in the utility. 'I use it when I go to the local shops.'

'Why?'

'Because my legs get tired.' She threw him another cold look, resenting the dubious note in his voice.

'And you have only your father to help you. No handy husband around? Or do you just not wear a wedding ring?'

'I'm not married,' she said between her teeth.

'You could be.' He was still studying her closely. 'You're a lovely looking girl.'

Eve shrugged to show she wasn't impressed. The only man she had ever wanted to marry was Brett. She wasn't interested in anyone else.

'Did you work before your accident?'

'Yes.' Eve felt so annoyed by such a stream of what she considered impertinent questions, she almost forgot to put the ham in the sandwiches. 'I was top of my secretarial course, and within two years was personal secretary to the owner of the firm which employed me. When he retired, he recommended me to the man he sold out to and I was with him until my accident.'

'Did you never think of going back?'

'No!' she almost shouted at him, angry with herself now for having told him about it. 'Who would want me, anyway?'

'If you're a good secretary,' he said, 'I could get you a job any day – if you wanted one. My – I mean our firm employs plenty of disabled people, one way and another.'

'Well, I'm not interested.' She began piling the sandwiches on a tray along with plates and cups, then added pickles and mustard. 'I can keep myself occupied here.'

He nodded, as if accepting this, and picked up the tray. 'I'll take this through,' he said, 'then come back for the tea and milk.'

Eve's mind worked quickly as she watched him disappear through the doorway. He was tall, she noticed, as if seeing him for the first time. Early forties, she guessed. Nondescript appearance, especially when compared with someone like Brett. The only thing he and Brett might have in common, she thought frowning, was a kind of understated determination to achieve their own ends. Well, she would soon fix him, Eve decided disparagingly. When he returned for the milk, she would ask him to tell her father to stay away from the building site, and say that the only way he might achieve this was by not seeing him again. If he took offence, perhaps so much the better? All she wanted was to be rid of him, so did it matter if she wasn't too particular as to how she did it? Apart from her father, she'd had enough, she told herself, of Simon Wentworth and his questions!

Feeling relatively satisfied with her planned course of action, Eve was dismayed to suddenly realize it might not be as clever as she thought. Before her father discovered the building site a few months ago, he had stayed at home most days. Now, if he was banned from the site and reverted to his old habit of rarely going out, it could be days – crucial days – before she got an opportunity to ring Gaby. John knew, of course, that she did ring Gaby sometimes, but she'd never had more than an ordinary conversation with her. They had never bothered with extensions, probably as the house belonged to Brett. The only phone they had was in the hall, and if John should happen to overhear her asking Gaby a lot of probing questions about Brett's marriage, and perhaps passing a caustic remark, she wouldn't put it past him to somehow get in touch with Brett and warn him. What he would warn him about, exactly, she wasn't sure, but lately he'd been grumbling a lot about taking money from him. John had, in fact, made her furious by informing her that he didn't need it and, as Brett still insisted on sending it, he had started giving it to charity, and that it might be prudent for Eve to consider doing the same.

While Eve had no intention of listening to her father over this, she knew better than to push him too far by letting him overhear a conversation about Brett which he might believe was detrimental to him. No, she had to get John out of the house, and the only sure way of doing this might be to adopt a more conciliatory attitude towards Simon Wentworth. Somehow she had to persuade Wentworth that John might fade away or something if he couldn't get to the building site. It might not be easy after the disapproving remarks she had made about it, and the cold shoulder she'd been giving him since she met him. But she was a woman, wasn't she? There were ways and means and it might only be for a few days. Whatever happened, no matter how much it cost, she musn't allow anything to stand between her and the possibility – even if it was a remote one – of destroying Brett's marriage. More importantly, perhaps, of doing everything she could to make sure it didn't happen in the first place!

CHAPTER 7

Two weeks after Brett proposed to her, Miranda was married to him and on her way to New York. Brett had told her that he had lived there for years and conducted most of his business from there now. The main purpose of their going there today, though, was apparently to see Brett's sister who'd said she wasn't well enough to attend their wedding. Afterwards they were flying to the Bahamas where Brett owned an island, to which he said he often sailed in his yacht from New York.

Miranda knew she had married a wealthy man, but from the odd bits of information he dropped, she suspected she had no idea how wealthy. They were still virtually strangers, which made their marriage no more acceptable to her now than it had been when he proposed to her. She had felt trapped when she was forced to say yes to him. She still did.

Not that she could complain that he had not done all he promised to do for her father and Alice. Already they were reaping the benefit of his generosity. Harry's debts were paid off, Well House was theirs for life, along with a sizeable income. They were so comfortable, Miranda doubted that they would miss her. But she was already missing them.

As the Concorde they were travelling on flew into Kennedy Airport, she stole a quick glance at the man sitting beside her. He had just fixed her seat belt and was busy with his own. He didn't smile much, or show her any of the gentler side of his nature, as he had done when he first met her. Perhaps she had imagined it, and it didn't really exist, she thought dismally.

He seldom talked to her, she realized though, during the past few days when they were together, he had watched her a lot. If she stumbled, as she still sometimes did, he was never far away, but she never detected any tenderness in his timely assistance, and couldn't recall having a conversation with him since the night he had discovered she could walk. Occasionally, when others were around, he kissed her lightly – to keep up appearances, she supposed, but that was all.

The question of why he had married her was beginning to plague her. And the more she thought about it, the more puzzled she became. His first proposal had obviously had something to do with her being crippled, but his reason for marrying her after he discovered she wasn't disabled and had deceived him remained a mystery. She just couldn't believe that a man of his intelligence and wealth would allow a little pique to drive him to lengths such as this.

He had let her father and Alice assume that, for him, his desire to marry Miranda was prompted by love at first sight, while Miranda suspected, though she knew little about such an emotion herself, that Brett had never been in love in his life. It amazed her how smoothly he had glossed over the true facts, in a way that saved both her father and aunt any undue embarrassment. And because she had feared what might happen to them if she didn't go along with him, she had been forced to pretend that her dearest wish was to spend the rest of her life with him.

They had been married quietly in London and spent the night there after Harry and Alice returned to Birmingham. Brett had booked a suite in one of the city's most prestigious hotels and Miranda was given her own room. He had said goodnight formally and closed the door behind him, leaving her feeling relieved but very much alone. His eyes had flicked over her briefly, without expression, yet something indefinable in them had made her shiver. She had been reminded of a panther lying in wait, like one she had seen in one of the jungle films her father was so fond of watching on TV. Brett had promised to give her time, she remembered, but she wondered how long it would take for her to trust him. Or if she ever would?

'Are we staying with your sister?' she asked, as they drove from the airport. They had been met by one of Brett's own cars, chauffeur-driven. Brett called the chauffeur Clive and introduced them briefly, but though the man had touched his cap respectfully and looked at Miranda curiously, he hadn't seemed surprised.

'We saw the announcement of your marriage in *The New York Times* this morning, sir.' He smiled.

'Staying with Gaby?' Brett frowned now. 'No, of course not.'

'I just thought – as she is a widow,' Miranda mumbled, feeling foolish for having spoken without thinking, 'that you might live together.'

'That will be the day!' Brett laughed drily. 'The last thing I would want to do would be to live with my sister.'

Poor Gaby, Miranda thought, feeling instinctively sorry for her. 'Do you live close to each other, then?'

'Everywhere in New York is just a cab ride away from everywhere else.'

Miranda frowned. He hadn't answered either of her questions – not properly, anyway. She glanced quickly at his indifferent profile, resenting the cold way he treated her. Yet, at the same time, she had to own that she appreciated the distance he seemed determined to put between them, feeling it protected her. From what? Staring down at her hands, a habit she seemed to have developed since meeting Brett, she felt her face grow hot. She didn't really have to try to work it out. If she got too friendly with him, he might believe this was a sign that she would welcome his lovemaking. She wasn't sure why this aspect of marriage frightened her, but it did. Nor could she account for it. It wasn't as if she'd had a bad experience – she'd had no kind of experience whatsoever. Perhaps this was the trouble? If she had slept with any of the boys who had wanted her to, years ago, she might not have felt so apprehensive at the thought of Brett approaching her and demanding his rights now.

Suddenly Miranda knew that, though her way of thinking must be out of date and old-fashioned, she couldn't bear to have Brett making love to her unless he loved her and he had showed no sign of doing this up to now. Since that ominous night two weeks ago, when he had more or less forced her to agree to marry him, he had reduced their relationship to almost a business arrangement. Hadn't he had a contract drawn up which denied any suggestion that he had even the slightest emotional interest in her? The agreement stipulated that Harry Ferris and his sister should enjoy the concessions he made to them, just as long as Miranda was married to him. If *he* ended their marriage, he would still provide for them, but if she did, they would get nothing. That was the bit which frightened Miranda. Did he intend torturing her, either mentally or physically, until she was desperate to leave him but, for her father's sake, couldn't?

Miranda had signed the form reluctantly, cloaking her fears with anger as she secretly belaboured herself for taking the easy way out. She wished she'd had the courage to tear it up, especially when she realized Brett was probably contemptuous of her for not doing so. Plenty of people lived on next to nothing. She ought not to have allowed her dependence on the security she was used to have persuaded her that neither she nor her family could do without it. She ought to have told Brett exactly what to do with his proposal and ambiguous marriage contract. Now, as it usually was with hindsight, it was too late.

New York was like a maze. To Miranda, who had never been here before, it was a labyrinth of fast, traffic-packed streets and impossibly high-rise buildings. From her first glimpse of the Statue of Liberty – a gift from the people of France to the

United States, commemorating the friendship between the two nations – she was continually startled
by the things she saw every time she tore her eyes and
her thoughts from Brett long enough to look through
the car windows. New York, she guessed, could
become both frightening and captivating.

Knowing it would be futile, she didn't try and keep
track of the route they took through the city. In the
space of a short time it fascinated her and aroused her
curiosity, but Brett's discouraging silence froze the
eager questions on her lips before she could utter
them. He didn't speak until they came to what looked
like a very smart district and the car stopped in the
concrete shadow of a skyscraper block where he gave
a few curt instructions to his driver, which she didn't
catch, then helped her out.

'This is it,' he said.

Thinking he meant they had arrived at his apartment, or where he lived, Miranda felt shocked when,
after the elevator deposited them on what seemed
like the hundreth floor – and probably was – he rang
the bell of a door which was eventually opened by a
young woman with next to nothing on, or so it
seemed to Miranda. She was wearing a skirt that
barely covered her bottom, a top which covered even
less, and her face was covered by too much make-up.
As soon as she saw Brett she gave a wild shriek and
positively launched herself at him.

'Oh, Brett!' she cried shrilly.

'Gaby!' he exclaimed, clearly not sharing her
enthusiasm, as he shook her away from him. 'What
the hell is going on?' he demanded, as the noise
behind them sounded deafening.

'What do you think it is, darling?' Adjusting a heavy gold earring, she giggled up at him.

'I thought you were ill?'

'I was, but I recovered.' Gaby's mouth went into a pout at Brett's disapproving tones. 'A few friends called to see how I was and somehow it developed into a party. And well . . . well, you know how things sometimes turn out?'

Realizing that this must be Brett's sister, Miranda drew an unconscious breath of relief. She had never imagined his sister would be like this. From the look on Brett's face, he was obviously doubting her story about being too ill to attend his wedding, but whether she had been or not, it was plain to see she was drinking too much.

Brett, however, after a brief hesitation, seemed prepared to be diplomatic and accept Gaby's explanation. Turning from her, he drew Miranda forward and said, 'I brought my wife to meet you, Gaby, since you couldn't be bothered to come to our wedding.'

As if she hadn't noticed Miranda before, Gaby turned slowly and stared at her coldly. She seemed to stare for a long time, her expression far from friendly. 'So this is the little bride?' she said to Brett spitefully. 'She looks sweet enough, but she'd have to be more than that to catch you, wouldn't she, darling? How she succeeded where countless others failed must still be keeping them guessing.'

Miranda stiffened. Gaby's remarks were anything but complimentary, but trying to remember the amount of drink the woman appeared to have consumed, she smiled, albeit half-heartedly.

Brett's hand tightened on Miranda's waist as apparently he was not prepared to be tolerant forever. 'I'm warning you, Gaby,' he said.

Gaby giggled again, but something in Brett's voice must have persuaded her to be careful. 'I'm sorry, darling, it's my tongue, you know. Never very tactful. But – ' she turned to Miranda again, to look at her even more closely ' – she's so young, isn't she? Haven't you been guilty of cradlesnatching?'

'That's something we need not discuss,' Brett rejoined tightly. 'Just say hello properly, Gaby, and Miranda and I will be on our way. We'll come and see you another day, when you aren't so – er – busy.'

'You aren't implying that I'm drunk, are you?'

Brett didn't speak.

'Or is it my friends? You never did approve of them . . .'

'Not those you made since Ed died.'

Fancying Gaby flinched, Miranda, feeling sorry for her again, said quickly. 'We don't have to rush off, do we, Brett? Perhaps,' she gulped, as two pairs of cold eyes were immediately trained on her, 'Gaby would like us to stay for a few minutes?'

This only seemed to make things worse. To Miranda's dismay, instead of appreciating the olive branch she was holding out, Gaby merely jeered at her, 'So you can speak after all, darling? And what a proper little English voice, so la-di-da.'

'You're half-British yourself, Gaby,' Brett snapped, but before he could say anything more – which he was obviously going to – another man appeared in the doorway behind them.

Placing a hand lightly on Gaby's shoulder, he nodded to Brett, as if he knew him. Then, turning to Miranda, his eyes lightened with more than just casual interest. 'Hi,' he exclaimed, 'I haven't seen you before, honey, or I would have remembered, but aren't you coming in? I'll get you a drink if you like. A lot better than standing on Gaby's doorstep.'

Miranda didn't know who he was, but he had a nice smile. Feeling warmed by it, she smiled back at him. She didn't realize that, when she smiled, she looked so beautiful it made people blink. It made her grey eyes sparkle and brought a warm glow to her translucent skin. The man took a deep breath as he digested her smile, her shining fair hair and delicate features.

'I'm Adrian Norton,' he introduced himself, as neither Brett nor his sister seemed inclined to.

'You're wasting your time, Norton.' Brett whipped Miranda away before she could so much as get her mouth open. 'Miranda is my wife.' Over his shoulder he added curtly to Gaby, 'I'll give you a ring some time. When you are sober.'

In the car, nursing a sore arm, Miranda made an effort to swallow her anger as she saw how grim Brett looked. 'Brett,' she asked, 'what is it? Does your sister worry you?'

Brett turned to her after instructing the chauffeur to drive on. 'Gaby's been like that since her husband and son both died in an air crash, five years ago.'

Miranda's eyes widened, horrified. 'Her son as well?'

'Yes. Didn't I tell you?'

100

'About her husband. No one else.'

Brett grimaced. 'It was tragic, but I feel she ought to be getting over it by now.'

'And she isn't?'

'Doesn't seem to be. These days, she's either ill or drunk or just plain bitchy.'

'And she never used to be?'

'Not that I can remember, but I'm beginning to wonder.'

Miranda sighed. 'Losing a husband and son must be a terrible thing to happen to anyone. We could have stayed with her longer.' She refused to wonder if Gaby had wanted them to. 'She seems to have a lot of good friends, anyway,' she went on when Brett didn't reply to her. 'Adrian Norton, at least, seemed very pleasant.'

'He's usually as drunk as she is.'

Was he? The derision in Brett's voice startled her but warned her against arguing with him. 'He seemed to know you.'

'He's no friend of mine, if that's what you mean.' Brett looked at her darkly. 'And I'd like you to remember he isn't the kind of man I want associating with my wife!'

If theirs had been a normal marriage, Miranda might have thought Brett jealous, but knowing he wasn't, she dismissed this out of hand. It must just be that he wanted a wife above reproach and meant to keep her that way. This would account for his warning her against someone whom she suspected was a well-known philanderer.

Another time, she might have told Brett that she was quite able to choose her own friends, but now, after all the hustle of the day, she felt too weary to bother. She did say, however, 'I'm not really interested in Mr Norton, you know. And I do have some sense. Dad took me around with him a lot, both before and after my accident, and I met a lot of people.'

'But the right kind, surely.'

Miranda nodded wryly. Harry had vetoed everyone, both men and women, and she'd often resented his over-protective attitude. If she hadn't been confined to a wheelchair, she wouldn't have put up with it. Glancing uncertainly at Brett, she hoped that, through marrying him, she hadn't exchanged one form of bondage for another.

This time when the car pulled up, it was outside a large house, not an apartment, in a district he called Upper Eastside. Miranda's breath caught as he ushered her inside and she saw for the first time how substantial and well appointed it was. A wide staircase rose up from the middle of the hall and on either side of it rooms branched off which, through open doorways, looked both gracious and spacious and as if they would be very pleasant to live in – if one liked a lot of space, which Brett obviously did. Compared with this, Miranda thought, Well House must have seemed extremely commonplace and she couldn't help wondering why Brett had wanted it.

As the manservant who let them in closed the door behind them, a woman, whom Brett introduced as Mrs Frank, his housekeeper, came forward to greet them. Brett had apparently rung ahead to let her know they were coming. Soon she met other members of his household staff, who all wished them well and every happiness. Miranda was glad that her father had employed plenty of people, one way and another, otherwise she might have felt overwhelmed by them. Even so, she felt relieved when, after thanking everyone, Brett said they would go up to his suite.

His suite turned out to be a sitting-room with two bedrooms attached. The master bedroom was huge with a king-size bed in the middle of it but, after enjoying the look of confusion on Miranda's face, he guided her into the smaller one and told her, in a silky voice, that it was hers, for the time being. Her luggage, she saw, was at the foot of the bed and she was so grateful to have a room to herself that she didn't pause to wonder whether Brett was being considerate or merely threatening. Dinner, she was informed coolly, would be served about seven-thirty. Which gave her an hour, he added, to bathe and get ready.

Miranda choose a short pink dress for dinner. The silky material was soft and complemented the faint colour in her smooth cheeks, which made her seem startlingly attractive. Before she joined Brett again, she viewed herself with some surprise in a mirror in her room. After spending years in a wheelchair, she had almost forgotten what she could look like out of one.

Brett wasn't in the sitting-room when she went out, but was waiting for her downstairs in the hall, talking to someone whom she remembered was Harris, the butler. As soon as he saw her coming, Brett left the man and strolled over to meet her. And, while she was still navigating the last step, he bent his tall head and kissed her.

It was one of his casual kisses, but even they were always able to make her pulses race and bring a flush to her face. Brett must have seen how disconcerted she was, for he murmured mockingly, 'If a light kiss bothers you to this extent, darling, how would you feel if I put some passion into it?

The butler, announcing dinner was ready, saved Miranda the embarrassment of answering and, during the meal served in Brett's elegant dining-room, she was relieved when he appeared to lose interest in taunting her. She just wished she could as easily lose interest in him. She couldn't understand how all her efforts to do this, over the past two weeks, had come to nothing. While they ate, she found herself shooting quick glances at him. When occasionally their eyes met, she felt her cheeks grow hot as, unable to sustain the sardonic regard in his, she was forced to look away. If only, she thought despairingly, he wasn't one of the best-looking men she had ever seen, how much easier the raising of adequate defences against him might have been.

As soon as she dared, after they'd had coffee in the lounge, she asked if he would mind if she went to bed. She had dreaded mentioning it, for fear Brett would read something into it which wasn't intended, but he merely nodded indifferently and said she could do what she liked.

'Are you feeling tired?' he asked curtly.

Miranda nodded reluctantly, while wondering if a silent lie was as bad as a verbal one? She wasn't, in fact, quite sure how she was feeling. The tight, burning feeling inside her was difficult to define, but she knew it had something to do with Brett, and suddenly she was desperate to get away from him.

Brett, observing her obvious discomfiture, smiled. 'You will soon feel better, once we're on the island and actually begin our honeymoon.'

Would she? Miranda wondered as, getting to her feet, she wished him a quick goodnight.

His reply was lost as the telephone suddenly rang. Dismissing Miranda with a brief wave of his hand, he sank into his chair again to answer it. As Miranda walked away from him, she heard him exclaim, 'Why, Eve, I didn't expect to hear from you so soon . . .'

After a restless night, during which she kept dreaming that a woman called Eve was dragging Brett triumphantly away from her, Miranda's spirits fell even further when, on dressing and going downstairs, she found he was gone. He had told her, she remembered, on the flight the previous afternoon, that, as well as seeing Gaby, there was one or two other things he might as well see to while he was here. Miranda had assumed he was talking about his business interests, but she hadn't thought he would be leaving the house this early in the morning.

'He doesn't expect to be home until this evening, madam,' the butler informed her as he escorted her into the dining-room for breakfast. 'And he left word that you aren't to go out alone.'

'Why not?' Miranda asked. Couldn't Brett have told her this himself? 'Is it dangerous?'

'Not particularly.' Harris poured her tea which she preferred at breakfast to coffee. 'But being a stranger here, you could easily get lost.'

'I do have a tongue in my head,' she said, trying to speak mildly.

'Sometimes, madam, it's not enough.'

Miranda refused anything cooked and settled for toast, saying she wasn't hungry. If Brett had forbidden her to go out, what did he expect her to do all day? She didn't believe Harris would try physically to prevent her from leaving the house on her own, but if she did, she suspected he might trail after her like some kind of watchdog or sleuth. And she fancied that even less than she did staying in.

To pass the time, after breakfast, she returned to her room and began sorting out her clothes. These had already been unpacked and put away by a highly efficient maid who had an irritating habit of popping in every now and again to see if she wanted anything. Suspecting the girl was acting on Harris's instructions, to ensure she didn't try to go out by herself, Miranda eventually told her she would ring if she wanted her, but that there was nothing she could do for her, for the moment.

She was back in half an hour, however, to say that Mrs Morley, Mr Deakin's sister, had called. 'Mr Harris doesn't know if you wish to see her, madam, but he said to tell you that he has put her in the library.'

Miranda hesitated. She couldn't think why Gaby had called, unless it was to apologize for her behaviour the night before, and she didn't want to make an enemy of her by refusing to see her. Brett might not get on well with his sister, but considering all Gaby had been through, this might be his fault as much as hers. He wasn't an easy man to get on with. He had little tolerance of human weaknesses, except, Miranda thought drily, remembering Eve, those of his own.

Telling Jill she would come down with her, she said hello to Gaby when Harris announced her – as he insisted on doing – and added cautiously, when Gaby turned her head to look at her, 'How nice to see you again.'

Gaby threw back her head and laughed as Harris, clearly doubtful, closed the door on them. 'You can't mean that, Miranda. Why bother to be polite?'

Miranda frowned. 'Then why did you bother to come?'

Gaby shrugged. 'Well, for one thing, I knew Brett would be out, and the last time I annoyed my dear brother he threatened to bar me from Luke, among other things.'

Miranda blinked at Gaby's somewhat garbled explanation, but refused to suspect these were not the real reasons for Gaby's visit. She didn't have to be suspicious of everything Gaby said or did, just because Gaby didn't like her. 'Are you feeling better this morning?' she asked politely.

'You mean – am I sober?' Gaby grimaced carelessly. 'I am right now, believe it or not, and I suppose I'd better stay this way while Brett is in New York.'

Miranda looked at her curiously, not knowing quite what to make of her. Gaby might be Brett's sister but she didn't seem like him, not even in appearance. She was dark and in her thirties, but there any resemblance ended. She had none of Brett's decisiveness and, though she was attractive, had far too many lines on her face for someone of her age.

'Brett likes a drink himself,' she said, trying to be tactful, though she hadn't actually ever seen him drink very much.

'In moderation!' Gaby made a poor job of imitating him. 'Not nearly as much as he likes women.'

'Women?'

Gaby took no notice as Miranda's eyes widened involuntarily. 'Well, you must have noticed he has plenty, even in Birmingham. That's where our Daddy came from, you know, and Brett still likes its women. One called Eve, in particular. It's a wonder you never heard of her?'

Miranda had – last night – but she wasn't going to tell Gaby this. She only said, 'I don't know what you are getting at, Gaby, but I'd be naïve to think I was the only woman Brett has ever had in his life.'

Gaby looked at her broodingly, as her thoughts seemed to leap erratically from one thing to another. 'I'll tell you one thing,' she said enigmatically. 'You're the only woman he's had who has been like you. I don't know where or how he found you, I have yet to find out, but wait until he's had you on the island a few days. He'll soon have all that prim and properness knocked out of you.'

Miranda, even as her cheeks flushed, felt she'd had just about enough. 'I don't know what your real purpose was in coming here today, Gaby – ' she began stiffly.

'Oh, gee, I'm sorry, Miranda!' Gaby broke in, before Miranda could go on. 'I've gone and done it again, haven't I? I meant to be so nice to you, to apologize for last night and to take you out for lunch. But now,' she groaned, waving her arms distractedly, 'you won't want to go anywhere with me!'

Miranda had to bite her lip to prevent herself from agreeing. Perhaps, she thought, looking at her sister-in-law, Gaby couldn't help inserting poisonous darts and hateful innuendoes into her conversation. Couldn't she be more mentally disturbed because of losing her husband and son than Brett suspected? Even so, the prospect of spending the next few hours in her company was not appealing. Yet, what else had she to do? Miranda asked herself. And, if she refused to have lunch with her sister-in-law, their relationship might never be any better than it was now. And wouldn't she rather have Gaby for a friend than an enemy?

'If you think we won't come to blows,' she said, trying to laugh over it, as Gaby still gazed at her remorsefully, 'I'd like to have lunch with you. If nothing else,' she tacked on, reluctant to have the other woman believe she was a pushover and could get away with anything, 'it will help to pass the time until Brett comes home.'

CHAPTER 8

Harris didn't seem too happy about Miranda going out with Gaby, but he refrained from saying anything and saw them studiously into the cab he called for them.

'Harris never did approve of me,' Gaby complained after giving the driver directions. 'You'll have to watch him, Miranda. Otherwise he'll be running to Brett about all sorts of things.'

Miranda didn't reply and a silence that wasn't particularly comfortable, but which she preferred to Gaby's barbed remarks, fell between them until they reached the restaurant where Gaby said she had booked a table.

It was obviously a restaurant favoured by the wealthy and famous, some of whom posed carelessly with practised smiles on their well-known faces for photographers on their way in.

To Miranda's dismay, though she wasn't sure why she felt uneasy, Gaby paused beside one of the photographers and spoke to him. 'Hi, Dave,' she said, 'I don't think you've met my sister-in-law yet. My brother's new wife, Miranda.' She drew

Miranda forward before Miranda realized what she was doing. 'They've only been married two days.'

'I saw it in the papers, but I didn't expect to get such an immediate scoop.' Dave laughed, clearly surprised but quick to raise his camera. Before Miranda could turn away, it nearly blinded her as it flashed in her eyes.

'Thanks, Mrs Morley,' he called after them. 'I owe you one.'

'What on earth were you thinking of?' Miranda frowned at Gaby as they went inside. 'I'm not looking for publicity and I don't think Brett would like it.'

'Calm down, honey.' Gaby shrugged. 'If he doesn't, he will soon get over it, and I just couldn't resist the temptation. Anyway, as Brett's wife, photographers will soon be a part of your daily diet, so you'd better get used to them.'

'But I don't have to encourage them.'

'They can be worse when you don't.'

Gaby's indifferent comment didn't help Miranda to feel any better. She felt even worse when she saw that the table they were shown to was already occupied by the man who had spoken to her the previous evening at Gaby's apartment.

He rose as they approached and it was perfectly obvious that he had arranged this with Gaby. Staring at him blankly, Miranda wished more than ever that she had stayed at home. But as she already seemed to be attracting considerable attention, she felt it might be wiser to accept the situation with as much self-possession as she could. She pretended, however, not to see the hand Adrian Norton held out.

Once seated, she looked at Gaby coldly. 'You didn't mention we were to have company.'

'You might not have come if I had.' Gaby lifted an eyebrow carelessly. 'Adrian is perfectly harmless, though, I can assure you. Even if Brett doesn't care for him.'

Adrian grinned sardonically. 'Approve might be a better way of describing it, but as your husband isn't with you this time, Miranda, I don't intend worrying unduly over what he thinks of me. I asked Gaby to bring you today because I wanted another chance to study your beautiful and charming face. And surely lunching with your sister-in-law and a friend couldn't be considered a crime for a lonely bride?'

'I am *not* a lonely bride!' Miranda emphasized sharply. 'I knew that, before we went to the Bahamas, Brett had some business to see to in New York.'

'Business?' Gaby laughed drily. 'I wonder how much of it has skirts on?'

Miranda flushed then felt her cheeks grow pale as this was something she had wondered about herself. But before she could say anything, Adrian broke in. 'Gaby has an odd sense of humour these days, Miranda. I shouldn't take any notice of her if I were you.'

For a moment, Miranda was tempted to ignore his advice. She had to remind herself that Gaby's reprehensible behaviour must have something to do with her tragic loss. Even so, she knew she would think twice before coming out with her again. She made a noncommittal reply to Adrian's suggestion, but none, whatsoever, to Gaby's.

Gaby, though, was clearly determined to stir something up, if only to relieve her all-too-obvious boredom. 'Tell me,' she asked Miranda smoothly, 'how you came to meet my brother? Was it at some social function?'

Miranda, with her new-found sense of caution, wondered how much it was safe to reveal? This time Adrian Norton appeared to be as curious as Gaby and didn't come to her rescue. 'We met when Brett took over my father's business,' she said reluctantly.

'And you?'

'If you like,' she replied coolly.

Gaby's scarlet mouth curled derisively. 'I can't see him remaining interested for long in a provincial little British schoolgirl. I'm still surprised he ever was.'

'Isn't that coming on a bit strong, Gaby?' Adrian frowned.

Gaby's pencilled brows rose unrepentantly. 'You've seen the kind of women he usually takes around. They can make even me feel gauche.'

'Sometimes,' Miranda interjected curtly, 'little provincial schoolgirl types get underestimated.'

Whether Gaby took this to be some kind of warning or not, Miranda couldn't tell, but for a moment, as she clearly thought about it, she was silent and Miranda felt grateful when Adrian Norton began to talk quickly of other things. Afterwards, though, she couldn't recall what she chose to eat. She could only remember feeling increasingly uncomfortable. She drank her coffee without really tasting it and made no effort to hide her relief when it was time to go. Suddenly, getting home was all she could think of.

Forgetting how, on occasion, her legs still had an irritating tendency to let her down, Miranda found herself stumbling unexpectedly as they went outside and might have fallen if Adrian, close behind her, hadn't caught hold of her. And, as the cameras she had forgotten about swung once more in her direction, he pulled her against him with a smothered exclamation, shielding her from the worst of them.

'All right, darling?' he asked gently, pushing her into a cab and jumping in behind her.

Striving to regain her breath, Miranda glanced at him unhappily. Gaby, having remembered an appointment with her hairdresser had, just before they left the restaurant, asked Adrian if he would see Miranda home. And everything had happened so quickly after that, that Miranda hadn't had time to tell him she didn't want him to. What Brett would say or do, if he ever knew about this, was something Miranda didn't want to think about.

Adrian, as if feeling slightly ashamed of himself, didn't say anything more until they reached Brett's house, where he dismayed Miranda again by asking her if she would consider having lunch with him the following day?

'Gaby needn't know and I promise to behave myself,' he assured her whimsically.

'I'm sorry.' Miranda shook her fair head firmly. Brett might be able to forget he was married, but, even though the circumstances of their marriage were unusual, she could not.

'Why not think about it?' Adrian persisted. 'I'll give you a ring.'

114

'I'd rather you didn't,' she replied too loudly. 'Brett wouldn't like it, for one thing.'

'Does he have to?' he murmured, she thought outrageously.

'Goodbye, Mr Norton!' Miranda snapped pointedly, sliding swiftly from the cab before he could move and slamming the door behind her on him.

Though Miranda tried not to not to think about it, she couldn't settle for the rest of the afternoon. She felt so restless and full of misgivings over her lunch with Gaby and Norton that she didn't know how she managed, after sitting down on her bed for what she intended to be only a minute, to fall asleep. When she woke, it was after six and Jill was standing over her, a look of concern on her face.

'I was just about to wake you up, ma'am,' she said.

'Oh!' Miranda sat up with a start, conscious that she was still wearing the dress she had put on that morning. Now it was sadly crumpled and she blinked as she saw that the maid was also looking at it. 'I must have fallen asleep,' she heard herself muttering, which must, she realised, be perfectly obvious.

Jill smiled. 'You were sleeping when Mr Harris sent me up to see if you would like him to serve tea.'

Miranda flushed as she became aware that the maid was dismissing her lethargy as the kind of tiredness that might beset any bride on her honeymoon, especially with the sort of husband which she clearly believed Brett to be.

'Is Mr Deakin home yet?' she enquired quickly, as the other part of the suite was strangely silent. She wondered if he had come in and changed and was waiting for her downstairs, as he had done the previous evening.

'No, ma'am,' Jill said. 'I heard he's just rang to say he has been delayed and you aren't to wait dinner for him.'

'Oh,' Miranda said again, feeling vaguely disappointed yet, at the same time, relieved. If Brett was late in getting in he might be tired, and her infamous lunch with Gaby need never be mentioned. And, her thoughts continued optimistically, by tomorrow he surely wouldn't be interested enough to ask what she'd been doing.

'I think,' she said carefully to Jill, 'that if Mr Deakin won't be in, I'd rather have something to eat up here, if you wouldn't mind?'

Jill was only too happy to oblige. She said Miranda could have dinner wherever she liked and, after bringing her a tray, returned later to collect it. After which Miranda thanked her and said she wouldn't be needing her again that night.

After Jill had gone, as Brett still wasn't in and it was almost nine o'clock, she decided to have a shower and to wash her hair. She had just finished drying it and was slipping into a thin robe when she thought she heard someone in her bedroom. Thinking that Jill must have returned about something, she tightened the sash of her robe around her slender waist and went out. But it was Brett, not Jill, she found there, and he looked so angry that she suspected – if she hadn't appeared – he'd been about to walk straight into her bathroom.

'Brett . . .' Her voice came out in a whisper she would have regretted had she not felt suddenly frightened. 'Is something wrong?'

'Wrong? I wonder you have the nerve to ask,' he snarled, waving a newspaper he was carrying contemptuously at her. 'You really have excelled yourself this time, have you not? You ignored my advice and brazenly disobeyed my orders!'

Miranda's eyes widened apprehensively as she stared at the newspaper he thrust before her and opened derisively. Above a picture of her, ostensibly wrapped in Adrian Norton's arms, was a caption which read: 'Brett Deakin's new wife, obviously passing the time very pleasantly as she waits for her husband to conclude his business in New York before they go off on their honeymoon. Or is the honeymoon already over? Watch this space.'

'It's a – mistake!' Miranda cried, chilled. She couldn't believe she ever clung to Adrian like that or looked at him so warmly.

'Fascinating, isn't it?'

Miranda tried to keep her wits about her, those which weren't scattered irretrievably. 'Gaby . . .' she began.

'Please leave Gaby out of this,' he snapped. 'It's Norton I'm talking about. Didn't I tell you not to go near him?'

'But it's not what it seems . . .'

He refused to let her explain. 'Don't the facts speak for themselves. You cheated when I first knew you, but let me tell you, Miranda, if you think you can do that again you're mistaken.'

Taking in his cold and furious face, Miranda took a deep breath. 'Brett,' she said, 'you're creating a situation that doesn't exist. I only had lunch with him . . .'

She was going to say '. . . and we weren't alone', but Brett gave her no chance to. 'Shut up!' he cut in. 'I might have overlooked a lot, but not this.'

'Please,' Miranda begged. 'You have to listen!'

'What to? More lies? We've talked enough as it is,' he said savagely, ignoring her protesting cry as his arms went out to jerk her to him. 'No one is going to wonder if our honeymoon is over before it's begun again.'

Miranda thought he was going to shake her. The iron grip he usually kept on his feelings appeared to be slipping. She couldn't remember him being as furious as this, not even when he discovered she was able to walk, after thinking she couldn't. Perhaps if he did shake her, even hit her, he might feel better afterwards and be prepared to listen?

Having worked this out, Miranda stiffened with shock and surprise when, instead of shaking her, he began kissing her. She hadn't time to escape his punishing mouth, it descended so swiftly. Her own lips were ruthlessly crushed and she couldn't move in his tightening grip. He held her so tightly that she knew she had no immediate hope of getting away from him.

He had kissed her on the night she had agreed to marry him, but that had been different. While he'd also been angry then, there'd been none of the harshness in his kisses that he was inflicting on her now. Did he kiss all his women like this? she wondered. Or was this kind of treatment reserved only for errant wives?

During their short engagement, Miranda had always refused to look too closely into her feelings, preferring to believe she hadn't any, as far as Brett was concerned. The first time he kissed her, she had been aware of her pulses quickening and something shooting through her, but she had put it down to repugnance, rather than anything else.

Now, as Brett went on kissing her, to her dismay, she began feeling the same kind of sensations shooting through her as she had then. She also felt a sudden heat as his hands began sliding over her, making her conscious of her body in a way she had never been before. It aroused in her an urgent desire to cling to him, to return his kisses instead of fighting him. She felt strangely bereft when he lifted his dark head and muttered grimly, 'I should have done that two days ago.'

Believing he considered the roughness of his kisses sufficient retribution for what she had done, and was about to release her, Miranda opened relieved eyes, but she couldn't, as she soon realized, have been more mistaken when, instead of letting her go, he merely straightened, picked her up, and carried her through to his bedroom.

'What are you doing?' she cried, as he paused by the bed and dropped her none too gently onto it.

'What I should have done on our wedding night,' he repeated, dropping down beside her and beginning to remove his clothes. 'And don't pretend,' he rasped, ripping off his shirt, 'that you weren't looking forward to it. I can tell by the way you respond.'

Miranda, as she looked up at him and saw he was still furious, tried desperately to think of something that might bring him to his senses. She could almost feel the force of his smouldering anger and it wasn't helping her much.

'You had me fooled,' he continued, searing her with another of his furious glances as she struggled futilely for words. 'How many men did you sleep with, I wonder, before your accident?'

'None.'

He dismissed her reply as obviously more lies. 'I'm sorry I disappointed you on our wedding night,' he said suavely. 'I should have listened to your doctors when they told me there is nothing to stop you from leading a more or less normal life. And that,' he added, 'though they didn't specifically say so, must surely have included sex?'

'You consulted my doctors!' Miranda flushed bright red with indignation.

'Don't worry, it was only one question, which they seemed to consider reasonable, in the circumstances,' Brett said. 'I didn't ask for a run-down on your medical history, which I probably wouldn't have got, anyway.'

'I still think you had a nerve!'

'To be concerned?'

'You don't seem concerned now,' she replied bitterly. 'You won't even listen to me.'

'I'm through doing that.'

'And you seem to think I'm no better than I should be?'

Brett laughed. 'Didn't Norton get the same impression? If a bride is willing to go out with another man, the day after she is married, what other category can one put her in? Where did you go after you left the restaurant, may I ask?'

'Nowhere!' Miranda's voice rose though she tried to control it. 'We came straight back . . .'

'Yeah!' Brett said, all too explicitly, beginning to remove her robe before she realized what he was doing. 'If you're so eager to make up for lost time and can't do without a man for five minutes, we will have to do something about it, won't we? We can't have you straying again.'

'Brett!' she protested wildly, as he cast her robe aside and pinned her to the bed while his eyes swept over her naked body. 'Please,' she pleaded, 'let go of me.'

He took no notice as his eyes continued exploring. 'You're beautiful,' he said grimly. 'Too beautiful for me to ignore any longer. I've a strong desire to make love to you.'

'No!' Miranda had fought him before. Now she tried again. He had a right, she knew, to make love to her, but though his kisses had proved she wasn't invulnerable to him, she didn't want the consummation of their marriage to be like this.

'Stop struggling,' he snapped, pulling her closer to him, disregarding how she trembled against him. Taking a firm hold of her chin, he lifted it to allow his mouth to plunder hers as devastatingly as it had done before. And, as her traitorous heart began once more to race, Miranda knew that, had things been different between them, all the defences she was trying to erect against him might have crumbled. As it was, it took a huge effort to say – as she somehow managed to wrench her mouth from under his, 'If you don't let me go, I'm going to hate you.'

Brett mocked her. 'You'll be the first woman who ever has.'

Angry that he should taunt her with the number of affairs he had had, she exclaimed, 'I think I *already* hate you.'

'Then I've nothing to lose.' He laughed, dropping his head to kiss her again, then, after effectively silencing her, trailing his mouth to her breasts. It was then that Miranda's resistance collapsed completely. A whisper of it might have remained but, as soon as his hands began caressing her and she felt the touch of his mouth on her bare skin, it was gone in an instance. Burned up in flames that licked through her veins as he left little of her without attention.

'You want me, don't you?' she heard him murmur some time later against her lips.

Miranda could only nod. The feelings inside her were escalating into something she had never previously experienced. Nor would she have believed them possible, if Brett weren't supplying irrefutable proof that they were. He was lying alongside her, imprisoning her with the weight of both his arms and legs, but suddenly she didn't want to get away from him. Her own arms, she realized, had gone just as closely around him, and though she wasn't quite sure, when she nodded, what she was inviting, she was vaguely aware that, whatever it was, it was inevitable.

Brett needed no further encouragement, though whether he would have desisted, had she shaken her head instead of nodding, was debatable. Miranda felt the full force of the rising passion which her slenderness seemed to arouse in him, but though a little apprehension still remained she no longer took any notice of it. She began returning Brett's kisses with an urgency she didn't try to hide, clinging to him in a way that must have clearly revoked her former reluctance.

Brett was arousing her to the point where she became wholly responsive to everything he did. Yet if Miranda's pulses, as well as her emotions, were spinning dizzily, he didn't seem totally under control himself. Suddenly a wild kind of insanity seemed to escalate between them, so that when he slid on top of her and, as if impelled by the strength of these feelings, parted her legs and thrust immediately into her, he was not as gentle as he might, in other circumstances, have been.

At first Miranda thought she might faint from the shock of his intrusion, but he didn't spare her, not even when she cried out and tried to push him away. He merely crushed her cries with his mouth and let the weight of his lean but strong body sink more heavily onto her, and made no attempt to stop his continuing invasion of her.

Then, to her surprise, as the unexpected shock of it gradually receded, she became conscious of other things. Her breath caught as a strange kind of warmth began flooding her, so that if Brett had offered to stop she might have begged him not to. It swept through her, taking her over, as something she couldn't resist, drew her towards a place she couldn't see, but which seemed to be promising incredible delights – if only she could reach it. Which, unhappily, she didn't.

Suddenly, with a final thrust of his powerful body, Brett appeared to reach this place before she did, then lay still. When, after a few moments, he moved and rolled away from her, Miranda not only felt confused and embarrassed, but a number of things she didn't wish to admit to, such as disappointment and resentment. Perhaps she had expected too much, she told herself, looking at Brett frustratedly. He was sitting on the edge of the bed, running a hand over his dark head, and she envied him his seemingly cast-iron composure. He had obviously got what he wanted and was already thinking of something else.

'I'm going back to my own room now,' she said, trying, while edging away from him, to refrain from adding, as she was tempted to, 'if you are quite finished?'

Brett turned to her quickly, his nakedness apparently not bothering him. 'Are you all right?' he asked curtly.

'Would it worry you if I wasn't?' she asked coldly, hating herself for finding it almost impossible to keep her eyes off him. She must be like a child with a new toy. One she hadn't seen before. Only Brett Deakin was far more dangerous than most toys and, before she either said or did something stupid and made a fool of herself, she had to get away from him.

'Will you please pass me my negligé? So I can go back to my room,' she repeated quickly.

His eyes darkened at her unconsciously imperious tones. 'If I had time,' he threatened, 'I'd soon have you imploring to be allowed to stay. As it is,' he shrugged, 'we have little more than an hour to be out of here. And I have other things to do.'

What did he mean – out of here? As he continued to stare at her, as if tempted to change his mind, she hastily grasped the garment he picked up and gave to

124

her and put it on. 'I don't understand.' She frowned, feeling slightly better for being even half decently covered. 'Where are we going?'

'On our honeymoon,' he informed her curtly. 'At least, I am going to the Bahamas, and naturally people will expect me to take my wife with me. Of course, it may not be like a conventional honeymoon. I can't guarantee you are going to enjoy yourself. But I will promise that, by the time we get back, Norton will no longer be interested in you. Or you in him.'

CHAPTER 9

So he still believed the construction those media men had put on an innocent luncheon? Miranda opened her mouth to try again to explain what had really happened, then suddenly paused. Perhaps, to a casual observer, her behaviour that morning hadn't seemed so innocent? The wrong impression the media got might have been her fault as much as theirs. She had a horrid suspicion, as well, that if she blamed Gaby for the whole affair and Brett rang, as he might, and confronted her with it, that Gaby would deny it. She might be too smart to deny taking Miranda out for lunch, but she would, almost certainly refuse to take any responsibility for Adrian Norton joining them. And Brett was hardly likely to check with anyone else about it, in order to discover if his wife was telling the truth or not. Bitterly, Miranda realized how she'd probably been used to create a malicious diversion by a woman who'd allowed a terrible tragedy in her life to unbalance her so much that the only pleasure she now found lay in destroying the happiness of other people. Biting her lip, Miranda knew she was going to need more proof than mere words – her words, anyway – before she convinced Brett of anything.

'Couldn't we spend our honeymoon here?' she asked, after deciding quickly that it might be wiser, for the time being, to ignore what he said about her and Norton. She wasn't surprised, though, when he dismissed her suggestion immediately.

'No way,' he snapped, reaching for his own discarded clothing and walking, without looking at her again, into his bathroom. 'You have an hour to get ready and join me downstairs. Otherwise I'll send Harris up for you.'

They flew to Nassau, the famous holiday resort and capital of New Providence, an island in the Bahamas, by private jet. During the journey, Miranda mostly slept, while Brett talked to the pilot and other members of the crew, or just sat beside her, keeping a close eye on her. When she didn't appear to be suffering any stress, apart from sleeping a lot, he relaxed and turned his attention to studying some of the numerous documents concerning his ever-increasing business empire which he had brought with him.

At the International Airport, they switched to a chartered plane to go to the island, which he told Miranda belonged to a group known as the Exuma Cays – pronounced keys. In the light of a new day, Miranda felt fresh energy flowing into her limbs, and a renewed interest in Brett's island stirring within her. She had heard plenty about the Bahamas from friends who had been there, but as the distance, when she was disabled, would have made such a journey difficult, she had never thought of going there herself.

She felt both excited and impressed by the kaleidoscope of spectacular scenery unfolding before her as, wide awake now, she gazed through the windows of the plane. Crystal-clear stretches of blue, green and aquamarine water lay beneath them, broken at various intervals by islands with white beaches rising out of the sea. Patterns under the water, of what looked like mountains, plains and canals between ridges of sand, fascinated her. Occasionally, on some of the islands, she saw villas and roads leading to quite large clusters of houses and tiny harbours, but most of them looked deserted.

When her curiosity drove her to asking Brett about them, he explained that there were hundreds of islands in the Bahama group, but only a few inhabited. 'They were a Crown Colony but gained their independence in 1973,' he said. 'Over sixty per cent of all Bahamians live on New Providence, where Nassau is the seat of the national government and has a sizeable share of the international financial pie. Otherwise you might visit most of the other islands without finding a crowd. And, like my own, it can get pretty lonely, if you don't care for that kind of thing.'

'How did you come to own it?' she asked curiously.

He looked at her drily, reading her mind accurately. 'You obviously don't see me as the right type – for lonely islands?'

Miranda didn't. She could see him in one of the popular southern Caribbean resorts, perhaps. She couldn't help associating him with places where there were plenty of people, most of them as sophisticated as he was. Hadn't Gaby described the kind of people, especially women, he was usually seen with? It made her wonder how long it would take him to tire of someone whom he might consider exactly the opposite for a wife?

'I hadn't thought about it,' she said stiffly. 'But now you come to mention it . . .'

Brett shrugged. 'I couldn't see myself on Luke at first, but I've become very fond of it. The island was part of a deal,' he revealed, before she could ask: if he felt like that, why he had bought it? 'Someone was in my debt and this was the only way he could even partly repay what he owed me.'

'How big is it?'

Brett smiled into her eyes, which were turned to him enquiringly. 'Big enough, I suppose. Actually, quite a few people live there. But not so many that you'll be able to ignore me.'

Miranda shivered. What did he mean? Did he think that was what she was doing? Miranda's cheeks grew hot, then paled. She knew she had scarcely spoken to him since they left New York. Did he believe she was sulking? Was this his way of letting her know that, no matter how badly done to she felt, he wouldn't put up with it much longer? He didn't seem to understand that she needed time to come to terms with what had happened between them. Until she did, she found it difficult sometimes to even look at him.

Being unable to express her immediate feelings, she said defensively, 'I didn't realize I was ignoring you, but if that's what I've been doing, maybe it's because we haven't much in common. To talk about, that is.'

'Nothing in common?' His brows rose.

'Well, we haven't, have we?' She looked at him defiantly. 'You forced me to marry you – '

'Now wait a minute,' he broke in. 'I gave you an option, which in my book, if not in yours, isn't quite the same thing.'

'But you knew I was trapped!'

'Maybe,' Brett replied, while knowing this was all he would admit to. Initially he had intended marrying Miranda in order to try and rid himself of feelings which irrationally haunted him. When he discovered she was not disabled he had decided to marry her for revenge – something he was beginning to realize might be a sheer waste of time. Even if he divorced Miranda, it would mean a few wasted years. Years which he might have devoted in better ways to getting rid of the guilt complex his mother and Eve Martin had left him with. 'Listen, Miranda,' he went on. 'Whether you – I could say, we – like it or not, we will be on Luke together for several weeks, so it might be a good idea to try to tolerate each other. We might even,' he quipped deliberately, 'learn to do more than that eventually?'

'I shouldn't count on it.' Miranda wasn't sure why she was pretending she didn't like his suggestion when she really wanted to go along with it. 'As I just said, we haven't much in common.'

'We might have more than you think,' he muttered pointedly. And, as her cheeks flushed, 'Reject me on Luke and you're going to regret it.'

After this, on the last lap of their journey, their conversation was limited to polite utterances again. Miranda returned to gazing through the window.

She felt she would rather look at the fascinating wonders of the sea than meet the glint in Brett's dark blue eyes, which had a disturbing effect on her.

As they approached the island, she found herself surprised by the size of it, as well as the number of houses she caught glimpses of on it. When she asked Brett about them he said they were used mainly by members of his staff who worked on the island for him. He didn't say at what.

After the pilot landed the plane expertly on the wide airstrip, and they got down from it, he took off immediately again to return to Nassau. Miranda watched until it was no more than a tiny speck in the clear blue sky, an expression of unconscious anxiety in her eyes. She didn't know that she looked as if she was saying goodbye to her last link with civilization for ever.

Brett glanced at her grimly as a station wagon raced towards them to pick them up. 'I'd rather you didn't make it so obvious that you would have liked to go back with it, Miranda. I can assure you this will change, but, meanwhile, I'd appreciate it if you made some attempt to keep your feelings to yourself.'

When the truck stopped beside them, he put the driver in the back and, with Miranda in the passenger seat beside him, set off along what proved to be a fairly rough track.

'How do you get off the island?' Miranda asked, aware that the young man behind them, whom Brett introduced as James Hamilton, was looking at her curiously. 'I'd have thought you'd have your own plane. Or do you use boats?'

'I keep a plane in the hangar back there,' Brett told her. 'I usually only use it for inter-island journeys, though, or in an emergency of some kind, when it's quicker and more practical to use than a boat.'

Miranda nodded, even as her heart sank. It couldn't have been more obvious that, without help, there was no way she could escape from the island by herself.

When they reached an intersection, the track from the airstrip gave way to a harder surfaced road which, after what she judged to be another mile, took them to the rear of a large and attractive villa. Behind it the ground rose slightly and was substantially fenced, while at the front of it – which Miranda saw when Brett took her around the side – was a swimming pool set in wide green lawns and beyond this a beach, then the sea. The view was truly magnificent. It almost took Miranda's breath away. Forgetting her husband for a moment, she stood gazing at it.

'Impressed?' Brett was watching the vivid expressions crossing her expressive face.

Miranda had to confess she was. 'It's beautiful!' she breathed. 'But what is it like in a storm?'

'Memorable.' Brett grimaced. 'Especially if you're outside and caught in the middle of it.'

Miranda nodded, then a woman appeared from behind them. 'I've just been seeing to your luggage, Mr Brett,' she greeted him. 'That no-good James just brought it in. Welcome back to the island.'

Brett laughed. Putting his arm around her, he hugged her. 'Nice to be back, Linda.' And, as Miranda turned, 'This is my wife, Linda. Her name is Miranda. She is already keeping me in my place, so I expect the two of you will get on. Linda,' he added to Miranda, 'is a veritable treasure of a housekeeper. I don't know what I should do without her.'

'Same as you always do, I expect, Mr Brett.' Linda's broad smile lit up her dark face warmly as she looked happily at Miranda, who said hello and shook hands with her. 'I never thought I'd see the day that Mr Brett would bring a bride to the island, and such a beautiful one at that. I'd almost given up all hope of him ever getting married.'

Brett said thoughtfully, 'When I rang and told you I was getting married, Linda, though you didn't say so, I somehow got the impression that you already knew?'

'It was your sister, Mr Brett,' Linda replied. 'She was here for a few days, as you maybe know. Anyway, she only left two days ago. She told me.'

Miranda saw Brett frown. 'When did you say Gaby was here?' he asked abruptly.

'Last week.' Linda shrugged her heavy shoulders. 'Had some people with her. Never seen them before . . .'

'You didn't like them?'

'Well, it's not my business to either like or dislike any of your family's guests, Mr Brett.'

'I'll have a word with you about them later,' Brett said, taking Miranda's arm and steering her towards the house. 'Right now, I think we should get settled in. What time is lunch?'

'Any time you like, Mr Brett.' Linda was fussing behind them. 'S'all ready – same as your rooms. But you needn't hurry, nothing's going to spoil.'

Miranda was sorry when Linda, still talking, disappeared into her kitchen. Somehow she'd felt safe when the woman was around, though safe, she knew, glancing at Brett's uncompromising face, was not a word he would approve of. She gazed nervously over the suite he drew her into. There was a large bedroom and off this quite a sizeable dressing-room, then a bathroom and, adjoining this, what looked like a shower room. There were no carpets on any of the floors, just large rugs, and though the other furnishings seemed just as spartan, she realized that anything else would be impractical in the kind of climate enjoyed by places like the Bahamas. Already she was becoming aware of the difference in the weather between here and New York. It had been snowing when they left New York, while on Luke the sun was shining, and the air tropically warm.

As the suite wasn't as big as the one in Brett's house in New York, Miranda's eyes went apprehensively back to the dressing-room. Would he allow her to sleep there? she wondered.

Almost as if he had guessed what she was thinking, Brett said, as he closed the door behind him, 'Before you start getting ideas about separate rooms again, let me tell you that, from now on, you sleep with me, Miranda. I'm the one who is going to be using the dressing-room, if I get tired of having company.'

Miranda swallowed, striving to stay cool, but finding what he said disturbing, even frightening. He had thrown off his jacket and the way he was looking at her made her feel almost afraid of him. Or was she afraid of how he could make her feel? Since he had made love to her, she had tried to convince

134

herself that she hated him. But now she wasn't so sure. And it was humiliating to suspect that if he made love to her again, she might not have much left to fight him with.

Trying to avert this happening, she said coolly, 'Brett, don't you think separate rooms might be a good idea? At least until we get to know each other better?'

'No, I do not!' he snapped. 'We tried that before and it didn't work, remember?'

'We didn't try very long. Or at least you didn't.'

He laughed. 'I've always found it better to start as I mean to go on.'

There must be some way of getting through to him, of convincing him she had no intention of cheating on him, that all she needed, as she had told him before, was a little time. But before she could even begin to reason with him, as if he had guessed her intentions, he reached her in a couple of strides and, before she could draw back, had her in his arms. In what seemed like seconds, she was crushed against his broad chest and gasping in sudden fear that he might feel how wildly her heart was beating. Belatedly she tried to push him away, but he held her so tightly that though she managed to struggle feebly, she had no real hope of fighting him. And when she lifted her head to plead with him verbally, his only response was to bring his mouth down on hers before she could say anything.

Unable to move and not sure she wanted to, Miranda closed her eyes as he pressed her slender body closer and she became a virtual prisoner under the probing of his experienced fingers. One of his hands went to her waist, the other to her nape. She could feel their insistent pressure on her skin, even through her dress, and suddenly, instead of fighting him, she was holding tightly on to him.

For a while longer he went on kissing her – then slowly released her. 'If that doesn't put an end to your sensible, if slightly outdated theories,' he mocked as he steadied her, 'I don't know what will.'

'What do you mean?' she asked, breathlessly.

'If Linda wasn't waiting with our lunch,' he threatened, 'I could be more explicit.'

Miranda opened dazed eyes and looked at him. He was laughing at her and it didn't help to realize that when he set her free she had not been as quick to let go of him. Feeling her cheeks colouring with embarrassment, she heard herself jabbering, 'I don't want you to be more explicit, thank you! But if you'd just give me a minute, I'd like to rinse my hands and face.'

Brett nodded. 'And after lunch you can rest,' he said. 'You don't want to overdo things.'

Glancing at him over her shoulder as she went into the bathroom, Miranda was surprised to catch a look of reluctant concern in his eyes. It was gone in a second, yet she was sure she hadn't imagined it. Why, she wondered, when she so often got the impression that he was intent on punishing her for something, should he look at her like that?

After a light but delicious lunch, Miranda insisted on helping Linda to clear the table. Brett had changed and disappeared as soon as they had coffee, saying he had to see someone at the other side of the island. He

136

didn't say who it was, or what he wished to see them about, and she didn't ask. She was learning fast that Brett didn't like being questioned, and anyway it was probably just one of his staff.

Linda looked both startled and surprised by Miranda's offer and, for once, a ready answer seemed to desert her. She demurred at first, then gave in. 'Well, if you really want to,' she agreed, 'but not when Mr Brett is around, mind you, or he will be angry.'

'Leave Brett to me.' Miranda spoke more confidently than she was feeling. 'Men shouldn't interfere domestically,' she went on grandly. 'Anyway,' she confessed, subsiding a little, 'it's been so long since I did anything like this that I can't guarantee to be much help.'

When Linda glanced at her questioningly, she found herself explaining briefly about her accident, which she had not intended mentioning. Linda was so kind and motherly that Miranda found her easy to talk to, but she didn't say anything about how she had met Brett.

'As long as you're okay now, that's all that matters,' Linda said cheerfully, after listening carefully until Miranda stopped speaking. 'For long as I remember since I've known him, I wanted to see Mr Brett married, but not to some of the women he's brought here. It seemed too much to hope for, that he'd find a girl like you.'

While Miranda was pleased that Linda appeared to have taken to her, she knew she would rather not have heard about the women Brett had invited to the island. Especially if, as Linda seemed to suggest, there'd been plenty of them. Had they slept in the same bed that Brett now expected her to share with him? Would she ever be able to sleep there happily, she wondered, knowing that the imprint of other female bodies must be, figuratively, at least, stamped indelibly on his sheets?

She sighed and tried not to think of it as she dried the last of the dishes. 'Have you lived on Luke long?' she asked Linda, as she hung up the tea towel when she was finished.

'I was born here an' hope to die here,' Linda said. 'Ten years I've worked for Mr Brett an' he's the best. Can't say the same for that sister of his, though. Once I thought I liked her, but now I just don't know . . .'

Brett was gone all afternoon and Miranda tried not to mind. After all, he had never promised her a conventional kind of marriage. They didn't love each other, and though Miranda hoped this might change, it didn't seem likely to happen immediately. Even so, she was beginning to feel curiously lost without him.

To pass the time during the afternoon, Miranda explored the bungalow, which was large and rambling and, as Linda explained as she showed her around it, big enough and well enough equipped to entertain any number of people. Miranda liked the spacious lounge especially, with its muted colours, comfortable chairs and fabulous views through wide windows of the ever-changing colours of the sea. Afterwards, she wandered by the pool, admiring the size and clear aquamarine depth of it and the changing cabins set back from it under the shade of overhanging trees, so you wouldn't notice they were there unless you looked hard enough. The whole house and surrounding grounds, she could see, had been meticulously planned and she wondered if Brett was responsible for it, or if it was like this when he took over the island? She must remember to ask him.

She would have loved to use the pool straight away but felt strangely uncertain about wearing one of the brief bikinis which, among other things, Brett had bought for her in New York. He had apparently given her size to a buyer he knew in a famous New York store who had supplied her with a wardrobe more suitable, he said, for the climate down here than what she had. The clothes were beautiful, she had to admit, but on examining them closer, after Brett went out, she couldn't help feeling rather doubtful about them. As well as being beautiful, many of them were too flimsy for her taste, and she wasn't sure that she'd ever feel really comfortable in them.

Yet Miranda knew that, at nineteen, she would have loved them, wouldn't have been able to wait to put them on. What, she frowned, still by the pool, had the years done to her? Had they frozen, or even completely done away with, all those youthful, adventurous instincts she'd once had? Surely not, when she was still only twenty-four? While five years in a wheelchair might have turned her into a more serious, more considerate person, she felt a sudden nostalgia for the impulsive, slightly reckless young girl she'd been then. Would a few weeks on Brett's island help her to recoup something of what she seemed to have lost? She wouldn't wish to have everything back, she thought with a half-amused grin. Just enough to enable her to do something without thinking of the consequences, now and then. But when a voice suggested this could mean falling in love with Brett, or even just making love with him, she flushed and walked on. Suspecting she was half in love with him already made her think of the old maxim which her grandmother, when she was alive, used to quote. Make sure, she would say, you really want what you wish for, as it might just come true.

CHAPTER 10

Brett was late in getting in, and when, as she began feeling worried, Miranda asked Linda if she knew where he could be, Linda would only say that there was a sizeable farm on the other side of the island and when Mr Brett came back he often had things to sort out: disagreements, genuine problems and the like. Miranda was beginning to realize that Linda could be very ambiguous about Brett's movements. She clamped down on an immediate suspicion that the farm might, in reality, be another woman. On a lonely island like this, couldn't he have a positive harem of them tucked away, with no one any the wiser? Feeling positively ashamed of herself for being so quick to jump to these kind of conclusions, Miranda went to get ready for dinner. If she thought like this every time Brett left her, she might soon know no peace of mind whatsoever.

She was, though, even as she tried to hide it, relieved when he did come in.

'Sorry I'm late,' he said without explaining why, disappearing into the dressing-room and closing the door. Believing he intended changing quickly

141

because of being delayed, Miranda was startled when, not more than a minute later, he came out again, wearing only a short robe and, without looking at her, went into the shower room, this time without closing the door. Miranda, who was sitting in front of the dressing-table, brushing her hair, had a clear view of him through the mirror as he threw off his robe and stepped naked under the shower. As her eyes widened involuntarily, she heard the brush she was using drop with a clatter to the bare floor before she wrenched her eyes away. But even as she managed to stop looking at him, this didn't prevent her breath from quickening, or a peculiar heat from sweeping through her, as this reminded her of how she had felt when he made love to her in New York. She had been both confused and frightened, yet, at the same time, she had known a surge of something very similar to the feelings running through her now. This forced her to admit, if against her will, that if Brett tried to make love to her again, she might be tempted not to fight him. This way, she might at least discover if the only thing to be gained from what she supposed more experienced girls than herself would simply call having sex was disappointment.

Quickly, lest Brett should emerge from the shower and guess her thoughts, she bent and picked up the brush she had dropped and, after replacing it on the dressing-table, hastily left the room to wait for him in the lounge.

During dinner which Linda served, like lunch, in the villa's dining-room, Brett watched Miranda broodingly. He never mentioned the shower, or her possible embarrassment. Was he so used to women seeing him naked that he no longer remembered the meaning of the word? By contrast, Miranda's own glances at him were almost furtive, but occasionally they lingered. He was casually dressed in a pair of cream pants and white shirt. The shirt, open at the top, exposed the strong, clean lines of his neck and the tanned darkness of his hair-covered chest. Closing her eyes, she tried not to remember what it felt like to be crushed against it and to feel again the sensations it aroused.

After dinner, she asked if they could go for a walk along the shore – she wanted to see the island by moonlight. But she also knew that she wanted to try and convince him once more over her innocence concerning her lunch with Gaby. If Brett made love to her again, she didn't want it to be merely because he believed she had betrayed him with Norton.

Brett appeared to be considering her request with mock seriousness. 'Any particular reason for requesting my company?' he wondered, smiling at her with glinting blue eyes. 'You haven't shown much enthusiasm for it so far.'

Miranda flushed, but refused to rise to his baiting. 'Do I have to have a particular reason?' she asked. 'I just thought you might like to come with me, that's all. I can easily go by myself.'

Brett laughed. 'And risk having some passing pirate snatching you away from me?'

'Don't be ridiculous!' she snapped, jumping to her feet.

Rising from the table, Brett caught up with her as she stumbled away from it. As he glanced at her flushed young face, one eyebrow rose in continuing amusement. 'It's not hard to see how long you've been out of circulation. You lose your cool at the least thing, and colour enchantingly.'

To Miranda, her cheeks were merely regrettably hot. But as Brett might have been paying her a compliment, she was ready to forgive him for teasing her. Especially when, as he caught her arm protectively and guided her outside, he went on to say, 'This evening you're looking quite beautiful. Is the dress you are wearing one of those I bought for you in New York? It's quite tantalizing, isn't it?'

Miranda bit her lip as she looked down on it, trying to ignore the mocking look in Brett's eyes. She'd been so busy earlier wondering where he could be that she just grabbed the first dress she came to in her wardrobe. It was white, with narrow shoulder straps, but she didn't think the material so transparent that it left nothing to the imagination. Not that she'd taken much time to really study it before leaving the suite before dinner. The sight of Brett in the shower had driven all thought of doing something like that from her head. 'I wish I'd had my own clothes here,' she said.

Brett shrugged. 'They're being shipped out from England, but mightn't have suited this climate so well.'

'I did have some summer things. If we hadn't been married in such a hurry, I might have had more time to sort them out.'

Brett merely shrugged again, as if he'd lost interest and, for a while, after leaving the house, they walked in silence, a silence Miranda was reluctant to break.

The sea rolled in, with only the mildest of waves, along the shore and, unable to resist it, she took off her sandals and let the water wash over her bare feet.

'Aren't you going to join me?' she asked Brett.

He regarded her laughing face solemnly, then shook his head. 'I've always been scared of the water since I lost a toe to a crab, when I was a kid.'

Miranda giggled, unable to take him seriously. 'I hadn't noticed one missing . . .'

'Perhaps,' he suggested, 'you were concentrating too much on other parts of my anatomy?'

'Brett!'

'Well, anyway,' he said, still solemnly and taking pity on her hot cheeks, 'you're quite right, as it happens. The judge ordered him, the crab, I mean, to put it back again, so if I have any flaws they aren't in my feet.'

Miranda giggled again, then sobered. 'If I'm expected to believe your tall stories, Brett, why won't you believe mine when I'm telling you the truth?'

'Come again?'

Miranda paused doubtfully. Impulsively, she'd decided, as he was in a better mood, to try and talk to him about Gaby, but now, as a steely glint returned to his eyes, she feared she had made a mistake. But as she could think of no other reason for her slightly obscure statement, she forced herself to continue. 'You wouldn't believe me when I tried to tell you the truth about my lunch with Gaby . . .'

'So we're back to that again?'

'Only because I think it's necessary.' She looked at him pleadingly. 'I don't know why you married me,

Brett, but if we are to live together, I shouldn't like to think that anything I'd done since we were married has made things worse than they already were between us. Which is why I keep trying to tell you I didn't lie about Gaby!'

'You did about being crippled,' he snapped. 'And very easily.'

'I didn't – find it easy, I mean,' Miranda protested. 'You don't know the half of it, Brett. I do know, though, that it was wrong to marry you, and I shouldn't have done, whatever the reason. But, as I've told you before, I intend to stick to my side of the bargain, or whatever you care to call it, which won't, I promise you, include any more lying. If we can't trust each other, what have we left?'

'Probably all we had to begin with,' Brett said cynically.

Miranda would liked to have asked him to enlarge on this. For her, to begin with, there'd been only fear and reluctance, but she still didn't know how it had been for him. He knew why she had married him, but she had no idea why he had married her. The more she thought of it, the more mystified she became. She might, in the end, be forced to conclude it could only have been for revenge. And because he was already regretting this, his ultimate way of taking it might be even worse than it was before.

'You may be right,' she acknowledged evenly, 'but I'd still like to clear up our misunderstanding over Adrian Norton.'

Brett halted abruptly and stopped exactly where he was, the gentle lapping of the sea at their feet contrasting oddly with the hardness of his face.

Miranda, suddenly nervous, thought he was going to hit her, but he merely looked at her and said, 'Go on.'

His obvious anger, along with the curtness of his voice, was scarcely encouraging, but Miranda persevered. 'Gaby called at the house, inviting me to lunch, after apologizing for her behaviour the night before. I didn't want to go. For one thing I felt tired. I expect it was just jet-lag catching up, but I didn't feel like going out. And, when I thought of it, I wasn't sure that you would want me to.'

'So, why did you?'

Couldn't he speak softly? 'Well, for one thing, she is your sister, and you said, yourself, she's been through a lot. And, as well as this, I didn't want her to think we could never be friends. She still seemed rather distraught and when she said she'd already booked a table at a famous restaurant, just to please me, I wasn't sure how she would take it if I refused. I could see that Harris didn't approve when he saw us leaving, but I didn't know what else I could do.'

'Pray continue,' Brett said as she paused.

Miranda did, and though she wished his eyes had been kinder, she was grateful that at least he appeared to be listening. 'As we were going into the restaurant – the Four Seasons, Gaby called it – some newspaper men began taking photographs. I didn't recognize any of them, of course, but Gaby seemed to know them. She spoke to one of them, Dave, I think she called him, who seemed to be a personal friend, though maybe I was mistaken. Anyway, she told him I was your wife and that we'd only been married a few days. I could see then that he couldn't wait to snap us. He said he had seen the announcement in the papers, but hadn't expected to see me around . . .'

Brett's eyes narrowed. 'What the hell did Gaby think she was doing?'

'I don't think she appreciated what he was doing, any more than I did.'

'No?' Brett laughed derisively.

Miranda gulped. Gaby may have treated her badly, but she wished it was over something she didn't have to relate to Brett. She wasn't sure how close Gaby was to her brother but she'd hate to be the one to cause trouble between them. Brett was clearly waiting to hear what happened next and suddenly she wished, despite everything, that she'd never started.

Drawing a steadying breath, she began again, though not without difficulty. 'I don't like having the media focusing cameras on me, but it has happened before, in Birmingham, so it didn't seem anything to make a fuss about. Even in the restaurant where Adrian Norton was waiting for us, obviously by arrangement, I tried to accept it, rather than cause a scene with Gaby over it or walking out.'

'You must have enjoyed yourself, all the same?'

'I might have felt better if I had,' Miranda said shortly. 'Gaby wasn't much fun and though Adrian was quite pleasant, I didn't feel comfortable.'

'What did Gaby talk about?'

Did he look suddenly wary? Miranda's soft mouth pursed slightly as, in the half-light, she tried to read his shuttered face. Should she tell him? Well, why not? 'Your women, for one thing.'

'My women?' He laughed ironically. 'Anyone special?'

'The only one she mentioned by name was the one who rang you on our first night in New York. Eve, wasn't it?'

Brett didn't reply. For a moment he neither moved nor spoke. Then, catching hold of Miranda by her bare shoulders, he stared down into her mutinous eyes. 'I'm in my thirties – *late* thirties, Miranda,' he emphasized. 'I won't deny there have been plenty of women in my life. If a man is single and well off, it gets difficult to avoid them. Even marriage is no deterrent to some of them, so don't expect the Eves of this world to stop ringing me, or trying to get in touch with me, just because I am married. All I can say, for what it's worth, is that if you persist in listening to gossip, even my sister's, you'll only have yourself to blame if you get hurt.'

Miranda looked at him uncertainly. Was he warning her that he didn't intend changing his ways, and she'd be wiser turning a blind eye to it? Or was he assuring her that, now he was married, he meant to be faithful? But before she could find the nerve to ask him, he was telling her impatiently to get on with her story.

Miranda nodded numbly and tried to pull away from him. His hands on her shoulders seemed to be burning into her flesh, making it almost impossible for her to think. Or even to remember where she had got to. She was relieved when, as if guessing the confusion he was causing, he decided to take pity on her and let her go.

'You were finishing your meal,' he reminded her.

'Oh, yes.' Miranda drew a more relaxed breath and

nodded. 'Gaby had apparently forgotten a hair appointment and asked Adrian Norton if he would see me home. I didn't want him to and we were arguing about it as we left the restaurant, which made me forget that the cameras might still be outside. This made me jerk back against Adrian and gave the impression in the newspapers that he had his arms around me, when some of them caught me by surprise. They nearly blinded me, and before I knew what was happening Adrian was pushing me into a taxi and jumping in beside me.'

'He came all the way home with you?'

'It seemed easier, after that, to let him.'

'You invited him in?'

Surely they'd had this out before? 'No! Ask Harris if you don't believe me.' Miranda's voice rose but she didn't care. 'I scarcely know Mr Norton. I'm not sure I even like him, and I certainly didn't wish to see any more of him.'

Brett said nothing for a few moments as he watched her narrowly. Miranda, meeting his contemplative blue eyes, drew a sharp breath as she suddenly felt suspended between heaven and that place far below it, awaiting his judgement. Another part of her was vaguely conscious of the isolation and loneliness of their surroundings. It was like being on the edge of the world, with the scent of wild herbs on the wind along with a faint saltiness from the sea. A wave of regret swept over her. How lovely it might have been, had Brett loved her.

Before her thoughts could wander along even more treacherous paths, he interrupted them by saying, 'I believe you, Miranda.'

'You – do?'

Brett ignored her wide-eyed surprise. 'However,' he said, 'I had warned you about my sister and it wouldn't have been impossible, when she asked you out to lunch, to have got in touch with me and asked my advice. In future, remember that.'

'I only accepted what I thought was a perfectly innocent invitation,' Miranda protested. 'I may have felt uncertain about it, but I didn't think I was doing anything wrong.'

'Not if simply joining people for a meal was your only motive.'

Did he have to sound so arrogant? Miranda looked at him resentfully. 'What other motive could I have?'

'A rich lover, perhaps? Someone to keep you amused when your husband is busy.'

'You know I'm not looking for anything like that!'

'Aren't you?'

'No – but I've no way of proving I'm telling the truth.'

'Nor can I prove you aren't.' Brett shrugged. 'So shall we call a truce?'

'If you like.' As usual, when Brett held out an olive branch, she felt slightly distrustful. He was older than she was and she sometimes had a feeling that he was playing with her like a cat with a mouse. But because she was, at that moment, beginning to feel exhausted by the grilling he was giving her, she was willing, when he suggested a truce, to agree.

As Brett, as if he considered there was nothing to be gained by discussing her unfortunate luncheon with Gaby any longer, turned to walk back to the house, Miranda stumbled after him. Why did he always make her feel so young and naïve when he was talking to her? It wasn't as if, come to think of it, at twenty-four, she was so young any more. How was it that each time she tried to appear more sophisticated, it didn't seem to work? It frustrated her to realize that, despite trying to keep up with everything over the years, she was probably far less worldly now than she had been at eighteen.

She wasn't to know that she often looked no older than eighteen to the man by her side. It made him wonder, not for the first time, why he'd never stopped to ask himself if he knew what he was doing when he decided to marry her. He seldom made mistakes – that was a luxury he rarely allowed himself – but he was beginning to think that Miranda was going to be the biggest mistake of the lot. Frustratedly, when he thought of all the other women he knew, who might have made this night satisfactory for him, he clenched his teeth.

Moodily he walked on. He had to admit there had been something about Miranda, when he'd made love to her in New York, that he hadn't encountered before. But the fire he'd imagined tearing at his guts, making him lose control, might have been caused by anger as much as anything. The whole episode was now so veiled in obscurities that, though this faintly surprised him, he couldn't recall anything about it clearly. One thing he did know – he would sleep in one of the guest rooms tonight. Until he got a few things sorted out in his mind, he wasn't looking for more complications.

Miranda was having some difficulty keeping up with him. Her white dress, now blowing in a rising wind, kept tangling about her legs, so she had to keep stopping to unravel it. In the end, she was forced to pick it up and hold it high above her knees in order to catch up with him.

She didn't know how it happened, but she was so busy holding on to her dress with one hand and keeping her hair out of her eyes with the other, that when Brett, on hearing her running, turned to wait for her she crashed straight into him.

'Something the matter?' he asked abruptly, his arms coming out to steady her.

'No!' she gasped, her heartbeats more rapid than could be justified, even by her wild flight. Whenever Brett touched her she was beginning to feel as if she was fighting something she didn't really want to. And, finding it confusing, she began to tremble. 'I – I was just trying to catch up,' she stammered, staring up at him.

'Sorry,' he said absently, his gaze going over her. She looked, he thought, like a beautiful bewildered child, but the tender curves clearly visible under the gauzy transparency of her spray-dampened dress suggested something else. For a few moments, as his eyes returned to hers, they seemed to be wrapped in a kind of mutual, if antagonistic, awareness of each other which neither of them could immediately break.

Miranda, as if unconsciously sensing danger, tried to move away from him, but he wasn't allowing it. As had happened in New York, when she'd tried to struggle against him, he merely tightened his arms about her, pulling her closer, then brought his mouth down hard on hers. She would have cried out from

153

the unexpected shock of it, had she been able to, as the flames she had known before in Brett's arms began once again to consume her.

He went on kissing her. One of his hands came up behind her, holding her ruthlessly, while he forced her lips apart to explore her mouth sensuously. Then he was tugging the thin straps of her dress off her shoulders until the top fell to her waist, allowing his mouth to slide in its wake and create further havoc within her. She could feel the heat in her limbs matching the blood pounding through her veins and a throbbing desire for him burning through the whole of her body. It seemed that her bared skin caught on fire wherever his mouth touched her. It was so incredible that she thought she was going to pass out from the sheer intensity of it, but was unable to prevent herself from clinging to him and returning his kisses fiercely.

Curled up against him, she felt her heart go out to him and she somehow knew, even in those moments of unnerving sensation, that it might never be hers again. Brett, she sensed, was not immune to her either. She could feel his need for her in the hardness of him and, though it was probably only physical, she knew that if he wanted her now she would welcome him. She wanted him to lay her down on the sands, even if it was uncomfortable, and make love to her, there and then. Being suddenly convinced that this time she would not be disappointed, it didn't seem important anymore that Brett didn't love her, If nothing else, they were married, weren't they?

When he lifted his head, though his heartbeats still hammered into her, there was such an obvious struggle going on inside him that she dared not either move or speak. Was he about to reject her? Had she not responded enough, made her own feelings clear enough to him? Then, just as she feared he was about to thrust her from him, she could have cried with relief when, instead of doing this, he merely picked her up and strode with her into the house. In a primitive urge, she had wanted to give herself to him on the beach, with only the wildness of the elements about them to bear witness. Nevertheless, as her thoughts swung inconsistently, she tried to be grateful that Brett was being considerate enough to put her comfort before his own, all-too-obvious needs. Something, she sensed, that with other women in situations like this, he seldom did.

'Linda?' she breathed as, still holding her, he strode over the hall.

'She lives on the other side of the grounds,' he told her. 'Only comes in during the day.'

Afterwards Miranda realized that the harshness of his voice should have warned her that something was wrong, but right then, the wanton feelings still running hotly through her weren't helping her to think straight. Much of the warmth was quickly knocked out of her, however, when, on entering their suite, he dropped her none too gently on the bed and, before she could protest, was moving swiftly towards the door.

'I'm sorry I kissed you,' he said curtly over his shoulder. 'It won't happen again.'

'Brett!' she cried, tears springing to her eyes as she suddenly became aware he was leaving her. 'I didn't – I mean, I don't mind you kissing me . . .'

'But that wasn't part of our marriage contract, was it?' he replied, pausing in the doorway.

'Wasn't it? But, if it wasn't, does it matter?' Miranda asked, feeling desperate.

'I believe it does,' he gave her a final glance. 'And, come the morning, you might be glad I decided to stick by it.'

CHAPTER 11

Struggling up on one elbow, Miranda stared at the door Brett closed behind him. He didn't slam it or anything as uncivilized as that, but it sounded so final. What did he mean about kisses not being part of their marriage contract? Of course they wouldn't be. All she recalled of the contract was that she wouldn't get anything if she left him, and the allowance he was paying her father and Alice which Harry had told her, when she rang him from New York, they were already getting. It seemed to Miranda that Brett had merely been talking at random in order to confuse her. A state, she thought bitterly and with not a little chagrin, he must know she was in already. Well, to hell with him, she thought, with a return of something like her old spirit, if he ever came near her again, she would tell him what he could do with his kisses!

During the following days she didn't see much of Brett. When she did he seemed determined to keep her at a distance. According to Linda, he spent a lot of time on the plantation where the main crop was sugar. When, however, Miranda tried to talk to him about it, he was curiously reticent. And once, when she asked if he would take her with him, he refused. He said, quite unjustly, she thought, that there was nothing there that would interest her – that she'd only be a nuisance. Naturally, such a rebuff only made Miranda more determined to see the sugar plantation for herself, but one day when she tried to follow him she found the track too rough for her. Before she had walked more than a few hundred yards it had ruined the sandals she was wearing and, though she searched through the luggage Jill had packed for her, she found she had nothing stronger with her.

As well as keeping himself busily occupied on the island, Brett also spent hours each day in his office, a specially equipped room with a system with which he could reach almost any part of the world. Occasionally personnel from some of his companies flew in and he would be closeted with them all day in the large dining-room that he sometimes used for business purposes as well as entertaining, and where he would ask Linda to serve them a working lunch. Miranda seldom saw any of these people before they went away again.

Her own relationship with Brett she could only describe as static. It puzzled her when she clearly recalled him warning her, on their way here, that if she rejected him on Luke she would live to regret it. Yet wasn't he the one, when she had more or less offered herself to him, who was doing the rejecting?

Miranda wasn't unhappy, though, to be left to her own devices. During the weeks before Christmas, she swam a lot and explored the beaches, or just lay around soaking up the sun. Linda spoiled her disgracefully. She seldom let her do anything and regularly brought out long cool drinks for her on to the patio. Now and then, when Miranda could persuade her to, she would bring out something for herself and talk to her of life in general on the islands. Miranda loved hearing about it, but it made her curious that when she questioned her about Luke specifically, Linda was strangely silent.

It was a lotus-eater's life and it showed. Miranda blossomed. She had always been an attractive teenager, but now she was developing into a beautiful woman. Her skin had a bloom on it which made it look like satin. Her fair hair grew long and literally shone, despite being frequently exposed to too much sea and sun. Her figure filled out. She still remained incredibly slender but in certain places she became considerably more rounded. So much so that, though she wasn't aware of it, Brett often had some difficulty in keeping his eyes off her. A tendency he put down drily to lust and the lack of the kind of women he used to relieve it.

Miranda was surprised to find that a doctor paid regular visits to the island. The same as the Flying Doctors in the outback of Australia, Brett told her, when she asked him. He made sure that she was booked to see the doctor, and, when she protested, he insisted.

The doctor, a youngish man, was called Lou Mitford and, when Miranda asked him, he said he usually visited Luke to check up on the people living there – a service which she later discovered Brett paid for. Brett had apparently told Lou about her being disabled, and of her operation, but the doctor, after a brief examination, pronounced her remarkably fit and well. He also talked to her about birth control, remarking that Brett thought it wiser to wait a while, after what she had been through, before starting a family. This infuriated Miranda so much that she almost told the good doctor that Brett had his own methods regarding birth control that might prove far more effective than a handful of pills.

They spent Christmas on another island, to which they flew in Brett's plane. Some friends of his owned it, he said, but rarely spent more than a week or two there each year. Miranda would rather have stayed on Luke. She didn't know if she would have liked to live there permanently, but she had wanted to spend Christmas there this year. It depressed her somewhat, though she tried to hide it, that Brett obviously had no desire to. Not with her, at any rate.

Brett had been to New York for two days, immediately preceding Christmas. Business, he said, but he came back with an armful of presents. For herself and the staff, he explained, and his friends on the other island, whom she had yet to meet. When Miranda complained that, as she had not expected their honeymoon to last so long, she had nothing to give him, he told her not to worry – that she could get him something when they returned to the city. Which, to Miranda, though she tried to convince herself it didn't matter, wouldn't, she knew, be the same.

* * *

Brett's friends on the other island turned out to be old acquaintances – business people from Los Angeles who had once lived in New York. They had known, they said apologetically, that Brett was on his honeymoon, but as they hadn't seen him for some time, they weren't able to resist the temptation of inviting him and his bride over for Christmas Day. Especially as they unfortunately had to leave on the following one.

'We hope you don't mind, dear?' Lisa Gordon smiled at Miranda warmly. 'We saw a lot of Brett when we lived in New York, but since we moved out, far too little. And while we both have places here, Bill and I – ' she grimaced at her husband ' – rarely get down often enough to meet up with him.'

They were obviously much taken by Brett's bride, as Lisa continued calling her, and Miranda liked them as well, though, as there were several other guests there, and she and Brett were only there for one day, she had neither the time nor much opportunity to really get to know them. Most of the women, Miranda noticed, appeared to be old friends of Brett's and flirted with him continually, while their husbands looked on, seemingly tolerantly. Miranda wished she was even half as sophisticated and beautiful as they were as she watched Brett laughing with them. Brett was so tall and ruggedly handsome, he made most of the other men look puny by comparison and, as she saw him responding to their wives, she felt something stir inside her which she feared must be jealousy. She had come to care for him more than she'd thought possible, she realized, though she never allowed herself to use the word love. Even 'care for' seemed to make her too vulnerable when Brett, nowadays, never gave even the slightest indication that he reciprocated her feelings in any way.

They were going to return to Luke later in the evening, but before then the weather broke. There had been, Miranda heard, a weather warning, but no one had expected it to change so suddenly and dramatically. When Brett told her it would be too risky to use the plane, she stared at him in dismay.

'It's just something that happens here occasionally.' He shrugged. 'The weather can be unpredictable on the Atlantic side of the islands. We don't usually get the devastating hurricanes they sometimes get in the southern Caribbean, but it can be pretty frightening. As well as bloody inconvenient,' Miranda heard him muttering.

'Can't we get home any other way?' she asked, one eye on the storm-tossed seas.

'I might have risked it on my own,' Brett said absently. 'But not with you.'

'Then – what will we do?'

'Stay here and return to Luke in the morning,' she was told. 'By then the storm will have blown itself out. I can almost guarantee it.'

Miranda found it difficult to believe it would be gone by then as she watched the churning ocean, which looked as if it was being stirred with a gigantic spoon by the force of the wind. The sea rose in great swirling waves, pounding against the shore-line, throwing huge sprays hundreds of yards towards the house. She was surprised that no one but herself seemed alarmed by it, and when Bill Gordon assured her, as Brett had done, that all might be calm again in a few hours, she still felt doubtful.

She didn't think about where they were going to sleep until later when someone mentioned they were going to turn in. The house didn't seem big enough to accommodate over a dozen people.

'They have guest cabins,' Brett said, when she asked him about this. 'They rent them to friends when they aren't here themselves, and use them for stressed-out executives in between.'

The Gordons must be as wealthy as Brett, Miranda thought, if they could afford to do such things.

She heard Brett adding, 'We've been allocated the end cabin, furthest away from the house. It's the only one left because, when Lisa and Bill invited us, I said we wouldn't be staying. There wouldn't have been even that one if another couple, who were supposed to be coming, hadn't dropped out at the last minute.'

Only one? Miranda glanced at Brett warily, while wondering how much more hassle she was to suffer over sleeping arrangements with him? London, New York, Luke. Every time they went somewhere new, would she be exposed to such nerve-racking uncertainty? She didn't think Brett would wish to share a cabin with her after the way he had pointedly ignored her and slept in another room on Luke. But she didn't wish to spend another night lying awake, wondering about it.

Attempting to discover what he meant to do, she asked, trying to speak casually, 'I expect you'll be spending the night drinking and talking to Bill?'

163

'No way,' Brett answered sardonically. 'I think most of us have had too much to drink already. All I want to do now is to get some sleep.'

'The plane . . .?'

Brett laughed. 'You aren't suggesting I spend the night in that, are you? It's quite safe in Bill's hangar. It certainly doesn't need a nursemaid to look after it.'

Miranda felt her cheeks colour as Brett obviously saw through her questions, but before she could speak again, he was saying goodnight to Bill and Lisa. Then, holding her firmly by the hand, he pulled her to join the others outside who were making their way towards their cabins. It was a struggle. Miranda didn't think she would ever have made it on her own. But with Brett half-dragging, half-carrying her, she was inside the cabin before she realized it, and he was closing the door.

'Lisa mentioned there's always spare nightwear in one of the drawers. If you need it,' he told her, still keeping hold of her as she swayed dizzily from the battering the elements had given them, even over the short distance.

'Why shouldn't I need it?' Miranda panted contrarily, as what he said – or was it the taunting way he said it? – put her back up. 'I can't imagine,' she went on recklessly, as she tried to pull away from him, 'that I'm like most of your women, who probably sleep naked.'

'What do you mean, my women?'

She hadn't meant to say anything about them, and had hoped he hadn't heard. 'Oh, forget it!' she cried, impatiently.

'Okay,' he agreed, looking at her oddly. 'Let's forget everything, shall we? At least temporarily.'

Miranda frowned as she became aware of the way Brett's dark glance was roving slowly over her. The last few yards had caught them in a torrential downpour which soaked them both. Miranda's dress, she suddenly realized, was plastered to her figure, showing every bit of it – she might as well have had nothing on. And she hadn't much to start with!

'Don't you think it's a good idea?' Brett asked suavely.

Miranda's frown remained in place as she shrank back from him. His voice sounded strange, slightly slurred. *Had* he had too much to drink? While she had not, herself, seen him drinking excessively, she had overheard some of the other men joking earlier in the evening that, when Brett liked, he could drink anyone under the table. There had been affection, rather than criticism, in their voices, which had made her curious over the amount of respect Brett seemed to command. Even though he had not exactly discouraged their wives from fawning over him, it appeared to make no difference to the regard the men had for him.

'It – depends . . .' she replied cautiously, as Brett repeated his question.

Brett laughed and merely hauled her close and, as if deciding he could answer her better with a little action than with words, he began kissing her. And, even as the thought struck her that he might again be only going to kiss her and then leave her, Miranda found herself clinging to him and returning his kisses passionately.

She took no notice of the small voice which enquired where her pride was. Why, after the way he had rejected her on Luke, she was willing to risk this happening again? Or why she wasn't struggling, even briefly, against the overwhelming desire flooding through her to respond to him? In New York, when he made love to her, she'd been full of apprehension and undecided feelings. She had felt it wrong to go so far with him when they didn't love each other. But now, though she knew Brett didn't love her, she had discovered, amazingly, that she loved him. And so deeply that it was rapidly overcoming any remaining doubts she had over making love with him. This, combined with the clamouring of her body, was making it impossible to resist him. As he divested them both of their wet clothing, then carried her swiftly to the bed, she found she couldn't do anything to try to stop him.

Perhaps it was the wildness of the night that aroused a kind of violent hunger in both of them. As Brett continued kissing her, Miranda felt something like potent wine pouring through her veins; even if it had been wine it couldn't have acted faster. Her arms went around his neck as he caressed her almost roughly, and when his mouth found her breasts, all her senses blazed in time with his until they appeared to be enveloped in a furnace of fire.

She wasn't really conscious of lying on the bed beside him, but she couldn't prevent herself from pressing wantonly against him. And if she was vaguely aware that she shouldn't be surrendering so eagerly, she could find no will, or even inclination, to do anything else. Not with the hot, searing turmoil within her, rapidly turning her into a mindless puppet under Brett's exploring hands and rendering her completely helpless.

When he pushed her legs apart and slid into her, he was so impatient that she winced with discomfort. But, unlike the first time, Miranda's own passion now leapt to meet his and, instead of fighting him, she let him know she welcomed him by clinging to him tightly. She heard him groan under his breath as he moved heavily against her and everything melted and began spinning. She forgot where she was. There was only sensation, which mounted quickly as Brett's mouth covered hers and he went on kissing her. And as his powerful body stretched over her he aroused her to an even greater extent.

Her response was so intense and naturally sensuous that it brought from him a grunt of satisfaction. As his strong limbs pinned her to the mattress under them, she began sharing his impatience. Immediately she knew an urgent craving for something just out of reach which she had been cheated of previously.

She wasn't sure what she was seeking but when, with new consideration, he paused and guided her towards it, she heard herself crying out his name against his mouth and begging him not to stop. And he didn't. He took her right with him until the last minute, when she was convulsed by feelings she would not have thought possible. Brett's own gratification was unmistakable and he was bathed in sweat when he eventually drew a deep breath and rolled a little away from her.

Miranda felt dazed and incredulous as she stared at him. She found it difficult to believe that anyone could feel as she did. Brett seemed to have taken her on a trip to heaven, or somewhere very like it. It was only the evidence of her still throbbing but satisfied body that convinced her it hadn't all been a dream.

'Surprised?' Brett asked softly, reading the thoughts crossing her vivid young face.

Miranda was not only surprised, she didn't know what to say to him. In the end, all she could think of was, 'Yes.'

'Ah,' he teased her, bending his mouth again to her breasts, as if he couldn't get enough of them, 'it was better this time, was it?'

Miranda, feeling her body beginning to stir again and thinking it might be greedy to want more so quickly, tried to twist away from him, but Brett wasn't having any. Instead of letting her go, he began tugging gently with his teeth at her nipples and caressing them with his hands until she thought she was going slightly crazy. Then his hand was sliding further down, and finding her warm and waiting for him, again slid deftly into her. Immediately she was carried away by the same sensations she had known before, and an even greater culmination.

'Now, are you going to tell me?' Brett asked drily, after obviously obtaining his own satisfaction. He raised himself on one elbow looking down at her, willing her to look at him. 'Miranda?'

'It was better,' she admitted slowly.

He laughed with gentle mockery. 'So much enthusiasm. There was more in your body.'

'Well, I'm sorry!' Her eyes widened indignantly. 'But no one told me . . .'

'Because you've never had a lover before. Didn't you ever want one?'

'I suppose I did,' she confessed. 'Before my accident, I remember I used to wonder what it was all about.'

'So now you know?'

'I think so.'

'I wonder how long it will be before you feel more certain?'

Her eyes were still indignant. 'I'm sorry if I can't discuss it as easily as you do.'

He laughed again. 'You will, in time. But, for now, why don't we forget our differences and take a shower?'

'You mean . . .?'

'Yes, together.'

Miranda wasn't sure what happened to the night after that. It seemed to dissolve into snatches of sleep and making love, with Brett deciding that talking was no longer necessary. Come the morning, Miranda felt so taken over by him that she couldn't seem to think straight. Even in a few hours she was becoming addicted to how he could make her feel and she was reluctant to do anything that might cause him to ignore her again, as he had done on Luke. So though there were several questions she had wanted to ask him, she decided they were no longer important. What mattered more was the new closeness between them, and though Brett, if she mentioned it, might laugh and say it was only physical, to Miranda it represented at least some hope that other things might be better in the future between them.

* * *

The following day Brett took her sailing. They had returned to Luke early that morning and, after lunch, as the weather was fine again, he suggested it would be a good way to spend the afternoon.

'That's if you would like to?' he said.

Miranda said she would. 'Though I haven't done any sailing,' she warned. 'I could be seasick, I suppose, or anything.'

Brett laughed and told her he thought it unlikely. 'We won't be gone long enough for that.'

He took her about a mile up the shore of the island to a small harbour where a small cruiser was anchored. There were several medium-sized houses nearby, Miranda noticed, with several women and children sunning themselves outside them.

'Their menfolk work on the plantation,' Brett explained, drawing up beside the boat, which had obviously been made ready for him, and helping Miranda on to it.

'Disappointed?' he asked, as she looked at it curiously.

'Oh, no,' she said quickly. 'This looks much more fun than the yacht you once mentioned in New York.'

'That's up for sale, actually.'

'Why?' She shot him a puzzled glance as he navigated them, clearly expertly, away from the harbour and houses, and headed for the open sea.

'Would you rather I kept it?'

Miranda's pink lips tightened at the habit he had of often answering her question with one of his own. 'I love the sea, but I don't think I'd care for being cooped up with several other people for days. Not that I suppose your decision to sell your yacht had anything to do with me?'

'I haven't used it much,' he shrugged. 'Gaby is the enthusiast.'

'She likes sailing?'

'She likes lying on the deck all day drinking gin. But, apart from that, the boat is too big. Like everything else I own,' he added brusquely.

Miranda stared uncertainly at his hard profile, as he sat at the wheel. 'I thought most tycoons considered big to be beautiful?'

'I did once,' he admitted. 'I'm not so sure now.'

'My father once said,' she recalled, 'that if things go on as they are doing, most of the worlds businesses will be owned by a mere handful of people.'

'He could be right,' Brett said grimly, as if he didn't think it would be a good thing. 'And you can get too obsessed by possessing, if that makes sense, and too cluttered up with things you don't really want. Or need.'

Miranda's stomach gave a sickening lurch that had little to do with the way they were skimming over the water. Did Brett intend getting rid of more than his yacht? Would his wife be the next to go? Once the novelty of taking her to bed wore off, how long would it be before he was demanding a divorce? Until she discovered she loved him, Miranda might have welcomed a divorce herself. It didn't make her feel any better to realize that now it was the last thing she wanted.

Miranda sighed as Brett turned his attention to the boat again and she unobtrusively studied him. As the temperature rose he flung off his shirt and she noticed the flex of his powerful shoulder muscles as he steered through some strong currents and the boat rolled. For weeks she had been conscious of his hard vitality but now, for the first time, she was fully aware of his powerful sexuality. Through the night, he'd controlled her as he was controlling his boat, wringing from her a response she would never have believed possible if she had not experienced it. It made her grow cold to think of him – if he divorced her – married and making love to someone else. Even the thought of it was so painful that she had to turn away from him for fear he read the thoughts which might be all too obvious in her face and taunted her with them.

CHAPTER 12

It was a beautiful afternoon, with the sun high in a sky as incredibly blue as the sea. The air was balmy, rather than hot and Miranda drew it deeply into her lungs, enjoying the saltiness and pureness of it. She could feel it soaking into her, slowly dispersing the apprehension tormenting her, and, as she turned from Brett to look at the small cay they were approaching, she found her whole body relaxing almost wantonly. As long as Brett wanted her, she would forget about the future, she decided.

It was a small, deserted island, Brett explained, as he let down the anchor before wading ashore with her. 'We can swim.'

'We didn't bring anything to swim in,' Miranda said as they reached the silvery beach and he dropped her onto it.

'We won't need anything. There's no one to see us.' Brett smiled. 'You can, of course, swim with what you have on, if you like, and you'll soon dry.'

Miranda, blushing, refused to even glance at him as he swiftly stripped out of the little he still had on and dived into the water. When she looked his way at

173

last, although she'd heard a splash, he was nowhere to be seen, and suddenly terrified that he might have hit a submerged rock and be in difficulties, she hastily flung off her own clothing and dived in after him.

It was a trick, as she realized afterwards she might have known, for as she held her breath to try to search for him, she immediately found herself seized from behind and crushed tightly against him, as the sea washed over them. It was an incredible sensation, and even though she felt mad with him for deceiving her in this way, she couldn't stop herself from clinging to him and experiencing again the thrill she had known the night before by pressing herself to the whole solid length of him.

'Sorry,' she heard him murmur, but with a teasing note in his voice which cancelled any remorse he pretended to be feeling, as they came to the surface.

'I thought you were in difficulties – had hit a rock or something,' she spluttered, as he began wading ashore with her again. 'You must be insane!'

'Sometimes it feels like it,' he agreed enigmatically when, as if to justify her remark, he lowered her to the sand and, with the sea still washing over them, began making love to her.

Miranda's heart stood still, then began leaping and racing as his mouth crushed down on hers and the hardness of his powerful body made no secret of how much he wanted her. As heat flared instantly between them, she felt herself becoming weightless, drowning in an increasing volume of surf and surging desire. When he moved, slipping a hand over her breasts, so that her rose-pink nipples

174

immediately sprang to life, she gave an involuntary cry which she knew must have betrayed her own feelings.

'You want me?'

How could she deny it, with every inch of her so eager for him she couldn't hide it? She could actually feel waves of desire overwhelming her as she nodded blindly and was aware of nothing more until she reached the same heights as she'd reached so often the night before.

After this, with his arms still around her, Brett swam back to the boat, where they spent the rest of the afternoon in the cabin. The bunk was narrow but Miranda didn't notice. The hours passed in a haze, with Brett pleasing her and teasing her, then teaching her how to please him. But never once, she realized afterwards, during the hours they were there, did he ever express any affection for her. And later, as they were leaving the small island and she said she was sorry she hadn't seen more of it, he laughed and said that though he had been here several times before, he hadn't seen much of it either. Which made her wonder unhappily how many other women he had brought here?

The following day two men flew in and Brett was closeted with them in the office for most of the morning and all afternoon. Linda served them with a light lunch while they were working and when they left it was time for dinner.

'Who were they?' Miranda asked curiously, as she and Brett sat down to eat. 'I didn't think anyone would be working during Christmas week?'

'Directors,' he replied indifferently. He looked tired with the lines on his forehead suddenly more noticeable, but, at the same time, burning with his usual vitality.

Miranda reached for a piece of Linda's delicious crusty bread, which she baked fresh every day. 'How many directors do you have?'

He glanced at her narrowly. 'Are you really interested?'

'Isn't a wife supposed to be?' she asked shortly. 'You could have introduced me.'

'We are on our honeymoon. They didn't expect to meet you.'

'You aren't ashamed of me?'

He frowned impatiently. 'No – why should I be?'

'I was handicapped. Sometimes I wonder if you can forget it?'

Brett glared at her, his blue eyes glinting as they often did when he was angry over something. 'Will you stop talking nonsense? You forget that I asked you to marry me believing you would be handicapped for life.'

Miranda looked quickly down at the chicken curry Linda had just served them with. Why did he sound as if she had cheated him out of something? It was uncannily like the impression she'd got on the night he had, more or less, forced her to agree to marry him. 'You could still,' she insisted stubbornly, 'be ashamed of me.'

Brett thumped a clenched fist on the table, something she hadn't seen him do before. 'I'm not sure what brought this on, Miranda. You are young and beautiful and,' he added sarcastically, 'what is known as socially acceptable. Even if you were still disabled, which you aren't, I'm sure you would never let me down.'

'I'm sorry, Brett.' Miranda looked at him quickly but, sensing his continuing impatience, looked away again. 'You've been working all day while I probably haven't enough to do.'

'Make the most of it.' His eyes glinted mockingly. 'We have the whole night before us.'

She ignored this, though colour flared under her cheeks. 'I wish I had a career. I have a degree, you know.'

'I don't want you to have a career,' he said curtly. 'I like you – available.'

The colour in Miranda's cheeks deepened, but even as his eyes smouldered over her, making the meaning of his words unmistakable, she refused, for once, to be diverted. 'I should at least like to do something for handicapped people. There's far more that could be done than people often realize. Even a few gadgets can often make life a lot easier. And I should know.'

'You didn't have just a few gadgets, Miranda. You had a positive arsenal of them,' Brett said gently. 'And most of them expensive.'

'My father did too much to make life easier for just one person.' Miranda's grey eyes clouded regretfully. 'I realize that now.'

'You don't have to feel guilty about it.'

'I know,' Miranda replied quickly. 'He was only doing what any parent might have done – if they could afford it – for a handicapped child. It's just that I can't forget. When I first came home from Switzerland, I

177

thought I could,' she confessed. 'I was going to have a good time. I was – well, whole again, if you like, and determined to forget I was ever anything else. But I find I can't.' She frowned. 'I shan't allow it to become an obsession, but I will find a way of helping people who are disabled, as I was.'

'We'll see.' Brett frowned. 'You have to give yourself time. Anyway, there's no need to get too virtuous about it.'

Miranda didn't care for the way he said that. She began to wish she had never confided in him. Once they returned to New York, she was sure there must be organizations to whom she could offer her services, without Brett knowing anything about it.

After serving them coffee, Linda said goodnight and retired to her own quarters. Having swum and wandered by the sea for most of the day, Miranda didn't feel like going out again so stayed in the lounge and read, while Brett pursued some business papers. It bothered her, however, when she found she was concentrating on Brett far more than on her book.

By eleven she gave up and announced she was going to bed. 'My book mustn't be as interesting as the papers you're looking at,' she said.

He glanced up, then startled her by jumping immediately to his feet. Tossing the articles he was holding aside with a carelessness that Miranda suspected was in no way relevant to their importance, he pulled her straight into his arms. His face was hard but his eyes smouldered darkly as he buried his mouth in her luxuriant hair and muttered thickly,

'I was wondering how long you would keep me waiting?'

Brett's lovemaking that night seemed to plumb depths they had never reached before; hours later, Miranda woke from an exhausted sleep to find him leaning over her. Her breath caught as it seemed only minutes since he had left her utterly satiated, yet she found herself responding to him instantly. He had only to touch her to make her forget everything but the sensations he could arouse so easily within her – sensations that rendered her immediately and completely responsive.

As she tried too weakly to protest, his hot mouth covered hers and he slid heavily between her legs and into her. Breathing raggedly, all objections faded from her parting lips as his hands sought the softness of her breasts, engulfing her in fire. As excitement rushed through her, Miranda became fully awake and began moving impatiently against him.

'Don't fight me,' he muttered, his grip on her tightening, as if he believed this was what she was doing.

Miranda wasn't, but couldn't find her voice to deny it. As always, the contractions beginning in her stomach rendered her less than coherent. And, as the continuing movement of his hands increased this, she could only murmur incomprehensibly against his invading lips.

A shudder went right through Brett's strong body as he felt her response and was unable to subdue his own fully aroused emotions. He was savagely remorseless but Miranda, sharing his urgency, welcomed it. Even when he pushed her to the limits she could

179

hold nothing back. Hazily, she was convinced she had been born to belong to this man who alone could make her feel like this, and unconscious awe mingled with the ecstasy she experienced as he took her every inch of the way with him.

During the days that followed Brett made love to her frequently and not always at night. Often he took her sailing and would anchor in a quiet cove and spend most of the day in the boat's cabin with her. Miranda always went with him willingly. He was like a drug she couldn't get enough of. He was beginning to obsess her to an inordinate degree. They were, she realized, physically compatible, very much so, but she had secretly hoped he might come to love her, as well as being physically attracted to her.

But when he showed no sign of doing this, she began to fear it might never happen.

Despite this, the days flew by. Miranda couldn't recall time going as quickly. She still wasn't sure she would care to live on Luke permanently but for a few months, if it was what Brett wanted, she wouldn't complain. Daily she was becoming stronger and so full of vitality that she rarely felt tired. Her increased energy was reflected in pink cheeks and eyes that sparkled, and a mouth forever laughing and responding to Brett's kisses. She looked so well that even Linda commented on it.

'You make me feel old, child,' she would sigh, then tease Miranda laughingly about the health-giving properties of a good marriage.

In moments of misgiving, which she usually tried to dismiss, Miranda wasn't sure she had a good marriage. She often suspected that, even when she felt optimistic over it, she could be living in a fool's paradise. Instead of coming to love her, as she was always hoping he might, some days Brett didn't appear to have any feelings of even friendship towards her. Sometimes he was so distant that it frightened her, but she couldn't think of anything more she could do than she was already doing to improve matters between them.

She was dismayed when, after never suffering from even a headache for weeks, she felt really ill on the evening Gaby arrived. It must have been something she had eaten for lunch, but she didn't mention it to Linda, for fear Linda thought she was criticizing her cooking. When she stopped to think about it, Miranda realised she hadn't felt well since she'd got up.

When one of Brett's men, who was working near the airstrip, drove up with Gaby and her friend, Miranda didn't know who was the most surprised, Brett or herself.

'Hello, folks,' Gaby cried. 'Surprised?' And before either Brett or Miranda could reply she turned to the man by her side and introduced him quickly as Clem Walker, from Texas.

Brett was polite, but made no attempt to be more than that as he shook Clem Walker's hand. 'Why didn't you let us know you were coming?' he asked his sister.

Gaby didn't give him a straight answer. Instead she said, 'You've been gone for weeks and I've been worried.'

'Worried?'

As Brett's dark brows rose in a way which clearly annoyed her, Gaby said, in an obvious attempt to annoy him, 'Not half as worried as several of your girl friends, though.'

'That's enough!' Brett snapped.

Miranda felt a chill joining the sickness in her stomach at Gaby's remark. Gaby hadn't mentioned anyone specific, but she had little doubt that the mysterious Eve would be among them.

Noticing Miranda's paleness, Brett held his sister responsible. 'I'm warning you, Gaby,' he continued, 'I won't have you coming here making trouble. In fact, knowing your liking for it, I'm inclined to ask you to leave. I *am* on my honeymoon.'

Clem Walker rounded on Gaby, his eyes cold. 'When you invited me here to meet your brother, you said nothing about him still being on his honeymoon.'

'Didn't I?' Gaby's eyes widened innocently. 'Well, as I just said, they've been married for weeks and I thought it would be over by now. This is my sister-in-law, Miranda, by the way.' As he acknowledged Miranda with a polite bow of his head, Gaby added, 'Clem lives in Kentucky. He breeds horses and is quite famous.'

'Gaby, will you shut up!' Clem Walker, tall, middle-aged and handsome, and more authoritative than his easygoing demeanour first suggested, refused to be mollified. 'I think we should go straight back to Nassau.'

'I don't want to,' Gaby muttered sullenly, but Miranda noticed her glancing at Clem Walker uncertainly, as if his disapproval bothered her more than she cared to admit.

Miranda unconsciously sprang to her defence. 'I'd like you to stay,' she said. 'Brett and I – ' she forced herself to smile ' – must be an old married couple by now and I'm sure we'd both appreciate some company.'

'Speak for yourself,' Brett said, his mouth tightening.

Miranda bit her lip. She had spoken impulsively; she should have chosen her words more wisely. Brett was staring at her thunderously, which surely wouldn't help to disperse the peculiar tension that seemed to have been growing between them lately.

She wasn't sure that Gaby was pleased at her support for her eyes narrowed suspiciously, but she did manage to look at Brett and say reluctantly, 'At least your wife doesn't want rid of me.'

'I wonder why?' he replied.

Linda came in and her obvious doubts, when she saw who had arrived, didn't exactly lighten the atmosphere. 'I hope you aren't here to make trouble, Miss Gaby,' she exclaimed, exercising the privileges of an old and trusted servant, 'Been enough of that in the past, don't you think?'

'I'll be as good as gold,' Gaby protested, gazing around the ring of sceptical faces with an injured expression on her own. 'Why must you all think the worst of me?'

'Because that's all we ever see, nowadays,' Brett said drily.

'Are you staying?' Linda asked resignedly, as if she already knew the answer.

When Gaby replied wilfully that she was, Linda merely shrugged her huge shoulders and turned away, saying she would get some rooms ready.

Miranda, glad of an excuse to escape, went to help her. Then wished she hadn't when Linda glanced at her and said sharply, 'You look a bit done in, honey. Was the way Miss Gaby arrived a shock to you?'

Miranda shook her head. 'No, not really.'

'Well, I shouldn't let her worry you,' Linda cautioned. 'I'm not saying she isn't worth it, but she's changed so much since her husband died that I sometimes wonder about it. The gentleman she has with her looks nicer than a lot of those she's had here over the past few years. I only hope he can make something of her.'

'I don't really mind her.' Miranda shook out a sheet and passed Linda one end of it. 'It's not her fault if – how did you put it – I look a bit done in. I was feeling queasy before she arrived. I expect it's just too much sun.'

Shooting her another quick glance, Linda said ambiguously, 'Even so, we don't want anything upsetting you at the moment.'

Miranda was just putting the finishing touches to Gaby's room, to allow Linda to get on with dinner, when Gaby came in. Her pencilled brows rose as she watched Miranda straightening the silk bedspread.

'Surely Brett doesn't allow you to do this kind of thing? Where is all the help he usually insists on supplying Linda with?'

'They went home early today, I believe.' Miranda smiled at the other girl brightly. 'And it's not a case of

Brett allowing me. I like to help Linda, though she doesn't often let me.'

Gaby shrugged. 'I thought domestic wives went out with the last century. My mother – she was the American half of our family, did Brett ever tell you? – spent her time entertaining herself with various lovers, one in particular. Not that I blamed her, not with Papa and Brett in the UK most of the time making money. Which interested them far more than what dear Mama was doing. She did do odd bits for charity, but that was merely a cover.'

Miranda frowned. Brett had told her that his father was an astute British businessman who had set up many of the companies Brett still ran today, but not that his father had ever neglected his mother. But even if what Gaby said was true, she knew she wouldn't be asking Brett about it. It might only make him angry and it was, after all, none of her business.

Gaby, as if not expecting an answer, wandered restlessly to the window. 'You and Brett must be having a great time here,' she said mockingly. 'Hasn't he gotten you pregnant yet?'

Pregnant? Miranda felt shock move through her. Then quickly she pulled herself together as she remembered this was the kind of provoking remark Gaby enjoyed coming out with. 'No, of course not,' she exclaimed, though her cheeks went pink. 'Brett and I haven't even discussed a family yet.' Well, not exactly, she thought guiltily, recalling what Brett had asked her to see Lou Mitford about.

CHAPTER 13

In England, in Birmingham, Eve Martin spent some frustrating yet rewarding weeks. In November, when she tried to get in touch with Brett Deakin's sister and was unable to find her, she didn't know what to do. Without Gaby's help she didn't see how she would be able to do anything to make Brett leave his wife. And until she had more information than her father had vaguely supplied her with regarding the Ferrises, she felt her hands were tied.

When she did get hold of Gaby, about the same time as Brett was married, she was relieved, especially on learning that Gaby was as furious about Brett's marriage as she was. Gaby was invited to the wedding but hadn't gone. Which seemed to suggest a lot of ill feeling, at least on Gaby's part.

Gaby had literally snarled. She'd said she knew nothing about Miranda Ferris except that her father had owned a factory or something, and lived on the outskirts of Birmingham. Like Eve, she had no idea why Brett had married this other girl. She said she had always believed he was in love with Eve. Why else had he always visited her, been devoted to her

186

and never married anyone else? She had wondered if Miranda Ferris had been, in some inexplicable way, part of a deal Brett had made with her father over his business. If Brett was really interested in something he always went straight for it, and if Ferris had stipulated unusual terms, he might have complied in order to get what he wanted.

'That sounds a bit far-fetched,' Eve had said, 'even in this day and age. Or perhaps especially in this day and age.'

'Well –' Gaby had snorted ' – I'm sure there was something strange about it.'

There hadn't seemed much to say after that, but before she rang off Gaby said she would be grateful if Eve could find out more about Miranda Ferris and give her a ring.

Eve Martin was no fool. If she helped Gaby to get rid of her brother's wife, the woman was unlikely to welcome Eve as a replacement. All the things she said about Eve making him a better wife would soon be forgotten. And Eve considered that, in realizing this, she could be one step ahead of her.

She would need Gaby. There was no doubt in her mind over that. But by the time they broke up Brett's marriage – if they were able to – she would make sure Gaby was in so deep that she wouldn't be able to extricate herself, even if she wanted to. Eve was determined to collect enough evidence to incriminate Gaby, even if it meant bugging the telephone, that would leave Brett in no doubt as to what his sister had been up to. That is, if Gaby ever decided to get rid of her, the way she was trying to get rid of Miranda Ferris.

Eve, however, soon became aware that without the services of perhaps a private detective, her own investigations regarding Miranda Ferris might come to nothing. There were plenty of businesses owned by different Ferrises in Birmingham listed in the phone books, but apart from stating what kind they were, that was about all she could find out about them And the owner's home number was usually unlisted. The only one she'd heard of as having a daughter was the one her father had told her about, and the daughter was crippled. Eve began to regret isolating herself so much over the past years. The business circles she had once moved in, if only on the fringes, no longer knew her – or she them. She was completely out of touch with what went on in the city, and had dropped all the friends she used to work with who might have been useful to her. Two days later, when she rang Gaby again, she had to confess she had nothing new to tell her.

Gaby did, though, have something for her. Brett and his wife had apparently arrived in New York and she'd succeeded in putting at least one spoke in the bride's wheel, good work which she hoped to continue. She also gave Eve Brett's private home number and suggested it might be a good idea to ring him on some pretext or another.

Which Eve had done. When Brett asked where she'd got hold of his private number, she wasn't sure if he believed her when she said he had given it to her years ago but she'd never used it. Or if he believed the excuse she invented for ringing him, but at least he had not been angry. Since then, Gaby had rung again and told her that Brett had taken Miranda to the

Bahamas for their honeymoon, but she'd heard nothing from Gaby since.

As she tried not to think of Brett and his bride sunning themselves in the Bahamas, it seemed to Eve – by this time steeped in self-pity – that everything was against her. Not least her father, who appeared to be doing his best to encourage Simon Wentworth to visit them. Which he did, in Eve's opinion, far too often. Since her father's accident, Simon began calling regularly and taking John out.

He took no notice when Eve protested that he mustn't allow her father to become a nuisance. 'He enjoys looking over building sites,' he would say, as Eve looked at him coldly. 'Why don't you come along with us one day?'

Eve always refused and grew heartily tired of his persistence. 'Why don't you let me take you out for dinner?' he would ask. Or, 'Why don't we go for a run in the country? I know a smashing little pub where they serve the most delectable food. It would be great fun . . .'

For whom? Eve wondered acidly. She wasn't interested in dusty building sites, or having meals with him in common little pubs where he would be, most likely, scratching around in his pocket for his last penny to pay for them. When her father hinted that Simon was attracted to her, she merely laughed scornfully and vowed silently that, one day soon she would tell the man exactly what she thought of him.

It wasn't until she was poking around one day through some of the city records available to the public that she accidently discovered exactly who he was. Simon Wentworth – and she double-checked that it was the same Simon Wentworth – was head of an old established family firm of architects, which did a lot of important work in the city. Suddenly Eve realized that, because of the influential position he held, Simon must be invited to most of the social functions, whether administrative, corporate or private, that took place in the city. He must hobnob with almost everyone who was anyone and would certainly know every Ferris who ever owned a company. What a fool she had been not to have looked into this sooner!

Eve was clever. She knew better than to change her attitude towards him too suddenly. Only gradually, over the next few days, did she let Simon Wentworth start to think she was at last beginning to thaw towards him. The next time he asked her out, she looked confused and said that though she would like to, she wondered how he could possibly bring himself to be seen with a cripple?

Simon, of course, immediately jumped to the conclusions she had expected him to. 'You don't mean to tell me you've been worrying over that?' He laughed. And when she nodded, he said more impatiently, 'You're far too sensitive, Eve. When you forget what you are doing you scarcely even limp. I'm sure it's become more of a habit than anything else. If you gave me a chance, I'd help you to forget it completely.'

Eve, still playing a game, pretended to be wary at first and insisted they only went to quiet places. But as Christmas drew nearer she agreed to attend one of the city's annual functions with him. And from then on, making him believe he had indeed worked miracles, she didn't object to going anywhere with him.

To say she didn't enjoy accompanying him wouldn't have been telling the truth. When she forgot about Brett, she didn't find it that difficult to transfer her attention to another man. In fact, she was often astonished at how easy it became. She even allowed Simon to kiss her, which he did with increasing frequency. And though she tried to convince herself that if she didn't it might arouse his suspicions, she couldn't resist the thrill she felt when he did this. At least, not very easily.

Nevertheless, Brett was always at the back of her mind, always the target she stubbornly set her heart on. She had been determined to be his wife for so long that she couldn't see herself in any other role. Not even the sight of Simon, tall and remarkably distinguished-looking in evening clothes, was allowed to do more than temporarily distract her.

Simon told her a lot about himself which she wasn't really interested in. He was forty-four and a widower, his wife, Lana, having been dead four years. He didn't actually say his marriage wasn't a happy one, it was just the impression Eve got, reading between the lines. He said, when she asked him about it, that the reason why he supervised the odd small job himself was that getting down to basics kept his feet on the ground and had helped him through some of the rougher times in his life.

'The sight of men digging foundations, laying bricks, transforming what was often a derelict piece of land into a place where new families can live, makes you feel you are doing something worthwhile. It can also make you feel very humble where poorer families are concerned, who might never have had a home before.'

Eve, though she didn't say so, wasn't really impressed. Simon was a very compassionate kind of person, she would think absently, rather as if she was making an observation about something inanimate which had nothing to do with her. The only thing about Simon that was important to her, she told herself, was the contacts he was supplying her with, with people whom she was certain would eventually lead her to Miranda Ferris's father, or someone who could provide information about him.

On the evening she actually saw Harry Ferris and learned something she believed could be invaluable to her, she was so triumphant that she almost let Simon make love to her. The cocktail party they were attending was an annual New Year one, given by one of the city dignitaries. Simon, as usual, introduced her to several people she hadn't met before, and was so obviously proud of her that she was glad she had taken so much care over her appearance. She was wearing a slinky, calf-length black dress, which had cost her most of Brett's last cheque, and with her hair freshly done, her make-up impeccable, she knew she looked her best.

'I think I'm falling in love with you,' Simon said, as they shared a quiet moment together.

Eve didn't understand why her heart should miss a beat, then begin beating faster as she met his adoring gaze. 'You've had too much of that,' she teased, glancing pointedly at the drink he was holding.

Simon shook his head drily. 'Haven't you noticed this is the only one I've had all evening? I have to drive you home, remember.'

As this, for some reason, reminded Eve too acutely of another night, years ago, when she insisted that a drunk Dan Greenly should drive her home, all she could respond with was a nod and a limp smile before excusing herself hurriedly to go and freshen her lipstick, which she didn't really need to.

After lingering a few minutes in the cloakroom, in order to get rid of Dan Greenly's ghost – if there was such a thing! – Eve went back to the reception rooms. Simon was still where she had left him but, in her absence, had clearly been pounced on by a group determined to have his attention. Relieved, even if just temporarily, to be deprived of it, Eve moved stealthily behind a pillar, where he mightn't immediately see her. It wasn't until she paused irresolutely that she became aware of the two men standing almost next to her. And heard one of them saying to the other,

'Hello, Ferris, haven't seen you for ages. Not since you retired anyway. Still living south of the city?'

'Yes. Edgbaston. Sutton's Road.'

'Ah, yes, I remember it. Well House, isn't it? Never think of moving to a smaller place, since you've retired?'

'No point,' Ferris muttered. 'Especially since Miranda was married.'

'Oh, yes, I forgot about that.' The other man laughed. 'Married Brett Deakin, didn't she? After he took you over.'

Holding her breath in an effort not to miss anything, Eve was disappointed when Ferris merely nodded and said something about wanting to catch someone before they left, and, before she could go after him, disappeared among the other guests. His place, however, was quickly taken by a slinky blonde Eve didn't recognize.

'I see you've been talking to Harry Ferris,' she said, raising curious brows to the man whom Harry had just left. 'Did anyone ever solve the mystery of Miranda's remarkable recovery? One day she's in a wheelchair, presumably unable to walk. The next, or practically the next, after someone saw her in one, she's walking down the aisle to marry one of the country's most sought-after bachelors.'

'I don't think old Harry is saying.' The man laughed as they moved away in the direction of one of the numerous trays of drinks. 'He clearly doesn't wish to discuss it.'

Eve had wanted to hear more, but didn't follow them. Perhaps, she thought, she had heard enough? For the first time since she began her investigations she had something to go on, but she had to have time to think. Firmly fixing the names of Harry Ferris's house and the area in which he lived in her head, she rejoined Simon and almost dazzled him by the smile she gave him. She didn't tell him that if what she planned to do went well, she might have no further use for him.

Two days later Eve arrived at Well House in the small car Brett had bought for her. She hadn't rung to tell Harry Ferris she was coming. If she rang – always supposing she could have got hold of his number – he might have refused to see her.

Even if he had not done this, it could have at least put him on his guard, which was the last thing she wanted. The element of surprise, she had long ago discovered, could be worth considerably more than anything else.

In the Edgbaston area she soon found Sutton Road. Harry Ferris's country-style home did not surprise her. Since the cocktail party to which Simon had taken her, she had learned, since having something to go on, that Ferris had owned a sizeable business he was forced to sell because of debt. His debts, which included horrific gambling ones, weren't supposed to be on the grapevine, but Eve soon found out all she wanted to know. And while she had the sense not to take everything the person had told her as gospel, she knew she could rely on some of it being true. There was only the mystery of Brett's marriage to be cleared up and, by visiting Harry Ferris, she hoped to get more information about this, which Gaby could put to good use. If, she laughed to herself, as she got out of her small car and and knocked on the door, good was exactly the right word to describe it?

A rather flustered-looking maid answered the door, and Eve asked if she could see Mr Ferris.

'He's just popped out, miss,' the girl said. 'An' the housekeeper's been taken ill an' Miss Ferris 'as had to run her to the hospital. My name's Hilda, by the way. Did you have an appointment?'

'No.' The girl reminded Eve of a character out of a TV comedy. She smiled at Hilda warmly. 'I know Mr Ferris would see me if he was in. What time will he be home again?'

'Well, like I said – ' the girl hastily adjusted her glasses as they slipped down her nose ' – he's just popped out. To post some letters, I believe. Wanted to get them off. He should be back any minute.'

'Perhaps I could wait? Inside?' Eve edged past her and was standing in the hall before Hilda seemed to realize what she was doing.

'Well, I suppose there'd be no harm in it, miss,' Hilda said, 'not if you go into the study. I'm busy in the drawing-room, you see, and Mrs Fellows, that's the housekeeper, you see, said she will skin me alive if I don't get it done by eleven. I know she's not here, but she always seems to know what's going on.'

In the study, with the door closed by a harassed Hilda, Eve glanced curiously around. She didn't worry about what Ferris would think of her practically forcing her way in – things like that never bothered her. The room contained the usual bookshelves, two chairs and an old oak desk. And on top of the desk was an envelope with an overseas' stamp on it.

Eve's heart beat faster as she drew nearer and stared at it. The address was machine printed. There was no obvious clue as to who it was from. It was only her intuition suddenly working overtime that told her who it was. Glancing quickly over her shoulder to make sure the door was still closed, she picked the letter up and drew out the sheet of paper from inside it. It was, as she'd instinctively suspected, from Brett.

Swiftly her eyes skimmed it, taking in the essence of what Brett said. He hoped Harry and Alice –

presumably Harry's sister – were both well. He hoped they would find the extra money enclosed useful to see them through the winter and promised this wouldn't interfere with their regular cheques. Miranda was well, he said. They were still on their honeymoon . . .

On hearing a car door slam loudly outside, Eve returned the letter to its envelope and hastily put it down again. When, a minute later, Harry Ferris opened the study door, she was standing innocently by the window, looking out.

'I'm sorry,' he said stiffly, frowning slightly at her now-smoothly composed face as she turned quickly to look at him. 'I don't think I know you – but should I?'

'No.' Smiling, Eve crossed the room, holding out her hand. 'I'm Liz Telfer,' she introduced herself, as he shook it reluctantly. She had thought it wiser to give a false name. 'I hope you'll forgive me for being in here, but your maid wouldn't hear of me waiting outside.'

'I still don't understand . . .'

'Oh, I'm sorry,' Eve apologized charmingly. 'Of course you don't. I'm afraid I haven't come to see you for any particular reason, other than that you are the father of the girl who married Brett Deakin.'

'You're a friend of Brett's?'

'An old friend.' Eve smiled. 'And when I couldn't make it to the wedding and he and his bride are no longer in the city, I thought the least I could do was to pay you a short visit.'

'Well, that is very kind of you, Miss Telfer,' Harry said, though he still looked uncertain.

'You see,' Eve went on, as if he'd never spoken, 'I happen to be disabled like your daughter and I wondered if you could tell me how Miranda found the courage to get married?' Here she paused, pretending to look anxious. 'That's not just an idle question, Mr Ferris – or even an impertinent one, if that's what you are thinking. You see, I'd like to get married myself, one day, but I'm not sure it would be fair to the man who has asked me.'

'You should have seen his face!' Eve laughed a few days later to Gaby over the phone. As usual Gaby had been away and this was the first time since Eve's visit to Harry Ferris that she'd been able to get in touch with her. And, as Simon Wentworth had just taken her father out for the day, she meant to make the most of it. 'I told him, when I called to see him, that Brett was an old friend of mine – which he is – and how pleased I was that Brett had married someone like his daughter – which, of course, I am not! Then I said how everyone in Birmingham was wondering how Miranda had had the courage to marry him, when she was disabled?'

'Hi, wait a minute!' Gaby broke in. 'Miranda isn't disabled. Is she?'

'According to what I've heard, she at least used to be,' Eve replied emphatically. 'But from the expression on Ferris's face, when I mentioned Miranda being crippled, I'd be willing to swear there's some mystery about it. He looked absolutely terrified and very green about the gills.'

'Miranda – disabled?' Gaby repeated. 'Gee, that's a new one on me!'

'Oh, and I almost forgot,' Eve lied as she rushed on, 'while I waited for Ferris to come home – he was out when I arrived,' she explained, 'posting a letter – I took a peek into the letter I saw lying on his desk.'

'Gee, Eve, do you think you should have?'

Eve wished Gaby would stop saying 'gee' like that. 'If it helps to destroy Brett's crazy marriage, isn't *anything* we do damn well justified?'

'Sure – I suppose so . . .'

Eve took no notice of the sudden uncertainty in Gaby's voice. Battles were never won by being too timid. 'Well, anyway, the letter was from Brett. I realize it was a remarkable coincidence, but it definitely was from him. And it was quite clear, when I read it, that he is more or less keeping them. Paying them a regular allowance, anyway. Apparently Harry Ferris was not only broke but seriously in debt when Brett, for some reason, rescued him.'

'I'm surprised Harry Ferris confessed to being broke. I mean, I don't know him, but men don't usually admit to things like that, do they?'

'Oh, it wasn't Ferris who told me.'

'Then – how . . .?'

Eve laughed proudly. 'I've been a clever girl, haven't I? I've got friendly with someone called Simon Wentworth who really fancies me. And while I don't return his feelings in any way, I've had sense enough to make good use of him. To cut a long story short, he's been taking me to a lot of Christmas and New Year civic parties where I've gleaned quite a bit of information. It's still Brett, of course, who I want. If Simon Wentworth is determined to make a fool of himself over me, I can't be responsible, can I? Gaby, are you listening?'

'Sure, yes, I guess,' Gaby responded after a moment. 'I'll, uh, see what I can do . . .'

Gaby sounded odd, but then she often did, Eve thought impatiently. 'I'll continue doing what I can as well,' she said. 'Between the two of us, we should soon be able to put an end to Brett's marriage.'

Eve was still burning with triumph as she rang off. She was sure that Gaby would soon, on the strength of the information she had given her, be generating enough mischief to cause a serious rift between Brett and his wife. Laughing aloud in anticipation of it, Eve did an excited twirl about the hall. It wasn't until she turned that her eyes fell on the tall, silent figure standing in the lounge doorway.

'Simon!' she gasped, stunned by the fright she received, as well as the coldly condemning expression on his face. How much had he heard, for God's sake? 'What are you doing here?' she asked, trying to speak belligerently.

'I came back for a map your father wanted.' Simon's voice was as cold as his eyes. 'He told me where to find it and gave me a key, in case you weren't in.'

Eve's mind, from being struck dumb, began working furiously. Their next-door neighbour had come round for a turnip. Her father had told him they had more than they could use. She had taken him to the bottom of the garden at the back of the house and told him to help himself. They'd only talked a few minutes before he'd climbed back over the fence, but it must have been long enough for Simon to enter the house and be concealed in the lounge where she hadn't noticed him as she'd hurried to the phone. 'Are you going now?' she asked, after giving him a brief explanation as to where she had been and he didn't speak. Maybe, she hoped with a peculiar feeling in her stomach, he had been so busy looking for John's map that he hadn't overheard her conversation with Gaby?

'I am,' he said, still staring at her coldly as he strode past her to the door. 'And I won't be coming back, Eve. I expect I should be mad but, somehow, I can only feel grateful that my eyes have been opened before it was too late. Of all the vindictive bitches I've had the misfortune to meet! But then – ' here he turned in the doorway to look her straight in the face ' – you never did envisage any future togetherness for us, did you, Eve?'

CHAPTER 14

Gaby merely shrugged when Miranda told her that she and Brett hadn't even discussed starting a family. 'I thought it woulda been his number-one priority,' she said carelessly.' He was always fonder of kids than I am. He practically ruined my son – while he was alive.'

Despite her anger at the underlying hint in Gaby's voice that a son and heir was all Brett had married for, Miranda was moved to compassion by the glimpse of pain she caught in the other girl's face. 'You still miss him?'

Again Gaby merely shrugged, but Miranda knew she wasn't far wrong when a tear ran down Gaby's cheek. 'Oh, damn!' she muttered, swiping at it impatiently. 'Here I go again!'

'Wouldn't it be better if you let yourself cry, instead of bottling it all up?' Miranda suggested unevenly.

'If I had a dollar for every time I've been given that advice, I'd be worth millions,' Gaby said fiercely. Then, sinking to the edge of the bed, she buried her face in her hands. 'I'm sorry, Miranda. It beats me why you're so nice to me when I behave like I do towards you. I wanted to hate you. I didn't want Brett to get married when I had nothing. I was convinced, if he had kids of his own, it would make losing mine hurt even more than it does. I told myself I'd be fully justified in trying to get rid of you, but all I succeeded in doing was being disgusted with myself.'

Here Gaby swallowed and paused, but while Miranda was still searching for words, she rushed on. 'I actually enjoyed involving you with Adrian Norton – putting you in a bad light in Brett's eyes. It helped to pass the time and, God knows, I've enough of it to pass. Then, after you and Brett came down here and I met Clem, everything seemed to change almost overnight. Suddenly I began to see what kind of person I'd become.'

'Oh, Gaby.' Miranda wasn't sure what to say to her. 'I think you're being hard on yourself.'

Gaby looked up with a grimace. 'Brett's always saying I'm not hard enough.'

Miranda frowned. 'Why do you and Brett not seem to get on?'

'I don't know.' Gaby's voice was suddenly shorter. 'Could be that I've always been jealous of him. Everything he touches is usually an instant success while, even though I'm just a year or two younger, my best endeavours rarely get off the ground. Even my marriage was a disaster.'

'Your marriage?'

'Because I never gave it a chance.' Gaby shrugged. 'Ed was okay, in a small way, but I soon lost interest in him.'

'And Clem?' Miranda asked tentatively. 'Are you going to be tempted to try again, with him?'

'I'm not sure,' Gaby replied. 'I think he wants to marry me, as he wanted to meet my family, but that wasn't the only reason why I came to Luke today. It was my conscience,' she confessed, 'that brought me here as much as anything. When Brett didn't bring you back to New York, you see, I began to believe I might have damaged your marriage irreparably.'

'Don't be silly.' Miranda tried to dismiss Gaby's misgivings with a light remark, rather than tell her that, far from being damaged by any mischief she might have caused, her marriage to Brett had probably been doomed from the start. 'I've got to like it here,' she prevaricated, 'and when Brett suggested we might stay a little longer, I agreed.'

'Nevertheless,' Gaby said, 'I'm determined to have a word with him. It will make me feel better to confess my sins, even if, as you insist, there's been no harm done.'

After Miranda went, Gaby remained seated on the edge of the bed, considering what she had just said to her. She stared speculatively at the door Miranda closed behind her. She hadn't told her about Eve Martin, that she had an enemy in her own country, one probably far worse than any she might have here in the USA. She wasn't going to mention Eve to Brett either. She might have, had Brett looked even the least bit pleased when she and Clem arrived. Recalling the look of displeasure on his face, she decided, with a brief return of her worst characteristics, that she wasn't that forgiving! No – she would confess to being responsible for tricking Miranda out to lunch with Adrian Norton, but that was all. That should be magnanimous enough for anyone! After all, there was plenty Brett hadn't told her. About Miranda being disabled, for one thing. Miranda might be fine now, but she hadn't always been. Eve Martin had collected too much evidence to the contrary for it ever to be disputed.

Gaby frowned as she thought of it. While Eve Martin had been busy, Gaby didn't really believe she could do anything to seriously upset Brett's marriage. She conveniently forgot it was she who had encouraged Eve to try to. At times, when she remembered, she excused herself on the grounds that Brett had announced his forthcoming marriage so abruptly that anyone might have reacted as she did. It wasn't until she met Clem a few weeks ago that she began seeing things differently and had a disturbing feeling that, if she didn't change her ways, she might alienate him as well as Brett, permanently. With this thought seemingly immovable at the back of her mind, the last time Eve Martin rang, Gaby was extremely cautious.

During their last conversation, she'd grown alarmed on discovering the lengths Eve had obviously gone to find out more about Brett's wife. When Eve recited how she had learned about Miranda being disabled, she was dismayed. Eve had even visited Miranda's father and tricked her way into his house. Gaby had shivered as she'd suddenly realized what the repercussions of this could mean to both Eve and herself, should Brett ever find out. Especially when, as well as this, Eve seemed determined to go even further.

Strangely enough, Gaby had heard nothing from her since. And, though the silence was somewhat unnerving, she hoped she wouldn't hear from her again. Now she was in love with Clem, she would rather put it all behind her. Miranda might not be exactly the kind of sister-in-law she'd envisaged, but she certainly had plenty of spirit. The way she'd quickly got rid of Adrian Norton in New York surely proved that? And she might be better, Gaby admitted grudgingly, than some of the women Brett might have married. Besides, if she did marry Clem and went to live in Kentucky, she wouldn't be seeing much of her. And with Clem's millions at her disposal, Brett's money wouldn't matter so much either.

As Miranda showered and dressed before dinner, she found herself remembering Gaby's remark about her being pregnant. Had she discovered at last why Brett had married her? she wondered. He might have thought it unfair to marry someone for the sole purpose of procuring a son and heir, but he might have no such scruples concerning a woman whom he believed had deceived him. Initially Brett had asked her to marry him as he'd wished to help her. When he found she didn't need help – at least not the kind he'd had in mind – he could have jumped at this other reason, considering it to be fully justifiable after the way she and her family had cheated on him. If she was pregnant, he would probably consider it evened the score between them and, even if she didn't like it, it was no more than she deserved. Brett never said why he had married her and, as he didn't love her,

Miranda thought this explanation might be more than feasible.

She didn't want to have a child under these circumstances and her heart sank as she realized how careless she had been. Brett, she had to admit, had told Lou Mitford they didn't want a family straight away, but he had obviously been thinking of her health, rather than an indefinite postponement. How naïve she had been not to have seen what could happen by ignoring the doctor's advice. Over the past few weeks, she had been too busy revelling in her new-found health and vitality to give it a thought. She might not, though, she told herself, be pregnant. It could be something she had eaten that was responsible for the sickly feeling she'd had all day. Tomorrow, she was convinced, she'd be feeling fine again and able to laugh at her irrational misgivings.

As Brett didn't come in until later to change, she joined Gaby and Clem in the lounge while he did. He mentioned he had been talking to Gaby, but she had to wait until bedtime before he told her what about.

At eleven, as Gaby and Clem were going for a walk along the shore, Miranda decided to retire for the night and Brett soon followed her.

'I'm sorry, Miranda,' he said abruptly, glancing at her as she sat at the dressing-table brushing her hair. 'It seems I was wrong about what happened in New York.'

'You mean, about Adrian Norton?' Miranda gripped her hairbrush tighter. 'I thought I explained . . .?'

He began pulling off his shirt. 'And I believed you. Well . . .' he confessed, 'maybe that's not quite true.'

Miranda put her hair brush down and tightened the sash of the short satin negligé she was wearing, with fingers which shook slightly. Brett was stripping unselfconsciously. She heaved a sigh of relief when he reached for something to cover himself with. 'But you do now?' she asked drily. 'Now you've spoken to Gaby?'

He came closer, struggling into his robe but leaving it partly open at the front. He seemed thinly amused as she stared at him through the mirror and flushed. 'I believe she was up to no good,' he replied. 'I have no proof, though, that you weren't attracted to Norton.'

'No, you haven't,' Miranda said, feeling suddenly angry. 'You'll just have to trust me, I'm afraid.'

His lips curled derisively. Miranda looked at him unhappily. He was contemptuous of women, en bloc, and wasn't going to make an exception of his wife. She'd been foolish to think he would. 'Gaby seems happier now, anyway,' she said, trying to change the subject. 'I admire her for coming to apologize.'

Brett was unimpressed. 'You don't know my sister as I do,' he said. Then, as if he was as keen as Miranda to let the New York episode drop, 'What to you think of Clem Walker?'

'He seems nice enough.'

'All men seem nice enough to you.'

Miranda shrugged. 'Gaby talked to me, as well, before dinner. She seems to have been terribly mixed up. Maybe she lost her bearings somewhere during the past few years, and Clem might have brought her to her senses again.'

'It might be wiser to wait until the novelty of a new boyfriend has worn off, before we believe in any great change for the better,' Brett cautioned drily. 'Walker looks like he could be the best she's taken up with yet, but let's wait and see.'

'She needs someone, though.'

'Don't we all?'

Miranda shivered unconsciously as he dropped his hands to her shoulders in a way even more explicit than his words. As he stared down on her, she was vividly aware of his uncompromising virility. He had rejected her a lot lately, but she knew he would stay with her tonight. He might not wish to, but he would. She looked at the breadth of his chest through the glass, noticing it move under its covering of dark hair as he drew a harsh breath. 'Brett,' she whispered, her hands going up to cover his, 'do you have to always act like we were fighting some kind of a war with each other?'

He didn't answer verbally but lowered his head, then his lips to her rose-tipped breasts after sweeping her white wrap to one side. When she flinched, he asked, 'Am I hurting you?'

'No,' she said, against the top of his head. It wasn't easy to explain her feelings to him, though it might have been if he'd loved her as she loved him. All the same, she tried to say something. 'Whenever you touch me, something seems to happen inside me.'

'Me too,' he said, if more reluctantly. Then, with a muffled groan, he crushed her mouth under his own and kissed her until Miranda thought she might faint

209

from the sensations sweeping through her. Then he picked her up and carried her to the bed.

Afterwards, while Brett slept, Miranda lay wide-eyed beside him in the darkness and her cheeks grew hot as she relived the past hours. Brett's mouth and hands could weave the kind of spell that might entrap a woman forever. He was a demanding but generous lover. He didn't want a passive partner. Miranda drew a shaken breath as she realized just how far from being that she had become, and it frightened her to even try and imagine how barren her life would be without him. Fear touched her heart as she recalled catching a glimpse of his eyes as he carried her to bed and seen both the hunger and repudiation in them. If he was so apparently contemptuous of himself for desiring her, how long would it be before he not only left her alone for weeks on end, but renounced her completely?

Miranda sighed as the heavy arm about her tightened. Even in sleep, Brett could make her heart beat faster and she snuggled up against him helplessly. For her, there would never be anyone else. She realized that now. It hurt to also know how he could probably leave her without a backward glance or even another thought.

The next morning, Miranda was again reminded of how much she had come to care for him, as she watched him on the beach. After swimming with the others, she was sitting by herself while they still lingered in the sea. She couldn't help noticing the contrast between the two men as, eventually growing tired of the water, they swam out of it and walked towards her. They were both tall and well made, but Clem Walker was slower and more patient, while Brett's vibrant energy was reflected not only in his body but in his face. Miranda was aware how it affected her greatly, even while he was still some distance away.

Brett had thawed considerably towards Clem over breakfast. They had discovered quite a few things they had in common and Miranda hoped, if only for Gaby's sake, they might soon become friends. The signs were promising. Brett had laughed more than she'd heard him laugh for a while, and had cancelled a member of his staff from flying in. He was even talking of taking them out for a meal to an island he called Barreterre, which she gathered wasn't far away. Miranda felt too languid during the morning to want to do anything but stay at home, but she never thought of refusing to go when he asked her.

In fact, she enjoyed herself immensely. They had visited several of the other islands, as Brett had promised they would, but not Barreterre. When they arrived, after landing on the airstrip, he had a car waiting for them which took them straight to a hilltop restaurant. It was an enchanting place, high above the sea, with an open dance floor, panoramic views, even in the moonlight, and excellent food. Miranda regarded it with eager interest, glad she had come, despite her prevailing lethargy.

Gaby, as though determined to change her ways, was being pleasant to everyone, but there was still an air of restlessness about her. While she and Brett might stop short of actually snapping at each other, Miranda sensed a continuing lack of sympathy between them. Gaby, however, did seem to be trying and Miranda decided that, if things worked out between them, Clem Walker could be the best thing that ever happened to her.

In the restaurant, Brett danced with Miranda several times between courses, holding her so tightly that sometimes she could scarcely breathe. On the dimly lit floor she didn't think anyone noticed, but his mocking glance told her he wouldn't care if they did. Once, when he let his mouth drop to her bare shoulder, a rush of delight swept over her, as well as the most primitive of feelings. In that instance, she thought he might easily guess how much she had come to love him, but for a few magic moments as she clung to him, it didn't seem to matter if he did.

She enjoyed her evening out very much and felt so much better for it that she was convinced she had imagined her sickness the day before. All she needed, she decided, was something to perk her up a little. And a rest, perhaps, from Linda's often highly spiced meals.

It was almost dawn when they returned and she didn't seem to have been asleep many minutes before she woke to find Linda at her bedside with a cup of tea. Brett was gone, but the memory of his lovemaking after they got in was still so vivid that she could almost imagine he was still with her. His place beside her was cold, but this wasn't unusual as he often rose early to work in his study.

Miranda struggled to sit up. 'Lovely,' she murmured appreciatively, then added, she suspected unnecessarily, as Linda still lingered, 'We were late getting in.'

'Miss Gaby's going back to New York today, did you know?' Linda asked abruptly.

'Today?' Miranda straightened with a start, nearly spilling her tea. 'She didn't say anything.'

'Well, she is.'

Miranda frowned. 'She did say she wouldn't be staying long, but I didn't expect her to be leaving as soon as this. I was sure she was getting along better with Brett.'

'Well I've just been packing her things,' Linda said over her shoulder, as she went out again.

Miranda felt puzzled as she stared after her. Why was she suddenly sure that, apart from Gaby's immediate departure, Linda had been trying to tell her something? I'd better get up and see what's going on, she sighed, just as Brett strode in.

He looked tired, she thought, and wondered where he had been. Then she stopped thinking about it as he said curtly. 'Gaby and Walker are leaving after breakfast and I'm going with them. I should be back in a few weeks.'

Was this what Linda was trying to tell her? Miranda went cold as she tried to think what she would do without him? A few weeks sounded like a life sentence! 'Couldn't I come with you?'

Brett hesitated as he met her pleading eyes, but his own immediately hardened. 'You'd only be bored and I'll get on faster without you.'

'But,' she protested, 'isn't it time we both went back to New York and resumed our normal lives, so

213

to speak? Luke is wonderful but I never thought of staying here forever.'

'There wouldn't be anything for you to do in New York,' Brett said tersely.

'I would find something to do. Didn't I tell you before that I intend working for charity?'

'And wearing yourself out.'

'I shouldn't,' she argued. 'Whenever I go back, I can't just sit around doing nothing. But I promise I shouldn't overdo things.'

'Maybe the next time,' Brett conceded.

'I'd still rather come with you this time,' she insisted, even as her stomach reacted involuntarily against the journey entailed.

'No!' Brett's jaw firmed as he noticed how white she had gone. 'You aren't up to it, for one thing. Any fool could see that. And I promised your father I'd take good care of you.'

Excuses, excuses! Miranda seethed. He didn't want her. It was as simple as that. If Brett had loved her, he wouldn't have let her out of his sight, not so willingly, anyway. This was probably his way of putting some more distance between them, distance which wasn't measured merely in miles. Lately he had been changing from hot to cold faster than the British weather, and she didn't doubt which would win in the end.

Gathering what little pride she had left, Miranda said stiffly, 'I'm sorry, Brett, if I appear to be making a fuss. Go to New York, stay as long as you like. Perhaps some time apart will be good for both of us. Maybe we married in too great a hurry and need time to think.'

Brett paled while his eyes glittered darkly. 'You want – out?'

Miranda swallowed, feeling too confused and increasingly miserable to be able to answer him properly. Instead, she decided to let him believe what he liked by remaining silent.

Brett stared at his wife grimly when she didn't reply, noting, as she sank back against the white pillows, how tantalizingly her thick masses of silken fair hair spread over them. She was just too damned attractive! A dull red stain crept under his cheek-bones as a narrow strap slipped off a slender shoulder, exposing the top of her breasts and a wealth of smooth pale skin. And, as she hastily righted it again, he felt a pulse jerk almost painfully in his throat.

He had to get away, he decided. Nothing was working out the way he had expected it to. This whole regrettable thing was getting out of hand. Marriage hadn't helped. It had merely made a lot of things worse. He needed time to concentrate on his business empire. There were plenty of good deals coming up that he should be looking into instead of frittering his time away on Luke. He liked taking things over. What he didn't like was the feeling that someone was now doing that to him. He wasn't sure if this was what Miranda Ferris was succeeding in doing. He couldn't believe it was. But she was beginning to affect him so insidiously that – even if it was only physically – he knew he was going to have to listen to his own sense of caution and self-preservation, which was telling him it was time to leave.

'Since you don't deny it,' he said harshly, 'I presume the answer to my question is yes?'

'I don't know, Brett.' Miranda looked at him unhappily. 'We'd have to talk about it. Some time,' she added vaguely.

Brett felt himself go strangely cold. He also felt angry. He hadn't expected Miranda to take the initiative. It was a shock to see her looking at him so defiantly. It was only the hint of distress behind it that gave him any satisfaction.

'When I come back, then,' he agreed grimly, swinging away from her.

As she had done the first time he was away, Miranda found the house curiously empty after Brett was gone. Gaby was disappointed, she said, that she wasn't coming with them, but she agreed it might not be worth it if Brett was returning to Luke in a few days. Miranda wasn't sure whether Gaby got this impression from herself or her brother, but she didn't enlighten her.

Gaby explained her own abrupt departure with a few simple words. 'Clem has to get back to Kentucky,' she said. 'And I have to go with him.'

If only it was that easy for her, Miranda thought, as the three of them left for the airstrip. If Brett had loved her, she knew it might have been. But, unfortunately, he did not. And though her lips felt bruised by his farewell kiss, she still felt miserable.

CHAPTER 15

The first day or two without Brett passed slowly. Miranda was aware of Linda watching her anxiously as she wandered aimlessly around. A few weeks ago she would never have believed she could miss anyone as much, and this made her increasingly aware of how much she had come to love him.

Since coming to the States, Miranda had kept in regular touch with her father and Alice, but while she missed them and sometimes longed to see them, she never fretted for them the way she did for Brett. Sometimes her unsatisfied need of him hurt so much it was like a pain, and she both deplored and was ashamed of her own vulnerability. If only she was in New York, she would think, then she might have found something to do, even if Brett disapproved, that might have stopped her from being so preoccupied with him.

'He will come back, Miss Miranda,' Linda said one morning, when she caught her looking despondent. 'He won't stay away any longer than he has to, you'll see.'

'It's been two weeks and I haven't even heard from him,' Miranda said.

'His overseer has, on the plantation,' Linda told her. Miranda wondered if that was meant to be consoling. 'I'm sure he's all right an' won't stay away any longer than necessary,' she reiterated.

'He must be busy,' Miranda agreed tonelessly.

'Business takes some men like that.' Linda shrugged. 'My man's just the same. Come the sugar-cane harvest, he forgets everything else. An' Mr Brett has a lot more to see to than a few bits of sugar cane! But, take it from me, he will soon be home again.'

Linda was proved wrong, however, when Brett rang at the end of the following week to say he didn't know when he would be back. His New York office was busy negotiating a big takeover of an overseas consortium too important to leave. Then, after asking Miranda politely how she was, and touching briefly on a few other things, he rang off – scarcely giving Miranda a chance to reply to him.

She sat staring at the telephone for a long time after he broke the connection. She had thought she would feel better if Brett rang, but she didn't. Now the persistent sickness that wouldn't go away seemed to be attacking her mentally as well as physically and she felt like weeping. She had been tempted to tell him how most days she was feeling ill and was frightened it might have something to do with her old disability, but he hadn't given her a chance to.

If her telephone conversation with Brett made her unhappy, Miranda felt even worse when a woman who introduced herself as Marcia Austin rang.

'You won't know me,' Marcia purred, 'but Brett does.'

'I see,' Miranda said, though she didn't.

'I thought you wouldn't mind if I rang,' Marcia went on. 'I didn't want to disturb you on Luke, which I know, from being there, is a wonderful island, but I felt I had to . . .'

'What do you wish to speak to me about, Miss Austin?' Miranda broke in, feeling unaccountably apprehensive. 'Are you a friend of Brett's?'

'Well, you could call me that.' Marcia laughed. 'I'm certainly looking after him.'

'Looking after him?'

Marcia giggled. 'Supplying his needs, you know, especially those at night, which are considerable. He regrets his marriage, of course. In fact, he told me, only yesterday, that he intends getting a divorce. He is only hesitating because he is concerned for you, after you've been – disabled, wasn't it? Which is why I felt compelled to get in touch with you. To ask you to assure him, if you would, that you're quite well again and able to manage without him, and to make things easy for us. Or I expect I mean him.'

Miranda didn't realize she had dropped the receiver until she heard it clatter. Shock seemed to ricochet through her so she didn't know what she was doing. Brett and another woman. A woman who'd been here before – slept with him in probably the same bed where he'd made love to her, Miranda. Suddenly she felt sick, very sick, and just made it to the bathroom.

Linda was standing in the hall when she fled past her. Seeing something was wrong, she came after her, clearly concerned.

'Miranda, honey!' she exclaimed, her eyes widening then narrowing in her dark face as she quickly realized what was happening and held Miranda gently until the worst was over.

Miranda was sure she was going to die. She couldn't remember feeling this bad in all the years since her accident. Eventually, under Linda's experienced administrations, she began feeling better, but she couldn't seem to stop shaking.

'What brought this on, honey?' Linda asked, carefully wiping the sweat from Miranda's brow with a warm flannel. 'You weren't too bad after breakfast.'

'I'm not sure,' Miranda said. She couldn't tell Linda about the phone call she'd had from Marcia Austin. If Linda knew, she might tell Brett. She could probably get in touch with him through her husband, or one of the many security men Brett employed throughout the island, and that would never do. He would be furious.

'Your operation bothering you?'

'No.' Miranda shook her head. She had tried to convince herself it could be the after-effects of it that were making her feel so queasy in the mornings, but in her heart she knew she was looking in the wrong direction.

'Then it can only be one thing!' she heard Linda exclaiming happily. 'Mr Brett is going to be over the moon, I should think!' She looked at Miranda closely, her smile fading as she saw the look of bewilderment on Miranda's face. 'You do understand what's the matter with you, don't you, honey?'

Miranda began to shake her head, then slowly nodded it instead. She realized it would be futile to go on denying it, especially to Linda. Linda had children of her own – she was even a grandmother. It would be foolish to continue trying to pretend, either to herself or Linda.

'How long have you known?' Linda asked gently, as she helped Miranda to her feet.

'I didn't. I mean, I wasn't sure,' Miranda stammered, trying to pull herself together. 'I haven't been married before, you see.' She paused, thinking that sounded terribly old-fashioned. 'I haven't had a relationship, either . . .' Her voice trailed off as she thought that sounded even worse. 'I should have asked you,' she said, like an apology. 'Told you, maybe.'

'You could have done, but I'd already guessed.' Linda smiled complacently. 'Don't you realize, child, that's why I've been keeping such a close eye on you? You told Mr Brett?'

'No!' Miranda flushed, then paled as her voice rose. How could she tell Brett anything, when he was involved with another woman, and wanted a divorce? 'I haven't had a chance to,' she replied weakly. 'Besides, I didn't really know for sure myself. I mean, I haven't seen a doctor yet, or anything . . .'

'Well, I don't think Doc Mitford's prognosis is going to be any different from my own,' Linda said drily. 'But I do think you ought to ring Mr Brett as soon as you can. Tonight, maybe? I'm sure, like I just said, he is going to be delighted.'

Sheer panic clutched at Miranda's throat as she pictured Brett's reactions to what might be a death blow to his plans. He wanted to marry Marcia Austin – or was it the mysterious Eve? Perhaps, Miranda thought bitterly, he hadn't made his mind up yet, despite what Marcia said. But he certainly wouldn't welcome a child by another woman to make things even more difficult for him.

'I'll wait until he gets back here,' she said quickly. 'Otherwise it may distract him from what he is doing. He rang, half an hour ago,' she explained, as Linda frowned. 'He's in the middle of an important business deal . . .'

'I can't think what could be more important to him than his own child.'

'Well, I would rather wait.'

'But not for long.' Linda was clearly not content with Miranda's decision. 'I'd feel much happier if he was here. A woman needs her husband around at a time like this.'

'Why?' Miranda asked, trying deliberately to sound amused. 'Haven't I enough people looking after me? What with you and your family and security men appearing to be hidden in every bush . . .'

'You seen them?' Linda sounded bemused. 'They were told to stay out of sight.'

Miranda laughed. 'Some of them are so big it would be difficult, and I asked James Hamilton about them. They must be costing Brett a fortune and can't be necessary.'

'They could be, in this day and age,' Linda said darkly. 'Sometimes, though not often, raiders come in from the sea and Mr Brett isn't one for taking chances. When he knows about the baby he will want to be extra vigilant, but then I expect he'll be taking you back to New York. He will want you to have the finest doctors, for one thing, if I know him!'

Miranda would rather stay with Linda, now she knew about Marcia Austin, but she didn't think Brett would allow her to. When she told him about the baby he might even pack her off to England. If he really wished to marry Marcia Austin – and there must be a reason why he was treating her like a stranger and staying away so long – he might even insist she had a termination, and this, Miranda thought, was something she couldn't believe she would ever agree to.

She had no official confirmation that she was pregnant. Doctor Mitford wasn't due on the island for another week or two. But while she might have doubted her own judgement, she didn't doubt Linda's. And as, for the first time, she really faced up to the possibility of having Brett's child, she knew she couldn't bear to think of losing it. She must, she decided, try to ensure he stayed away from the island until it was too late for him to do anything about it. Anything that could harm it, anyway.

It was with this in mind that, when Brett rang a few days later, saying he was coming to see her, she told him it didn't matter. That she knew he was busy.

'I'm always busy,' he replied brusquely, as if her obvious reluctance to see him angered him. 'We have to talk, Miranda.'

'About a divorce?' It was out before she could stop it, propelled by long, agonizing days of thinking of it and the need to know. 'You mentioned it the last time you were here.'

'Did I?'

Why did he sound so startled? 'I just thought,' she said coldly, 'that if that's what you want, there's no need for you to come all the way here to tell me.'

'I'm coming, all the same,' he said curtly. Without really answering her question, Miranda realized unhappily, as she heard him put his receiver down none too gently.

When Brett flew in a week later, he took Miranda completely by surprise. Since their telephone conversation, when the days went by and he didn't arrive, Miranda began to think he had changed his mind and wasn't coming. It was late afternoon, after she'd had a dip in the pool and was sitting on a recliner, near it, letting her hair dry in the sun, that she looked up and saw him walking over the grass towards her. Stunned, she stared across at him, unable to move.

'Brett?' she gulped.

'Yes,' he said sardonically, without taking his eyes from her as he halted beside her. 'I'm not a ghost, if that is what you are thinking?'

For a moment, Miranda wasn't able to think at all. Or if she did, it was only that he looked thinner. Or his face did. Still staring at him, she saw there were more lines on it than she remembered. Work and women – too much of both, she thought derisively, attempting to hide the sudden tension within her with anger.

'You startled me,' she said sharply. 'You told me you were coming but that's over a week ago. I was beginning to think you had changed your mind.'

Brett brushed a hand over his dark hair irritably. 'If I had given you a date and time, would it have made any difference?'

This jerked Miranda upright immediately as it reminded her of the reason why she hadn't wanted to see him. Even now he was here, she didn't want him to know about the baby. She didn't think she had put on any weight, but she might have done, and Brett's eyes were sharper than most. Nervously she looked around for something to cover herself with. Unfortunately both the towel and the wrap she was using were lying just out of reach.

Brett, following her almost furtive glance, picked up the cotton wrap and held it out to her. 'Is this what you are looking for?'

'Yes,' she said, taking it from him and draping it quickly around her bare shoulders before scrambling to her feet.

Staring at her agitated face, Brett frowned. 'You didn't think I was going to fall on you like some sex-starved maniac, did you? I'm not that desperate.'

Miranda looked at him mutinously. 'Well, you wouldn't be, would you?'

His eyes narrowed. 'What's that supposed to mean?'

Licking dry lips, Miranda tried to feel grateful that he appeared to be taking more notice of what she was saying than how she looked. All she wanted was to be in his arms, but there was no way she was going to let him see how much. Not after what Marcia Austin had told her!

'Maybe that you haven't been that lonely in New York.'

His expression hardened. Then, following a contemplative pause, 'Has Gaby been up to mischief again?'

'I haven't heard from Gaby since she went away.'

'No?'

'No!' Miranda raised her voice as he sounded so sceptical. 'I've neither seen nor heard from Gaby since she was here. Have you?'

Brett nodded indifferently, his eyes never leaving her face. 'She's in Kentucky with Clem, talking of getting married.'

'Oh, great!' Miranda exclaimed involuntarily. 'I'm sure Clem will make her very happy.'

'He can always try.'

'Can we go to the wedding?' Miranda asked, forgetting Marcia Austin for the moment, she felt so pleased for Gaby.

'Are you that keen to leave the island?'

Brett's terse query took her by surprise. 'Perhaps it's about time . . .'

'As you believe I'm keeping you here so I can enjoy myself in New York with other women?'

Miranda, much as she wished to, suddenly couldn't find the courage to challenge him over this. 'I just think,' she said, 'that I've been on Luke long enough . . .'

Brett frowned as his eyes travelled over her, noting how she was positively glowing with health, despite the hostile air about her which she wasn't attempting to hide. He smiled mockingly. 'Whether you're tired of being on Luke or not, it certainly appears to agree with you. You look well, and I do believe,' he added, his eyes sweeping over her again, 'that in certain places you've put on a little weight.'

Miranda flushed warily. 'I've been sitting with my feet up too much,' she said quickly. 'As I've told you before, I need something to do.'

Brett was staring at her mouth, as if recalling what it felt like under his own. Then his glance did a quick flick back over her, as though recalling other things as well. Suddenly the colour under his own skin deepened and he thrust his hands in his pockets and turned away. As Miranda's heart for some reason broke into gallop, he said tightly, 'How about going up to the house? I'm surprised that Linda hasn't been out to say hello.'

Miranda lowered her shining head. Linda would be keeping out of sight, giving her time to tell him about the baby. But she still didn't know how she was going to. If Brett had loved her, it could have been easy. If he had loved her, she would have been with him all the time and might not have needed to.

She didn't, however, have to tell him in the end. As they walked towards the house, after she said something about Linda being busy, she inadvertently stumbled and, as Brett's arms shot out to prevent her from falling, she guessed immediately that telling him wasn't going to be necessary. It could only be his sixth sense working overtime, but she suddenly realized he knew. As he glanced down at her, it was written on his face all too clearly.

'Miranda!'

If he had uttered the worst profanity, his anger could not have been more apparent. His eyes blazed as his grip on her tightened until the gasp of pain she gave made him aware of what he was doing and he slackened it a little. 'How long have you known?' he asked harshly.

Miranda pulled away from him miserably. She hadn't the nerve to ask him what he was talking about – to try and bluff it out. If she had been dressed, she was sure he would never have guessed. She wasn't sure, even yet, how he could? Something must have told him, as she'd thought, instinctively.

As Brett stared at her, Miranda stared back at him unhappily. If only she had told him over the phone. If only Marcia Austin hadn't rung. If only – she drew a sharp breath, stopping herself from going on. Thinking this way wasn't going to solve anything. It was no use pretending it would.

Trying to avoid Brett's angry gaze, she replied unsteadily, 'Just a week or two. I wasn't sure before then, as I haven't seen a doctor, but Linda told me . . .'

'And you didn't think to tell me?'

'I didn't know you'd be interested.'

'My own child and you didn't think I'd be interested?'

'Brett, please!' She hadn't thought blue eyes could be so cold, but when Brett was angry his appeared to lighten until they sometimes seemed almost silvery.

Miranda didn't realize that her own eyes were glistening with unshed tears which, when Brett saw them, made him pause. 'I'm surprised that Linda didn't let me know,' he said, modulating his voice and the cutting words he'd been about to utter, with difficulty. 'She had her orders. Did you countermand them?'

As he gripped her arm again, as if to emphasize what he was saying, Miranda said anxiously, 'She didn't say anything about getting in touch with you. She did say, though, that I should and I promised I would. Which I meant to do, eventually.'

'Eventually?'

'Yes!' Her voice rose at the dryness of his. Why was he going at her like this? As if she was the one in the wrong, while, all along, it had been him! 'When you rang from New York,' she said, 'I was going to tell you – at least that I was feeling ill, but you never gave me a chance to.'

He ignored this. 'Hadn't you seen Lou Mitford?'

'He's not due for another week.'

Brett nodded, mentally counting. 'No, he isn't. But you could have called him.'

'Why? To get rid of it?'

Uncomprehending, Brett frowned, then suddenly looked so grim that she shuddered. 'If you'd gotten rid of it, you would have regretted it when I caught up with you.'

Miranda's eyes widened indignantly. 'I never wished to get rid of it. I kept quiet about it because I thought you would. That is . . .' she hesitated then rushed on impetuously '. . . it's bound to upset your new plans, isn't it?'

'What – plans?'

Miranda gulped, never having seen him so coldly furious. She felt relieved beyond belief when Linda appeared, preventing her from answering.

'Oh, Mr Brett!' she exclaimed on reaching them. 'I'm so glad to see you!'

Brett smiled tightly as he let go of Miranda and laid a friendly hand on Linda's shoulder. 'You think I should have been here sooner?'

Linda hesitated and blinked uncertainly. Miranda could see she was suddenly suspicious of Brett's mood and felt uncomfortable. 'Well,' she said, 'we've been expecting you . . .'

'And I've turned up like a bad penny,' Brett quipped, though he didn't sound amused. 'I think Miranda was hoping I'd stay away. Permanently.'

Glancing quickly from one to the other, Linda patently decided she'd be wiser to keep out of it, that the little she had contributed so far hadn't helped any. 'You must be wanting something to eat, Mr Brett?' she said, as if she hadn't heard him.

'A drink, perhaps. Nothing else.'

Linda pretended not to see the uncompromising expression on Brett's face, but it made Miranda shiver. Suddenly she didn't want to be alone with him again. He would make her feel bad by lecturing her for not telling him about the baby, and probably worse by demanding a divorce. After this, he would most likely suggest she went home to her father and Alice. And while she didn't doubt he would arrange some kind of settlement to tide her over until she got herself sorted out, what kind of compensation would alleviate the pain of losing him?

Reluctant to even think of it, Miranda began walking towards the house. Once inside she went straight to the lounge, while Linda followed, looking both exasperated and slightly bewildered, as if she would like to shake them.

'If you can get your own drinks,' she said. 'I'll start dinner. I'll make something special,' she added firmly, 'seeing you have so much to celebrate.'

Miranda noticed, as Brett followed her, that he didn't ask Linda to join them, as he surely would have done had he shared her sentiments. Had he loved her and been pleased about the baby, she believed he would have insisted on champagne and invited the whole island to join them.

As Brett closed the lounge door behind them, then strode straight to the bar – which was unusual for him – and poured himself a large whisky, she watched his broad shoulders for some sign of relaxation, but they remained stiff. She breathed quickly as her eyes slid to his powerful thighs and a wave of longing shook her. It was so strong it startled her, as well as making her making her feel ashamed that such a thing could dominate her thoughts so forcibly at a time like this.

It just wasn't possible, Miranda told herself despairingly, yet had to clench her hands tightly against emotions so intense they was difficult to control. Her nails dug into her palms – a light sweat bathed her smooth brow. If Brett were to take hold of her, make love to her, there and then, she knew she might be weak enough to forgive him anything. Even his other women and the way he neglected her. As she stared at him she was conscious of an overwhelming need that threatened to blot out everything else. When he turned, his brows raised in silent appraisal, she was so scared he could read her thoughts that she swiftly averted her eyes.

If he had been able to guess what she was thinking – and the thought brought swift colour to Miranda's cheeks – he didn't mention it. He only asked if she would like a drink.

'No, thank you,' she said.

'Is it your – condition? Or just too early?'

Miranda looked at him bitterly. 'It hasn't taken you long to forget I rarely drink much. Either before dinner or after it.'

Regarding her grimly, Brett tossed back his whisky, then referred to something she'd hoped he had forgotten. 'Would you mind explaining,' he asked softly, 'exactly what you meant, before Linda disturbed us, about upsetting my plans?'

CHAPTER 16

Miranda bit her lip. She had hoped he had forgotten what she'd said as, after having second thoughts, she had decided she wouldn't mention it again. Other women managed to ignore their husbands' infidelity, didn't they? If others could do it, why couldn't she? Did she really wish to bring up a child on her own, with a father who only visited, as many did, occasionally?

Then, as she pondered on this uncertainly, her thoughts swung erratically, and suddenly she knew it wasn't the baby she was thinking of as much as herself. But while she still wanted Brett, and might be prepared to do almost anything to keep him, she didn't think she could make an exception of a continuous succession of other women. And hadn't Marcia Austin talked of divorce and remarriage, which had to be worse than merely an extramarital affair? And if Brett did want a divorce, but decided to put it off until after the baby was born, how could she live through all those months not knowing? She couldn't, Miranda admitted simply.

Having reached this conclusion, she found it impossible not to blurt out, as Brett impatiently repeated his question, 'You must know!'

'If I did, would I be asking?'

She couldn't hold his stony gaze and sat down uneasily in the nearest chair. From where she was sitting, through the wide French windows, she could see the placidness of the ocean, blue in the distance, and a light whisper of evening breeze stirring softly through the palm trees on the beach. She wished she could find some of the same gentleness in Brett. He seemed older and harder than he had been when he was last here. Snatching another look at him, she thought he looked strained. Marcia Austin couldn't be making him that happy, she thought, unless it was the niggling problems which often accompanied such relationships that were bothering him. Brett, not having been married before, might find it irritating having to balance that side of his life with his married one.

Lifting her chin, Miranda looked at him steadily. 'You are having an affair with someone called Marcia Austin, aren't you? I realize this kind of thing is so common today that you'll probably laugh at me for even mentioning it. If I didn't know you wanted a divorce, I don't think I would have . . .'

There, it was out. Miranda wasn't sure if she felt better or worse, but she did feel relieved. Brett was staring at her, but she could tell nothing from his expression of what he was thinking. Nor could she deduce anything from his voice as he said, 'Who told you about Marcia?'

Miranda shook her head, feeling sick. He hadn't denied it. Had she been crazy for somehow hoping he might? She couldn't let him think his sister was still trying to make mischief. Yet how could she tell him the truth?

'It wasn't Gaby,' she said, hoping he might leave it at that.

He didn't. 'Norton, then?'

'No . . .'

Brett turned to pace the room, a frown darkening his face. Halting beside her again, he said grimly, 'There is no one else you know in New York, so you'd better come clean, Miranda. Unless you are making it up?'

'How could I?' Something glittered in his eyes she didn't like the look of. Was it anger – anger because he had been found out? Miranda swallowed a hysterical desire to giggle. That must sound silly when applied to someone like Brett Deakin, but it was what she and her friends were always scared of when breaking the rules at school. And Miranda remembered she had usually been among the ringleaders. Only with Brett's icy eyes on her, she didn't seem able to find the same kind of courage now.

Yet where was the role of a shrinking violet getting her? Precisely nowhere. Mustering some of her almost-forgotten boarding-school courage, she decided to be frank with him. She didn't like betraying people, not even those like Marcia Austin, who had shown little concern for her feelings, but it might be the only way to get anything out of him. While he had not denied knowing Miss Austin, he hadn't admitted to anything else.

'Your friend rang me here,' she said, meeting his grim gaze. 'She said you wanted a divorce so you could marry her.'

'In so many words?'

Miranda nodded, trying to remember exactly. 'She also asked me not to make things difficult for you. She seemed to think I might be inclined to.'

Brett watched her coldly for several seconds, as if waiting for her to continue. 'Was this all?'

'Isn't it enough?'

'More than enough!'

Miranda said, she knew sulkily, 'It wasn't easy to tell you even that much. It probably wasn't easy for Miss Austin, either. When she told me,' Miranda added, 'I'm sure she wasn't enjoying herself.'

He laughed harshly. 'I'd forget the Miss, if I were you. Marcia hasn't been one for years. She just divorced her third husband.'

'And you're going to be the fourth?'

'Miranda!' Brett snapped. 'Do you really believe I should let a woman negotiate that kind of thing for me? When I want a divorce, I'm quite capable of asking for one myself.'

Her voice shaking a little, though she tried to steady it, Miranda persevered. 'We weren't exactly enemies while you were here, Brett. I thought perhaps because of this you might be unwilling to hurt me, and asked Marcia to . . .'

'Do my dirty work for me?'

'Something like that,' she confessed.

His mouth thinned and she shivered at the condemnation in his eyes. 'It's amazing the amount of trust you have in me, Miranda. I presume this is why you didn't tell me about my son?'

The way he said this made Miranda fear it was a son he was suddenly interested in more than herself.

236

Before, because of Marcia Austin, she had been scared he would demand a termination, but now she was frightened that, unless the baby was a girl, he might take it from her as soon as it was born and divorce her then.

'Don't you think that's a good enough reason?' she asked. 'And what was I to think when you left me here for weeks on end?'

'Just over two,' he snapped. 'And because, as you know, I had business to see to in New York. And I thought we both decided we needed time to think?'

'But not that long!'

'It was for your own good,' Brett replied evasively. 'I wanted to give you a chance to consider our marriage clearly. Without your view of it being distorted by sex.'

'Sex?'

'Yes.' His eyes went over her coldly. 'You enjoy it as much as I do, Miranda. No use pretending otherwise. But no marriage can survive on that alone.'

Miranda wasn't so naïve that she didn't follow him, but though her traitorous body leapt in response to his words her cheeks went scarlet with humiliation. 'I never had the feeling you wanted it to survive,' she said sharply. 'When you went away,' she continued, nearer the mark than she realized, 'wasn't it to plan to put an end to it?'

Brett shrugged, resorting, she noticed, to his habit of ignoring questions he didn't wish to answer. 'Whatever I planned for the future,' he said curtly, 'I don't think a child – not an immediate one, anyway – came into it. I should have guessed, though, what might happen,' he admitted bluntly. 'Too much sea and sun and nothing much to do. A lethal combination. As well,' he added, as if for good measure, 'as too many nights we didn't sleep.'

And days, Miranda remembered involuntarily, spent on the boat or on some deserted beach. Her cheeks went even hotter as she recalled her own enthusiastic part in it. Though she might have discovered she loved Brett, did that excuse all the lust?

Defensively, she drew her thin wrap closer about her, as if silently, while acknowledging it, declaring it would not happen again. 'What do you intend doing about the baby?' she asked anxiously. 'If you don't want it, I do.'

'I intend taking you back to New York,' he said, again not answering her directly.

'I'd rather stay with Linda,' Miranda said quickly.

'Impossible,' Brett snapped, losing patience. 'You can't be more than, say, two months gone, but I want you where I can keep an eye on you.'

'Until it is born?'

'If you like. It doesn't pay to look too far ahead.' Brett was determined not to commit himself further. He had married Miranda with every intention of divorcing her in a year or two. He had probably been a fool to marry her in the first place, but he hadn't counted on having a child to complicate things. But then, he reminded himself derisively, he hadn't married Miranda to solve anything. It was because it had not solved anything and he'd allowed this to infuriate him.

'But what about afterwards?' Miranda persisted, refusing to be put off.

Brett shelved the complication of his thoughts. Women wanted everything worked out to the bitter end. Every small detail. Which was probably why he had always valued his freedom. They demanded guarantees of both time and devotion, among other things, which he wasn't, even now, prepared to give. Miranda, he thought, looking at her grimly, must have sought to trap him into a permanent relationship by deliberately ignoring Mitford's advice and becoming pregnant.

'Let's take one step at a time,' he said shortly.

Miranda's soft mouth set stubbornly. 'Haven't you forgotten Miss Austin?' she demanded. 'Are you hustling me off to New York so you can be with her?'

'I have to be in New York. You know that.' Brett sounded as if he was having to explain something to a particularly obtuse child. 'My affairs – and I'm talking about my business ones – ' he said grimly, 'won't run on their own. Even with good staff there has to be someone to guide them and often take the final decisions. I can delegate so much, but not everything. As for Marcia Austin,' he went on, 'you can leave her to me. I can assure you she won't be bothering you again.'

And with that, especially as Brett declared he wanted to hear no more about it and was going to take a shower, Miranda was forced to be content.

Two days later they flew into Nassau, then on to New York. They might have gone sooner, but Brett had insisted Miranda saw a doctor first, to ensure she was fit enough to travel. After Lou Mitford, who was delayed by a bad accident on another island, had flown in and told Brett that his wife was in excellent health, they left the following morning. Miranda said goodbye to Linda and to the other people on Luke whom she'd got to know better while Brett was away. But, though she tried to look cheerful, her heart was heavy, as she wondered if he would ever allow her to come back again.

The journey proved uneventful. Brett saw to it that she had everything she wanted, and insisted that she rested immediately they got home. Dismissing Harris and a tentatively hovering Jill, he took her upstairs himself.

'If I don't stand over you,' he said, as they entered their rooms, 'you might forget.'

Miranda sighed. Was he determined to have a clear conscience by making sure nothing happened to her while she was bearing his son and heir? He might pretend he wished to take care of her, but he didn't love her. And though he might have hinted he had no long-term plans for Marcia Austin, there must be plenty of other women . . .

Absently Miranda sat down on her bed and kicked off her shoes. Then, still without paying much attention to what she was doing, she began taking off her coat. Seeing her struggling with it, Brett came to help her. He'd had a heavier coat waiting for her at the airport, as the climate in New York in February was totally different from the one they'd left behind in the Bahamas.

'Thank you,' she murmured politely, trying to hide the fact that his hands, even touching her lightly, made her tremble. He had left her severely alone during the two days he had spent on Luke, but ever since they were married, hadn't he always kept his distance at regular intervals? And though Miranda often told herself she was tired of him treating her like this, when he wanted to make love to her again she had never been able to resist him. Her longing to be in his arms always seemed greater than her pride, or any strength she could find to say no to him.

Now, as he not only removed her coat but unzipped her dress as well, the sight of her in her brief satin teddy, her long slender limbs and still-slender body, seemed to rivet his attention against his will. 'You're beautiful,' he said, coming down beside her on the silk sheets and drawing her roughly to him.

Miranda closed her eyes as he swept her thin underwear to one side and her burgeoning breasts appeared to welcome his seeking hands, while her mouth moved in helpless response to the urgent assault of his own. Their passion rose quickly, almost animal-like in its swiftness.

'Turn over,' Brett said thickly.

Miranda didn't fight him. Rather she obeyed him blindly, as she did as he said and he rolled, after swiftly throwing off his clothes, on top of her. It was over in minutes, but the degree of feeling involved stunned her, especially when he turned her back again and again entered her.

Some time later – she wasn't sure how much – she heard him apologizing. 'I'm sorry, Miranda,' he said. 'It won't happen again, but I never could resist a beautiful woman.'

241

Still slightly disorientated, Miranda blinked up at him. She had hoped that everything was all right between them again, but apparently she was mistaken. Brett had merely given in to a temporary weakness and had no compunction over letting her know. Or – suddenly she paused in her silent condemnation – did he believe that, in her present condition, too much lovemaking could be bad for her?

'Please, Brett,' she begged, 'I don't think we were doing anything wrong.'

She had obviously expressed herself badly, for he said harshly, 'Being unwise could amount to the same thing. You were disabled for years. We don't know how fit you are yet.'

'I was well enough on the island.' Miranda watched as Brett got off the bed and carelessly pulled on his clothes again. 'I saw Lou . . .'

'Yeah, well, Lou's fine as a general practitioner, but you have to see a specialist; in New York, we have some of the finest.'

Miranda frowned. Why did she feel he was looking for excuses? He'd made love to her, told her she was beautiful but would he still think she was when she began gaining weight in all directions? Brett might feel embarrassed by even the thought of it. If he had loved her, he might not care what she looked like, but it could be a different matter as he didn't.

'What if the specialist – if you insist I see one – says it is all right?' Miranda asked, her cheeks pink.

'Let's wait and see,' Brett said briefly, picking up his jacket and, after slinging it indifferently over his broad shoulders, leaving the room. 'I'd get

242

some rest, if I were you,' he advised, closing the door behind him.

Miranda wasn't keen to rest, but she felt so miserable after Brett left her that she cried a little, which must have sent her to sleep. When she woke the bedroom lights were on and she found Jill standing over her.

'Where's Brett?' she cried, without thinking.

'Dressing for dinner, ma'am.' Jill smiled. 'It's nice to have you home again, Mrs Deakin. How are you? I didn't get a chance to ask you downstairs.'

'I'm fine.' Miranda smiled back while thinking nostalgically of Linda. Linda had been the mother she had never known. Aunt Alice was kind in her way and had done her best, but she had never been a motherly sort of person. Jill was warm and friendly, though, and could be a great help during the following weeks. She needed someone to help her find her way around New York, for one of the first things she was resolved to do was to get to know Brett's city better.

Tightening the sash of the negligé she was glad she'd put on before she fell asleep, Miranda suddenly swallowed and put a hand quickly to her mouth.

Seeing Miranda do this, Jill asked anxiously, 'Are you all right, ma'am? I ran your bath, but can I get you something?'

'No, thank you.' Miranda shook her head as Jill looked concerned. 'I felt sick for a moment, but it's gone.'

'Sick?' Jill frowned.

Miranda shrugged wryly, thinking she may as well tell her. It wasn't, anyway, a secret she would be able to keep much longer. 'I'm going to have a baby,' she said. 'I've been feeling a bit queasy, especially in the mornings, but I'm a lot better now.'

'Oh, gee, that's great!' Jill exclaimed, beaming. 'Mr Deakin must be thrilled!'

Why did everyone think Brett was thrilled? After Jill asked whether they wanted a boy or a girl and when it was expected, Miranda had her bath while Jill, still smiling, went to find her a dress to wear. Brett might be pleased about the baby only if it was a boy but, even if it was, would he be able to give him any more love than he gave his wife?

Gaby arrived from Kentucky full of wedding plans and congratulations about the baby. 'Brett told me when I rang to say I was coming. Somehow I thought I would feel bad about it, after losing mine, you know, but surprisingly I find I don't. Maybe,' she pondered, 'falling in love with Clem has something to do with it?'

Miranda agreed.

'I take it,' Gaby rushed on, in her usual effusive fashion, 'that everything is okay between you and Brett again? Don't get me wrong . . .' she paused '. . . he never said it wasn't, but he was like a bear with a sore head, the day we left the island.'

'That was a while ago,' Miranda frowned. 'I don't recall exactly, but I think his sudden departure for New York had more to do with business than me.'

Gaby nodded. 'Come to think of it, he did say at the time that there were things coming up he wanted to see to personally.'

Like Miss Austin? Miranda thought, though she was reluctant to suggest this to Gaby. Instead she managed to smile and insert a teasing note in her voice as she asked about Clem. 'Brett told me you are thinking of getting married,' she added.

Gaby clasped her hands together excitedly. 'Clem's just wonderful, Miranda. He loves me, bitchiness and all, and swears I'm everything he wants. We are going to be married in Kentucky, in two weeks' time.'

'A big wedding?' Miranda asked, after saying how pleased she was.

'Not very. Just a few of Clem's relations who live near him. And you and Brett, of course.'

'What about all your friends here?' Miranda frowned. 'Won't they be disappointed?'

'Probably.' Gaby shrugged. 'This is why Clem insists on giving them a kind of prenuptial party to make up for it. I believe Brett wants to pay for it as he considers that, as head of our family, it's his place to do this, but at the moment they are still arguing over it.'

A few days later, the party was all arranged for the following week. Though the invitations merely stated an impromptu party and people were given little notice of it, there were few refusals. It was clear that Gaby's friends soon guessed what it was about and no one was going to miss out.

Miranda tried not to feel hurt when Brett seemed reluctant to even talk to her about it, let alone let her help with it. She was told impatiently that everything was being taken care of. Apparently Gaby was to keep her town apartment, for when she visited, and most of the arrangements were being conducted from there and Brett's office. All Brett said he wanted Miranda to do was to relax and rest up for it. An order she found it extremely difficult to obey, as, despite being pregnant, she was finding it almost impossible to sit around all day doing nothing.

She couldn't help viewing the forthcoming party with some trepidation. Somehow she was unable to forget Gaby's fondness for stirring things up by creating a little mischief. And though she tried to convince herself that her sister-in-law had changed since she had first known her, she still found it difficult to ignore her misgivings.

Since making love to her on the day they returned to New York, Brett hadn't come near her again. Miranda, though used to his moods by now, couldn't pretend she appreciated them. He never came with her when she retired to their suite at night. Not even when the specialist she saw said she was fit and well in every way did it make any difference. She had no proof, no reason to suspect he was seeing other women, but as he seldom spent a whole evening at home, it seemed a bit improbable to suppose he was working all the time. After Gaby's wedding was out of the way, he told her, they might give a few parties of their own, so she could meet some of his friends. And this concession, though Miranda doubted it really was one, was all she could get out of him.

CHAPTER 17

On the night of the party Miranda was determined to look so good that Brett would be proud of her. Hurt feelings weren't allowed to interfere with her efforts to put an end to the present strained situation between them. He might have other interests in New York but, whatever they were, they weren't visible. And she'd caught a glimpse of something in his eyes, once or twice recently, that made her feel more optimistic. While Brett might not love her, she felt suddenly sure he did feel something for her, and she was willing to try anything that might bring them closer together again.

Not having found it necessary to wear maternity clothes yet, she decided to buy a new dress. Though her own clothes had arrived from England, she thought they'd looked better when she had worn them sitting down. She had to do something, she told herself. If Brett didn't fall in love with her while she was still reasonably slender, seeing her relatively shapeless in perhaps only a few weeks' time might put him off forever.

When she told Brett that she intended going shopping and would take Jill with her, he didn't object. He did insist that she used one of his cars and kept in constant touch with its chauffeur. The chauffeur, he said, would take them to the 5th and Madison Avenues with their wide variety of boutiques and department stores, for a start. He had, he told her, opened accounts in several of these for her – he gave her a list, advising her to try those he had marked first. And she had only to mention his name to get all the attention she wanted. When Miranda protested that there was enough money in the bank account he had opened for her to more than cover any purchases she wished to make, he had merely shrugged and told her to use that as pocket money or to keep it for a rainy day.

Trying to remember she was his wife and had no need to feel humiliated because she had no money now of her own, Miranda set out. To begin with, she had resented Brett's insistence on providing her with an escort, but it didn't take her long to realize she would have been hopelessly lost without it. That, even with Jill's help, the extra convenience of having a car always waiting for them as they emerged from a shop proved invaluable. Soon, she hoped to be able to scoot around New York by herself, but she knew this would take time and wasn't something she could expect to do immediately. True independence, she admitted, even in small things, wasn't going to be achieved overnight.

It had been the same concerning Jill. The day after they returned from Luke, she had told Brett that she didn't need a maid to look after her, but it wasn't until he saw she really meant it that he relented.

248

'She will be useful to you,' he had insisted to begin with. 'When her last employer died – she was secretary–companion to one of New York's leading socialites – I was lucky to get her.'

'So would I be – if I needed her,' Miranda said. 'But until I make some new friends and learn to find my way around, if you deny me the right to even look after myself, I'm going to find the days intolerably long.'

Brett had said nothing for a few minutes, but in the end he gave in. Mrs Frank, he said, was beginning, as she got older, to find the household accounts and the general running of the household almost too much for her. He would appoint Jill to assist her, which should leave her plenty of time to accompany Miranda about the city when she felt like going out. If the way he said that seemed to suggest he didn't want Miranda going out by herself, she was so relieved to have got at least this one concession out of him that she didn't dwell on it.

In fact, she was indeed glad of Jill's company today. She was ten years older than Miranda and had lived in New York all her life. Her late employer, she said, before her health failed, had bought new clothes continually so she knew the city stores like the back of her hand. Soon, with Jill's help, Miranda found exactly the kind of dress she was looking for and the right accessories to go with it. Jill also advised her, a day or two later, where to go to have her hair cut.

Miranda's hair had grown long on Luke and she wished to have it trimmed. She liked the newer, shorter styles, which the hairdresser said should suit her admirably. He exclaimed rapturously over the thickness and beauty of her hair and said he rarely saw any as healthy as this! When she remarked to Jill that flattery was probably all part of a very expensive service, Jill laughed and said that in all the years she had come here with her last employer, she'd never heard even one complimentary remark escape the head stylist's lips.

As it was the night of the party, Miranda decided to have a facial as well. Might as well have everything, she thought recklessly, if it would help Brett to fall in love with her. When the beautician was finished, however, she gazed at herself with some surprise in one of the salon mirrors. She had always had a near-perfect skin, but now it looked satiny and brilliant. Almost too good to be true, she thought in amazement.

Though she had no wish to steal Gaby's thunder, Miranda did everything in her power to make herself as attractive as possible that evening. Her hair and skin looked immaculate and beautiful, her dress fitted her like a glove, revealing no sign of her pregnancy, and she felt convinced that she looked the kind of woman most people would expect someone like Brett Deakin to have for a wife.

Satisfied that she looked her best and could do nothing more to improve her appearance, she knocked tentatively on Brett's bedroom door to see if he was ready. He was, but instead of telling her how good she looked, as she eagerly hoped he might, his eyes merely darkened with disapproval.

Feeling somewhat dismayed, Miranda stepped back and heard herself asking uncertainly. 'Don't you like my dress? It's my new one.'

'I can see what it is.'

'Then . . .?'

'You look wonderful,' he said, as if he could read what she was asking plainly in her face. 'I like your hair, but I don't know about the dress.'

'What's wrong with it?' Miranda glanced quickly down at it.

'Don't you think it's rather low at the front? People won't need a lot of imagination.'

'Oh.' Miranda felt her face flush. She was sure it wasn't that low! Both Jill and the saleswoman in the boutique where she bought it had assured her it wasn't. Very discreet, the woman had said.

'You can see the tops of your breasts.'

Miranda felt the heat in her cheeks increase wildly when Brett said this. Feeling utterly mortified, she offered shakily, 'I'll go and change it.'

'No time,' Brett answered curtly. 'We're late enough as it is.'

Suddenly Miranda found the strength to retaliate. 'You can't blame me for that! You were late getting in.'

'I'm not blaming you,' he snapped, steering her almost roughly out of the suite, down the long staircase, past the ever-subservient Harris, into the waiting car. 'I've been busy.'

Miranda struggled for breath as she clutched at the wrap he had grabbed from her hands and thrown around her shoulders before they came down. He was so busy he scarcely had time for her these days.

251

To add to this, this evening, he had criticized her dress and taken away most of any little confidence she'd had in her appearance. In that moment the party she'd been so looking forward to seemed to lose its appeal. She just wished it was over and she was back home again.

If the evening, from which she had hoped to gain so much, began badly, it seemed determined to continue that way. To begin with, as Brett had predicted, they were late and found Gaby in a bad mood because of this. She positively scowled at them and the short altercation she had with her brother didn't seem to make her feel any better. When Brett, with an impatient shake of his dark head, walked off, leaving Miranda to calm her agitated sister-in-law, she felt even worse than she had done when they arrived.

'I'm sorry – ' she looked uncertainly at Gaby ' – Brett really was held up. He did try to get home earlier,' she added, while wondering dubiously if this was true.

Gaby's shrug was clearly as doubtful as Miranda's thoughts as her eyes followed her brother's tall, lean figure. The large reception room, where the party was being held, was full, with more people coming in all the time. Miranda though, like Gaby, was taking more notice of Brett than of the other guests. She saw a tall, graceful woman approach him and slip her arm through his. Something in her manner made Miranda feel suddenly chilled as she continued to watch them. Brett was smiling as he turned and spoke to her, and the woman's face was curiously animated as she raised herself on tiptoe and kissed him. How did

Brett have such an effect on women? Miranda wondered, recalling the way they had all fawned over him when they spent the day with the Gordons and their friends at Christmas.

'Who is Brett talking to?' she asked, as Gaby turned from greeting the last influx of guests. Clem had apparently just been called away to take an important telephone call.

'Marcia Austin.' Gaby pretended not to see the startled look on Miranda's face. 'An old friend of Brett's,' she tacked on, almost viciously.

'And you asked her?' Miranda, when her first moment of shock was over, didn't try and hide that she felt disgusted. Gaby might have changed, but not that much. When she and Brett annoyed her by turning up late, she'd retaliated the way she knew best. And for all she must be aware that Marcia was trying to destroy Brett's marriage, she'd had no compunction over inviting her here this evening. The chance to make a little mischief must prove, for Gaby, to be irresistible.

'Why not?' Gaby looked at her, then away again sullenly. 'We've known her for years. I could hardly leave her out, could I? She's old money – old family. Brett might easily have married her. And very advantageously.'

Quickly Miranda moved away from her sister-in-law, not trusting herself to stay for fear she said something she might regret. While Gaby was obviously quoting facts, she wished they weren't quite as painful. Brett might have seemed to deny any serious intentions towards Marcia Austin, but he clearly felt something for her?

Feeling distressed by such thoughts, Miranda stumbled and, failing to notice where she was going, ran straight into Adrian Norton. Gaby had excelled herself, she thought bitterly, as he caught hold of her and steadied her with an amused grin.

'So, we meet again?' he greeted her. 'And still without a husband, despite the prolonged honeymoon.'

'He's around,' she said, somewhat breathlessly, though she realized he hadn't actually asked a question.

'Ah, but where?' Adrian was still smiling and looking at her intently. 'Isn't he aware that you're the loveliest thing here? With your golden hair and gauzy dress you're the nearest thing to an angel I guess I'll ever have the good fortune to meet. If I were Brett, I'd never let you out of my sight.'

'Mr Norton . . .!'

'Why not Adrian?'

'All right – Adrian,' she conceded unenthusiastically.

'And you were about to say – before I interrupted?'

Of course he knew! Miranda sighed with exasperation. She could see it in the way his eyes were twinkling. 'I'm a married woman,' she said briefly.

His brown brows rose, perhaps deliberately, until they almost disappeared into his hairline. 'Surely I'm not meeting one who takes that seriously?'

'Well, I do.'

'Well, I'm not trying to run off with you.' He smiled ruefully, 'Much as I'd like to. I'll admit, when I first met you I acted somewhat brashly, but now I only wish to admire you respectfully.'

Suddenly, though she wondered if she could trust him, Miranda felt herself warming to him. She didn't want to admit to feeling mortally wounded by the way Brett was treating her this evening. It was Gaby's party, but it was also the first time she had been anywhere with him in public, and he was ignoring her. She had expected him to introduce her to people, to be with her for at least some of the time, but this appeared to be the last thing he intended doing. And he must know that there were those who were noticing it. They must be wondering what was wrong with her that she couldn't keep her husband by her side after just three months.

She heard Adrian Norton going on. 'Marriage, these days, is a funny business, isn't it? Doesn't seem to conform to any particular pattern. I've been curious about yours, especially when you went away on your honeymoon and Brett returned alone.'

Startled, Miranda looked at him. 'Brett sometimes had to return to New York to see to his affairs, but you must have been following our activities very closely?'

Adrian didn't bother to deny it. 'I have – still do, I confess.' He paused abruptly, faint lines of strain on his face. 'I've gotten to the stage where I can't sleep at nights for thinking of you.'

Miranda forced a teasing smile to her lips. 'I'm sure you could think of better things to lose sleep over.'

Adrian shook his head and returned her smile soberly. 'Sometimes I wish I could, but there's something about you I don't seem able to forget.

'Why not try to?'

'Do you want me to?'

Miranda said firmly, 'Isn't this conversation getting a bit out of hand?'

'That's how my feelings are getting about you.'

Miranda sighed as she glanced over the room to Brett again. Marcia Austin was still with him, but other people had joined them, since she'd last looked, and were talking to him. How was it, she wondered dully, that one man's admiration should leave her cold, while she would have sold her soul for even one hint of it from another?

'I'm in love with my husband, Adrian,' she said, believing it might deter him if he was seriously thinking of pursuing her. Even if he wasn't, it couldn't do any harm to let him know how she felt.

Brett took her home shortly after midnight, despite Gaby's protests.

Clem added his. 'It's early yet.'

Brett eyed him grimly. 'If Gaby is ever in Miranda's condition, I hope you realize she will need taking care of.'

Unable to contain herself, Miranda snapped as they left, 'Was there any need for such hypocrisy, seeing how, for most of the evening, I've had to take care of myself?'

Brett laughed shortly. 'Norton appeared to be doing that quite nicely.'

'I spent most of the time with Gaby and Clem.' She didn't say anything about also having to put up with Gaby's taunts about the way Brett was neglecting her. Clem, at least, had been kind to her. 'They introduced me to a lot of your friends, which Clem must have thought should have been your job, but where were you? Talking to people like Marcia Austin and completely forgetting everything else.'

'I didn't forget,' Brett said, so acidly that Miranda lapsed into silence until they were home.

Once in their suite, however, with the door closed behind them, Miranda found she couldn't leave it alone. Swinging around to face him, she said accusingly, 'You told me to leave Marcia Austin to you. I see now what you meant.'

Brett followed her when, as if not trusting herself to say more, she went into her bedroom. Tossing off his jacket, he looked at her as he said, 'Perhaps you should feel grateful that there are such women to divert me.'

How cool he sounded while she was seething with unrest. 'You always use the baby as an excuse.'

'Shut up,' he said tersely.

Miranda flopped down on the bed, kicking off her shoes. When Brett used that tone of voice she always felt herself tremble. When she obeyed him she thought he would leave but suddenly, to her dismay, he was sitting on the bed beside her with his arms coming out to haul her to him.

Anger rushed over Miranda that he dared do this after neglecting her all evening and she tried to push him away. Did he mean to kiss her? Did he think the hurt she had suffered over the past few hours, could be healed by perhaps a mere kiss? 'Let me go,' she cried tautly. 'Please – Brett!'

The words were smothered against his mouth, her cry of protest lost under the pressure of his lips. He was too strong for her – he always had been. Despair swept sharply over her, but there were other feelings as well. The familiar weakness she knew whenever he touched her made short work of her desire to fight him, and she found herself responding to him helplessly. Her mouth opened passionately under his as she slipped her arms around him. Suddenly she didn't care if he did guess how much she wanted him. Within seconds, with Brett's usual expertise, their clothing was off and flung on the floor and she was pressing herself against him, feeling every movement of his totally aroused male body.

Miranda thought she had never known such ecstasy. Begging him shamelessly not to stop, she clung to him as his hands found her tender breasts, then his mouth caressed them. Melting into him, she raised herself involuntarily to meet his demanding invasion of her. They were both impatient, perhaps too urgent in their shared hunger, but Miranda was grateful that Brett didn't hesitate. He devoured her until her whole being was consumed by fire, then he took her with him to the stars and back. She still couldn't find any sense of reality as she floated reluctantly down to earth again. She meant to tell him how much she loved him, and ask him to forgive her for annoying him that evening, but after he made love to her again she must have fallen asleep, for when she woke he was gone and she didn't have the courage to go after him.

When word came that Miranda's father was ill, she could think of nothing but going to England to be with him. She wanted to book a flight immediately.

She wasn't sure what it was that made her decide to ring Brett first and ask his advice.

'Don't do anything until I get home,' he said, after she contacted his office and waited while his secretary decided whether he could spare her a few minutes or not. 'I can't talk now. We'll discuss it this evening.'

What was there to discuss? Miranda wondered. Her father was ill. He needed her. It was as simple as that. And it wasn't as if there was anything here to prevent her from going to him. It wasn't as if she had to cook Brett's meals or iron his shirts. He had an army of servants who probably made a better job of doing these things for him than she ever could. And though she was learning to find her way around New York, she hadn't found anything yet to really fill in the days which, as Brett was rarely around, were beginning to feel curiously empty.

For once he was home reasonably early but, with Harris and a maid hovering around, it wasn't until after dinner that Miranda felt able to talk to him about her father.

'Harry's ill,' she said, amazed when Brett made no attempt to mention his father-in-law himself. 'Alice says it's his heart again and . . .' her voice faltered '. . . he is in intensive care.'

Ignoring the coffee Harris poured for them, Brett told Miranda to drink hers and poured himself some brandy. 'You could be worrying unnecessarily,' he said coldly. 'His heart was never that bad, he told me so himself. By tomorrow he could have recovered.'

'Alice sounded worried,' Miranda said, 'and she isn't one to make a fuss over nothing.'

'You rang the hospital?'

'Yes.' Miranda thought wistfully that it would have been nice if Brett had done this for her. He might, being Brett, have got more out of them than she had done. 'They will only say he is comfortable and improving gradually.'

'There, you see.'

Miranda looked at him, her grey eyes like jewels with the tears behind them. 'All the same, I have to go, Brett. Don't you see – he's done such a lot for me . . .'

'You are his daughter.'

'I know that, but many parents might not have done half as much, and if I didn't go and he had a relapse, or something, I would never be able to forgive myself. Besides,' she uttered huskily, 'I happen to love him.'

'How nice,' Brett murmured sarcastically. 'For him, I mean.'

Miranda swallowed, refusing to feel more hurt than she was already. 'You wouldn't like to come with me?'

'No, I would not. And aren't you forgetting Gaby's wedding?'

'But Gaby isn't ill.'

'You could still wait and go to the UK afterwards. We've arranged to go to Kentucky at the weekend, but will be back by Monday.'

Miranda looked at him despairingly. She had wanted his permission to visit her father, but she could see she wasn't going to get it. For some reason he didn't want her to go to England. He didn't seem to understand she had to! 'I'm sorry, Brett,' she said, 'I'm afraid I'll have to miss Gaby's wedding. You'll have to go on your own and I'm sure she won't mind that much if I'm not with you. I'll ring the airport in the morning and hope they will have a cancellation.'

Brett's mouth tightened grimly, as if he was forcing himself to accept she meant this. 'How long,' he asked, 'do you propose being away?'

'Perhaps two or three weeks.' Miranda hadn't really thought about it. 'It depends, I suppose, on how Harry is.'

'Well, I'll only let you go if you take a nurse with you.'

'A – nurse?' Miranda exclaimed, startled.

'No use looking like that,' Brett said grimly. 'We have a child to consider, remember? And your gynaecologist believes you are inclined to be depressed.'

'That's not the child's fault,' Miranda muttered bitterly.

'I realize that,' Brett agreed enigmatically. 'But I still don't want you taking unnecessary risks.'

'A few hours on a plane, where every passenger is always well looked after, couldn't surely be called taking unnecessary risks?'

'No one would have time to be with you every minute.'

Miranda thought Brett was being ridiculous. Of course it would be his son and heir he was worried about, not his wife. 'Well, I'm not taking anyone with me,' she said stubbornly. She almost added, 'If you can't come, I don't want anyone else,' but of course she didn't.

Brett appeared to be making one last attempt. 'A nurse could stay in London and come back with you?'

'No!'

Brett frowned but, to Miranda's surprise, didn't continue trying to get her to change her mind. Instead, he said. 'You can leave your flight arrangements to me. I'll have someone see to it in the morning.'

'Thank you.' Miranda knew that if Brett used his influence she would be in England very quickly. 'Will you come to see me off?'

'No,' Brett said, while refilling his glass with more brandy. 'I'll get Harris to do that. He will look after everything.'

CHAPTER 18

Miranda arrived at Birmingham late the following day. To her surprise, Brett arranged everything after she went to bed. That he had done this himself after letting her believe he would leave it to his staff soothed her a little, if it didn't wholly alleviate the hurt she felt that he hadn't chosen to come with her. Brett, she knew, by this time, had offices and enterprises all over the world. He could have looked after his affairs just as well from the UK as he did from New York.

Alice looked nearer to tears than Miranda had ever seen her when she arrived at Well House and walked in.

'Oh, darling!' she exclaimed, rushing out to meet her. 'I'm so glad to see you. You couldn't tell me exactly what time you'd be here, but I've been counting every minute . . .'

'How's my father?' Miranda asked anxiously, after she kissed her aunt and they moved into the lounge and she managed to get a word in. 'I've been so worried.'

'He's recovering – gradually,' Alice said cautiously. 'I think he's making more effort since he knew you were coming. Brett rang an hour ago, by the way, to see if you'd arrived yet. He was on to the hospital earlier and arranged for Harry to be transferred to a private ward as soon as he is out of intensive care – which they expect he will be in another day. I'm sure Harry will appreciate it.'

'What do you think brought this attack on?' Miranda asked, as Alice settled her in a chair by the fire, and the housekeeper, despite the lateness of the hour, bustled in with sandwiches and tea. 'He hasn't had a serious one before, has he?'

'No.' Alice began pouring out as she shook her head. 'Apparently, there doesn't have to be any particular reason, though sometimes, of course, there is.'

'He hasn't been worrying over something?'

'Not that I know of.' Alice put milk in Miranda's tea and remembered no sugar. 'I have a feeling, though . . .' she frowned, '. . . that he's had something on his mind. Something that, if it hasn't exactly worried him, has been niggling away at him.'

'What kind of thing?' Miranda took a drink of the hot tea Alice gave her then, putting it down, held her hands out absently to the blaze. She felt almost embarrassed to mention it but felt she had to. 'Brett told me he gives him plenty of money.'

'Yes, he does,' Alice said quickly. 'Harry is very grateful, but I'm sure, if it's anything, it's not that. I could be wrong. In fact, most probably I am. It's just, as I said, a feeling I have.'

'Perhaps he has been wondering why I haven't been over?' Miranda said. 'I'm not suggesting he's missed me that much, but he spent a lot of time looking after me and could have thought I'd forgotten about it? Ungrateful daughter, you know.'

'Well, he certainly missed you.' Alice smiled at her warmly. 'We both have. But Harry knew you were on your honeymoon and it pleased him enormously when Brett rang occasionally and told him how well you were looking. And then he had your calls too, which had the same effect.'

Miranda frowned. Brett never once mentioned ringing her father. She wondered why? 'I expect,' she said to her aunt, 'we could go on speculating for ever without coming up with the right answer. And, as you say, it may be nothing much. Most of us, I suppose,' she added with a sigh she was scarcely aware of, 'have something on our minds from time to time that – while maybe not important – bothers us.'

Alice said she was sure Miranda was right.

Miranda was silent for a moment than asked tentatively, 'Did Brett tell you about the baby?'

'Yes, he did.' Alice looked at her eagerly. 'I've been dying to talk to you about it but wasn't sure if I should. You see Brett thought – though I felt he was wrong – that you might decide not to tell us about it yourself, for fear it worried your father and made him worse. And he asked me, in case you didn't, to keep an eye on you, to see you didn't do too much.'

Miranda pretended to be amused. 'Much chance I'll get to do that if everyone is as hardworking as your housekeeper.'

'Whom he ought to know about as he pays her salary,' Alice said wryly. 'As well as the wages of a maid and part-time gardener. But I expect, like any adoring husband, he just wished to be sure you would be well looked after. Anyway – ' she smiled ' – I'm so thrilled about the baby. And I know your father will be too, when you tell him about it.'

'I'll tell him tomorrow,' Miranda promised. 'I suppose it is too late to visit tonight?'

'I'm afraid so as it's almost midnight, but he knows you are coming – which is almost as good as a visit.' Looking at Miranda, Alice hesitated before continuing rather awkwardly, 'I've never tried to take your mother's place, Miranda, and perhaps you've sometimes thought I've not been very loving. I've enjoyed looking after the house and you and your father, of course, but I've never dared allow myself to grow too fond of you. I was always aware that if Harry married again, for instance, it could all be taken away from me. I was so busy trying to hang on to the only family I had yet, at the same time, keeping my distance, that I think I lost sight of what is really important.'

'I'm sure no one could have looked after us better than you have,' Miranda said quickly, strangely moved by her aunt's obviously difficult confession. 'You've devoted the best years of your life to Dad and me, and I've never doubted your affection for us.'

'Thank you, dear.' Alice smiled at her again warmly. 'And I hope you'll let me be a grandmother as well as an aunt to your child when it arrives as, with both your dear mother and Brett's no longer with us, it won't have a proper one.'

The following morning Alice took Miranda to the hospital. Miranda had spent a restless night thinking of Brett, though she had felt the heaviness of her

266

heart easing a little when she'd gone into her old bedroom. For a few moments it was as if she had never been away. So many memories, both painful and cherished, but it had always been a refuge to her.

Alice's confession had troubled her and kept her awake as well. How often, she thought guiltily, despite denying it to her aunt, had she thought her rather hard and uncaring? No one should judge another person indiscriminately, she realized remorsefully, no matter how well you thought you knew them.

Miranda couldn't help wondering, as she tossed and turned and her thoughts, as always, returned to her husband, why Brett hadn't told her he was keeping in touch with her father? She also wondered what Harry had been worrying about? It wasn't his nature to worry over anything, but she supposed there were very few people who didn't worry occasionally over something. Perhaps if he really had a problem he would tell her about it when she saw him and she could help him to solve it. Though heaven knows, she admitted to herself, she wasn't that good at solving her own. The news of the baby would please him, she knew. And, after all, it might be all they were left with when this whole sorry business was over. What exactly she meant by that, Miranda wasn't sure. It was just a feeling she had of impending doom and disaster she couldn't get rid of.

When Miranda and Alice arrived at the hospital, to their relief they found Harry out of intensive care and ensconced in the private room Brett had booked for him. He was pale and obviously tired, but his consultant told them he was now out of immediate danger and should make steady progress.

Miranda thought privately that he looked ten years older than when she'd last seen him. She felt her heart ache as she summoned a bright smile and hugged him as she said hello to him. She wasn't unaware of how, rightly or wrongly, Harry had devoted himself to her since she was born. And, in the end, he had let her go, happy in thinking she was happy, putting any possessive instincts behind him. She didn't want to believe that the money Brett had offered had anything to do with it. It was better, she thought, not to!

Harry, as Alice predicted, was delighted about the baby. 'A grandson,' he said slowly and, to Miranda's surprise, with tears in his eyes. 'What a pity that I won't be able to leave him anything, but I expect Brett has enough.'

'It might be a girl,' Miranda said, with gentle irony, wondering why neither he nor Brett had thought of that.

'Yes, of course.' Harry smiled ruefully, then raised a bushy eyebrow thoughtfully. 'Do you know, I think a girl might be better? She'd probably love her old grandfather more.'

'Well, I'm just going to wait and see and love it whatever sex it is,' Alice said wisely.

Miranda visited her father every day after that. She actually spent the greater part of each day with him. Alice, though pleased to let her, began to worry that she wasn't getting enough proper exercise and rest. It was a relief when, after a week, Harry was allowed to come home, providing he promised to take things easy.

'Don't know what else they imagine I have to do?' he pretended to grumble. 'I don't know that it's good for me, but Brett does so much for me I don't have to lift a finger unless I want to.'

Miranda, in turn, wondered why Brett was doing so much? She couldn't help feeling disturbed about it. She had known about the monthly cheques, if not the exact amount contained in them, but not about all the money for extra expenses. Had he done this in order to keep her tied to him? Or for the pleasure of taking it away from them when he no longer had any use for them? Her heart went cold even to think of it.

She had thought she would miss Brett terribly – just as she had done on the island. And, to a certain extent, she did. But she had to admit that, this time, being away from him also brought a sense of relief. She wasn't aware of how much tension there had been building up inside her until she felt it draining out of her, as the calm atmosphere of Well House, along with the quiet of the grounds in which she still liked to wander, gradually restored in her a feeling of peace. It was only early March, but it was this and the touch of spring in the air which lifted her spirits and helped her to feel better.

She hadn't quite believed Alice when she said she thought something might be worrying Harry but, surprisingly, once he was home and there wasn't a constant retinue of nurses and doctors interrupting them, it was an impression that Miranda somehow got herself. Yet when she tried tactfully to get something out of him, he clammed up.

'You've too much imagination, my dear,' he said. 'What could be worrying me?'

Miranda affected a light shrug. 'I just thought that something must have been responsible for your heart attack?'

'Perhaps I ate too much.'

'Dad!' she protested, 'I'm serious.'

'And being silly,' he growled. 'But if we're being serious, of course I don't eat too much. I've always taken care not to put on weight, and it's not as if I just sat around doing nothing. I take plenty of exercise – play golf, as you know, that sort of thing, and go out a bit socially. Take Alice with me occasionally. And apart from an odd drink,' he added drily, 'I've given up almost everything else that Alice says might damage my health. Probably not many monks live as frugally in some ways as I do.'

Miranda nodded. Though still unconvinced, she knew better than to go on pestering him. Whatever it was that was bothering him, it couldn't be that much or he would never have kept it to himself. And he would know, she tried to tell herself, that in his state of health it wasn't wise to.

Brett rang every day. Miranda wasn't sure why as he had little to say. She decided at last that he could only be checking up on her, or rather the son and heir he expected her to provide him with.

'He must be very much in love with you,' Alice would tease, having obviously concluded, from his frequent phone calls, that Brett was a devoted husband. 'Do you know,' she would sigh, 'even at my age, I feel quite envious.'

If only she knew!

'I hope Brett doesn't want you to go home too soon,' she said, when Miranda had been with them two weeks. 'Harry seems more content when he has you to talk to. When he is able to get out and about again, it mightn't matter so much, but I hope Brett will let you stay until he gets properly on his feet.'

Brett, however, refused to. 'A fortnight or so,' he said, 'is long enough. I don't want you travelling when you are more than a few months' pregnant.'

'I'm scarcely three,' Miranda protested, 'and . . .' she hesitated before rushing on precipitously, 'I thought, if I stayed a little longer, Alice and Dad might be able to come back with me and I could take them to Luke for a few weeks?'

'No!' Brett snapped adamantly. 'I'll bring them over later, with some medical staff, if needs be, and we'll see about Luke then. Meanwhile, I've booked a flight for you next Thursday morning – ' he gave her the details ' – and you'd better be on it.'

'Brett – please!' she felt like shouting at him, but forced herself to speak meekly. 'Won't you let me stay, even a few more days? My father really has been very ill and I can't pop back to see him from New York, as I might have done had we lived, say, in London.'

'No,' Brett snapped again, just as curtly. 'Please don't argue with me, Miranda. I want you back here immediately.'

'Very well,' Miranda agreed listlessly, feeling suddenly so depressed by the lack of any tenderness in his voice that it didn't seem to matter any more what she did,

For two days Miranda hesitated over announcing she was leaving. Eventually, however, with time so short, she had to. To her surprise her, father didn't seem half as dismayed as she'd expected him to. If she had been asked to try and define exactly how he felt when she told him, she might almost have said relieved.

'On Thursday, you say?' They were having coffee in the lounge. 'Shows how much he cares for you.'

Miranda smiled, which she hoped he took for agreement, and when she promised recklessly not to be long in coming to see him again, he told her not to be in a hurry, and not to worry.

'Your place is at your husband's side now, y'know, m'dear,' he stressed firmly. 'Leave a man to his own devices too long and he might go astray. Not that Brett would, but you're better to be safe than sorry,' he assured her somewhat ponderously.

Miranda frowned as she listened to him. Had he heard of Brett's womanizing? She knew, of course, it would be no use asking him. He would merely look embarrassed and innocent and, even if he had, would deny it. Men had a funny habit of sticking together, like an endangered species.

'I'm not worried about Brett straying. Not yet, anyway.' She tried to look more amused than she felt. 'It's you I'm worried about.'

'Then don't,' Harry said, though his eyes were wary under his bushy brows. 'I'm well on the way to a complete recovery.'

'If Brett hadn't been in such a hurry, I'd have liked to have taken you back with me,' she confessed impulsively.

'Well, never mind.' Not even then did Harry seem disturbed by Brett's insistence that she returned to New York. 'You go back and in a few weeks' time Alice and I might pop over to see you. If I have that to look forward to, it will help me to get better more than anything.'

'You're sure?' Miranda asked doubtfully.

'Very sure,' Harry answered staunchly. 'Your husband is missing you, which is as it should be. He wants you with him and you shouldn't disappoint him.'

Brett might be missing her, but for what? Miranda wondered as she sat in the private car he had sent to take her to the airport. She was flying direct from Birmingham and though it was a beautiful morning for early March, she'd refused to let her father and Alice come to see her off.

'It just isn't worth the risk,' she told Harry. 'You could easily get a chill and suffer a setback.' And to Alice, 'You know how airports confuse you? About the only thing that does,' she teased, 'but I should only worry, if you came with me, that you might get lost.'

'Well, it's a comfort to know Brett will be at JFK to meet you,' Alice said as she kissed her goodbye.

Would Brett be there to meet her? Miranda asked herself as she looked through the car's rear window for a last glimpse of them standing and waving to her on the drive. Would he even bother to return to the house before his usual time? She thought not. He would merely send Harris to meet her and a message to say he hoped to be home in time for dinner. Or something like that.

To distract herself from what she feared might become a string of equally depressing thoughts, she spoke to the driver. He had insisted that she sat in the back of the car though he did leave the glass partition between them open. It would have been quite easy to have some kind of conversation, but he didn't seem interested. He merely grunted a reply and seemed more interested in his surroundings. They were passing through a built-up area which lay between them and the more open country approaching the airport. When he made no attempt to talk to her, Miranda decided he probably knew someone living around here and was trying to remember where it was.

Left to her own devices, she began thinking of Brett again and what she might find in New York. Though she loved him, she didn't think she could ever come to love the big elegant house he lived in. She found it too lonely and impersonal. There was a large staff but they were so efficient she seldom saw them. Sometimes, though she supposed in a way it was comfortable, it reminded Miranda of a museum. She thanked God for Jill.

Miranda's thoughts brooded on. It wasn't as if Brett's house intimidated her. After all, Well House wasn't small and since her accident there'd always been servants around, but in New York she often longed for something smaller. A place where she and Brett could live together without someone seeming to watch their every move. A modest place, where she could do things for him. Cook dinner, for instance. That had to be a joke of course, Miranda thought wryly, picturing herself as an efficient housewife when she had scarcely done more than try to boil an egg. Still, she could learn, couldn't she? Everyone had to start somewhere.

Here Miranda pulled herself up. Some dreams, as she ought to know by now, could never be more than that. Brett lived in the house his mother inherited from her family and generously bequeathed to her son. It had been in her family for generations. Brett was used to it. He probably even loved it, and would never be prepared to leave it. Gaby once said, in one of her cynical moods, that Brett only stayed there because his mother left it to him, but this wasn't the impression Miranda got. From what she could make out, Brett had seen too little of his mother when she was alive ever to feel obligated to her. Even if he had, he wasn't a man to let sentiment compel him to do something he didn't wish to.

Again, to try and divert her thoughts, she tried speaking to the driver. This time he answered her, even chatting for a few minutes when Miranda asked him if he was a native of Birmingham. Afterwards she partly blamed herself for what happened. If she hadn't taken his attention, he might have seen the van bearing down on them sooner and been able to get out of its way. Or even had time to call the police. As it was he didn't have time to do anything. Anything at all.

The van, a dark muddy-looking blue one, passed them swiftly where the road narrowed on a squalid part of the estate they were going through. A short cut, Miranda's driver had said. The van mounted the pavement, apparently in order to get in front of them, then stopped suddenly, entirely blocking the way. It caused Miranda's driver to slam on his brakes and swerve violently in trying to avoid running into it.

'Bloody fools!' he yelled. 'What the hell do they think they are doing?'

Miranda, flung forward helplessly, didn't hear the hint of apprehension in his voice beneath the cursing, or see his hand jerk futilely towards his mobile. Her seat belt saved her, but owing to the abrupt way they stopped, cut into her painfully. She gasped with fright as she clutched at her stomach, but before she could say anything the car door was wrenched open and she was released from the belt and dragged out.

It all happened so quickly that even had she been able to, she couldn't have taken it in. She was aware of different things, but only in a disjointed fashion. As she hit the road, the hands dragging her tied something roughly over her eyes so she couldn't see. She remembered wondering where her driver was, until she heard him being warned to stay where he was or he was dead. When he clearly didn't take the advice, there was a dull thud followed by a groan and the sound of someone falling, which seemed to suggest he had been hit over the head with something. Then she was lifted and thrown into the back of the van. After which there was more slamming of doors and excited shouts from her captors and she was being driven away.

Though Miranda didn't lose consciousness, the extreme roughness of the treatment she received made everything hazy. For a few minutes she couldn't even seem to think straight. She knew enough to realize she was being kidnapped but that was all. Surely the police would come, she thought, trying to control the panic rising within her. Perhaps if she screamed someone might hear her? But when she tried to something was thrust quickly in her mouth, so the only sound to come out was a useless smothered one.

'Be quiet or you'll get more than you bargained for,' the same voice that had threatened her driver hissed in her ear. 'Just shut up and you won't get hurt.'

Miranda subsided. She might not have actually seen what happened to her driver, but she'd heard enough to convince her that these men meant what they said. They must have planned this carefully. It could be no coincidence that they had known she was going to the airport that morning, though how they had puzzled her as she suddenly felt certain her driver was not involved. The car he had been driving was Brett's. She suspected he was one of Brett's top security men. As such, he would earn a good salary and she doubted that he would risk his job for a wildcat scheme such as this.

Questions related to this began moving sluggishly through Miranda's mind. Why hadn't someone come to her rescue? It was early, but there must have been people about. Even if they were too scared to do anything, surely someone must have seen what was happening and rang the police? Yet, if they had, where were the sirens? There was nothing to indicate that there was a policeman within miles of them. And why was she being kidnapped? And why now? Brett was a millionaire, but her father, before he mysteriously lost everything, had been wealthy and no one had attempted to kidnap her then. She was aware that kidnapping was more common in the States, but even there it only amounted to a small percentage of those with enough means to make it worth someone's while.

To begin with the van went fast, jerking her and the man beside her around on the wooden floor. Then it slowed down, but not before her hands were tied behind her to add to the indignity of her blindfolded eyes and gagged mouth. Then she was again warned not to try anything unless she wished to get knocked out.

If she had not been pregnant, Miranda would not have obeyed without a struggle, but she was thinking of her baby and didn't wish to do anything to endanger it. She didn't want to think of Brett. Not yet. For if she did, she knew she might blame him for this. If he had come over with her, or even let her stay in England a little longer, none of this might have happened. Thinking this way at the moment, she realized, wasn't going to do anything but make her feel bitter. It might be better, she thought, just to pray he would come now and get here in time to help her.

CHAPTER 19

Miranda wasn't sure how far they travelled, but after it slowed down, after a bump or two, the van stopped.

'We're here,' the man holding her informed her. 'Just be quiet and do as you're told.'

What chance would she get to do otherwise? Miranda wondered despairingly. She was beginning to realize, more with every minute, just how much danger she might be in and, despite trying not to, felt almost sick with fear.

Two other voices joined the one speaking to her. 'We've closed the garage doors and opened the house ones,' they said. 'We're certain no one has seen us. Either going out or coming in.'

'You're sure?' This from the man with her.

'As sure as we can be,' one of the others replied. 'We're lucky the house next door is empty and old Macbride on the other side is both blind and deaf. He might be better dead as well. We can't afford to take any chances.'

Miranda shivered as they hustled her from the van and into the house, almost carrying her through the door, then down some steps. Though two of them were lifting her, one on either side of her, so her feet scarcely touched the ground, she could feel herself getting colder as they went down. Where were they taking her? Somewhere where she might never be found again? As they descended, Miranda felt a fresh wave of fear wash over her.

At last they hauled her through another door – this time one that creaked – into a place that smelled damp. Damp and of something else. She shivered involuntarily. Here she was pushed on to some kind of a bench and, though they still held her immobile, her hands were untied while they spoke to her harshly.

At least one of them did. 'We've untied your hands, Mrs Deakin, but until your husband pays a ransom, you'll have to stay here, I'm afraid. It's not exactly the Ritz but, don't worry, we'll tell him that when we contact him. No one will ever discover where you are and, unless your husband pays up, you haven't a hope of getting out. Oh, and by the way,' he added, getting up and walking towards the door, 'we've freed your hands. You can do the rest yourself when we're gone.'

Miranda didn't reply because she couldn't, but as soon as the door closed behind them she grabbed hold of the cloth covering her eyes and wrenched it off. In a similar fashion she dealt with the gag in her mouth. This wasn't as easy to remove as her blindfold, for a few moments she sat rubbing at the soreness of her lips. Then, blinking dazedly in an effort to fully restore her sight, she began looking around.

She was in a cellar. A damp one. She could hear water trickling in at one end of it, probably from a broken gutter or drainpipe. Judging from the look of the stone slabs on the floor and walls, the house she was in was an old one. Probably a mouldering old terrace, one such as could still be found in many cities in the United Kingdom. Built in the last century, they might survive far longer than many more modern ones. Sadly a lot of them, like this one, suffered from neglect, as betrayed by damp and dry rot and other equally unpalatable things. She remembered seeing a programme on television about urban decay and knew from that that most old houses possessed deep and capacious cellars. Above her head she saw one small light, scarcely bright enough to justify its name. There was no fire. Already she could feel the cold biting into her. How long, she wondered, did her captors expect her to survive in a place like this?

Still sitting where they left her, she wished she could have had a good look at the men who brought her here. They hadn't sounded very old. No more, perhaps, than in their twenties. She could be wrong, of course. Voices could be deceiving. Some senior citizens, on the radio, sounded more like youngsters in their teens. One thing did occur to her, though, now she had time to really think of it. The men who held her had what Alice would call good voices. They sounded as if they came from upper-class families. And while Miranda was aware that criminals came from all walks of life, she somehow had a feeling that these weren't hardened ones. Then she derided herself for being naïve. Intuition was a fine thing, but it mightn't always pay to take it too seriously. Plenty of very clever criminals today were still scarcely out of their cradles and she'd be wise to be wary of them.

Suddenly she looked at her watch. Though the men had searched her, as if looking for hidden weapons, they hadn't taken her watch. She guessed they were playing for higher stakes, but for a moment, though she knew it was ridiculous, she felt grateful. Brett had sent a car to take her to the airport at eight. It was now eight forty-five, which meant it must have taken her kidnappers approximately twenty minutes to convey her here from where they had picked her up. Which didn't really tell her anything, she realized bleakly. Feeling the excitement inside her subsiding as she became aware of how foolish she'd been to think it might, she felt like weeping.

Miranda did indeed feel hysterical tears begin to roll down her cheeks, but she wiped them away, telling herself she mustn't give in. Though she also began to shiver with cold and fright, she forced herself to continue considering the desperate situation she was in. The driver of Brett's car must, by this time, have recovered from the blow he had received and raised the alarm. Soon the police would be out in force, looking for her, and Brett would be informed. She didn't doubt he would be on his way here immediately and, even before he arrived, would be doing everything he could to find her. If only, she thought bitterly, to save his son. Even so, she hoped she would be found before her father heard what had happened to her. If he did and had another heart attack, would she ever be able to forgive herself? Feeling worse than ever, Miranda thought not.

Brett was in his office when word came through that Miranda had been kidnapped. He knew an instant sense of shock when his secretary put his chief security officer in the UK on to him and he told him what had happened. As soon as he heard, Brett felt fury rip through him, along with several other things he couldn't put a name to, but which immediately threw him. He knew an almost uncontrollable urge to shout at Smith, to ask him what the hell he had been doing to let such a thing happen. It was only with the greatest difficulty he didn't.

Smith said he'd informed the police, just as soon as he'd recovered consciousness after being hit over the head. 'I'm sorry, sir,' he reiterated. 'We were just driving quietly along when this van appeared, out of the blue, so to speak. I should have taken more men with me.'

'You didn't suspect anything?'

'Not right away, sir. I mean, it just looked like an innocent old van carrying men to work, as thousands would be doing at that time of the morning. It wasn't until it mounted the pavement to pass me and stopped directly in front of me that I realized it mightn't be.'

'What did you do then?' Brett knew he was biting his questions out, but his fury was so great that he considered Smith fortunate that the Atlantic was between them. If Smith had been here beside him, he might easily have taken hold of the man and half-killed him.

Smith answered quietly, as if he understood how Brett was feeling, 'I had to swerve and slam on the brakes. It couldn't have taken more than a few seconds. Even so, they were too quick for me. One of them must have jumped out of the van before it stopped, for I was just reaching for my mobile when they wrenched open the car door and drew a gun on me. Told me one move and I was dead.'

'And did you?'

'Sure, boss. Maybe I wouldn't have done if I'd had time to think about it. But with Mrs Deakin sitting in the back and suspecting the men must be after her, I couldn't just sit there and do nothing.'

'Then they hit you?'

'Knocked me out.'

'Did you get a look at them?'

'Yes,' Smith replied, 'but not a good one. They were wearing hoods and seemed young.'

'Nothing else?'

'No, boss. By the time I came around, both they and Mrs Deakin were gone. There was only this ransom note pinned to my coat, which I've already read out to you.'

'Did no one come to help you?'

'No, boss,' Smith said again. 'Just this old woman who helped me up and let me use her phone. The rest of the street, if they did see what happened, were probably too scared to. Repercussions, you know, that kind of thing. I should probably have had the sense to bring more men with me, but kidnapping doesn't seem to happen much in Birmingham. Not this kind of kidnapping, anyway.'

Brett had thought this himself, though he didn't say so. Like his father before him, he was a millionaire. If his assets were totalled up, he might be more than that, but never once had any of his family been victims of anything like this. 'You still have the note?' he asked.

'The police have,' Smith said. 'I kept a copy.'

'And they're out looking?'

Smith laughed, though it sounded humourless. 'You don't need to worry about that, Mr Deakin. They are searching every nook and cranny and I believe one of the hierarchy's waiting to have a word with you.'

Brett made a quick decision. It was actually one he had made as soon as he heard Miranda was kidnapped. 'Tell him not to bother. I'll be over there myself on Concorde in a few hours and can talk to him then. Meanwhile, Smith, if you've quite recovered from your mishap, do what you can. Some heads are for the chop if my wife isn't found immediately. Just pray it won't be yours.'

Brett still felt sick as he put the phone down. In fact, he felt as if he had been kicked really hard in the guts. Smith might think he was being unfair, but he couldn't be suffering as much as Miranda, he thought furiously.

Only one thought, however, dominated him now. How quickly could he get to her? He had to reach Birmingham as soon as possible. Even if she wasn't found immediately, if he was there she might sense he was near her. If she had access to a TV or radio, she might even hear or see him.

Swiftly, with the speed and precision he was famous for, he arranged to take the place of a man he had been sending over to London that afternoon to deal with some pressing business. Nothing was more important than Miranda, though had someone suggested that a few hours ago, Brett realized bitterly he wouldn't have believed it. Even now he didn't know if he really wished to. The pain he was experiencing now was unbelievable.

Once in the air, he tried to relax but couldn't. Fear for Miranda's safety wouldn't allow him. He tried to tell himself that the police would be doing everything possible. Birmingham had a very well-trained and up-to-date police force – he had a great respect for them. At the same time he knew that some crimes were difficult to solve. The men who had taken Miranda might have hidden her away somewhere where no one might ever find her. In a city the size of Birmingham, there could be hundreds of places where people no longer went: derelict buildings and long abandoned factories, old railway tracks, even old drainage systems – the list was never ending. Places which might make people even in perfect health soon fall ill if they were incarcerated in them. And while there might be nothing wrong with Miranda's health now, she was pregnant. What, he wondered desperately, would she do without any medical help if she began to lose the baby?

Fear, such as Brett had never known before, began to assault him, as he imagined her alone and frightened with no one to turn to. Suddenly he knew that, though he didn't want Miranda to lose the baby, what mattered most was her. He would pay the ransom, do anything, give more. Here he paused, frowning imperceptibly. Two hundred thousand? Whoever was demanding it must know it was peanuts to a man like him. Why not a couple of million? Or did they think a small sum might be easier to get away with? And if so, why? It occurred to Brett that the men who had kidnapped Miranda might be amateurs, working on the theory that it was better to start in a small way. He tried to figure out who might be the most dangerous, amateurs or professionals but, being unable to reach any definite conclusions, only finished up cursing impotently under his breath.

Whatever category the kidnappers were in, he knew he would pay whatever they demanded. At the same time, he realized this might not guarantee Miranda's release. No matter how well planned a kidnapping was, the kidnappers had to pick up the ransom money. In an attempt to escape apprehension, they usually made it a condition that the pickup person be allowed to return to his or her destination before the prisoner was freed. What usually happened – or so Brett had heard – was that the kidnapper rarely returned to where the victim was being held. They escaped elsewhere, leaving the unfortunate victim to get out the best way they could. In many cases, because of the restraints put on them, they were unable to. And those who were found often suffered too much from exposure and hunger ever to recover.

Brett Deakin was a man who seldom prayed, but he did so then.

Eve Martin heard about the kidnapping over the radio and read about it in the evening newspaper.

Miranda Deakin, wife of Brett Deakin, a prominent businessman, had been kidnapped. The police were asking anyone with information, or who had seen anything, to come forward or to give them a ring, no matter how trivial they thought it was.

There were more details, but Eve didn't pay much attention. Why should she? she asked herself defiantly. Hadn't Brett Deakin messed up her life by letting her think he cared for her, then gone and married someone else? Some little fool who'd allowed herself to be kidnapped. If he was having a hard time, didn't it serve him right?

Unlike her, though, Eve doubted he would be suffering very much. She was the one doing that. All life ever dealt her was blow after blow. Brett Deakin, once so important to her, no longer was. But since she had stopped accepting anything from him, one would have thought fate would have given her some kind of recompense. But like hell it did! It never paused in its obvious determination to take more and more away from her. It made her sometimes feel she'd be better off dead. Sometimes she wished she was.

Eve stared moodily in front of her. Since the time at Christmas, when Simon Wentworth eavesdropped on her talk with Gaby, she had only seen him once. That was at her father's funeral. He was among the mourners, but hadn't so much as spoken to her. He hadn't even come to the graveside. After the service in church he had hurried off.

Some people must never have heard of forgiveness, she thought surlily, rather than remember how it had hurt. Okay, she had spoken disparagingly of him over the telephone, but did one short sentence – well, maybe one or two, but that was all – justify cutting someone off completely? Eve choose to forget it could have been the implications behind her short sentences, more than what she had actually said, that were responsible for Simon's reactions. No man liked being used and made a fool of. This was a fact Eve liked to ignore.

Eve was more inclined to look self-righteously at her attempts since then to put the past, in the shape of Brett Deakin, behind her, especially when Brett's sister made no further attempt to get in touch with her, to continue their vendetta against his marriage. She refused to admit that Simon Wentworth's contempt had anything to do with it. She'd decided, with an impulsiveness born of bitter anger, to cut Brett completely out of her life. Preferably not to see him again.

First, however, she was determined to have some kind of revenge on him for what he had done to her. Or what she imagined he had done to her. Convinced she was able to, and still blindly holding him responsible for Simon's desertion of her, among other things, she set about it.

To start with, she had agreed with her father that the bungalow they lived in was too large for them. She'd suggested they hand it back to Brett and buy a smaller place instead. The only stipulation she made, though she didn't offer any explanation, was that it was not on one of the estates Simon Wentworth was helping build.

'Are you sure?' John Martin had asked somewhat incredulously. The large garden here was slowly exhausting him, but Eve liked it tidy. She had rejected all his efforts to persuade her to move. She'd always refused to even consider leaving it so that now, when she suggested it, he could scarcely believe it.

'Certain,' Eve said, and so emphatically that John did. 'If we can manage it, that is.'

'Of course we can,' John replied. 'I still have the money from the house I sold after your accident. There may not be enough to buy a huge mansion, but there should be enough to purchase a smaller one.'

Another house, especially as they didn't have one to sell, had been easy to find. Within two weeks, they were installed in a two-up and two-down, Eve having told her father she was well enough now to cope with stairs. Secretly she had decided on a two-storey house rather than a bungalow, thinking it would provide more privacy. John Martin didn't tell his daughter that, even though the house was a modest one, he'd had to take out a mortgage for some of it as his savings, particularly after he cancelled the allowance Brett had made him, had gone rapidly down. That, he'd thought, could wait for another day. Little had he known then how few more days he had left to him.

Once settled in, Eve wrote a triumphant note to Brett, addressing it to his New York offices, where she knew he would be sure to get it. In it she said she had left the keys of his bungalow with the agent who'd overseen it. She told him she didn't need either the house or the allowance he made her any more. She told him she preferred being independent and, though still far from well, would try and find a job. She finished by more or less saying how she hoped none of this would send her to an early grave.

It pleased Eve enormously, in a twisted kind of way, to do do this. She felt almost as good as she might have done had she actually been standing in front of him and telling him where he could go to. She refused to think that her letter wouldn't bother him one way or another. Instead, she fixed it firmly in her head that it might cause him such a volume of remorse that he might never completely recover.

Eventually, Eve realized reluctantly that her grand gesture might only have hurt herself, as nothing had gone right since then. The smallness of their new house irritated her; she'd grown used to having plenty of room. Then she missed the allowance Brett had made her far more than she'd thought she would. She also missed her car, which she had felt forced to return to him. Her father let her borrow his, but it wasn't the same as having her own, and while John did give her some money each week, it wasn't nearly as much as what she'd had before. When she complained, however, John had reminded her unhappily how they now had their own bills to pay, as well, he said, as having to put something aside for possible repairs and decorating. And on top of this, there were the daily household costs of food, newspapers, etcetera. If Eve had been able to find a job, he said once, it might have been easier.

Eve, although she had told Brett she was going to find a job, had no intention of doing so. She had become lazy over the past ten years and even the thought of having to get up and go to work each morning horrified her. Instead she began using credit cards to pay for the goods and services she considered she needed, and hoped to be able to cajole her father into settling any money she owed on them at the end of each month. Though he grumbled a little over the lack of it, she believed he had more hidden away than he let on about. He was always too careful over money to be short of it now. She knew he was still curious as to why she no longer went out with Simon Wentworth – why Simon no longer came to see them – but she stubbornly refused to talk about him. If Simon had chosen to disappear from her life as abruptly as he had entered it, then she wasn't going to start on a lot of what might have to be lengthy, fabricated explanations. And while she knew her father wasn't a fool and might have his suspicions, she didn't think he would ever come near to guessing the truth.

Little did Eve know then that her father had little time left to guess anything. They were in the new house only a week when, one morning when he didn't bring her, as he usually did, an early-morning cup of tea, she went into his room and found him fast asleep. It was only an hour later, when she couldn't wake him, that she realised he wasn't just asleep, he was dead. Utterly shocked, she had called his doctor who, after examining him, had merely shaken his head.

For about the first time in her rather selfish life, Eve felt a surge of remorse. 'I should have called you an hour ago,' she cried. 'I might have saved his life. I thought he was sleeping and would let him lie in. I believed the move we did lately must have tired him . . .'

The doctor halted her hysterical outburst, but he did so kindly. 'It wouldn't have made any difference, my dear,' he said. 'Your father has been dead for quite a while. At a guess I would say he died about midnight, so you've nothing to rebuke yourself with.'

Maybe not, Eve thought, but she couldn't seem to think straight. The doctor, realizing this, took one look at her white, stricken face and drew her gently down the stairs into the living-room.

'There will be a postmortem, Eve,' he said, after finding her some brandy and making her drink it. 'That will answer most of your questions. I've been your father's doctor for years and he's never given me any reason to suspect he didn't enjoy very good health. The last time I examined him, when he complained about his back, I advised him to stop doing so much gardening, but his blood pressure was normal and there was certainly nothing wrong with his heart.'

The postmortem on John Martin merely seemed to confirm what the doctor had already told her. There was no evidence of an overdose or poison or anything which might have caused sudden death. John had apparently just died peacefully in his sleep, like elderly people sometimes did.

His gardening, Eve thought dully – she had insisted that the one at Brett's house was always kept in good condition while refusing to help with it herself – had it worn him out? Or had it done more good than harm? She remembered the doctor saying that the postmortem would answer most of her questions. Had his words contained a hidden innuendo? Had he implied there were ones she must answer herself? During the past ten years, when she'd refused to think of herself as anything but an invalid, she had sensed his hidden disapproval. She might have imagined it, of course, but whether she had or not, though he had fetched and carried for her a lot, no one was going to hold her responsible for her father's death! Just let anyone try to, she thought angrily.

Her second shock came on seeing Simon Wentworth at the funeral. The sight of his tall figure – after she recovered her breath – seemed to add to the turmoil she was experiencing, making her feel worse. To begin with, she had wondered if he was there to comfort her. Did he wish to apologize for being so brusque the last time she saw him? Was he going to ask her to forgive him? While the vicar conducted the service, she began rehearsing exactly what she would say to him. He couldn't expect her to welcome him back with open arms. The best he could hope for was that she would do so gradually. She didn't know what to think when he left without even trying to speak to her. After paying his last respects to John Martin, he made no attempt to heal the breach between himself and John's daughter.

That, unfortunately, was not the last blow to fall on Eve's hapless head during that period. When her father's will, made some years ago, was read, he left what he had to her, which she immediately discovered was precisely nothing. Or very little. Even the house was mortgaged. Eve had thought he'd had enough put away from the sale of his old one to pay for a new one. She found, however, that as he'd refused to take money from Brett for far longer than she'd known, in recent years he had had to dip heavily into his savings to supplement his pension with which he paid for their food and all the extras he was forever buying for Eve. To her horror, Eve realized she was virtually penniless since she had no income of her own and John's pension died with him. A part of it might have survived for a wife, but not for a daughter.

Returning from the solicitors to the house, Eve was so consumed by anger against her father that she could scarcely contain it. On her way home she had called at the agents who held what she supposed now was her mortgage, but they only confirmed what she'd already been told – that John had owed more on the house than she could ever manage to repay. The monthly figures alone were frightening.

Not even after getting home and making herself a cup of tea did things look any better. She would have to get rid of the house, put it straight on the market. But this was only one of the now indisputable facts which began plaguing her.

If there was anything left after selling the house and settling any debts, it might only be enough to enable her to rent a miserable room. As there was nothing wrong with her, she knew she couldn't hope to get invalidity benefit, or anything like it. Her uncooperative doctor would never sign a certificate. The most she might get was social security while she looked for a job. It made Eve feel sick even to think of it. It also made her begin to realize, if reluctantly, what she might have lost over the past ten years by hiding behind deceit and Brett's benevolence and refusing to work.

In the end Eve was lucky as far as work was concerned, though this didn't prevent her railing against what life had done to her. She didn't expect to find a job, but with the help of the impressive references she had kept from her last employers, it was only a week before she did. True, it was just a temporary one in large manufacture's office – and a lowly one at that. But the salary would be enough to buy food and was more than she might expect to get from social services.

Once she found work, the other things she had to do seemed to proceed quite smoothly. The house was sold, with a minimum of fuss, to none other than her next-door neighbour, whose daughter and her family suddenly decided to come home from Hong Kong and wanted a place of their own.

'They will probably move on again,' the neighbour, a kindly woman, said. 'This will give them a chance to take their time and have a look around. And, as the house is new, if they do, they shouldn't lose too much money on it. And where are you going, my dear?' she asked Eve. 'It was a shame about your poor father . . .'

Eve agreed, briefly. 'I'm actually trying to find a room somewhere,' she'd replied, feeling too embarrassed over her straitened circumstances to try and explain them.

The woman looked surprised. 'Why, do you know, dear,' she exclaimed, 'if you aren't too fussy about the district, my husband has a small flat which has just been vacated. It wouldn't have suited my daughter – too small, for one thing, having just a small kitchenette, lounge and bedroom. But as it is in a rather rundown neighbourhood, it would be cheap. Of course . . .' she smiled apologetically '. . . you may be looking for something quite different?'

A few weeks ago, Eve wouldn't have spared the flat, if one could call it that, a second glance. Yet, after looking at several others in the city, she began to realize that, though describing it as rundown was being kind to it, she would be lucky to find anything else she could afford.

She felt the same way over her job. Jobs were scarce, or she would never have taken the one she did. For the first week she hated it then, to her surprise, as her old, and what once was above-average, ability returned, she actually began feeling interested. There were so many things in this large firm's office that she saw could be improved, but she knew that even if they kept her on, it might be a long time before she got promotion and was in any position to do anything about it.

The nights were the worst. She missed her father more than she ever thought she would. And Simon, whom she'd begun thinking of a lot, though she tried to convince herself it was in anger. Nevertheless, try as she might, she wasn't able to forget him. Not even after she saw a picture of him with a glamorous woman companion in the same paper where she'd read about Brett's wife being kidnapped, and the caption below asking if an engagement was imminent?

The woman, whoever Mrs Anstane was, was welcome to him, Eve thought savagely, as she flung the newspaper into her wastepaper basket. Unhappily, though she tried to ignore it, this did nothing to alleviate the feeling of pain that rushed through her. Men just weren't worth wasting any kind of time over, she decided vindictively. In future she would concentrate on getting her working skills together again and finding a better job.

CHAPTER 20

The first thing Brett Deakin did when he reached Birmingham was to call on the police. He knew the city police well and had every confidence in them, but like many people facing a major catastrophe in their lives, this still didn't stop him wondering if they were doing enough to find Miranda. He had to curb his impatience and remind himself firmly that it was only hours, rather than days, since she had disappeared.

Brett Deakin was well known in the city. He was respected as a businessman who never forgot he was born there and, though he now lived in New York, still gave generously to its worthy causes. Apart from this, he was considered a man to be reckoned with. There weren't many, it had been heard in the streets, who would be brave enough to try and kidnap his wife.

The police, however, always did everything they could, regardless of who they were, to help people in trouble. They had not found Mrs Deakin yet, they told Brett, before discussing her kidnapping with him. They agreed, when he asked their opinion about it, that the size of the ransom demanded was unusual, and that it could be a gang who hadn't done such a thing before, who might believe they had a better chance of getting away with it if they asked for a smaller amount. And while Brett had agreed to pay what they asked, nothing had been heard yet about how the kidnappers intended to collect it or what would happen when they did.

Meanwhile, the police were working flat out to try and trace them. They had been to see Miranda's father, who hadn't been able to tell them very much, but they had officers and detectives everywhere with plenty of back-up available should anyone discover anything suspicious. The public were helping. They'd already had numerous phone calls from people who had either seen a blue van or knew where one was kept, but all the vehicles investigated so far had failed to turn anything up. Finding a suspect vehicle was always difficult if there was no registration number to go by. And it was more than likely, the police said, that after Miranda was taken to the place where the kidnappers held her, the van was disposed of.

After his meeting with the police, Brett went to Well House. He'd rang there immediately he heard Miranda was kidnapped. He had spoken to her aunt and Alice, though clearly shocked, had promised to break the news to her brother herself. It was better that Harry should hear it from her, she agreed, rather than through the media, or even the police who, she realized, would almost certainly be coming to see them.

On his way to Well House, driven this time by another of his security men – the one who had been

300

with Miranda was still not recovered from the blow to his head – Brett was consumed again by feelings of frustration. Though the police promised to keep in constant touch, they didn't suggest he should do anything himself.

'If you wish to pay it, have the ransom money available, Brett, in case they contact us,' the Detective Inspector, who knew him well, told him. 'And if, by some remote chance, they go straight to you, ring us immediately. These men – as demonstrated by the way they knocked out your security guard – are dangerous. Whatever you do, don't be tempted to play the lone hero and tackle them yourself.'

Fat chance he might get to do that, Brett thought cynically. Kidnappers didn't usually have the nerve to come face to face with the families of their victims. They usually did any negotiating from a safe distance and rejected any attempts to persuade them to do otherwise.

Brett had never felt so utterly helpless. He acknowledged that the police had given him good advice, but how could they expect him just to sit still and do nothing while they searched for his wife? In a city the size of Birmingham, of course, trying to find Miranda might be like looking for a needle in a haystack. And then, as the police reluctantly mentioned, she might not be in Birmingham. Nothing had been heard from her kidnappers since she was taken. She could, apparently, be in London or anywhere. Though the ports and airports had been alerted, clever men seemed capable of getting through almost anything. They could feel sure of perhaps only one thing: if the men were desperate for money, it wouldn't be long before they heard from them again.

Brett hoped they was right. He regretted for the hundreth time having insisted that Miranda came home when she'd wanted to stay. Or that he had not come over and escorted her back to New York personally. But these were only two of the things he regretted. There was a lot he dared not even think about. Things he knew he must put at least temporarily out of his mind if he wished to remain sane enough to take advantage of any opportunity that might arise for him to help her.

The police, as they'd told Brett, had already been to Well House, and Harry Ferris, though composed, was understandably upset by Miranda's kidnapping and subsequent disappearance.

Miranda's aunt answered the door when Brett knocked and spoke to him in the hall for a few minutes before taking him in to see her brother.

'I called his doctor and, like you, he thought I should tell Harry straight away,' Alice said, after greeting him. 'There was no way we could have kept it from him and, if he hadn't known until the police arrived, the shock might have been even greater. I feel devastated myself and Harry is, after all, her father. It doesn't seem possible but it must be worse for him.'

Brett felt at a loss for words as he saw a tear slide slowly down Alice's cheek. 'I'll speak to him.' He laid a sympathetic hand on her shoulder. 'It's probably debatable which of us feels worst.'

'Is there no news?' Alice asked urgently, when Brett told her where he had been. 'It's been such a dreadful day.'

Which just about summed it up, Brett thought bleakly, only he might have put it in stronger language. 'The police are doing all they can, but there's nothing yet. I want to get out there and look for her myself, but they won't hear of it. They seemed to insinuate that I might only get in the way and would rather I stayed where they can find me, if it is necessary.'

Alice looked at him, into eyes full of steely impatience he wasn't trying to hide. She guessed it was the first time in his life Brett Deakin had felt so frustrated. 'I think it might be wiser to take their advice, no matter how hard it is for you,' she said. 'The police – or so we get told in crime novels – usually have access to information we don't have, and I'm sure Miranda will soon be found.' This last she added more optimistically than she felt.

'She wanted to stay here longer. I should have let her,' Brett muttered, as if he wasn't really listening to what she was saying.

Alice replied quietly, 'We usually blame ourselves, Brett, when something like this happens. Harry has been doing it all morning, but I don't think it helps to reproach oneself too much.'

Harry, though, appeared to be as unconvinced over this as his son-in-law when Alice took Brett into the lounge where Harry was sitting staring unhappily at the fire.

After Brett had a word with him, he said without preamble, 'Both Alice and I wanted to go to the airport to see her off, but she wouldn't hear of it. Seemed to think I wasn't well enough and that Alice might get lost. We wish now we hadn't listened. If we had been with her, none of this might have happened.'

'Just as well you weren't with her,' Brett said grimly, as he and Alice sat down beside him. 'If only because you are you and not me. If I'd been there, I might have been able to do something, though I doubt if they would have tried anything if both Smith and I had been around.'

'But that's what I mean,' Harry broke in stubbornly. 'Another man!'

Brett shook his head. 'Aren't you forgetting something?' he asked. 'I'm a lot younger than you are, Harry, while Alice would just have been another woman. You might both have been killed, or at least badly hurt.'

Alice didn't know that she liked being described as just another woman but she let it pass. Harry, she'd noticed, had looked like a man with a weight taken off his shoulders when he saw Brett, and she felt so relieved that he was here herself that she might have forgiven him anything.

'I'm sure Brett's right,' she told her brother firmly, as he looked ready to renew his protests. 'Neither of us would have been up to it, and if you'd landed yourself in hospital again, how far would that have got us?'

'All the same, I wish I could have done something,' Harry said. 'Just sitting here, wondering what is happening to her, might kill me quicker than anything!'

'Nonsense!' Alice rebuked him almost sharply. 'At least this way you will be here for her when she does get home again.'

Brett nodded at Harry in agreement. Though he could understand how he felt, for he was feeling much the same way himself, he appreciated how Alice was doing her best to keep her brother's spirits up.

'Alice tells me the police were here,' he said.

'Yes, this morning.' Harry Ferris sat up straighter and looked a little brighter. 'Les Spanklehurst is an old friend of mine. If anyone can find her, he will.'

'Were you able to help them?' Brett didn't say he had already been told Ferris hadn't been able to.

'I don't think so,' Harry replied uncertainly. 'They asked a lot of questions, but I'm afraid I couldn't tell them very much.'

'What sort of questions?'

'Oh . . .' Harry looked vague, as if he had already forgotten some of them. 'You know the kind of thing. How long was she here? And why? Was it just an ordinary visit? Exactly what time she left? How many people, other than ourselves, knew she was returning to New York this morning . . .?'

As Harry paused – Brett noticed he had to do so frequently in order to regain his composure – he frowned thoughtfully. Before Alice could take up where her brother left off, as she was clearly going to, he asked quickly, 'How many people did know she was leaving this morning? Have you any idea?'

Alice shook her head. 'I don't think there can have been very many. Hilda, our maid, has been off with

305

the flu, and Mrs Fellows – housekeeper,' she explained briefly to Brett's questioning brows, 'wouldn't say anything. There was your driver, of course, but you say he is a security man?'

Brett nodded. 'It was early and he didn't mention what he was going to do. He thought he would be back before the others turned up at his office.'

'And you can trust him?'

'Smith has worked for me for years. I've never had any reason not to.' Brett paused as another thought struck him. 'Did Miranda go out much while she was here, seeing friends, things like that?'

'No,' Alice said. 'Mind you, she was going to, if she could have stayed a little longer. But, as it was, she spent most of the time with me and her father.'

'There's nothing in her room? I mean, no clue that she might have talked to someone?'

'If there had been, I'm sure the police would have found it.'

'They were there?' Brett felt startled, though he knew that in cases like this it could be normal procedure. It was essential that they missed nothing that might help the victim. And occasionally it was the smallest of clues, which to the untrained eye might seem insignificant, that proved vital.

'They certainly were!' Alice answered his question drily. 'Went through everything with a fine-toothed comb, but found nothing, and they must have been there well over an hour.'

Yet someone, somewhere, must have known something, Brett thought grimly. Someone must have gotten hold of information that Miranda's kidnappers had been quick to use.

He heard Harry Ferris muttering something tersely under his breath about being so useless, then Alice asking anxiously if he would stay.

'It would be easier for us if you did,' she said. 'We feel terribly cut off, just sitting here waiting for the phone to ring and almost dreading answering it when it does for fear it is bad news.'

Harry nodded in agreement. 'Even if you weren't here much, if you were here some of the time it would be a help.'

Brett would rather have stayed elsewhere. He doubted that he would sleep again, apart from on his feet, until Miranda was found, but having seen the look of relief on Harry's face when he walked in, he realized it might be cruel, at this point, to desert them. Or seem to desert them. Alice was obviously putting on a brave face but, whatever the outcome, she would come through it. Her brother, on the other hand, might not. Although he might not feel as near to Miranda as he would if he was in the heart of the city, he knew what she would have wished him to do.

'Of course I'll stay.' He glanced at the clock. 'It's getting late, anyway, and I don't suppose I would be of much use to anybody, prowling the streets in the dark. I'll have to go out tomorrow, though.' He didn't think he needed to explain why.

'We've been so frightened that Miranda might lose the baby.' Alice poured them each a drink after speaking to the housekeeper who said dinner would be ready in half an hour. Giving Brett his, she added, 'I'm praying she will be rescued in time to prevent such a thing happening.'

Brett felt a chill run down his spine as Alice spoke. 'The baby is important, but not as much as Miranda,' he said harshly, then wondered why Ferris glanced at him doubtfully. Had Miranda said something to him about the regrettable state of their marriage? He didn't think she would and he hoped he could put things right between them before she was tempted to. He had a lot of explaining to do – to Miranda as well as himself, but he had to find her first. That much was clear, even if some matters, such as why he had allowed certain things to cause him so much aggro in the past, were not.

At eleven, when he couldn't settle, he asked Alice for a key and spent the next few hours driving around the city. Though he realized that trying to find Miranda this way was no job for someone who didn't really know how to go about it, it was almost five in the morning before he gave up and returned to Well House. Here, after making himself some coffee in the kitchen, he had a shower, then went to Miranda's room. He had been there before he went out and, like the police, had searched it with Harry Ferris's permission, but found nothing. He'd thought it would help him now just to sit on her bed, but when he did all he could think of were the years she must have spent there in her wheelchair and how she must have suffered because of it.

When he thought he could bear it no longer he got up and went quietly, so as not to disturb anyone, along to the room where Miranda had once shown him she'd kept her wheelchairs. Alice had told him over dinner, the evening before, how Miranda had taken the opportunity to dispose of two of them to a well-known charity while she was here. She had kept the third one, Alice said, as it needed some attention and she would arrange to have it seen to the next time she was over.

Brett wasn't sure why he had a sudden desire to see it at this particular moment, unless he'd hoped, like sitting on her bed, it might make him feel closer to her. As soon as he opened the door he saw it. It was standing in front of the window, where she'd probably sat for a few minutes looking out over the gardens where she must have played as a child. Had she been thinking that her own child might play there one day? More than likely, Brett thought heavily.

Refusing to believe there could be anything to prevent such a thing happening, he walked slowly over to the abandoned chair. It wasn't until he reached it that he saw the small crumpled piece of paper lying on the floor just beyond it. It looked like something that had been accidently dropped or thrown away.

Brett didn't know why he bent down and picked it up, when it was so small he might not even have noticed it. It must have been, he decided afterwards, his instincts telling him it was important. Yet when he straightened it out and looked at it he felt immediately disappointed.

While he thought he recognized Miranda's handwriting, it was merely a brief memo and he frowned as his eyes skimmed over it. Ring Pam, it said. Tell her can't come to her party tonight as am leaving in the morning.

Nothing else. Yet as Brett stared at it, reading it again, a sudden feeling of excitement hit him. He tried to control it, tried warning himself he couldn't be sure Miranda had written the note as, when it came to her handwriting, he hadn't seen enough of it to be certain he wasn't mistaken. It might easily have been scribbled by someone else. The people who'd collected her other wheelchairs, for instance?

All the same, he decided to show it to Alice and Harry though he doubted they would be up as it was only – he glanced at his watch – six-thirty.

There was no sign of Harry, but Alice was in the breakfast room setting the table. As usual she was impeccably dressed, even at that hour of the morning, but she looked as pale and as worn as she had done the day before. 'I couldn't sleep,' she confessed. 'I heard you come in. I suppose it's no use asking if you found anything?' When Brett shook his head she said. 'You haven't slept either?'

'It would have been a waste of time even trying to,' he said flatly. 'But I'm glad you are up as there's something I want to show you.' Spreading the note he was holding on the table in front of her, he said, 'I found this in the room where Miranda kept her wheelchairs. I don't really know why I went there, but could she have written it, do you think. And, if so, who is Pam?'

Alice glanced quickly at the note, then at him, then back to the note again as she fumbled to put on her glasses to study it. 'That's Miranda's writing, all right,' she said. 'And Pam . . .' She paused, frowning thoughtfully. 'It could be Pamela Brent-Nordon. They used to be good friends, though I haven't heard of Miranda being in touch with her lately.'

Brett said, 'It could be a mistake, or something Miranda wrote years ago. She could have found it in a drawer she was sorting out and meant to dispose of it. I'd like to speak to this Pamela, though. Do you know her telephone number?'

Alice, still studying the note, lifted her head and looked at him. 'Well, not offhand, but I'm sure it must be in the study. Miranda usually kept her friends' numbers there; she used to say it was easier than going to her room all the time. Pamela, I believe, has her own flat,' Alice said vaguely. 'But as for her number, if Miranda hasn't got it and it's unlisted, I don't know where you will find it.'

It was, however, in Miranda's telephone and address book in the study. 'She took a duplicate one to New York. She thought it would be handy to leave this one here,' Alice explained, finding it for him surprisingly quickly.

To Brett's relief, the number he wanted was there. 'I'll have to use your phone,' he said, asking permission while already picking it up and dialling.

He got through but, when no one answered, he glanced at Alice, who was hovering anxiously. 'She doesn't seem to be there.'

'Probably still in bed.'

Brett was just about to give up when the receiver at the other end was picked up and a slurred voice mumbled, 'Do you know what time it is! Who the hell is it . . .?'

Charming, Brett thought cynically as he checked he was speaking to the right person. 'I'm Brett Deakin, Miranda's husband. Miranda Ferris.'

'Oh, my God!' Pamela exclaimed, clearly shocked from her half-awake state. 'I say, I'm very sorry – it's so early. What a terrible thing to have happened! Poor Miranda, I didn't realize,' she gabbled on. 'Have they found her . . .?'

'No,' Brett answered briefly. 'But I've just found a note in her handwriting, in which she reminds herself to ring and tell you she wouldn't be able to come to your party which, according to the note, was the night before last. Of course, it could have been written a long time ago, but I wanted to check. Do you know anything about it?'

'Why – yes,' Pamela replied slowly. 'I do. I actually bumped into Miranda in town a few days ago, when she was doing some shopping. Just something she wanted for her father and aunt, I believe. She couldn't stop, but before she rushed off, I suddenly remembered the party I was giving on the night you mention, and she agreed to come. At least she promised to try to. I was disappointed when she rang and said she couldn't as she was going back to New York the following morning.'

'Did you mention you'd been expecting her to any of your guests? And tell them why she couldn't come?' Brett asked tersely.

Pamela hesitated. 'I suppose I told quite a few,' she confessed. 'After all, a lot of people know her, even if she was out of circulation for a while.'

'Would you remember who you told, Miss Brent-Nordon?'

'Well, it was just a sort of drinks party – drinks and snacks with a few old friends,' she added defensively. 'And you know how it is. Tell someone something and you can't guarantee they won't blab it to someone else. There weren't that many there, though. Daddy's been insisting lately that I cut down. He's going to pay my rent and a few more things, but I have to find the rest myself. Do parents have any idea of the cost of living these days? Anyway, I only had about twenty here that evening – maybe thirty with hangers-on – so he couldn't grumble over that! But I can't remember specifically who I told about Miranda leaving . . .'

'But you did tell some?'

'Haven't I just said? Listen, Mr Deakin . . .'

Before she could ask, as she was obviously going to, why he kept on about it and why it was important, Brett thanked her and rang off. He wasn't sure, at this stage, that he could have answered such questions himself, or even wished to try to, but as soon as he cut the connection he picked up the phone again and rang the police.

CHAPTER 21

If Miranda had known how Brett was following his hunches, without any real proof that he'd come up with anything that might help to find her, she might have felt even more despondent than she did when she woke up that morning. Not that she had slept much. She'd been so cold that, despite the small paraffin fire her kidnappers brought her, she hadn't been able to. The previous day, after her kidnappers left her, she had walked around and around the cellar, trying to find a way out, but the door was locked and so substantial that she knew she would never be able to escape without help. Though she was thankful for the warm coat she was wearing, it soon proved not enough to keep out the cold and damp. Almost immediately she began shivering and prayed that someone would bring her some form of heating.

It wasn't until midday that the door of her prison, as she began to think of it, had opened and one of her kidnappers came in. He still wore a mask, as the others had done, but she thought from his voice he was the one who had sat with her in the back of the van.

'I've brought you some tea and soup,' he said. 'Haven't a lot, even for ourselves.'

'Why are you keeping me here?' she cried as soon as she saw him. 'The police will soon find me and then where will you be?'

'The police won't find you – they haven't a clue!' he muttered disparagingly as he dumped the tray he was carrying on the bench beside her. 'Neither will your husband,' he added menacingly, 'unless he pays what we are asking.'

'A – ransom?'

'You can't be that naïve!' he exclaimed incredulously, 'You didn't think we were keeping you here for the fun of it, did you?'

'But my husband is in America!'

'He won't be for long.'

'How do you know?'

'Well, you're his wife, aren't you?' The youth scuffed his feet on the stone flags on the floor. 'He's bound to come running when he hears what's happened to you.'

Maybe, Miranda thought to herself. 'You can't be sure,' she said.

'When you've only been married a few months!' the young man replied. 'Or so your friends told . . . What I mean,' he said, after breaking off abruptly, 'is that if you'd been married for years, he might have said we were welcome to you – but you don't get that kind of chat from a practically brand-new bridegroom.'

Little did they know! 'How much are you asking?' she'd asked tonelessly.

'Only a few measly thou,' he shrugged. 'And don't

say it's too much and we can't expect him to pay it. Not when we know he's rolling in it.'

Miranda thought for a minute, though she tried to be quick as she suspected he had his orders not to spend much time with her. 'If he did agree to pay, how are you going to collect it?'

The youth hesitated; she could almost see him frowning through his mask. 'That's not going to be as easy to work out as we thought it would be. Frank's still not sure of the best way to go about it . . .'

'Frank?'

The youth started, said quickly. 'That's not his real name. You don't use real names in a game like this.'

It didn't seem like a game to Miranda. It was her turn to frown. They sounded, even to someone with her limited knowledge of the average criminal, like a bunch of amateurs. Who might, she reminded herself, be just as dangerous, in their way, as more experienced criminals.

'Look,' she'd suggested, 'why don't you let me go? I would see you got paid, whatever you are asking, and that no one will prosecute you.'

'Ha!' The youth laughed mockingly. 'Do you think the police would swallow that?'

Miranda didn't and almost shook her head. For her baby's sake she had to keep trying. 'It could be worth thinking about, though. You could . . .' she searched desperately for a feasible plan '. . . simply free me, then disappear for a while and my husband would pay you privately.'

'You'd guarantee it, huh?'

'I would.'

316

'Without consulting your husband?'

'I'm sure Brett would do anything!'

'In that case, maybe we should up the ransom?'

Miranda sank back on the hard bench defeatedly, her shoulders brushing the dank wall behind her. Was she only making things worse? If the attitude of the youth in front of her was anything to go by, she wasn't making much progress. He was clearly laughing at her and just waiting to see what she would come out with next. She might be wiser to shut up, if she couldn't think of something he might be prepared to listen to.

Dully she said, 'You'd better be quick if you wish to do that for I'm sure I'll soon be dead if I have to stay here much longer. I've only been here a few hours but I'm already frozen with cold.'

'What a bloody shame.' The youth spoke carelessly.

'Couldn't you bring me a fire of some kind? A small one would do.'

'We don't have any fires,' he replied, 'except the one that's a fixture in the lounge and we can only afford to run that so long. We aren't all millionaires, like your husband.'

After saying that, he turned abruptly and went out, slamming the door behind him, grinding the key in the lock as if suddenly comparing himself with what he considered were the have-alls of the world and not finding the comparison to his liking.

To Miranda's surprise, however, he was back in just over an hour with what he informed her was a paraffin heater. While he was away, she had consumed the soup and tea, but the warmth she'd

317

derived from them hadn't lasted long. The temperature of the cellar was so low that a constant supply of even the hottest of food would have made little real difference.

She watched now as the youth put the fire down in front of her and lighted it. 'It burns paraffin,' he said. 'I was lucky to find it and you're lucky to get it as most are either gas or electric, which we have no means of plugging in down here.'

Miranda wondered if anyone had seen him buying it? Then she realised how foolish she was being. Plenty of people would be purchasing heaters at this time of the year. Though spring might officially be almost here, the weather might still be cold for weeks.

It seemed to Miranda that she was beginning to pin her hopes on the most improbable things. How long, she wondered, did it take for someone in her situation to lose control of their minds? It couldn't be long, she thought, looking at the dripping walls, if they were kept in a place like this. Dreaming up unlikely means of rescue could be one of the first signs.

The heater, as she'd suspected, wasn't big enough to warm her much. It might not be even worthy of its name. The glow from it was probably no more than what could be achieved from two or three candles and the heat from it even less. After the youth departed, she wished she'd had the nerve to physically attack him. If she had not been pregnant, she knew she would have tried to, but she had to think of the baby. If she'd attacked one of her kidnappers, he might easily have shouted for the others who could have been violent. They could have knocked her about and hurt her badly, and then what might have happened? It could have been the end of her, or at least her pregnancy.

After this visit, the youth came only once more that day and that was to bring her more soup and tea.

Some time before dawn she must have fallen into an exhausted sleep and when she woke it was seven o'clock and she was feeling ill. Ill and half-frozen. The fire, she saw, was out. It must have ran out of fuel during the night. She wondered if it was the fumes that came from it that were making her feel so terrible? For all it was no longer burning, the air was still thick with them. In the small space she was in, with little or no ventilation, it would probably have had a bad effect on anyone.

It was after nine before the youth appeared with a cup of tea, and when she complained that the fire was out, he said he would see what he could do, but wasn't making any promises. His friends, she was informed in a low voice, were not pleased about him buying the fire for her in the first place. They were still going on about it.

Whether this was true or not, even through the heavy door Miranda could hear sounds of raised voices. As they were obviously quarelling upstairs over something, though she couldn't be sure what it was, she began to fear she wouldn't be getting any more fuel. Bearing this in mind, she didn't drink her tea until it was cold, choosing to warm her numb fingers on the hot cup until the heat went, and when she drank it, it only made her feel worse than she already was.

After this she tried walking up and down in an effort to get warm. She feared she might not survive if she let the piercing cold get further into her. Unfortunately, though she had been walking for about five minutes without mishap, she suddenly slipped and fell heavily on one of the wet stone slabs of the floor. Pain shot through her as she pulled herself weakly to her feet. Sighing with frustration, she went back to sit on the bench. She felt no warmer and she could have broken her leg. Perhaps it might be safer to stay where she was?

During the afternoon she suspected she might be losing the baby. Though she tried to tell herself she could be mistaken, she knew instinctively what was happening. She had to get help, she thought desperately, before it was too late. Her stomach was aching and instead of feeling cold she now felt burning hot.

Brushing back her tumbled hair from her face, she struggled to her feet and went to the door and began banging on it. She had only her bare hands but she tried to make as much noise as she could. Surely, if her kidnappers knew what was happening to her, they would do something to help her? Even if they just let her out, she would promise not to tell anyone about them. She would even promise, as she had suggested to the youth the day before, to get Brett to pay their ransom privately. Anything – if only there was a chance of saving the baby.

She thought they musn't have heard her. Or if they did they were ignoring her. After knocking intermittently for about ten minutes she gave up. She felt faint and her legs started buckling under her, so that she had to go and sit down. It wasn't until more minutes passed that the door opened and the youth who usually attended her came in.

'Look,' he said sharply, 'if you keep on knocking we will have to tie you up. You're making a hell of a racket and we can't risk someone hearing you.'

'I'm ill,' she said.

'It's just the cold,' he shrugged. 'I'll get some more paraffin.'

'That won't help me now.' She stared at him, white-faced and trembling. 'I'm losing my baby.'

'You're – *what*?' If she had thrown a bomb he couldn't have been more shocked. 'You're kidding!' he exclaimed, 'Having me on.'

'I wish I was,' she said bitterly, her voice hoarse.

'Oh, my God!' he cried. 'My sister – it happened to her once. She nearly died . . .' Then he paused, as if again doubting her. 'How is it you never said anything before – or that no one mentioned you were pregnant?'

'I don't know what you mean by no one mentioning it.' Miranda gasped. 'But I hadn't told anyone, apart from my immediate family. It's true, though. My doctor in New York confirmed it over a month ago.'

The youth's eyes widened. She could see consternation in them winning over the doubt. 'I'd better tell the others,' he said, rushing out.

He forgot, in his apparent haste, to lock the door, or even close it behind him, but when she might at least have tried to escape, Miranda found herself attacked by cramp-like pains and unable to move because of them. Upstairs she could hear raised

321

voices again, but the sudden silence that followed a few minutes later was even more frightening. What were they doing, or going to do? she wondered.

She didn't have long to wait to get an answer. Almost immediately the door opened and the youth was standing in front of her again.

'Listen,' he panted, 'the others have scarpered. We don't want to be accused of murder . . .'

'Murder?'

'Which we might be if you had a miscarriage and happened to die here because of it. That wasn't our intention – murder, I mean. I'm going to ring the police and then be gone. I just wanted to say – well, the others told me to – that if you are lying about your condition, then you'd better watch out when they catch up with you.'

Miranda, disregarding the last bit, was so relieved by what he said that she had what she supposed was a crazy desire to thank him. But the pains gripping her stomach were so bad that she seemed to be losing the ability to even speak. The walls of the cellar appeared to be advancing, then retreating about her, – the light above her growing dimmer, then brighter as she fought a losing battle against unconsciousness.

In the last few moments before she gave in to it, however, it seemed to her that the youth had scarcely time to leave the house before there came the noise of loud sirens, screaming tyres and men shouting. Then doors crashing open and the sound of boots pounding the floors above her head. Then people were calling her name, saying they were the police and asking if she was there. But before she had time to find enough breath to answer them, everything faded completely.

When Miranda regained consciousness, she became gradually aware that her surroundings were entirely different. Slowly she realized she was warm and in a comfortable bed, but she felt strangely disorientated and though the pain she remembered was gone, her body seemed to be aching all over.

She didn't open her eyes immediately, fearing briefly she might be dreaming and still in the cellar. Then a greater horror struck her as she recalled how convinced she had been that she was losing her baby.

'Oh, no!' she whispered aloud, as shock caused her eyes to fly open and she saw Brett sitting on a chair beside her, looking at her intently.

'Is – it – all right?' she asked, while knowing in her heart it wasn't.

Brett swallowed visibly, knowing instinctively what she was talking about. 'I'm sorry,' he said heavily. 'They tried to save it but couldn't.'

'They?'

'The police and doctors, who worked tirelessly, but it was too late. What matters most, though, is that they were in time to save you. We can have another baby, but there couldn't be another you.'

Was she supposed to find that comforting? In her distress, Miranda almost laughed as she wondered how many times, during their brief, stormy marriage, had she asked herself that after one of Brett's brief observations? She stared at him now without speaking. His dark blue eyes were fixed on her face.

If he hadn't known better, she might have imagined he was memorizing every detail. He was pale and drawn, but then he would be, wouldn't he? He couldn't have had much sleep since she went missing. It wouldn't have looked good if he'd gone to bed while others were searching for her. And the baby must have been a blow, despite his dismissive words about it being replaceable. She just wished she could accept the loss of it as resignedly as he clearly did.

'Miranda?' he began, tightening his grip on the hand she hadn't realized he was holding, 'Darling. . .'

'How long have I been here?' she asked, not hearing him.

Brett hesitated, then said more evenly. 'Since yesterday, but don't talk now. What I have to say will keep as well. Just try and rest.'

She wanted to shout that she couldn't, but instead found herself obeying him, drifting off into the soft shadows beckoning her, where she could mourn in private over her baby.

The next time she woke she didn't feel so unwilling to, and when she opened her eyes, to her surprise, Brett was still with her. He smiled grimly when, after a moment, she asked him why he wasn't working.

'Obvious reasons, I suppose.' He shrugged. 'You've been asleep another day. The after-effects of shock, losing the baby and hypothermia, and I think the staff here have accepted me as a permanent fixture. There'll be plenty of time for work when you're better.'

Again she wasn't really listening, as she glanced around the room she was in. 'I'm in hospital?'

'Where else?' As if to convince her, he leaned over and pressed a bell. Almost immediately a doctor and two nurses came in and bent over her. As soon as they arrived, Brett got up and walked out, after telling Miranda he would be back in a few minutes. Miranda wished he hadn't gone. There were questions she wanted to ask him. About her father, for one thing. Did he know she had been kidnapped, and, if so, how had he taken it? Strangely enough, she could find no curiosity within her as to what Brett had thought when he heard of it.

The doctor said. 'I'm a gynaecologist, Mrs Deakin. I asked your husband to ring as soon as you woke up. Among other things, I would like to ask a few questions, if you feel up to it?'

Miranda wasn't sure she did, but she nodded dully.

'The police have some questions as well,' he told her. 'I have to make sure you're well enough to answer them.' After finishing a brief examination, he sat on the edge of the bed beside her. 'Your husband has told you about the baby, Mrs Deakin, I believe? We tried to save it. Unfortunately we couldn't and I'm very sorry. You are recovering well physically, though, and there should be nothing to prevent you from having another one. In time, that is.' He paused, then went on, 'We know from your medical records how well you recovered from the accident that crippled you in your teens. The doctors who looked after you then have, in fact, been in to see you . . .'

'They have?' she exclaimed.

'Yes, Mrs Deakin. When they heard you had been kidnapped they were very concerned. Not because they feared it would reverse the results of your operation – which would have been impossible – but after learning you had been pregnant they were genuinely sorry that you'd lost your baby.'

Miranda nodded. The doctors he spoke of had always been great with her, but she wished that this one, nice though he seemed, would stop talking about the baby.

'I don't wish to tire you or upset you, Mrs Deakin,' he said, almost as if he had guessed what she was thinking, 'But do you know of anything else, apart from the terrible conditions your kidnappers kept you in, that might have caused your miscarriage? For instance, did you feel all right when you set out for America that morning?'

Miranda said she had. 'And the men didn't try to rape me, or anything like that. I was terrified they might, but all they seemed interested in was the ransom. I did slip on the floor of the cellar,' she said, as it came back to her. 'There was scarcely any light and the stone slabs were very damp and slimy. I think I came quite a cropper.'

'Ah,' said the doctor, 'that could have been responsible. You were in pain afterwards?'

'Yes.' Miranda shuddered, remembering. 'Quite a lot. I believe my kidnappers thought I was dying.'

The doctor frowned as he watched her. He had rarely seen a more beautiful girl – he hated to think what might have happened to her.

'In normal circumstances,' he said, 'few women ever die from a miscarriage, uncomfortable and upsetting as it may be. But your situation was rather different from a normal one. In a freezing cellar, like the one you were imprisoned in, without proper heat, food or ventilation, even had you not been pregnant you would almost certainly have suffered from hypothermia and might not have survived more than a few days.'

The police said much the same thing when the doctor allowed them in, after he was satisfied she was well enough to be interviewed. There was a Detective Inspector Spanklehurst, whom Miranda knew through her father, two other detectives of lesser rank, and a policewoman.

After expressing the hope that she was feeling better and offering his condolences for the trauma she'd experienced, the Inspector said, 'We don't want to tire you, Mrs Deakin, but there are some questions we have to ask. Your husband has just been telling us that he hasn't had a chance yet to tell you how we managed to find you, but he will do when we leave. A lot of the credit for it goes to him, anyway, for setting us on the right track. Saw something my men didn't.' He cast a baleful glance at his sergeant, who looked as if he'd heard it all before and didn't think this was the last of it.

The Inspector continued. 'The morning after you disappeared, Miranda, when your husband rang with the first real clue we'd had, after following it up, we caught your kidnappers a few hours later. Two of them not far from the house you were being held in – the other, just coming out of it.'

Miranda frowned. 'The one coming out of the house must have been the one who was going to phone you to say where I was and that I was ill. You surely couldn't have been that quick?'

'Ah, well,' said the Inspector, 'we were acting on information received previous to that, though if we hadn't had it, we'd have known where to find you when that young man rang us.'

'I see,' Miranda said though she didn't. She could see, however, by the quick look the Inspector shot at the doctor that his time was limited and he wasn't going to waste it explaining something Brett was apparently able to. 'That young man,' she said, 'was actually quite kind to me. I know he must have been as responsible as the other two for what happened to me, but at least he wasn't as unpleasant. What will happen to him?'

The Inspector hesitated. 'Kidnapping is a serious offence, Miranda, and we'd like to know if, in their case, there is anything to add to it. For instance, how did they treat you after they put you in the cellar?'

Miranda wondered if he was trying to avoid being indelicate. She remembered he had a daughter about her own age. 'They didn't try to rape me, if that's what you mean.' She was beginning to feel too tired again to be anything but blunt as she repeated what she had told the doctor. 'They threatened a lot, but I only saw one of them after they took me down to the cellar. The same one every time and, as I've just said, he was quite civil. Considering.'

'Did they give you anything to eat?'

'Tea and soup.' Miranda grimaced as she recalled the funny taste of it. 'When I complained of being cold they brought me a fire, but there wasn't much heat from it and it ran out of fuel. If they'd kept me in a warm room, apart from the fright I got, I might have been all right.'

'That's debatable, Miranda.' The Inspector frowned. 'The suspense of not knowing what was going to happen to you could have done a lot of harm in itself. Now, I wonder, did your kidnappers ever say why they needed the ransom money? Or why they abandoned you – and presumably the plans they'd made – in such a hurry?'

'No.' Miranda shook her head, stirring restlessly in her bed under the impact of several pairs of eyes fixed keenly on her face. 'They never said why they wanted the money, but I somehow got the impression that they weren't hardened criminals and wanted it to get them out of some kind of trouble, rather than something to merely go off and enjoy themselves with.'

'That figures,' the sergeant grunted, though he didn't say why.

'If they had been hardened criminals,' Miranda went on, 'I don't think they would have panicked when they learned I was losing the baby. The one who looked after me said his sister nearly died of a miscarriage and, as I told Doctor Levis – ' she glanced towards him ' – this seemed to convince them it could happen to me if I didn't get some attention immediately. Anyway,' she added, remembering, 'my prison warder, the last time I saw him, said they didn't wish to be accused of murder.'

'And then,' the Inspector said, 'he rang us?'

'Yes.' Miranda nodded. 'I think so.'

CHAPTER 22

When Brett told Miranda of the part he had played in her rescue, he didn't do it voluntarily. It was because she broached the subject herself and he had agreed with the police that he would.

Miranda, for her part, felt more indifferent than curious. That Brett had rushed to the UK as soon as he heard she was kidnapped left her strangely unmoved. Whereas the old Miranda would have been thrilled, she couldn't seem to feel a thing. It was as if the loss of her child had taken away her love for Brett with it, so she could regard him as she might a stranger. Which, strangely enough, seemed to make asking him things like 'Why did you come over to look for me in the first place?' a lot easier. Now, as he sat beside her again, after the doctor and police went, she watched him trying to answer her question.

'Of course I had to come,' he said, believing this was not the time to tell her the exact reason. Any attempt to explain the hell he'd been through since his security man told him what had happened to her would have to wait until he was sure she wanted to hear it. Which, he suspected from her unconsciously hostile demeanour, wasn't then.

'Were you frightened of what people would say if you didn't?' she taunted him while amazed she could speak to him like this.

'Miranda!' He looked as if he was going to say more, then hesitated and shook his head. 'I had to come, you know that,' he said.

'I'm sorry,' she muttered quickly, having no real wish to goad him. 'Perhaps we'd better stick to what happened when you did? Get here, I mean.'

Brett paused, then said, 'I think the police exaggerate the help I gave them. I believe your rescue had more to do with the note you wrote reminding yourself to ring your friend, Pamela Brent-Nordon, to tell her you couldn't go to her party as you were returning to New York the following morning.'

'But I didn't know what route we were taking.'

'There's not much choice, is there? Your kidnappers must have followed you from Well House, or just got lucky and guessed the right one?'

Miranda frowned, going back a little. 'My note – where did you say you found it?'

'I didn't, but it was in the room where you kept your wheelchairs.'

'What were you doing there?'

'I'm not sure.' Brett didn't want to say he was out all night looking for her and when he went there, in a way, he still was. 'The police missed it, apparently.'

'Yes, I remember now,' Miranda murmured retrospectively, 'I bumped into Pam in the city and half-promised – I think to escape her – that I'd look in on her party. I had no intention of going, but when

I had a good excuse not to, I decided to ring her and apologize. Hypocritical of me, I know, and I remember making a note of it.'

'Which you must have lost or thrown away when you were probably sitting in your wheelchair. You asked me why I went there, Miranda. Can I ask you the same question?'

'Old memories, I suppose.' She shrugged, after a slight hesitation. 'Thinking of the past, perhaps, and wondering if, despite everything, I wasn't happier then than I am now.'

'Memories often get distorted,' Brett replied somewhat harshly, while again deciding to stick to what they were talking about. The new wariness he had sensed in Miranda when she first recovered consciousness after the ordeal she'd been through was still there, still warning him to keep his distance. Maybe it was all part of the shock of that and losing her baby, but he had to give her time. He'd meant, though, what he said about memories. Hadn't he allowed his to dominate him until they might, if this crisis hadn't brought him to his senses, almost have ruined his life?

'I expect you are right,' Miranda said abstractedly. 'I don't remember throwing the memo I wrote about Pam away, but I must have done. Probably just before I rang her . . .' Miranda's eyes suddenly widened incredulously as she looked at him. 'You don't think Pam had anything to do with my kidnapping, do you?'

Brett shook his head. 'Not directly, or intentionally, I'm quite sure of that. After I found your note and Alice found your friend's number, and she

332

confirmed you'd rung and told her you were going back to New York, and that she'd probably mentioned it to quite a few people, I got in touch with the police.'

Miranda frowned. 'You aren't suggesting that my kidnappers were among Pam's guests?'

'It was possible. And the police weren't overlooking anything. After asking Miss Brent-Nordon a few question, they got a list of her party guests from her, which included two young men.'

'But there were three.'

'They didn't all have to be there,'

'I know Pam can be a bit wild,' Miranda said, 'but I don't think she would be associating with criminals.'

'Neither did she,' Brett said drily. 'It seems she actually only invited one of these young men, whom, like you, she'd just bumped into accidentally. She hadn't, in fact, she told the police, seen him for a few years, but because he said his parents had thrown him out, she felt sorry for him and asked him along. And the police decided, with the instinct they often have for such things, to investigate him first.'

'And . . .?' Miranda looked at him expectantly.

'Well, his father, it turned out, is a wealthy man called Brown, and James is his only son. James, though, after leaving university, refused to enter the family business, or seek any other kind of work. For two years he lay about at home, getting deeper into drugs, wild rave-ups and other questionable activities until they could stand it no longer and told him to go.'

'And did they know where he was?'

'No, they swore to the police that they didn't. All they could say was that they had reason to believe he was living in a rundown part of the city, in bad company. They hoped he had nothing to do with your kidnapping, even though the police, with no real evidence to go on, hadn't accused him of anything.'

'So how did they find him?' Miranda asked. 'If his parents hadn't his address, he must have been well hidden.'

'Well, the police have their own methods,' Brett said briefly. 'I've no doubt they would have found James Brown using these, eventually, but time, especially when someone is kidnapped, can be imperative. Some men haven't survived more than a few days and you were a woman and pregnant.'

'Not any more,' Miranda said bitterly, but rushed on before Brett could say anything. 'I could have been there for days if I hadn't been found since they couldn't decide, as I told the police, how to collect the ransom. But,' she repeated, 'how did they find him?'

'Through the lad's sister,' Brett explained. 'His parents gave us her address, but were sure she would know no more of his whereabouts than they did. Unfortunately, it took an hour or two to find her as she wasn't in, and when they did, she was at first very suspicious of the police. It wasn't until they said what James might be involved in that she broke down and told them what she knew. Apparently, her brother had been in touch with her only the previous week and was in bad trouble. He was desperately in need of money. Since his father's generous supply of it had dried up, he'd got deeply in debt to the wrong kind of people. He and the two men, with whom he lived, had been forced – or so he said – to traffic in drugs to earn a living and it had all gone wrong. Now they were being threatened by people who might easily kill them.'

'Did his sister give him some money?' Miranda asked as Brett paused. She sensed that Brett, like the police, was trying to spare her as much as possible but there were things about her kidnappers she felt she had to know.

'She didn't.' Brett met Miranda's intense gaze anxiously, wishing he could just pick her up and put this whole thing behind them, fly with her to Luke and make a fresh start. Realizing this wasn't going to happen for a while yet, he said, 'It wasn't, apparently, because she didn't want to help him but, though she worked for their father and he was generous to her, she'd just had an extravagant foreign holiday and, until her next pay day, could do with some money herself. She doubted she could have found the kind of money her brother was in need of, anyway. Nevertheless, he'd insisted on leaving his address in case she could manage to borrow some for him. He'd sworn her to secrecy over both this and his phone number, which was why she was so reluctant to give it to anyone.'

'So when James and his *friends*,' she emphasized the last word cynically, 'learned I was leaving for the States the morning after Pam's party, it must have seemed like a heaven-sent opportunity to find the cash they were so urgently in need of?'

'Things are seldom that easy,' Brett grunted. 'Once the police had their address and everything in place, they were around to confront them almost immediately.'

'Yet the two I often heard but didn't see almost got away?'

'They might have done, but I doubt if they'd have got very far. Their blue van was soon spotted and the police apprehended them . . .'

Miranda said somewhat sadly, 'They didn't wait for poor James.'

Brett's face went white with anger. 'I'd forget about poor James, if I were you. It was thanks to him you were kidnapped in the first place. You might have been killed!'

Miranda couldn't argue with it. 'I'm sorry, Brett,' she said slowly. 'I seem to have put a lot of people, including yourself, to a lot of trouble.'

Brett, struggling to recover his equilibrium, said, 'It was my fault, Miranda, for making you come home when I did. Things are going to be different in future, believe me.'

Miranda looked at him uncomprehendingly, wondering why she was feeling so exhausted? She slept, but what little energy she derived from that was gone when she woke, almost instantly. 'I don't want to even think of the future just yet, Brett. It's not just losing the baby, which has been a blow for both of us. It's our marriage . . .' She tried to find the most accurate words to explain her feelings. 'You must know as well as I do it's been a mistake from the beginning. Hasn't the time come for us to admit this and begin again?'

Brett frowned. 'Isn't that what I am saying? We'll begin again?'

'But I don't mean the way I think you do – by patching something up, which would have no better chance of succeeding than it did in the first place. I'm talking of a clean break, Brett, before we end up hating each other.'

Brett went pale. 'I realize I married you for the wrong reasons, Miranda, but if you listen I can explain . . .'

'I don't want to hear your reasons,' Miranda broke in, certain nothing he could say now could make any difference. 'Never mind,' she taunted him, dry mockery in her eyes, 'you'll have your other women to console you – or celebrate with you, whichever way you choose to look at it. The Eves and Marcias of this world to help fill your huge house and any empty days.'

'Is it the house?'

Miranda flinched at the sudden harshness of Brett's voice. 'I can't deny I've never felt comfortable in it, but it's not that bad. I could have put up with it if other things hadn't been against us. Such as our relationship.'

'I can soon alter that,' he assured her.

'I don't think you could, not now,' she said flatly.

'Miranda.' Brett stared at her in frustration. He couldn't remember feeling as desperate over anything in his life, or as powerless to do anything about it. When he heard she was kidnapped, it was as if his eyes had been suddenly opened and he realized exactly what she meant to him. Never having been in love before, he'd been stunned by the sheer volume of emotion rushing through him and, despite the seriousness of the situation, not altogether sure he welcomed it. Yet, looking at Miranda now, though he still felt distinctly nervous of the depth of his feelings, he knew she was no longer just a beautiful young girl with the rare gift of being able to satisfy him physically, the way no other woman had done, but a woman with whom he wanted to share the rest of his life. Still staring at her, Brett controlled an urgent desire to sweep her into his arms. Instinctively he knew, as he had done before and a few minutes ago, he had to give her time. Never being a patient man, he realized this wasn't going to be easy. But he refused to believe he could be on the brink of losing her forever.

'Miranda,' he repeated, 'I'm not convinced about this, but, for the moment, I'm willing to go along with it. What would you like me to do?'

'Return to America and divorce me,' she answered stonily, with such determination in her voice that Brett paled visibly. 'There's just one more thing,' she added, not noticing. 'When we are divorced, I don't want anything for myself – I've had a good education and, being young, can work for my living – but there's my father and Alice . . .'

'Say no more,' Brett broke in, mentally tearing up the marriage agreement they'd made. 'I still think you are being too hasty, but whatever happens, as far as they are concerned nothing will change. I'll continue to make them an allowance. You, too, even if you do find a job.'

'Brett, please – I don't want . . .'

'Will you just shut up, Miranda!' Because he couldn't be sure he wasn't making a mistake in letting her go, even for a little while, Brett almost snapped at her. 'If you want rid of me, that's my last word.'

On his way back to Well House that evening, Brett decided he would stay in the UK until Miranda was discharged from hospital. He talked to Harry Ferris about it, the following morning. Both Harry and Alice had visited Miranda often and, though sad over the baby, were extremely thankful that Miranda had been rescued and was going to be all right. Or so Harry had thought until Brett told him of her decision to divorce him.

'I'm hoping it won't come to that, that she will change her mind once she's had a chance to get over being kidnapped and losing the baby,' Brett said.

Harry looked shocked. Alice was out and when Brett had asked to speak to him privately, he couldn't think what it could be about. Now he stared at his son-in-law, aghast. 'What brought this on, Brett, do you know? Is it, as you seem to suggest, what she's been through? Or is it something else?'

'I'm not sure.' The hard expression in Brett's eyes seemed belied by the hand he raked impotently through his hair. 'Probably a combination of several things. I think, for instance, I married her too quickly.'

Harry frowned uncertainly, not caring to go into the implications of that. 'It's not something silly, is it?' he asked, with a hint of embarrassment. 'Like you and another woman?'

Brett hesitated. Another time, he wouldn't have tolerated such a question, but could this, he wondered, be a clue? Did Miranda believe he was having an affair? Since they'd married, he admitted, if only to himself, he had been to bed with another woman, trying to prove Miranda meant little to him when he feared he was getting too involved. But it hadn't worked. He had found no pleasure with her, and had certainly not even dated anyone since he learned about the baby.

'What has Miranda been saying?' he asked Harry now.

'Oh, nothing. Nothing at all!' Harry stuttered in alarm, wishing belatedly he hadn't said anything. 'It was just,' he went on, not knowing where or how to stop, or if he should, 'something that once came up . . .'

'Yes?' Brett prompted tersely, as he paused.

Harry, though clearly nonplussed, said, 'I suppose I'd better come clean, but if you tell me it's none of my damn business and that I've been making mountains out of molehills – '

'Harry!' Brett interrupted impatiently. 'Spare me the clichés. Just get on with it.'

Harry nodded. 'It was a few weeks after you and Miranda were married, just after Christmas, I think, when a woman came to see me. I was out, but Hilda, the maid, let her in. Not only let her in, but put her in my study, where I'd reason to believe she was poking about. As soon as I got back she introduced herself as someone called Liz Telfer. Said she'd been invited to your wedding and couldn't make it, then produced some far-fetched story about coming to see me to apologize. Anyway, to cut a long story short, she left me with the impression – deliberately, I believe – that you and she had been lovers for years, and still were.'

While Harry paused to cough gruffly, as if his last words were stuck in his throat, Brett stared at him in amazement. 'I can't remember the last affair I had in Birmingham, Harry. What did you say the lady's name was?'

Harry repeated it. 'I wouldn't like to tell you how much sleep I've lost over this, Brett. Nearly worried myself to death. Of course I'm not so straitlaced as to get in a state over a man having a mistress, but I was worried for fear Miranda got to hear of it. Women don't always take such a tolerant view of these things.'

'What was she like?'

Though nervous at the way Brett barked at him, Harry, nevertheless, obliged. 'Tall, dark, walked with a limp.'

Eve! It could be no other, for all she'd obviously given a phony name. 'How did she get here?' he bit out.

'By car,' Harry told him. 'As a matter of fact, Hilda took her car number. She and a friend, she said, were competing with each other as to who could collect the most old Mini numbers. I don't know why I asked her for it, but I did. I still have it, if you would like to see it.'

Brett didn't need to. The make of the car and Harry's description of the woman who visited him were enough to convince him it was Eve. 'I think I know who it is, Harry, without further evidence. I'll go and see her,' he added grimly, then proceeded, as he saw this was still festering at the back of his father-in-law's mind, to tell him briefly about his involvement with Liz Telfer, alias Eve Martin, since the beginning. There was a lot he left out which he realized wouldn't make sense to Harry, or even perhaps to himself, were he to try and explain it. But what he did tell Harry appeared to convince him that the woman who came to see him had merely been out to make mischief and that there had never been anything sexual, or anything even remotely of that nature between them,

Finding Eve took Brett longer than he thought it would. When he went to the bungalow he had bought for her, he was told she had moved. It wasn't until then that he remembered she had given it back to him and cancelled her allowance. His PA had said something about it, he recalled, but being busy at the time he had put it to the back of his mind and forgotten all about it.

Feeling impatient with himself for overlooking something like this, he pretended he was a personal friend of Eve's who'd been abroad and was given her new address, to which she had asked the present occupants to forward any mail that came for her. Unfortunately, when he got there, he was again told she had moved. The young woman he spoke to, however, took him next door to see her mother, who was able to provide him with the name of the street where she said Eve now lived, and the number of the flat she rented from her husband. She also said that after Miss Martin's father died, she'd been forced to look for a smaller place.

With the early evening traffic getting heavy, Brett had some difficulty in finding the street and the flat the woman sent him to, even though she had given him fairly clear directions. If he had been surprised to learn that Eve's father had died, he was even more surprised by the change he saw in her. She had just returned from work, from what she said was a new job, and she looked so pale and thin he almost didn't recognize her. When she asked him in she didn't apologize for the obvious shabbiness of her surroundings. She merely said that after losing her father she had had to economize, as she had no money of her own and John's pension had died with him.

When Brett accused her of trying to destroy his marriage she made no attempt to deny it. It seemed that so much of the life was knocked out of her, she couldn't find the energy to. She hadn't, though, she assured him, had anything to do with Miranda's kidnapping and was glad she'd been found, and was sorry she had lost the baby.

Eve didn't mention Gaby. What would be the point, she thought, on recovering a little from the shock of Brett's sudden appearance? Why try to make more trouble? What good would it do? Instead, knowing it was something she had needed to do for a long time, she found herself confessing everything and leaving Gaby out of it. She told Brett how she had merely pretended to be crippled. How, because he appeared to believe her, she had hoped he would eventually offer to marry her. And how her anger, after he married someone else, had led her to do stupid things, like ringing him in New York and even visiting Miranda's father.

There was more, for she didn't want to leave anything out, but eventually Brett stopped her. If

Eve had cheated him all these years, had he not been far too willing to let her? Had he not been using her as much as she'd used him, even if he had not been consciously aware of it, to get rid of the guilt he'd always felt because of something he hadn't tried to do for his mother?

In a pause of seconds, he went back to the day his father refused to leave London in the middle of an important business deal, when his wife, Julia, rang from New York, asking him to come home immediately to go on vacation with her.

Brett, at twenty-three, as keen to clinch the deal as his father, hadn't tried to get him to change his mind. And when his mother, in a fit of pique, went off on the trip alone, met with an accident, was seriously injured and died shortly afterwards, he had always felt partly to blame. When her doctors stated that, had she lived, she would have been permanently disabled, he got no comfort from it. Had she lived and been crippled, he might have got rid of some of his guilt by helping her.

Which was probably why, he realized now, when Eve was injured in the accident she'd hinted he was responsible for, he'd been determined to assist her in every way he could, believing it might at last absolve him from whatever he had failed to do for his mother. He had known Eve wasn't as badly injured as she made out, but it had suited him, for this purpose, to go along with it.

When Miranda appeared on the scene, he'd persuaded himself that if he married her and made her well again, it would all contribute to this end. He knew now he had been fooling himself. He had fallen for Miranda, he suspected, from the first moment he saw her. But as he had never been in love before and thought himself immune from it, he'd been convinced his other reasons for marrying her were the true ones. When he discovered she wasn't crippled, he was furious, but as he hadn't been able to let her go, he'd used the fact that she'd cheated on him as another excuse for marrying her. Now, as he regarded the ghost of his twenty-three-year-old self, by which he had seemingly allowed himself to be driven beyond a point which now seemed comprehensible, he could only feel relieved that he might at last be able to put it behind him.

Aware that Eve was waiting and beginning to look at him uncertainly, he turned to her grimly. 'It's okay, Eve,' he said, briefly. 'I'm probably as much to blame as you were for not making certain things clear from the beginning. But I don't think we need go on about it. I'd just like you to promise you won't go near my wife or her family again.'

'I won't, Brett,' she assured him.

After this Brett decided to leave immediately. In a way he regretted looking Eve up. She had lost her father and, in various ways, had probably suffered enough without having him rubbing salt in her wounds. She was obviously paying for the past and, from the look of both her and her flat, it didn't seem as if she had much hope of a better future.

Though Brett didn't know it, in thinking this about Eve Martin, he might have been mistaken. To Eve's surprise, that very day as she left work she'd bumped into none other than Simon Wentworth.

345

'Why – Eve!' he'd exclaimed, halting abruptly and saying goodbye to the man he was with, whom she recognized as the boss of the huge conglomerate she worked for.

'Hello, Simon,' she replied, watching the other man walk away, rather than look at him. 'How are you?'

'I'd rather not answer that,' he said slowly, putting a detaining hand on her arm when she would have gone past him. His eyes went swiftly over her strained face and thin figure. 'You've lost weight?'

Eve merely shrugged as she tried ineffectively to free herself, not liking the feeling from his fingers which seemed to be speeding to her traitorously beating heart. 'I'm working these days,' she said flippantly, 'which maybe explains it.'

For a moment he simply stared at her, now as pale as she was and saying nothing. Then, drawing an audibly deep breath he said, 'It's no good, Eve. I have to see you again. We can't talk here. This isn't the time or place. Will you meet me, perhaps later on this evening?'

'Where?' she asked quickly, but when he suggested seven-thirty at a quiet but exclusive restaurant, she only drew a deep breath herself and wrenched herself away from him. 'If you care to risk it, I might be there, but I won't promise anything,' she cried, making an unconscious sop to her pride, as she hurriedly left him and lost herself in the crowds of factory workers surrounding them.

Now, after seeing Brett Deakin out into a stormy March evening and recovering a little from the ordeal of his unexpected visit, Eve was surprised to find a new peace within herself. For the first time in weeks she didn't feel so tense and despondent. Suddenly she believed she was ready for a new beginning – somewhere or with someone. She couldn't be sure whether this would be with Simon or someone else, or maybe just by herself. She might never be as selfish again as she was in the past, but she realized it wasn't just Eve Martin she had to convince of this. She might have to be as straight with Simon as she had been with Brett. And, afterwards, he might be as unwilling to forgive and forget, as he had been previously. Her heart might feel lighter, the world brighter, but she could, she knew, be deluding herself. Completely.

Nevertheless, as Eve stood there pondering over it and listening to the rain coming down, she suddenly made up her mind that she was not going to be a coward and stay at home that evening. If nothing came of her meeting with Simon, could she be any worse off than she was now? When the answer to this appeared to be no, whichever way she looked at it, she didn't allow herself to think about it any longer. Instead, she went to run her bath and get ready. If fate was giving her another chance, shouldn't she at least be trying to cooperate? she thought drily.

CHAPTER 23

Miranda couldn't remember time going so slowly. It seemed more like four years than four months since Brett had returned to New York, and though she tried to convince herself this was what she wanted, she wasn't finding it easy to begin again without him. He had promised she would have her divorce by the autumn. He said he would be too busy before then to get around to it. But she knew, until he did, she would still feel threatened by him and, because of this, unable to see her way ahead clearly.

It had taken her longer than she thought it would to get over being kidnapped and losing her baby. Before he left for the States, Brett arranged for her to have what she'd thought must be every kind of medical help available. Most of which she'd firmly rejected, having complete faith in the doctors she was familiar with, who had looked after her so well and patiently during her handicapped years and childhood illnesses.

While physically she was in excellent shape, she still had nightmares occasionally. During the night she would wake up bathed in sweat and certain she'd been screaming. Several times, when she first came home from hospital, Brett, in the room next door, heard her screaming and would come rushing in to talk to her and stay with her until she was calm again. But gradually the worst of her bad dreams had passed and she hoped they would disappear altogether, eventually.

The psychiatrist she sometimes saw at the surgery had helped her a lot over this. He was a pleasant man who assured her that her kidnapping would be directly responsible for her nightmares, but that other factors could be contributing. Losing her baby the way she did might be one of them, along with perhaps some hidden worries at the back of her mind over other things. He also suggested she might have married too quickly after the operation which had enabled her to walk again.

'Too many traumatic experiences over a short period of time,' he said with a wry smile, 'often means that something has to give.'

Miranda didn't tell him her marriage was over. There were some things she couldn't bring herself to discuss with anyone. She suspected he knew this and it probably wasn't fair to keep so much back, but never having been used to sharing her deepest thoughts, she didn't find it easy to start now.

She heard nothing from Brett after he left. He stayed for a week after she came out of hospital, but she had found the strain intolerable and been relieved when he decided to return to New York. Before he went he asked if she had changed her mind about a divorce, since she'd had time to think about it, but when she merely shook her head he hadn't argued. He'd merely looked grim for the rest of the day and departed the following morning.

Often Miranda wished she could have gone to Luke and talked to Linda. Linda, she felt certain, would have done her more good than a dozen psychiatrists. She would dream of the islands and the endless blue-green panorama of the ocean surrounding them. Of brilliant, beautiful mornings when Brett had taken her sailing. She tried not to dream of the times he made love to her, either on the boat or in some sandy inlet, with the soft sea breeze washing waves gently over them. Of wonderful days and equally enchanting evenings when it seemed that their marriage had every chance of succeeding. How naïve can one get? Miranda thought now.

Alice often tried to persuade her to go back to Brett. 'We aren't trying to get rid of you, darling,' she would say. 'But Brett is still your husband and both your father and I would like you to try again. Losing your child was a blow, I know, but you could have others and I'd hate to see your marriage fail.'

Today, as she listened to what she must have heard a dozen times since Brett went away, Miranda looked at her aunt impatiently. 'My marriage had already failed, Aunt Alice. I wish I didn't have to keep telling you this.' Going further than she had done before, she said, 'I've stopped loving Brett and I don't believe he loves me.'

Alice frowned. 'How do you know he doesn't?'

'What makes you think he does?'

'You didn't see him when you were missing, but I did,' Alice replied. 'Perhaps I shouldn't tell you this, as he asked me not to, but as soon as he arrived he spent the night searching for you. It was almost six in the morning before he came in and found the memo you'd wrote reminding yourself to ring Pam. He acted so quickly, even after no sleep, it had to be seen to be believed. He rang Pam, suspecting she might have mentioned your departure to someone at her party. Then he got in touch with the police.'

'Brett's mind always works twice as fast as other people's.' Miranda was woodenly unimpressed. 'It just comes naturally to him.'

'But, in your case, I could see, though he didn't make it obvious, that he was under considerable strain. The police,' Alice claimed, 'couldn't get rid of him, and he was the one who carried you from that terrible cellar.'

As Alice paused with a delicate shudder, Miranda said, 'I think he felt responsible for not letting me stay here longer.'

'Nonsense,' Alice rebuked her sharply, hating the deadpan expression on what used to be a lively, animated face. 'Well, perhaps he did,' she conceded reluctantly, 'but feeling responsible for something seldom drives a man to the lengths he went to. I admit,' she went on, 'I did have my doubts over your marriage at first, but not any more. I still think you should try again, or at least see him.'

Miranda shivered. How could she try again when it would mean going back to that huge empty house in New York, with Brett out all day and almost every evening? Back to having mostly only Jill for company. To return to that was something she refused to even think about. Marriage to Brett might have helped her to grow up, given her a new maturity, but if she had known the price was to be so high she doubted, even in the circumstances, that she would have gone through with it.

'I'm going to get some training and find a job. Then I might think about seeing Brett,' she promised her aunt vaguely. She guessed, though, that long before then she and Brett would be divorced and he might well be married again. Dully she wondered why the thought of Brett being married again, and to someone else, didn't hurt?

As most of the training courses Miranda was interested in didn't begin until the autumn, she decided to spend the weeks until then getting really fit. But as time went by she couldn't understand why it was, when she was able to jog now for miles each morning, swim, play tennis and even have a moderate social life, that she seemed to derive no pleasure from such things. It was as if her physical and mental states were poles apart and one had nothing to do with the other. Not even going on holiday with her father and Alice made any difference. She came back full of a glowing vitality that seemed to stop a little short of her brain. She could only find there a growing uninterest in almost everything.

When Gaby rang it startled her a little but that was all. Recognizing her voice, Miranda frowned for a moment before murmuring a response. She hadn't heard from Gaby since she married Clem and had no idea what she could want. Gaby hadn't tried to get in touch with her after she was kidnapped and lost the baby. If Gaby had been sorry, she hadn't cared enough to send even a simple message. Miranda couldn't believe she was ringing to offer her sympathy now.

She was quite right, as it happened, in her deductions. Gaby said, after they exchanged brief greetings, 'I'd like to speak to you, Miranda. Are you alone?'

'Yes,' Miranda replied, for she was then.

'It's about Brett,' Gaby said.

'Brett?'

'Yeah.' Gaby was obviously deaf to the sudden coolness in Miranda's voice. 'You haven't heard from him?'

'No,' said Miranda, 'I haven't. I've heard nothing from him for months.'

'I wondered . . .'

'Gaby!' Miranda exclaimed, beginning to feel irritated, 'You must know as well as I do that everything is over between us.'

'He hasn't said anything.'

'Well, we're getting a divorce.'

'A divorce?' Gaby sounded surprised. 'Are you sure? He hasn't mentioned it.'

'He probably hasn't had a chance to – if you're still living in Texas with Clem?'

'Oh, I am,' Gaby cried. 'You've no idea what a good time I'm having. Clem loves me and I'm crazy about him.'

Miranda tightened her hold on the phone angrily. Talk about salt and open wounds! Then she wondered why such a thought had crossed her mind when her wounds, regarding Brett, had healed long ago?

Or had they? As such a question disturbed her, she said sharply, 'Would you please get to the point,

Gaby? What do you want? You said you wished to speak to me about Brett but that was five minutes ago and I could do without a summary on wedded bliss. If, on the other hand, you just wanted to satisfy your curiosity as to what is happening between us, well, since you know now about our divorce, perhaps that's it?'

'No!' Gaby shot back, 'that's not it. I realize I'm dithering, but what I have to say isn't easy. Not when I'm not sure how you're going to take it.'

'How can I tell until I hear what it is?' Miranda was rapidly losing patience again.

'It's Brett,' Gaby said. 'He has – ' her voice broke ' – some terrible disease.'

Miranda's smooth forehead creased as she stared across the study, where she had taken the call, to the window. A robin fluttered on to the window-sill and stood looking in. His perky stance would have amused Miranda any other time, but all she could see and hear was what Gaby had just told her. Brett had developed some disease. He had always enjoyed such excellent health; she found it difficult to believe it had suddenly failed him.

'Is he ill?' she asked uncertainly.

'Of course he's ill!' Gaby was clearly upset. 'Aren't you listening to what I'm trying to tell you? He won't recover. It's fatal.'

Miranda still found it difficult to take in, or to feel upset herself about it. An incurable disease? There were many, of course. 'Is he confined to bed?' She thought it was the kind of question Alice would have asked.

'No,' Gaby replied. 'He's still working, but he's

354

lost a lot of weight and looks terrible. I doubt if he will be able to carry on much longer.'

Miranda frowned. 'He was all right when he was here in March. At least, I think he was.'

'Sometimes something can kill someone just weeks after it is diagnosed. He may have felt all right and not known something was wrong.'

Miranda supposed this was possible, but she still didn't feel anything. 'Is he in pain?'

'Quite a lot, I should think, though he doesn't say anything.'

'Isn't that rather silly?'

'Brett's proud.'

'What has pride to do with it?'

Gaby paused as if for once she was stuck for an answer. 'You're reacting real peculiar, Miranda,' she said. 'You sound as if we're talking about a stranger, and Brett's still your husband.'

Miranda sighed. 'It's a long story, Gaby, and you mightn't understand. Brett and I are no longer together. I do feel for him, of course, but he's no longer my business.'

'I can't believe it,' Gaby argued. 'You used to love him!'

'Used to. Though sometimes I wonder.'

'But you doted on him!'

'Not any more.'

'Well, sure, okay.' Gaby sounded as if she was going to go on about it, then changed her mind. 'I guess it happens. But even if you've stopped loving him, do you think you could bring yourself to come over and see him? If only because you once did. Love him, I mean.'

The robin flew off the windowsill while Miranda considered it. Following Gaby wasn't always easy. 'What good do you think seeing me would do him?'

'Maybe not much, but you never know.'

'I could be wasting both my time and his.'

'So you could, but one visit wouldn't be wasting that much. And even if it didn't help, what have you to lose?'

Nothing, Miranda supposed. Yet while what Gaby suggested might seem harmless enough, she couldn't bring herself to promise anything. 'What if I ring him?' she asked. 'Suppose I spoke to him over the phone, told him I'm sorry he is ill? It would save him getting in a state over it, if he didn't wish to see me.'

'Then he would want to know where you'd gotten your information from and he'd never forgive me! What's to stop you from coming over?' Gaby demanded.

Feeling driven into a corner, Miranda floundered. 'Well, the most I can promise is that I'll think about it.'

'Oh, gee, that's great!' Gaby exclaimed derisively. 'A man's dying and when I beg his wife to visit him, she says she'll think about it!'

'Gaby!' But Gaby was gone as, with a contemptuous snort, she broke the connection.

Miranda didn't tell Alice or her father about Gaby's phone call. Nor did she intend to, for she wasn't going to New York. She decided this within five seconds of talking to her sister-in-law. For once Gaby would have to accept she couldn't have her own way over everything. Pushing back her glossy blonde hair off her fretful face, Miranda went to join her father in the garden.

He was sitting under the shade of the willow trees near the goldfish pond, as it was late morning and the sun was hot. He was reading the morning papers and, as she sat down beside him, looked up with a smile and a few words before returning to his papers again.

Another reason why she didn't want to say anything to Harry about Brett being ill, was that she couldn't guarantee his silence. Miranda thought about this as she watched a light breeze ripple the surface of the water. He would be concerned as he appeared, since she was kidnapped, anyway, to have become one of Brett's greatest admirers, and might be tempted to get in touch with him, even should she ask him not to. And, if this happened, wouldn't she be guilty, if only indirectly, of getting Gaby into trouble with her brother? Something, Miranda tried to convince herself, she might have forever on her conscience.

Picking up a spare paper off the garden table where Harry had placed it, she opened it then put it down again, unable to concentrate. Why did she feel so numb? she wondered. Why didn't she feel sorry that Brett was suffering? Why did she feel it had nothing to do with her? Stirring restlessly, she shook her head, as if finding an answer to any of these things was beyond her.

Harry, not always the most observant, looked up suddenly and asked if something was wrong. Quickly Miranda concentrated her abstracted gaze on a nearby herbaceous border which an unusually stormy night had partly devastated. 'Nothing's wrong,' she assured her father glibly. 'I was just thinking I might help Bernard to tidy that lot up. Alice did say she could do with some fresh flowers for the house. Perhaps I can salvage something . . .'

Harry frowned, her answer, for some reason he couldn't think of, not altogether satisfying him. 'I thought you were going shopping this afternoon?'

'I might later,' she said, while suddenly knowing she wouldn't be going anywhere. Not until she put the after-effects of Gaby's phone call behind her and managed to dismiss it completely from her mind.

It angered Miranda that, despite all her determined attempts to do this, she was still thinking about Brett as she got into bed that night.

'Damn, damn, damn!' she said aloud, as there didn't seem to be any logical reason for it. Okay, Brett was ill, but she couldn't see how a visit from an estranged wife would help him. Nor did she feel she owed him one. Had he ever said he loved her? No. He had merely married her, then discarded her, as he might a pair of shoes he was tired of. If he had loved her even a little, could he have left her alone all this time? A visit from her would only embarrass him, do him more harm than good. No, Miranda decided, she wouldn't even think about it. It wouldn't be fair to either of them. Having made up her mind, for what she didn't realize might have been the hundreth time, she put out her light and tried to go to sleep.

She didn't remember falling asleep, but woke up pouring with sweat after having a nightmare again. It was the first one she'd had in weeks. She had thought she was cured of them, but they seemed to have returned with a vengeance. It was just after midnight, she ascertained, with a quick glance at her watch. Stumbling to the bathroom, she had a quick shower to cool herself down and, after changing her nightgown, slipped back into bed and tried to forget about it, but found she couldn't. Somehow she had to keep going over it.

She had been back in the cellar, telling her kidnapper she was having a miscarriage. She still remembered how he'd looked, as if she was accusing him of murder. What would she have done if they had merely locked her in and fled the country – as they usually did in her dreams? It wasn't likely they would have got far, but they might not have been caught straight away. They might not, in fact, have been caught until for her it was too late. The police had told her afterwards that the panicky instructions her kidnapper had given them as to where to find her had been vague. Had it not been for Brett finding Pam's note, they said, with the information they'd got through that, she might not have been found for days.

Miranda went over this twice before she realized what she was trying to tell herself. Even if Brett had only acted out of a sense of duty, conscience, or some remote concern for the welfare of another human being, or even just an awareness of public opinion, he had probably saved her life. And now, she was refusing to even visit him when he was apparently in danger of losing his.

For two days Miranda thought about this, going over it again and again, but in the end she knew she would go to New York to see him. If Brett had more or less blackmailed her into marrying him, then neglected and deserted her, did two wrongs – if one looked at it that way – ever make a right? She thought not. She became certain she might be as wrong as Brett had been if she didn't at least call and see if there was anything she could do for him. Especially when he'd been so instrumental in saving her life.

Determined not to hesitate any longer, for fear her courage failed her, she booked a flight to New York. Not until then did she tell her father and Alice what she was about to do. She didn't mention she was going to New York because Brett was ill. After all, he might refuse to see her. She merely said she had a few things to see to over there and they weren't to ring Brett and tell him where she was. Not even if by some remote chance he was to ring them while she was away. If they did, she threatened she would never forgive them.

To her relief, she had no trouble in getting to the airport this time. Since she and Brett were now living apart, she guessed that people with kidnapping in mind had lost interest in her. Very few men might be willing to pay much for a wife they were in the throes of getting rid of. Nevertheless, she couldn't help an occasional glance over her shoulder as Bernard and Harry drove her to the airport.

In New York she had made a reservation in a hotel on East 61st Street, where some of her friends had stayed and highly recommended. It was expensive, but as she wouldn't be staying long this didn't, she told herself, really matter. With her fear of being kidnapped not altogether gone, to be central seemed safer.

It was late when she arrived and had a light snack sent to her room. The hotel was comfortable and well furnished; the beds were large and looked inviting. Viewing her slightly weary face in one of the mirrors in the bathroom, she decided that, after a night's sleep, she might be more able to think of the best thing to do. She had come to New York to visit Brett, but though on the plane she had thought of little else, she felt ashamed that she still had nothing worked out as to how she was going to set about it.

CHAPTER 24

The following morning Miranda got through two cups of coffee and a slice of toast before she managed to work out what to do. She decided not to go to the house. If Brett was there and refused perhaps to even let her in, she knew she couldn't face the humiliation this would bring. She could just imagine Harris looking down his snooty nose at her. Nor did it seem a good idea to try to catch Brett as he left for work, as this could be as early as five oclock and he often didn't return until late in the evening.

There seemed nothing for it but to go to his headquarters. She had remembered to bring a pass he once gave her, which might gain her entry. She had used it only once or twice before and he could have cancelled it. This was a risk she would have to take, though, as it might be her only chance of getting to see him without first letting him know she was here. And this she didn't want to do.

Having made up her mind, Miranda had a shower before dressing quickly. She chose a shirt and slim jeans. She used make-up carefully but lightly, then brushed her hair until it shone and slicked it back the way her Manhattan hairdresser had once taught her to. It had grown longer since she last saw Brett and clung to her small head like a pale gold cap. Staring at herself before leaving, she wished her eyes didn't look too big for her face, or her mouth so vulnerable. While aware that her reflection showed a slender, well-groomed young woman beautiful enough, as she often noticed, to turn heads, she was sure this was until people looked closely and discovered her sophisticated appearance wasn't what it seemed to be. She decided, however, that as Brett had seldom noticed how she looked when he was well, he was even less likely to do so when he was ill.

New York, that morning, under a brilliant blue sky, was positively seething with an overabundance of just about everything. It wasn't for the fainthearted. Traffic roared, people of every colour, creed and nationality crowded the sidewalks. When Miranda first came here with Brett, she had thought she would never get used to it, or get to know it. Now she was surprised to find she had a pleasant sense of homecoming she couldn't account for. She had gone about a lot with Jill, of course, so she guessed she had come to like it more than she'd realized. If Brett had taken her out more and helped her to make new friends, she knew she might have settled there quite happily.

When the cab she had engaged dropped her off outside Brett's offices, she was relieved that she didn't feel any notable reaction. Her heart beat a little faster, probably with apprehension, but this was all. She certainly didn't feel consumed by belated love or pity for her husband, which merely caused her to wonder at the seemingly impermanent state of human emotions.

Despite believing that Brett might have cancelled her pass and she wouldn't be allowed in, Miranda was gratified when she discovered it wasn't even questioned. The porter who examined it looked startled, but as if he was suddenly confronted by royalty, rather than someone he had orders not to let in.

'Why, sure, Mrs Deakin,' he stammered, when she asked if it was all right. 'If – if you like, I can take you upstairs myself.'

'No, thank you.' She gave him a smile which made him her slave for life. 'If you just buzz me through I can manage.'

When she reached Brett's private suite of offices, though it was still early, the day was well under way. Telephones were humming, computers and fax machines busy, while Mrs McGrain, his personal secretary, was snapping out instructions to a retinue of assistants, which would be small in number, Miranda knew, compared to Brett's hundreds of other staff employed on projects below.

'Ah!' Jean McGrain looked up and saw Miranda as she came in. 'Lindhern just buzzed me. I haven't had time yet to tell your husband . . .'

Which meant, of course, that she'd declined to. While she couldn't be sure Jean McGrain actually disliked her, Miranda was sure she had never approved of her. Not as a wife for Brett, anyway. And it wouldn't be helping her now, Miranda thought drily, that she had stayed away so long when he was ill.

Meeting McGrain's cool glance with an equally cool one of her own, she asked, 'Is my husband in?'

'Yes, but he is busy and has appointments for the rest of the day. But if you'd like to wait, I'll go and see.'

'No, please.' Miranda, holding up her hand, halted her immediately. 'No need to put yourself out. I'll just go in.'

'Oh, I don't know . . .' The woman started towards her, then paused uncertainly, but Miranda, ignoring her, merely swept past her. In another moment her hand was on Brett's door and, almost before she realized what she was doing, she was pushing it open and confronting him.

He was standing by the window with his back towards her and, on seeing him, she stopped abruptly. She heard the door swing shut behind her, but for some reason she couldn't find her tongue.

'What is it?' he asked curtly. 'Didn't I tell you, Jean – '

'Brett?' Miranda found her voice at last, but though it sounded no better than a croak the effect on the man in front of her was electric. For a second he seemed to freeze then, with a muffled exclamation, he swung around to face her.

'Miranda?' he said, pausing as suddenly as he had moved and staring at her.

Miranda stared back. She couldn't help herself. Though Gaby had warned her what to expect, she still felt shocked. The light was behind him, but she saw at once that his face was gaunt. Gaby had not been mistaken. He was ill – and thin. Or, she frowned as her eyes skimmed over him, thinner than he had been. He must be dying! Oh, God, she thought. Oh, God, please no!

Scarcely aware she was silently praying, Miranda clenched her hands together until they hurt. Why was fate doing this to her? And why was she suddenly feeling so anguished over it when, after Gaby told her about it, she had only felt frozen and numb? Yet, as she stood there looking at him, trying to think, the most amazing thing appeared to happen. All of a sudden the ice which had surrounded her heart for months seemed to dissolve in a massive flood of feeling that swept it away. She knew now that during all these weeks when she'd thought she had stopped loving him, it had only been a misconception. The state of her marriage, the shock of being kidnapped and losing her baby must have paralysed her emotions until she believed they had genuinely changed. Now she realized ironically, when she was about to lose him, that she was not only in love with Brett, but that she loved him. She remembered how he had begged her to think again about a divorce and she'd refused to. Would he, she wondered bleakly, allow her to try and make up for it now, in what little time he had left to him?

'Brett,' she repeated, knowing he was waiting for her to explain why she had turned up like this. 'Gaby told me and I'm sorry. I had to come . . .' Her voice trailed off as he continued to stare at her, paler than she had ever seen him.

'What did Gaby tell you?'

He wasn't making it easy. Miranda swallowed painfully in an effort to stop trembling. Would Gaby kill her if she told him? 'That you're ill.'

'Ill?'

'An incurable disease. She wouldn't say what it was and I found it hard to believe at first, as you always seemed so healthy.'

'So – ' Brett laughed harshly ' – what convinced you?'

'Well, what motive could she have had for making it up?'

'Or did you decide you couldn't risk not believing it? Was it conscience or pity that brought you here? Or perhaps something else? Were you going to try and make sure you weren't cheated out of anything by my fatal – er – illness?'

Miranda felt despair wash over her as he sat on the edge of his desk and surveyed her with icy blue eyes. If only she could have told him she had come because she loved him, but she hadn't begun loving him again then. And how could she confess she loved him now, when he was looking at her so coldly?

'You must think what you like, Brett,' she said, lifting her chin slightly, 'but I didn't come for any mercenary reasons. Didn't I tell you that as soon as I get some training and begin working I won't want anything from you?'

'There must be something?' he persisted.

'It probably had to do with my conscience.' Better to let him believe his first guess was the correct one. 'You did save my life when I was kidnapped. Perhaps I felt I owed you something.'

'Something? Maybe you could be more explicit?'

He was playing with her as a cat might play with a mouse. For a moment Miranda's eyes blazed. She remembered how ill he was just in time to bite back the half-angry, half-hysterical words she was about to shout at him. Calming herself with difficulty, she said, 'I couldn't be more explicit. I just thought I might be able to help you somehow.'

'In other words, you feel sorry for me, and that I can do without.'

'Can't one help a person without feeling sorry for them?'

'Rather difficult, I should say.'

He was tripping her up again and she hated him for it. Her cheeks bright red, Miranda wondered why he took such pleasure in tormenting her? She felt a sob rise to her throat as suddenly it all became too much and this time she was unable to hang on to her precariously wobbling equilibrium.

'Brett,' she choked, tears scalding her cheeks from which the colour was fading rapidly, 'I don't think I can take any more of this and I realize it isn't doing you much good either. But before I go, I'd like you to know I love you. You may not believe it, or even wish to hear it, but I bloody well do!'

As if suddenly realising the enormity of what she was saying, Miranda paused, gulped, then gasped and made a rush for the door. 'I'm sorry,' she cried, but before she could escape Brett had straightened and, with his hand shooting out like lightning, stopped her in her tracks.

'Say that again,' he snapped.

About to refuse, Miranda felt so churned up that it no longer seemed to matter what she said. Or did.

'Okay.' She tried to look at him boldly but failed hopelessly, had she but known it. 'If you want the whole truth – and nothing but the truth –' she added wildly, ' – you may as well have it. If you must know, when Gaby told me you were d-dying, I didn't feel a thing. I didn't feel anything, either, on the plane. It didn't happen until I saw you again. Only this time it's worse.'

'It couldn't be worse than what I've got,' Brett said grimly.

Miranda knew this and it didn't help. He was weighing the mental against the physical and as what she had wasn't fatal she could see he was wondering what she had to complain about. When he didn't release her, she raised pleading eyes to his face. 'I have to go, Brett,' she said, aware that she must, unless she wished to make an even greater fool of herself than she was doing.

'No!' Brett's voice seemed as hard as the anger in his eyes. 'I want you to come somewhere with me, Miranda.'

'Where?' She didn't want to go anywhere with him. Not now. All she wished to do was to get back to her hotel, to compose herself and accept that she might never see him again.

He didn't answer her query directly. 'It will take only a few minutes.'

Miranda shook her head, a gesture he either didn't see or took no notice of as he drew her forcibly through the room, out into the outer office and through that as well. She heard McGrain's agitated voice reminding him of an urgent appointment and the order he snapped back for her to cancel all his appointments for the rest of the day.

'And make sure Carl is waiting outside,' he said, before the door swung shut on the woman's astonished face.

In the car, which Miranda knew was kept on permanent stand-by for him, she asked again where he was taking her, but all he would say, in curt tones, was that she would soon see. Unhappily she stared through the car window. He was sitting beside her in the back of the limousine, still holding her arm, as if determined she wasn't going to get away from him. The contact of his fingers through the thin cotton shirt she was wearing wasn't doing much for her self-control, but when she tried to free herself, he merely tightened his grip. She didn't struggle as she guessed she wouldn't win if she did. Knowing he must feel her trembling was humiliating enough without exposing herself to more of it.

After having considered several alternatives as to what he intended doing with her and resigning herself to being drowned in the Hudson or packed off immediately back to England, Miranda was startled to find the car drawing up outside a large apartment block which, if outward appearance was anything to go by, must be among some of the most luxurious in the city. 'Why here?' she asked uncertainly.

'Shut up,' Brett said tersely as, after a brief word to his driver, he manoeuvred her swiftly into the building, then to the elevator, which whisked them immediately up to one of the top floors. When it stopped, still without providing any explanation, he dragged her out of it across a wide hallway into one of the apartments, then closed the door.

Miranda glanced about her, trying to regain her balance in more ways than one as at last he released her. 'What are we doing here, Brett?' she asked again.

'I live here.' This time his hand was gentle under her arm as he drew her into a spacious lounge.'

Miranda felt bewildered. 'What about your house?'

'It's sold.'

'Sold?' Miranda couldn't keep the astonishment from her voice. 'But it was your mother's house and you loved it.'

'I never loved it, but I'll tell you about that later.'

Miranda wasn't listening. 'Perhaps you wanted to make sure it was in good hands before you . . .'

'Went?' Brett said it for her as she hesitated unhappily. 'Death. How is it, when it happens to thousands every day, we are so reluctant to talk about it?'

'Perhaps –' Miranda swallowed painfully ' – because it is so final?'

'Well . . .' Brett followed her as she wandered absently to the window and stood looking blindly out '. . . I'm hoping I won't be dying of anything now. Not for many years, anyway. It all depends on you, of course.'

'On me?' Miranda swung around quickly to face him. 'What can I do about it?'

Brett stared down into her puzzled eyes for a moment before replying, 'I have to talk to you, Miranda. I've a lot of explaining to do which may take some time, so you'd better come and sit down.'

Miranda had no wish to sit down. Nothing he was saying made much sense, but he had made it clear, hadn't he, that he didn't want either her love or sympathy, so what could they have left to talk about? Nevertheless, she didn't protest when he

371

took her over to a soft cushioned sofa and, after seeing she was comfortable, sat down beside her.

Miranda,' he said, without taking his grim eyes from off her face, 'before I go back to the beginning, I want you to know I'm not dying – if that is what Gaby told you?'

Miranda looked at him in amazement. 'But she said you were suffering from a terrible disease and wouldn't recover.'

Brett shrugged. 'She certainly chose a droll way of putting it, but it's only my heart, I'm afraid.'

Only his heart! Miranda's sank. For a moment she'd thought he was going to say that what Gaby had told her wasn't true. 'Can't your doctors do anything for you?' she asked. 'I know when my father had a heart attack, his did a lot for him.'

Feeling oddly shaken by the concern on her beautiful face, Brett had difficulty in speaking evenly. 'You are the only cure I need, Miranda, if you love me enough to forgive me?'

Miranda frowned, not following.

Brett, seeing her bewilderment, continued before she could say anything. 'I'd better tell you that it's what's known as unrequited love that my heart is suffering from. My fatal disease, as Gaby calls it. I didn't realize, unfortunately, until you were kidnapped how much I loved you, or indeed that there was such a thing. Sexual attraction, yes. But not love.'

Staring at him, Miranda wasn't able to hide how stunned she felt. It just wasn't possible, she warned herself, not after all this time. 'If you love me, why didn't you say something when you were in England?' she asked cautiously.

372

'I thought it was too late,' he said. 'I had married you for all the wrong reasons. Love didn't come into it. It was only after you were kidnapped and I thought I had lost you that I discovered the truth. I was going to tell you as soon as you recovered consciousness in hospital, but all you wanted was a divorce. You didn't seem to want to even talk to me and I believed that, by treating you as I had done, I had killed anything you might have felt for me. I didn't give up immediately. I kept hoping you would come back to me, but when you didn't I began to believe you never would. I think Gaby guessed what was wrong with me, though I never dreamt she would ring you and tell you I was suffering from something fatal.'

'I'm glad she did. Though,' Miranda remembered, 'I didn't appreciate it straight away. I still find it hard to believe you love me. Why didn't you say something as soon as you saw me today?'

Brett looked into the grey eyes in which a measure of doubt still lingered and his own darkened. 'I thought you were only there out of pity. Like you, I wasn't sure what to think when you said you loved me. But I believed you enough to know we had to talk about it. That if there was even a small chance of making things right between us, I had to take it. Which is partly why I brought you here.'

'Partly?'

'And this.' Suddenly he was pulling her into his arms, bringing her over his knees, his face close as he stared down on her. 'When you said you loved me I had a desperate urge to kiss you, but I knew that if I did and what you'd told me was true, I might not be able to stop. Six months' abstinence can do strange things to a man's appetites, my darling, and – ,' he added whimsically, 'Yours, too, I hope?'

Silently agreeing, Miranda grimaced. 'And that urge to kiss me,' she murmured innocently, 'do you still have it?'

'Sure, yes, but I have a lot of explaining to do.'

Miranda could feel the iron control Brett was exerting over himself and felt suddenly exultant as she began to experience a little the power she might have over this man. 'Can't explanations wait?' she asked.

A light leapt into his eyes. 'They shouldn't.'

'Brett?' she murmured pleadingly, and the longing in her eyes and voice was enough. With a smothered exclamation, he pulled her closer and, as she slid her arms around his neck and their lips met, the blazing physical attraction that had always been between them sprang into life. Miranda's eyes closed as her whole body and being accepted this as something that would never alter between them. But as her senses soared to heights she hadn't previously known, she recognized how the addition of reciprocated love was adding a new dimension to them.

She wasn't conscious of Brett carrying her to a bedroom, of their clothing being swiftly removed, or of the bed giving softly beneath them as they descended on it. There was only fire and lightning and impatience. If there was one thought in her mind, it was that she had to have him at any cost. She was beyond control, beyond any need of preliminary lovemaking as she opened herself to him and let passion engulf them.

She felt his hands on her nipples as he plunged into her and the stimulus was so erotic she cried out. She felt his arms tightening, his breathing quickening as a fierce urgency grew between them, and while his hardness hurt her almost as much as the first time, it also threatened to drive her wild. Brett might have lost weight but he was still heavy and didn't spare her. It was as if he sensed the violent need for him within her and was not averse to satisfying it. Soon he had her writhing under him and their mutual orgasm when it came was beyond anything she had ever imagined.

Irrationally, though, Miranda wanted more. They both did, the hunger of so many barren weeks not being lightly appeased. Even hours later, lying naked on rumpled, silken sheets drinking champagne, they were still hungry for each other. They might be temporarily sated but an unslaked craving was rapidly mounting again.

Brett, however, had something to say, which he insisted he couldn't put off any longer. 'Miranda,' he said, putting down his empty glass and turning firmly on his back, 'I told you before I have to talk to you – to try and explain, if you like, why I married you. And I think the best way to do that is to begin at the beginning, as it might help you to understand better.'

CHAPTER 25

Miranda shifted her position to look at her husband; her heart, which had slowed a little, beating fast again. It was three in the afternoon and the past few hours had been magical, and the sight of his lean, perfectly proportioned body lying beside her made her incapable of thinking of anything but one thing. She knew she was willing to let go of the past without a backward glance, but when she told Brett this, he merely shook his head.

'No.' He remained lying on his back, but put a hand up to gently remonstrate with her. 'It's something I should have talked to you about before now, but it's not easy for a man of my age to confess to feelings which have long proved irrational. I suppose I did, in a way, recognize them long ago for what they were, but instead of putting them sensibly behind me, I merely pandered to them.'

Miranda frowned as she pulled a silk sheet half over her bare body. She didn't do it because she was cold, or out of a belated sense of modesty. She did it because she suddenly sensed Brett was serious and could do without the distraction. The way he was clenching one of his hands, even if he was doing it unconsciously, somehow warned her that what he was about to tell her was important to him and that she might hear it only once. And if she didn't listen she might never get a chance of hearing it again.

Suddenly as serious as he was, she said quickly, 'Go ahead then, Brett, I'm listening.

Brett nodded briefly. 'As you know, Miranda, I'm a bit of a mongrel, my father being British, my mother American. I believe the plan was, after they married, that they should divide their time between the UK and the States, only it didn't work out quite that way. My father's interests were based in Birmingham and London. He did have business in other parts of the world, but his time was never divided equally. He had offices in New York, but not his headquarters as I have today. It was merely to keep my mother happy that he ever spent any time here.

'I believe for that same reason he agreed I should go to Harvard, after which I joined him in London. He was a brilliant man, Miranda, and I was determined to follow in his footsteps. My parents, by this time, were spending more time apart than together and I not only saw less of my mother, but I'm afraid scarcely even thought of her. Then, one day, there was a call from her. She wanted my father back in the States to go on vacation with her. When he said we were finalizing an important business deal – which we were, by the way – and couldn't come over immediately, she said that, if he didn't, she would go it alone.

'I was there when he took the call and I could see he was dithering over it, but when he asked me what I thought he should do I advised him to take no notice. I didn't actually stop him from going, but I didn't think I could manage the final settlements on my own. And the takeover was an important one.'

'Then what happened?' Miranda prompted curiously, as Brett paused.

He smiled grimly. 'The worst thing that possibly could. When the old man didn't turn up, my dear mother went off, like she'd threatened, but the plane crashed on take-off and she was badly injured. A lot of passengers were killed.'

'But she wasn't?'

'No,' Brett's mouth tightened. 'She died a week later, her doctors implied mercifully, as, had she lived, she would have been a cripple for life. My father, of course, blamed himself. He never seemed to get over it. When he died, five years later, I think it was because of it.'

'Of a broken heart?'

'A guilty conscience, more likely. Maybe a bit of both?'

'And you?' Miranda asked uncertainly. 'Did you blame yourself as well?'

'Yes, I did. Looking back I guess, at twenty-three, I was at an impressionable age, but I did. I believed I might easily have persuaded my father to go to New York, and if I had, Julia might have been on another plane and not lost her life.'

'You can't ever be sure about such things,' Miranda broke in, on what she imagined was Brett's still lingering pain. 'It's not always wise to blame oneself.'

Brett said curtly. 'I remember thinking that at the time and believing I would eventually believe it.

That didn't happen, though. I don't know why, but my feeling of guilt only grew worse. Which, paradoxically, often angered me. I wasn't exactly lacking in ego in those days, I'm afraid. I could manage almost anything the business world threw at me. I was quite aware that my reputation in this direction was envied, and my personal life was nothing to complain of, either. Yet something I wasn't really responsible for continued to haunt me. It made me sympathize with a man I once met on a plane who said the number thirteen had such an effect on him that if he saw it before a business meeting, he cancelled.

'To cut a long story short, Miranda, I began giving more and more to charity, not out of concern for the disadvantaged, but in an attempt to get rid of what I now considered my nemesis. Unfortunately that didn't work and when, a few years later, a secretary of mine in Birmingham had a bad accident – which I'll tell you about later – and pretended it had crippled her, I think initially to get my sympathy, I decided that if I helped her, put my involvement with the handicapped on a more personal basis, it might provide the cure for my neurosis which had so far evaded me. I continued,' Brett went on, 'to pay her a salary and provided her and her father with a house, rent free. That kind of thing. I didn't realize Eve believed I was doing this because one day I hoped to marry her.'

'Which you didn't?' Miranda asked, looking at him wryly.

'I never gave it a thought,' Brett confessed. 'The whole project was a waste of time anyway, as far as I was concerned. Certainly my interest in Eve was never a romantic one. I wasn't aware that I'd dashed her expectations in that direction until I called to tell her I was going to marry you. Apparently this infuriated her so much that she tried, in various ways, to make trouble between us. A few weeks afterwards she even visited your father, under a false name, with mischief in mind. I think that had worried him, and when I discovered it was Eve I went to see her. I don't think we will be hearing from her again.'

'Was this the Eve who used to ring you in New York?' Miranda asked, and, when Brett nodded, 'I hope you weren't too hard on her?'

Brett smiled drily. 'I thought I may have been and, as what had happened was probably, with hindsight, as much my fault as hers, I got someone to check up on her. They discovered she is now living with one of the city's chief architects. That's all I know. It appears there has been a happy ending, but I didn't ask for details.'

Miranda wasn't going to ask for any either. She was too busy formulating her next question, which had nothing to do with Eve. 'So why did you marry me?' Her grey eyes swept curiously over him before returning to his face. 'I always believed you proposed because you felt sorry for me, then married me out of revenge when you found I had cheated and was no longer a cripple.'

Brett hesitated before replying. 'I was coming to that,' he said. 'Because what I was doing for Eve Martin hadn't helped and I was still beleaguered by a guilty conscience, I believed if I married you and my money could make you well again, it might do more for me than my previous efforts in other directions had done. When I discovered you weren't crippled, instead of weakening my resolve to marry you it merely strengthened it. This time, however, crazy as it seems, I intended punishing you by allowing you to get used to a life of luxury, then divorcing you. Ironically it didn't take me long to become aware I was really punishing myself. I didn't know on Luke that I was falling in love with you. I felt sure it was only a powerful physical attraction. If it was anything else, I refused to acknowledge it. It wasn't a case of ignorance being bliss, though, my darling.' Putting out a hand, he gently clasped her small, slender one as it lay beside his. 'I suffered. And this, I think, was why, when I thought you were getting too great a hold over me, I reacted by totally neglecting you. But again that was something I wouldn't even try to define. When I learned you were pregnant, it was like a bomb under my plans to get rid of you, though heaven knows I hadn't thought of that for some time. All I could think of was you and the baby. It didn't help to make the overall picture any clearer, but it did put everything else out of my mind.'

'But, Brett – ' Miranda clutched his hand tighter ' – why didn't you at least try to explain?'

'I couldn't, Miranda.' His voice was full of self-mockery. 'I was in such a state of unwelcome chaos, I couldn't explain it even to myself. I used to sit at my desk wondering what the hell was the matter with me. It wasn't until you were kidnapped that I realized.'

'Yet, even then, you didn't say anything?'

'Well, as I told you a few hours ago, I wanted to, but it didn't work out that way.'

Miranda nodded ruefully. 'Perhaps that was my fault as much as yours. When I woke up in hospital I really believed I had stopped loving you. I began loving you on Luke, but while I knew I attracted you physically, I wanted more than that. But with Marcia and all the other women around, I didn't think I stood a chance. I kept on loving you, though, despite everything. Being kidnapped and losing the baby was probably what caused me to think I no longer did. I was actually relieved when you accepted my decision about a divorce and went back to New York. Nobody ever said anything about you being ill, which was why, I suppose, I didn't know what to think when Gaby rang – ' Breaking off, Miranda frowned and turned quickly to look at him. 'Why did Gaby ring and tell me what she did, when she must have known it wasn't true?'

Brett smiled grimly. 'Maybe she thought it was true. At least in a way. You see,' he went on, 'she caught me one evening last week, when she arrived unexpectedly on a flying visit from Texas. I'm ashamed to admit – ' he grimaced ' – I had nearly finished a bottle of whisky and was probably half-drunk when she showed up. When she accused me of drinking too much, however, that was another thing and we traded a few insults. Anyway, though I don't remember how she got round to it, she began talking about Julia and I told her to shut up – that the state I was in, the mess my marriage was in, might be entirely due to our dear mother. I didn't tell her everything, but it must have been enough for her to grasp the rudiments of it.'

'You mean you told her about your guilty feelings since your mother's accident?', Miranda said.

'I must have done,' Brett nodded, 'for she positively gasped and exclaimed, in that elegant way she has, "Oh, shit, Brett, I had no idea. If only I'd known, I could have told you the truth."'

'"What – truth?" I guess I mumbled.

'Gaby continued to look stunned. "Well, didn't you know," she said, "that our dear mother, as you call her, was running away that day with a bum she'd been having an affair with for years? Keeping, as well."

'I couldn't believe it,' Brett said to Miranda. 'I asked her if she was sure? "Of course I'm sure," she said. "I'm only two years younger than you are, Brett. At twenty-one, don't tell me I wasn't old enough to know what was going on."

'I didn't know what to think,' Brett said to Miranda. 'I expect I was shocked, but I did ask why she hadn't told the old man, instead of letting him think that an innocent woman had met her death because of him?'

'And what did she say to that?' Miranda asked.

'She only said, why should she have done? That her father had never had any time for her. That when she came to the UK we were both busy, so she decided her mother was the lesser of a few evils. She hated her mother's lover, but at least Julia was always there for her.'

'But didn't you say,' Miranda frowned, 'that Julia had asked your father to go on holiday with her?'

'According to Gaby, that was just a gamble,' Brett replied. 'The kind Julia loved to take. She did, though, Gaby said, leave a letter for her to give to her father when he did turn up. Gaby wonders, even now, if Julia didn't have a premonition of some sort that something bad was about to happen, for in it she confessed to everything.'

'Oh,' Miranda was genuinely dismayed. 'Your poor father!'

'As it happened,' Brett said tersely, 'Gaby never gave it to him. When Julia never regained consciousness and her lover had already met his death on the plane, she said she didn't see much point in causing any more pain. Or so she maintains.'

'But it could have saved both your father and you pain of another kind,' Miranda murmured shrewdly.

Brett nodded grimly. 'I suspect my dear sister knew this. It could have been her way of getting back at us for what she considered our neglect of her. Though why she decided to tell me about it now when she didn't then, I'll probably never know.'

'She may have let time go by, then never found the right opportunity. What did she do with the letter, by the way? Did she say?'

'She still had it, hidden in her flat,' Brett replied to Miranda's surprise. 'She actually let me read it the next day. It was all there, a bit faded with age. A confession of adultery and worse, on my mother's part, a strange sense of release on mine from feelings of guilt which should never have been.'

'Do you think,' Miranda wondered, 'that Gaby tried to make amends by ringing me in the hope that it might bring me over and give us a chance to start again?'

'Maybe,' Brett said. 'I must admit, though, that I might have looked as if I was dying, because of the strain of losing you.'

Miranda glanced at him speculatively. He had seemed gaunt when she saw him that morning, but that look at least had gone from his face. And he wasn't as thin as she'd thought he was. Had it been a case of autosuggestion? Gaby had wanted her to believe Brett had lost weight and, because of this, she had consequently seen him that way.

She said slowly, 'Things often have a strange way of working out. If Gaby, instead of reading Julia's letter, had given it to your father, he might not have told you about it. So perhaps Gaby did you a favour, even if it took time for her to get around to it?'

'I guess that's one way of looking at it,' Brett agreed, though he didn't sound convinced.

'But about your mother's house – ' Miranda's thoughts veered curiously ' – you must have parted with it before Gaby told you about this?'

'No, I didn't,' Brett said. 'I didn't sell it. I simply gave it to Gaby last week and moved out at the weekend. Julia left it to me. It belonged to her parents, and Gaby believed it should have come to her. I never told her I didn't like it and only kept it as I felt partly responsible for Julia's death.'

'A kind of atonement?'

'If you like. Anyway, after Gaby showed me the letter and I thought of all the years I'd been burdened by unnecessary guilt, all I wanted to do was to get rid of it.'

'What will Gaby do with it?'

'Sell it, I should think. It's not much good to her now that she's living in Texas. Meanwhile, of course, there is a lot to see to. Jill is packing your belongings, for one thing. I was going to send them to you in England.'

'And this apartment?' Miranda wasn't going to pretend she was sorry about the house when she wasn't. 'Will we be living here?'

'Only until we find somewhere else,' Brett said. 'It's a service flat. I just have to ring for anything from tea and toast to a full-scale meal. I just couldn't face looking for another place on my own.'

'I should like something not too big,' Miranda said.

'So would I,' Brett agreed.

Miranda stroked a hand along his side. 'There are usually different ways of looking at almost everything, aren't there? I mean, if you hadn't been so interested in the handicapped, as a way of pacifying your guilty conscience, you might not have spared me a second glance. Perhaps I, at least, owe your mother something?'

'Maybe.' Brett refused to commit himself over that. He remembered feeling instantly attracted to Miranda Ferris and he doubted he would have let her go. 'I think fate meant us to be together, my darling. Even if it had a strange way of going about it. Oh, Miranda – ' his voice was suddenly husky as he turned towards her again and drew her closer ' – I've thought so much about you and our little lost baby. I've been through such hell. I wanted to mourn with you, but you weren't there.'

386

Miranda's eyes misted over as she gently touched his face. 'It wasn't very old, Brett, but I grieved for it as if it had been full-term. And it was a part of you which I never expected to have again . . .'

Brett swallowed, a painful movement in his strong throat. He said, his voice still husky, 'I'm going to take you back to Luke, my love, before we begin a proper honeymoon. We'll get Linda to make us a small wreath and, one evening, toss it out on to the island seas, for after all that was where our child was conceived.'

'And it might come back in the form of another one?'

'Other ones,' Brett teased, smiling down at her tenderly before his eyes darkened. 'I want you to myself for a while first, though. I want to make up for all the distress and pain I've caused you.'

Miranda's arms strayed around his neck as, for a moment, they lay quietly. 'We have the rest of our lives to make it up to each other,' she breathed.

'Amen to that,' Brett said, then proceeded to show her just how good it was going to be.

EPILOGUE

Miranda and Brett had a daughter to begin with then, two years later, a son. They spend their time between the States and England, with visits to Gaby and Clem, who now have two children of their own, and the island. On Luke, Linda insists on spoiling both Miranda and the children as if they were all the same age.

In New York and wherever they go, Miranda devotes both time and energy to improving the lot of the handicapped, never forgetting she was once one of them herself, while Brett, though no longer plagued by a guilty conscience, helps her in every way he can.

# THE EXCITING NEW NAME IN WOMEN'S FICTION!

PLEASE HELP ME TO HELP YOU!

Dear *Scarlet* Reader,

Don't forget we are now holding another super Prize Draw, which means that **you could win 6 months' worth of free *Scarlets*!** Just return your completed questionnaire to us **before 31 January 1998** and you will automatically be entered in the draw that takes place on that day. If you are lucky enough to be one of the first two names out of the hat we will send you four new *Scarlet* romances, every month for six months.

So don't delay – return your form straight away!*

Looking forward to hearing from you,

Sally Cooper

Editor-in-Chief, *Scarlet*

*Prize draw offer available only in the UK, USA or Canada. Draw is not open to employees of Robinson Publishing, or of their agents, families or households. Winners will be informed by post, and details of winners can be obtained after 31 January 1998, by sending a stamped addressed envelope to address given at end of questionnaire.

Note: further offers which might be of interest may be sent to you by other, carefully selected, companies. If you do not want to receive them, please write to Robinson Publishing Ltd, 7 Kensington Church Court, London W8 4SP, UK.

QUESTIONNAIRE

Please tick the appropriate boxes to indicate your answers

1 Where did you get this Scarlet title?
Bought in supermarket ☐
Bought at my local bookstore ☐ Bought at chain bookstore ☐
Bought at book exchange or used bookstore ☐
Borrowed from a friend ☐
Other (please indicate) _____

2 Did you enjoy reading it?
A lot ☐ A little ☐ Not at all ☐

3 What did you particularly like about this book?
Believable characters ☐ Easy to read ☐
Good value for money ☐ Enjoyable locations ☐
Interesting story ☐ Modern setting ☐
Other _____

4 What did you particularly dislike about this book?
_____

5 Would you buy another Scarlet book?
Yes ☐ No ☐

6 What other kinds of book do you enjoy reading?
Horror ☐ Puzzle books ☐ Historical fiction ☐
General fiction ☐ Crime/Detective ☐ Cookery ☐
Other (please indicate) _____

7 Which magazines do you enjoy reading?
1. _____
2. _____
3. _____

And now a little about you –
8 How old are you?
Under 25 ☐ 25–34 ☐ 35–44 ☐
45–54 ☐ 55–64 ☐ over 65 ☐

cont.

9 What is your marital status?

Single ☐   Married/living with partner ☐

Widowed ☐   Separated/divorced ☐

10 What is your current occupation?

Employed full-time ☐   Employed part-time ☐

Student ☐   Housewife full-time ☐

Unemployed ☐   Retired ☐

11 Do you have children? If so, how many and how old are they?

_____

_____

12 What is your annual household income?

under $15,000	☐	or	£10,000	☐
$15–25,000	☐	or	£10–20,000	☐
$25–35,000	☐	or	£20–30,000	☐
$35–50,000	☐	or	£30–40,000	☐
over $50,000	☐	or	£40,000	☐

Miss/Mrs/Ms _____

Address _____

_____

_____

Thank you for completing this questionnaire. Now tear it out – put it in an envelope and send it, before 31 January 1998, to:

Sally Cooper, Editor-in-Chief

USA/Can. address
SCARLET c/o London Bridge
85 River Rock Drive
Suite 202
Buffalo
NY 14207
USA

UK address/No stamp required
SCARLET
FREEPOST LON 3335
LONDON W8 4BR
Please use block capitals for address

MISCON/11/97

Scarlet titles coming next month:

HARTE'S GOLD Jane Toombs
No-nonsense rancher Carole Harte can't believe that she, of all people, would fall for a film star. But that's exactly what she's done! Trouble is, she's never heard of 'the star', Jerrold Telford, and fears he's out to con her grandmother!

THE SECOND WIFE Angela Arney
When Felicity decides to marry Tony she thinks the decision is theirs alone, and that love will conquer all. What she's forgotten is that other people have a stake in their future too, and then Felicity realizes just how difficult it is to be *the second wife* . . .

WILDE AFFAIR Margaret Callaghan
Rich, powerful, ruthless – the Jared Wildes of this world don't make commitments. Oh yes, Stevie has come across men like Jared before. Her daughter Rosa's father for one!

A BITTER INHERITANCE Clare Benedict
'A scheming little gold digger. Her husband not cold in his grave and she's involved with another man!' That's how Sam Redmond thinks of Gina. How can she change his mind, when he clearly can't forget or forgive how badly she treated *him* in the past?